D1053540

continued . . .

Also by John Mackie

Manhattan South
Manhattan North

Published by Onyx

EAST SIDE

JOHN MACKIE

AN ONYX BOOK

ONYX
Published by New American Library, a division of
Penguin Group (USA) Inc., 375 Hudson Street,
New York, New York 10014, U.S.A.
Penguin Books Ltd, 80 Strand,
London WC2R 0RL, England
Penguin Books Australia Ltd, 250 Camberwell Road,
Camberwell, Victoria 3124, Australia
Penguin Books Canada Ltd, 10 Alcorn Avenue,
Toronto, Ontario, Canada M4V 3B2
Penguin Books (NZ), cnr Airborne and Rosedale Roads,
Albany, Auckland 1310, New Zealand

Penguin Books Ltd, Registered Offices:
80 Strand, London WC2R 0RL, England

First published by Onyx, an imprint of New American Library,
a division of Penguin Group (USA) Inc.

First Printing, July 2004
10 9 8 7 6 5 4 3 2 1

PUBLISHER'S NOTE
This is a work of fiction. Names, characters, places, and incidents either are the
product of the author's imagination or are used fictitiously, and any resemblance to
actual persons, living or dead, business establishments, events, or locales is entirely
coincidental.

For my terrific sister, Patti Capwell

ACKNOWLEDGMENTS

As always, my deepest appreciation to Sharon Townley, Sue Mather, and Emily Cole, the "Three Wise Ladies" who work so hard to keep me honest and on track. Thanks also to John Talbot, of the John Talbot Literary Agency, and to my skillful editor at NAL, Doug Grad. And for her early guidance, unflagging encouragement, and instilling of the belief, I need to express long overdue thanks to Kay Oderkirk.

ONE

Father Thomas J. Gilhooley made the sign of the cross as Mrs. Reardon's annoyingly thin and crackling voice slowly recited the Apostles' Creed. He gave the woman absolution and a penance of five Our Fathers and ten Hail Marys and quickly closed the hatch. He knew the fifteen-prayer penance was a piece of cake for Mrs. Reardon. She might even think she'd been shortchanged—he usually hit her with twenty. Her worst reported sin again this week had been "having impure thoughts"—whatever the hell an old woman's impure thoughts could possibly be. He didn't ask—he didn't want to know. Gilhooley did know, however, that when confession hour was over, he would find Mrs. Reardon still kneeling in the third row, Saint Joseph's side, doing the Rosary. The poor soul actually thought she was a sinner. Sweet Jesus!

The widow Reardon was a regular. Rain or shine, she made confession every Saturday afternoon and High Mass every Sunday. The regulars were dwindling, Gilhooley thought; dying off. And the younger people were drifting away from religion in general, and Catholicism in particular. Not only at Blessed Sacrament Church, but all over the country. He shook his head in sorrow; how the world had changed during his lifetime. Maybe His Holiness' visit to New York City next week would reinvigorate lazy and failing parishioners and help improve future Mass attendance. Who knew? Word was that the pontiff's scheduled New Year's Eve Mass and celebration of the Eucharist at St.

Patrick's Cathedral was by invitation only, and that it was completely booked. At least that was what Mrs. Reardon had just told him, though how the hell she knew these things he could never quite figure.

The portly priest squirmed on his padded seat, repositioning to relieve the raging hemorrhoids that were flaring again. The Preparation H suppository wasn't helping today. Yawning widely, he slid back the little window to his left. There were no new customers. Yet.

How many confessions had he heard in his forty-two-year priesthood—thousands . . . millions maybe? He had listened to it all, he thought, every wacko story there ever was. In the old days, before the Vatican made the sacrament of confession optional, long queues—a regular production line—would form on both sides of his booth and he'd be opening one slider while closing the other. He wondered if Father Dominguez, in the confessional across the nave, was getting any action this afternoon.

Gilhooley raised his old Casio to eye level; it was ten minutes to six, thank God. He always wore the watch when hearing confessions. Press a tiny button and the digital face would glow in a muted green so he could keep track of the time while in the darkened booth. By six his bladder would be screaming, and he'd be out of there like a shot to hit the closest john just inside the sacristy.

Of course, there was always the possibility of some last-minute penitent wandering in, someone with a lifelong litany of sin and degradation to unload, who didn't have the decency to arrive earlier. That was especially prone to happen now; there was always a sudden rush to get straight with the Big Guy Upstairs in the week before Christmas. It was a time when past sins sat heavily on the soul. Gilhooley sighed; he hated being stuck late in the confessional. He heard a stirring in the left-side booth, checked his watch, sighed again, and slid back the door.

"Bless me, Father," a breathy, almost whispery male

voice began, "for I have sinned. It has been thirty-five years since my last confession."

Here we go, Gilhooley thought, grimacing and crossing his legs. Did I call this one or what? "Tell me, my son, why have you come back after so long?"

The man coughed twice, wheezing as if he were on the verge of an asthmatic attack. "I have to make things right, Father."

"The Lord is a forgiving God. How have you sinned against him, my son?"

"I have killed people, Father."

"Who have you killed, my son?"

"Many, many people, Father," said the penitent, his thin voice labored. "Men mostly, some women. Must be fifty or more, I guess."

"You guess?"

"There were fifty confirmed. I know there were more I killed but couldn't claim. They were gooks."

"Sounds as if you were in a war, my son."

"'Nam."

"Unh, I see," Gilhooley muttered. Poor bastard's probably been carrying this around for thirty years. "How long ago was that?"

"Got out of the army in January '68. Two days before the start of the Tet Offensive."

"You must have been very young."

"I was sixteen when I went in." There was a short hesitation, just long enough to let loose a gagging cough. "Forged my birth certificate so I could enlist."

Good God Almighty, Gilhooley thought, what could possibly cause a kid to run off to Vietnam? "What did your parents have to say about that?"

"Had none. Never knew my old man. My mother was pregnant with me when he got it in Korea."

"And your mother?"

"Cancer. Died when I was ten." Melancholy draped his next words. "She was the most important thing in my life."

"Who became responsible for you when she died? An aunt, an uncle?"

"I was raised in a Catholic home for boys."

Gilhooley stared at the screen partition that separated them. As a young Christian Brother he'd spent several years on staff at St. Malachy's Home for Boys, teaching, disciplining. Not a favorite memory, he decided to say nothing of that connection.

"Have you come here because you're feeling great guilt now for all those killings?"

"No . . . not really. Back in 'Nam, sometimes I used to wake up screaming in the middle of the night. I'd be soaked with sweat and wishing to God that I were dead." Hesitating briefly, he added in a barely audible whisper, "But then I would lie there and pray the Rosary in my head, and the Blessed Mother would make everything okay."

"I see. . . ." Gilhooley murmured.

"I was doing God's work."

"*God's work?* All the killing you did was part of God's work?"

"Oh, yes, very much a part. Just look at St. Michael the Archangel. He killed in the Lord's name."

"Yes, he slew dragons, agents of the devil."

"Precisely."

Gilhooley rolled his eyes. "Why have you come here, my son? Have you come to seek the Lord's forgiveness and return to his flock?"

"I have the Lord's forgiveness, Father, *and* the Blessed Mother's."

Confused, intrigued, Gilhooley forgot he had to piss. He hadn't had a good confession like this in years. "How did it come to pass that you killed so many people in Vietnam?" he asked, switching back to the original subject, his morbid curiosity getting the better of him.

"I was a tunnel rat."

"Oh, I see. Go on."

"Whenever our unit would find a VC tunnel opening," the man continued, his voice at times almost inaudible through the wheezing, "my platoon leaders would always come right to me . . . they'd ask me . . . to crawl in and flush it out." He slipped then into a thirty-second fit of roiling, rumbling coughs.

"You would actually crawl into one of those places? It must have been an incredibly hard thing to do."

"I liked it, Father. I liked doing it. It gave me some kinda . . . satisfaction. Know what I'm saying, Father? *Satisfaction*?"

"Not exactly." Sweet Jesus in heaven, Gilhooley thought, that terrible war really screwed up a lot of people. "Tell me about it, my son."

"Sometimes the tunnels were real long. Once I crawled a whole mile and a half until I came to a chamber that had four people in it."

"What did you do?"

"I killed them."

"Could you have just captured them instead of killing them all?" he asked gently, striving for a nonjudgmental tenor.

"I guess."

"Well, then," Gilhooley stumbled, looking for the right words. "Why did you decide to kill them instead?"

"I hadda."

"Had you been ordered to?"

"It was kinda generally understood. Know what I mean? They were the enemy, and I was doing . . . God's work."

Holy mother, Gilhooley thought. Got me a real dyed-in-the-wool wack-a-do here. Where in *God's world* can I go with this guy? Just have to be very careful and keep winging it. He checked his watch; it was a few minutes after six. The priest repositioned himself, trying to take some pressure off his high-tide bladder and his aching butt. He had to pee badly but couldn't just get up and walk away. Not now. He hated when this happened. This guy's gonna be here till six thirty at the very least, he thought. Why couldn't he have gone to Father Dominguez?

"If these people you killed were a wartime enemy and you were doing God's work, why are you rehashing it now? All these years later?" Gilhooley asked, the demanding bladder bringing an edge to his voice.

"I've been having the dreams again."

"You're dreaming about all those people you shot?"

"Yes." The man coughed the answer. "When the dream first starts and I round them up in a chamber, they're all gooks: small, with gook features, and they wear gook clothes. You know what I'm saying—those black pajamas they always wore."

"I think I do."

"First I gather them in a semicircle, see. But when I do, they start to change. They grow bigger and taller and stronger than me—much stronger. Their black pajamas become black pants and shirts . . . sometimes even cassocks. Their black hair becomes Irish red, and suddenly they all have Roman collars."

"Roman collars?" Gilhooley uttered, raising pudgy nail-bitten fingers to rake nervously through his mane of graying red hair. A foreboding shiver flashed down his spine.

"Yes. Then they all drop their pants. Before my very eyes . . . all them North Vietnamese gooks become priests. Naked priests. They're all standing in a semicircle, smiling, getting ready to do things to me. Just like the drunken priests up at St. Malachy's."

Gilhooley caught his breath. "St. Malachy's Home for Boys?" he blurted in a troubled whisper, feeling the small hair on his arms and at the back of his wrinkled neck spring to tingling attention. He cleared his throat and swallowed deeply.

"That's what I said, Father. Saint Malachy's Home for Boys," came the answer in a sinister monotone.

Gilhooley's palms felt moist; his pulse pounded at his temples.

"So I jack the first round into the chamber, see, and I shoot them, first in their privates, and make every one of them scream and beg and cry like little frightened boys. Then I put one right between their fucking Irish eyes. But then, when they're all dead, in a pile . . . they all turn back into black-haired little gooks again. . . . *Weird, hah, Father?*"

Shameful recollections—forcibly drowned in the deepest ocean of Thomas J. Gilhooley's mind—broke their weighted shackles. They surged like reinflated balloons to the surface of his consciousness.

"Do you remember a little kid named Emilio Buffolino?" the faint voice asked, then he coughed.

"Emilio . . . *who?*"

"You probably remember him better as Buffo, Father. That's what everybody called him. He was one of your favorites back in the middle sixties; him and me, that is. Remember the rides you used to make us go on in your gold Plymouth? Down to that lonely stretch of beach? Do you remember the day Buffo killed himself?"

Shit, yes, Gilhooley remembered. The Buffolino kid *had* been one of his favorites. He instantly recalled how one very rainy night—after a bit too much of the grape—he and a few of the other brothers from the home had taken the Buffolino kid down to the basement of St. Malachy's for a little group sport. The very next day the kid climbed to the building's fifth-story parapet and dove off.

Gilhooley slammed the partition slider and sprang from his seat. Sweat beaded his brow. He had to get away from this rip-roaring psycho. He pushed against the confessional booth door; it was jammed. He pushed harder. *What the hell?* Frantically, he twisted the knob back and forth. Nothing was happening. *"Jesus Christ Almighty,"* he whimpered angrily, feeling sudden urgency in his bowels. *"Why can't I get out?"* Frenzied, he barged with all his weight against the door until it finally swung open.

A faceless figure, cloaked within the enveloping cowl

of a dark and long-flowing outer garment, completely blocked his exit. Gilhooley knew it was no phantom; it was real, and it held a very big, very real pistol aimed directly at his midsection. He felt a scream boil up from his chest, but no sound escaped.

The figure raised its free hand. It gently peeled away the cowl to reveal the grinning white face of a circus clown, its hideous exaggerated features frozen in bizarre convulsive laughter. For one guilt-driven nightmarish second, the harsh blare of a sideshow calliope played in Gilhooley's head.

"This is for Buffo," the figure uttered in an eerie whine.

Frightened beyond anything he had ever known, the Reverend Thomas J. Gilhooley sank back heavily onto his cushioned seat. Beneath the fear, some recess of his brain registered the spreading warm, wet feeling of his pants between his legs. The muffled spit sound, a curl of gray smoke at the gun's barrel, and searing pain as a bullet ripped through his groin—all seemed to happen together. In total disbelief he looked up at the malevolent creature and opened his mouth to speak. The words died with him.

Eight minutes later, Father Roberto Dominguez found Father Thomas J. Gilhooley slumped inside his confessional booth. Gilhooley had a massive crater between his still-open eyes, his pants were soaked with blood and urine, and a prayer card depicting Our Lady of Fatima had been neatly placed on the center of his chest.

As Dominguez ran for help, the widow, Mrs. Dorothy Reardon, knelt nearby, blessed herself with her beads, and started mumbling yet another Rosary.

TWO

When Detective Sergeant Thornton Savage arrived at the Thirteenth Precinct that Monday morning, the vapor plumes rising randomly along the street surfaces of the East Side were huge and plentiful. To the uninitiated, they resembled the steam-belching hot springs at Yellowstone or a forbidding backdrop on some strange, uninhabited planet in a sci-fi flick. The city phenomenon came about when warm underground air rose up through manhole-cover vents and condensed into the freezing winter air above. The lower the outdoor temperature, the greater the steamy evacuations. Sometimes, when the pressure became too great, it would blow a two-hundred-pound cast iron manhole cover fifty feet in the air.

The weatherman, Savage recalled, had promised a "drop in temperature," but nothing quite like this. A bitter eighteen degrees—with a vicious windchill pushing it down to two below—had settled in overnight on the New York Metropolitan area. Lady Liberty must be freezing her butt off in the harbor, he thought, and a ride on the Staten Island ferry would probably seem like a passage up the Yukon. It was the kind of cold that stung like needles through earmuffs, mittens, and scarves. The first breaths of outdoor air would freeze-dry mucous membranes and petrify nose hair into annoying rigid bristles. When it was like this in New York City, even the sidewalk concrete seemed harder.

As was his practice, Savage avoided the slow-moving

elevator in the station house and took the back stairs two at a time up to C-deck. As he let himself into the offices of Manhattan South Homicide—his home in the department for the last dozen years—he geared himself for the palpable tension and pressure he knew would greet him the moment he got inside. Almost two days had passed since Father Thomas Gilhooley was executed inside his church over on East Twenty-second Street, a mere block and a half away, and it was his case.

Savage and his team of detectives had beaten the bushes all weekend, working till well after midnight on Saturday—and doing sixteen hours on Sunday—but had come up dry. They had two .45 caliber shell casings found beneath a pew inside the church nave, and the mating bullets dug from the sixty-six-year-old priest at autopsy. They also had a religious prayer card that had been left on top of the priest's body. Aside from that, they had nothing else to go on. Nobody had seen or heard a thing.

Deep in thought, almost transfixed, about the perplexities and oddness of the latest case, he scrawled the time—0830 hours—and his signature on the next available line of the command log. Still fatigued from the marathon weekend of interviews and canvassing, Savage offered only an abbreviated good-morning nod to Eddie Brodigan, the unit's wheelman. Brodigan was preoccupied, gazing dreamily at the long legs of Carmen Lugo, the hot-looking, newly assigned civilian clerical aide, who was busy tacking the latest department personnel orders to the office bulletin board.

The little Hispanic number, who had cascading black hair, ebony bedroom eyes, and a penchant for skirts that sometimes revealed more thigh than they should, had been getting lots of attention from several of the guys in the unit. It wouldn't be long, he thought, before one of the horny sons of bitches would be wining, dining, and nailing the former "Miss Ponce." His money was on either Herbie Shaw from Team 1 or his Tex-Mex partner Diego Sanchez, who, Savage figured, because of the Latin connection, probably had the inside track.

"Just got a call from Lieutenant Crowley, down at the Chief of D's office," Brodigan said, snapping out of his mini wet dream. He handed Savage a Post-it square with the info. "He's waiting for the Monday morning update on the Gilhooley case."

"Well, he can wait a little longer," Savage said, checking his watch. "It's not due till nine."

Savage wanted to put off making the call to the chief of detectives operations coordinator until the very last minute. For starters, he didn't much care for Jake Crowley, a matinee-idol-handsome windbag and one of the department's greatest self-promoters. Everybody in The Job knew how Crowley loved to get his Bushmills-blushed mug in front of a TV camera. Chief Wilson wasn't crazy about Crowley either, and it was still a mystery how the pompous hump had wangled into the cushy job he had; it must have taken a monstrously big hook. More importantly, though, Savage hated disappointing the chief with a nothing-to-report report, and leaving him to blow in the breeze.

As a cop, Savage had long ago accepted the fact that murders—like the ice-cold certainties of death, taxes, and Midtown parking summonses—were just another troubling fact of life for the toiling masses that struggled within the orchards of the Big Apple. Like the sun bubbling up into the eastern sky each morning, or oozing out of sight into the western horizon each and every night, they simply occurred. Most never got a drop of ink, let alone made headlines in any of the New York dailies—why report the sun rising or setting? Nor did the victims get so much as a brief mention on the six o'clock news. What those unnoted souls *did* get was a medical examiner's toe tag, a UF-61 complaint number from the NYPD, and a case referral to Homicide.

Then there were the killings that *everyone* heard about.

They became major news because of their particular outrageousness, or the notoriety of either the victim or perpetrator. The Father Gilhooley story had been *Daily News, Post,* and *Times* front page—the presses having been stopped to hastily reset headline copy—and the lead on every local TV and radio newscast. The anchors at Channels 2, 4, 7, and 11 had sent forth stringers for live on-the-scene reports from Blessed Sacrament Church where Gilhooley had been gunned down. It was, in every sense, a true media event.

At city hall, the phones had been ringing off the hook, and the rattled mayor did what rattled mayors always do: He passed along the frenzy to the police commissioner's office at One Police Plaza. Needless to say, the PC went right to work, cranking up the Btus on the boys below, who were already up to their bloodshot eyeballs investigating all those other killings that no one ever heard about.

Uptown, at Gracie Mansion, the usually calm and cool mayor was getting nervous and hot; downtown at One PP, heat and pressure from the mayor was rapidly building on PC Thomas C. Johnson III. Again, for the uninitiated, it was just another city phenomenon; sometimes, when the mayoral heat and pressure became too great, it could blow a two-hundred-pound police commissioner fifty feet into the air. Therefore, in clear defiance of the warm-air-always-rises rule of thermodynamics, it was extremely warm in the lowly offices of Manhattan South Homicide, and likely to get much warmer.

In the thirty-nine hours since the event, Savage and his crew hadn't been able to produce even a mild breeze to cool off either the PC or the mayor, or assuage the hungry media who were busy fanning the flames at the feet of chief of detectives, Ray Wilson.

Savage passed through the larger eight-desk squad room to the smaller office he shared with the unit's two other sergeants, Billy Lakis and Jules Unger. Cramped with three large lockers, three full-size desks, a huge four-drawer file cabinet, and an old mahogany hat rack, the room was tight quarters, especially at those times when all three bosses were working. But today Savage had some elbow room. Lakis and his Team 1 were on RDO, and Unger's Team 2 was scheduled in for an evening tour.

Savage draped his topcoat on the hat rack, hung his Hickey-Freeman glen plaid jacket beside the sharply pressed blue uniforms inside his well-organized locker, and was reaching for his New York Yankees coffee mug when the phone on his desk rang. The voice on the other end belonged to Joe Ballantine, crime reporter for the *New York Post* and Savage's onetime drinking buddy. Ballantine had given up the sauce eight years ago to spare whatever was left of his pickled liver. If the man hadn't hooked up with AA and permanently ceased his intimate nightly relationship with Johnny Barleycorn, he'd probably be banging out the gossip column at the *Paradise Press*, the *Purgatory Picayune*, or . . . maybe the *Hades Herald*.

"Thorn," Ballantine opened with his scratchy, booze-coarsened voice. "How the hell you been?"

"Good, Joey," Savage replied warmly. "What's doin' with you?"

"Quite a damn bit, actually!" Ballantine whispered cryptically.

"Whoa!" Savage said. "Sounds like you got a handful of something. Anything good?"

"You gonna be at your office for the next hour?"

"Just signed in; haven't had so much as a sniff of caffeine to get my heart started. Don't think I'll be going anywhere for a while. Why?"

"You're in charge of that priest-killing investigation, right?"

"Uh-huh."

"How's it going?"

"Next question!"

"That good, hah?"

"Yeah, that good."

"Got anything at all?" Ballantine pressed.

"We know the two rounds that killed him came from a .45 caliber," Savage said, offering the reporter a pacifying tidbit. He declined to mention the Hail Mary prayer card that had been left on the priest's body, and that Crime Scene had been unable to recover any usable fingerprints from it or the surrounding scene. He also failed to mention that no eyewitnesses had come forward or been found, or that any kind of apparent motive had been established. Trace evidence—a few hairs and some fabric fibers—had been collected from the two curtained booths that abutted the priest's confessional, but it would be a while before they heard anything back on that stuff. Of course, then they still had to find someone to compare that trace evidence to.

"Forty-fives are monster guns, for crissakes," Ballantine said. "Weren't there any other people actually inside the church when it happened?"

"A few that we know of."

"Are you telling me that none of them heard at least two shots go off from a goddamned thug of a weapon like a forty-five? Inside an echo chamber of a church?"

"That's what I'm telling you. The thing had to have a terrific silencer on it."

"Hmm."

"But you know all this already, don't you?" Savage said. "What is it you really want, Joey?"

"Sounds to me like you've got yourself a pressure-packed heavy," Ballantine said. "Afraid I'm about to make matters even worse for you, though."

"How's that?" Savage asked, nodding at Detectives Diane DeGennaro and Richie Marcus, who had slipped quietly into his office.

"Stand by," Ballantine said. "I'll be up there in five minutes. I want to meet with you and your CO. *Only* you and your CO, got it? By the way, what's his name again?"

"Pezzano," Savage replied. "Lieutenant Pete Pezzano."

"I'm on my way. Got something frightening to show you both."

Joe Ballantine's assessment of "frightening" remained to be seen, Savage mused as he hung up the phone. But the reporter's assessment of the priest's murder weapon had been right on. The forty-five *was* a thug of a gun. It was big, heavy, loud, cumbersome, and kicked like a mule on crack. But as any firearms expert would tell you, the weapon certainly did have its redeeming qualities. First and foremost, forty-fives were designed to knock men down and knock them down fast. And they usually stayed down.

"Just heard from Davy Ramirez over at Ballistics," Diane DeGennaro said, breaking into Savage's thoughts. The looker First Grade Detective handed over a freshly typed DD-5 and continued. "The bullets taken from Father Gilhooley's body were fired from a Colt auto."

"Ramirez said it was one of them model 1911s," the somewhat paunchy—but not soft—Richie Marcus growled in his blunt-instrument Brooklynese. The veteran third-grader would never win any awards for elocution or polish, but his finely tuned police instincts and street smarts were Olympic gold. "Used to carry one when I was in the Corps," he added. "It is one nasty freakin' piece, I wanna tell ya!"

"Can you believe how cold it's gotten outside?" Diane said softly, gazing down at Savage through sparkling, Gaelic blues. A shiver crossed her lightly freckled face. "We were wondering if the car would even start when we left the apartment this morning."

"The car was gonna start, Diane. I never had any doubt," Marcus quickly piped up, giving her a macho-assaulted, how-dare-you glare.

Richie and Diane sometimes bickered, usually at his instigation. They were partners on The Job and played house together off The Job. Considering they spent twenty-four hours a day virtually joined at the hip, it was a miracle they didn't bicker more, often. Or worse. Everybody at Manhattan South Homicide—sixteen detectives, three sergeants, one lieutenant, and the newly assigned Carmen—loved Diane, and almost everybody liked Richie. The pair had long ago become known in the office as Beauty and the Beast. Marcus, as a solo, also bore the title of the Swami, for his willingness to opine from on high on virtually any topic.

"Yeah, I'm a little worried about this cold spell," Savage said. "After that freeze last night, Ray never came home."

"How can you tell?" Marcus asked. "Maybe he came in during the night, ate, and went right out again. Who knows," he added with a shrug, "maybe he had a date." A cat lover himself, Richie's question was etched with obvious concern.

"Nah," Savage said, shaking his head. "The cat door that leads to the fire escape is built right into my bedroom window. When he comes and goes, I usually hear it swing. Besides, I'd left half a slice of pepperoni pizza down for him. It was never touched."

"That doesn't sound at all like the Ray *we* know," Diane said, glancing over at Marcus. "The little bugger can smell pepperoni pizza from a mile away."

"And they're talking about a freakin' blizzard hitting the city sometime today or tonight," Marcus said. "He better get his furry butt back before that shit starts."

"He's been MIA for a day or two before, so I'm not fearing the worst yet," Savage said casually, knowing he was trying to convince himself. "And speaking of MIAs, has anybody heard from Jack? I see he's not in yet." It was the third time in recent weeks that the normally punctual Jack Lindstrom had been late for duty.

Marcus and DeGennaro shrugged helplessly.

"He'll be along, boss," Diane assured him, then suggested, "Maybe he had to stop and meet with somebody."

"Yeah," Marcus snickered, "like maybe he's meetin' with Jack Daniel's or Johnnie Walker for breakfast."

"Richie!" Diane snapped.

"Hey," Marcus responded in a calming tone, "we've all worked together here for a long time. We're pretty much like family, you know. Dysfunctional at times, maybe"—he chuckled and flashed an impish grin—"but still family." Marcus nodded toward Savage. "You think the boss here don't know what's going on? Get real," he said with a confident smirk.

Maintaining his silence with an innocuous expression, Savage hoped the revealing dialogue between the pair would continue. He wanted an uninfluenced view of their thinking on Lindstrom's recent behavior.

"Well," Diane said softly, "we all know Jack's got problems. First his sister got killed in the Twin Towers disaster. Then he went through hell with that killer divorce. His ex-wife really ran him through a meat grinder—"

"Divorce happens," Marcus interrupted unsympathetically.

"—Joan got the house, the car, big-time child support, and alimony."

"She got child support?" Marcus questioned. "Their daughter's grown-up. She's away in college, for God's sake—Villanova."

"That's right, Richie," Diane replied in a high tone, exasperated. "And Jack's paying that big tuition nut. But the girl still has to be supported—she's still gotta eat." Facing Savage, she added in an even tone, "Joan also left Jack with a mountain of lawyer's fees. He probably doesn't even have the *price* of a bottle of Jack Daniel's . . . or"—she turned to stare coldly at Marcus—"Johnnie Walker, for that matter. Why don't you just leave him alone?"

"Yeah, well he's suckin' on sumpthin' with an alcohol base," Marcus responded with another smirk. "Besides, he was a sap. Put up absolutely no fight. Went along with every damn demand Joan and her vulture lawyer made. He deserves exactly what he got, for crissakes. Guy's got no balls."

"You know he's still crazy about her, Richie. He thought he was doing the right thing," Diane said compassionately. Flashing a withering glare, she added, "The damn irony here is that it was Joan who was fooling around on Jack, not the other way around. That's gotta hurt. Worse, she's still tied up with that shady used-car salesman who broke them up in the first place, although I've heard there's been some trouble in paradise."

"That guy's got a pretty good sheet, you know," Marcus said. "Jack had somebody down at BCI run the hump's name on the QT a coupla months ago: falsifying business records, insurance fraud, false advertising, and a scheming to defraud, for which he was never convicted."

"Guy's got real problems with the truth, eh?" Savage said.

"Yeah," Marcus replied. "But his real specialty seems to be assaults. He's a tough guy; likes to beat people up. A barroom brawler."

"Not surprising," Diane replied. "I heard the guy was a real slimer, but I've also heard that Joan's supposedly about ready to dump him. But getting back to Jack . . . he's a real nice guy. A little on the brainy side sometimes maybe, but—"

"Brainy?" Marcus sneered. "Son of a bitch is a fugitive from Mensa, for crissakes."

"You sayin' that that makes him a bad person?" Diane asked, her steamy glare morphing into a look of incredulity. "Any woman would be lucky to have Jack Lindstrom. Really lucky."

"Yeah, well . . . " Marcus said, taking a beat as he cleared his throat nervously, "then maybe you and him could stay home nights and cuddle up with a nice game of chess or Trivial Pursuit."

Diane nibbled at the inside of her cheek and simmered in exasperation.

"Sarge," Eddie Brodigan, leaning into the small room, interrupted in the nick of time. "Someone here to see you." He stood aside and motioned a lanky, unmade bed of a man carrying a manila folder into the tight office. After a subtle get-lost nod from Savage, Marcus and DeGennaro let themselves out.

Joe Ballantine, thinner and grayer than the last time Thorn had seen him, wore a wrinkled jacket with suede elbow patches. Savage recognized the brown herringbone Harris Tweed from their previous meeting. It didn't have patches then, but the threadbare elbows had sorely needed them.

"Boy, Joey," Savage began, standing to shake the man's hand. "You sure know how to get mileage out of your duds."

"Huh?" Ballantine grunted, clearly oblivious to the dig.

"Never mind," Savage said. Chuckling to himself, he led the reporter from the cramped space. "Come on, let's get with the boss."

Petey Pezzano's office was immediately adjacent to the sergeants' room and only slightly larger. Like every other room in the building, it was painted the same boring semi-gloss municipal beige and illuminated with tired ceiling fluorescents. The unit's Stat-Board, which broke down Manhattan South's annual homicides and clearance rates into six categories, hung squarely on the long wall opposite Pezzano's desk. Framed eight-by-ten glossies, one of Police Commissioner Thomas C. Johnson III, the other of Chief of Detectives Ray Wilson, hung on either side of the official NYPD calendar. They were the only wall adornments in the entire office.

Savage leaned into the commanding officer's spartan space and rapped twice on the metal doorjamb. "You busy, boss?"

"No, not at all," Pezzano replied, looking up and casually sliding a dogeared copy of *AARP* into the kneehole drawer of his desk. "Come on in."

"Lieutenant Pete Pezzano," Savage announced. "I'd like you to meet Joe Ballantine from the *New York Post.*"

The hulking Pezzano, sometimes referred to as Big Bird by his troops because of his sheer size and gentle nature, stood and extended a ham hock of a hand. He was also notorious throughout The Job for having the balls of a lion and the heart of a submariner. Savage closed the office door.

"Good to see you, Joe," Pezzano said. "Take a seat." He motioned the men to the two chairs facing his desk.

"Joe's an old friend of mine," Savage started. "We go back a long time."

"I know that," Pezzano interrupted. "Think I've forgotten the shooting incident you had with that Russian hitter a few years ago, and the part Mr. Ballantine here played in it?"

Savage nodded. "Joe's asked to meet privately with just you and me. He's got something of importance to share with us."

Pezzano turned his wide inquisitive eyes toward the reporter. "What have you got, Joe?"

Ballantine tossed the letter-size manila folder onto Pezzano's desktop. "There are only a few other people who have seen this," he said, "and they've all been sworn to secrecy. It's related to that priest's murder the other day. I felt obligated to show Thorn before I considered doing anything else with it."

Savage rose from his chair and moved his limber six-foot frame around behind the lieutenant's desk.

"By the way," Ballantine added, "the envelope was sealed. And as soon as I got the gist of the letter, I ceased handling it. No one else but me, and probably the guy who typed it, have actually touched it."

Careful himself not to touch its contents, Pezzano opened the folder and laid it flat on his desktop. Loose inside were two pieces of yellowed stationery and a two-and-a-half by four-and-a-quarter prayer card that bore a picture of Our Lady of Fatima on one side and the Hail Mary on the other. Each piece of paper was typed on one side only and bore creases where they'd been folded into thirds to fit into the envelope that was clipped behind them. The plain white envelope bore the typewritten words, JOSEPH BALLANTINE, NEW YORK POST, PERSONAL AND CONFIDENTIAL.

Savage looked up briefly at Ballantine; then began reading over Pete Pezzano's beefy shoulder.

21 December

Mr. Ballantine,

The Catholic Church in America anymore is a big joke. It is a laughingstock. The bad bishops have cost the church all its moral authority. They're the ones who allowed all this garbage to happen. For starters they let faggots into the seminaries, because real men weren't becoming priests anymore. That's cause the seminaries needed money from paying students in order to stay in business and the church needed more priests to work in more and more priestless parishes. One more thing, the scandals we read about every day anymore are nothing new. Its been going on for a long time. Believe me, I know.

God bless the three peasant children of Fatima. It was them who let us know that the church is being run by the Antichrist. And judgment day is here for those who are under the spell of the Antichrist. The church must change, from top to bottom. The Third Secret of Fatima must be revealed to the world according to the command of the Blessed Virgin, for it will end the loss of faith in the Church and it will stop the abuse of the pastors, most who are nothing but fakers anyway. It will stop the petty fighting within the whole Church, and it will free the world from the evil powers of the devil.

I'm just a lowly grunt, enlisted in the army of people who work for Our Lady of the Rosary. And I am a short-timer, with only a few days left. Believe me when I say I have nothing at all to lose in this world anymore—and everything to gain in the next. Jesus once ran the money changers from the temple, now Our Lady will rid the Church of all those snakes that have hidden in it, and fouled it and tainted it. Snakes like Father Geoghan who got what he deserved in prison, and snakes like Father Gilhooley who was on the wrong side of the confessional.

There's an important mission for you too, Mr. Ballantine. It will be your job to keep the Lord's flock informed. They must be made to understand that this surgery—this gutting—is absolutely necessary to remove the terrible cancer and stop it from spreading any further within our beloved mother Church. Amen.

You must do this, Mr. Ballantine, for Our Lady has ordained it to be so. Do not disappoint her.

The time has come to wield a mighty sword placed in our willing hands by the Blessed Virgin herself. Our orders have been cut. The operation has been mounted. Father Gilhooley was only the beginning. Stay tuned . . .

The Soldier

"Jesus *K.* Christ almighty," Pete Pezzano uttered slowly, then blew out a long breath, turning to look over his shoulder at Savage. "Just what the freakin' city needs for Christmas, right? A rambling letter from goddamned Son-of-Sam-type maniac. A voice-hearing nut with a fucking mission to murder."

"Well," Ballantine uttered through a sardonic laugh. "At least this guy isn't getting his orders from his neighbor's dog. His come right from the top."

"Unh," Pezzano grunted.

"And by the way, Lieutenant," the reporter added with a sly grin. "Isn't it supposed to be Jesus *H.* Christ?"

"Afraid even he's got an alias now," Pezzano murmured, deadpan.

"When did you get this?" Savage asked.

"This morning," Ballantine replied. "Got into my office at about eight. It was sitting on my desk with a few other pieces of mail. It could have been dropped on my desk anytime between Saturday afternoon when I left and early this morning.

"The envelope isn't stamped or postmarked," Savage said, "so it didn't go through the post office."

"That's why I thought it was in-house stuff at first," Ballantine replied. "All someone needed to do was drop it in anybody's out-box at the paper, and I'd eventually get it."

"Who's to say that it *isn't* just an in-house prank?" Pezzano offered with a slight shrug. He did not mention the prayer card as being identical to the one from Saturday's murder scene. "Or something from some nut perpetrating a hoax."

"Who usually handles this in-house mail?" Savage asked.

"Copy boys," Ballantine responded.

"Find out which copy boys worked the weekend," Savage said. "We'll have to rule out their fingerprints on the envelope."

Ballantine nodded.

"What's this Third Secret horseshit?" Pezzano asked.

"I remember hearing a lot about that business when I was a kid in parochial school," Ballantine replied.

"Me too," Savage said. "And I clearly remember my parents talking about it. It was supposedly some secret letter from heaven that the pope was going to read to the world."

"Right," Ballantine agreed. "But it never happened. So just to refresh my memory, I jumped into our archives for some research before I headed over here." He pulled a piece of paper from his pocket and unfolded it.

Pezzano leaned his huge frame forward, resting his elbows on the desktop; he cradled a lantern jaw on massive fists. "Do tell," he said quietly.

Ballantine began to read from his notes. "On the thirteenth day of May, 1917, and on the thirteenth day of each successive month until October 1917, the Virgin Mary—Our Lady of the Rosary—supposedly appeared in a series of apparitions to three shepherd children at Fátima, Portugal. It was on the visit of July thirteenth that Our Lady confided a three-part secret to them.

"The oldest of the three children of Fátima was Lucia, who later entered the convent and became Sister Lucia. Sister Lucia had a long life, but her younger cousins, a boy and a girl, did not survive the decade. Years later, in 1941, Sister Lucia revealed the first two parts of the secret to the world.

"Supposedly, at about that time, she was again visited by the Virgin Mary, who told her that God wanted the third part of the secret to be written down and given to the pope. Which she supposedly did.

"And it was announced that the pope was to reveal that secret to the world no later than 1960," Savage interjected.

Ballantine nodded. "But never did. Supposedly, in 1960, Pope John XXIII broke the letter's seal and read the Third Secret. It's said that upon reading it he cried, but never revealed its content."

"Supposedly . . . supposedly . . . supposedly," Pezzano piped in. What the hell *supposedly* became of the damn thing?"

"It was said by Cardinal Ottaviani that John XXIII then placed the secret 'in one of those archives which are like a very deep dark well, to the bottom of which papers fall and no one is able to see them anymore.' *Supposedly,* every pope of the Church since has read the letter but—against God's wishes—has remained mute to its divine word."

"Sounds like a hoax," Pezzano said disgustedly, sitting back in his chair. "A bunch of bullshit religious hokum. Am I right?"

Savage and Ballantine exchanged you-got-me shrugs.

"There's an awful lot of people in this world who truly believe it," Ballantine finally said, scratching contemplatively behind his left ear with the cap of a Bic ballpoint. "The big question is, do I publish the letter and make the big news story out of it that it could be?"

"You want to go out on that limb?" Savage asked, not really believing what he was about to say. "The letter might just be a bad prank—"

"Or . . ." Ballantine interrupted, "the real thing. And if it is the real thing and I print it, will that encourage this nut to start bumping off other priests left and right? Would it be playing into his hand?"

"The letter clearly states *all* the snakes from the Church," Pezzano commented.

"And it stated that Father Gilhooley was only the beginning," Savage said. "Which can *only* be interpreted to mean that more priests may be targeted; that this is *just* the beginning of some nut's bloody crusade."

"And we certainly can't forget that the pope is coming to town next week," Ballantine inserted. "The letter clearly stated that the church must change . . . from *top to bottom.*"

"So who's forgetting?" Pezzano said, sounding like a yenta. The big lieutenant shrugged his ample shoulders and asked, "Would you consider sitting on this for a short while, Joe? Will your paper allow it?"

"Gotta tell ya, I'm up in the air on that," Ballantine responded. Leaning forward in his chair, he dropped his volume and added, "If it were not for my longtime association with Thorn here, I can tell you this, it would already be set in type. But I know I can trust Thorn not to leave me hanging, should I sit on it for now. Whatever agreements we make on this, I know he'll live up to."

"My guess is this," Pezzano said. "Monsignor Dunleavy, who has just been named by Cardinal Hammond to be our liaison with the archdiocese on the Gilhooley case, would probably want you to sit on it forever. Because of the papal visit, they want this thing totally played down. The mayor and the PC ditto. But I know you've got a job to do."

Savage stared directly into Ballantine's watery eyes; the whites were tinted a shade of reformed-drunk beige. "Give us forty-eight hours before you pop it. That'll get us past your Christmas Day edition and give us at least a little time to run this stuff for prints. Maybe we'll get lucky, come up with an I.D. and be able to drop a net on this psycho."

"I can do that," Ballantine said without hesitation. "But I'll need a quid pro quo to pacify my bosses. How about when you clip the Soldier's wings, I get an exclusive with him ASAP? We square?"

With a pair of quick knocks on Pezzano's office door, Jack Lindstrom let himself into the room. The tall, balding, third member of Savage's investigative team was a bit watery-eyed himself and, judging by the nicks on his face and neck, looked as though he'd shaved that morning using the ragged edge of a broken tall neck as a razor. His dated Sears suit needed pressing, and his shoes hadn't seen a shine in weeks.

"Sorry to disturb you, Lieutenant," Lindstrom announced in his polished baritone, "but Operations just notified us. We've got a priest dead in a construction site down on Allen Street—a Father Jean Brodeur. Shot twice."

"Jesus!" Pezzano murmured.

"Tell Marcus and DeGennaro to saddle up and get down there right away to preserve the scene," Savage said to Lindstrom. "You and I will be a few minutes behind them."

"Methinks this letter just might be the real McCoy," Ballantine said to no one in particular.

"You better get down there now, Thorn," Pezzano said. Looking up at the clock, he added, "It's five to nine. I'll take care of making the update call to Lieutenant Wonderful down at Ops. I'll also call Chief Wilson direct. Based on this letter and this new killing, I don't think there's any doubt that he'll want to form a task force."

"Do me a favor, boss," Savage said, moving to the door. "Have a copy of that letter hand delivered immediately down to Harvey Wallbanger." Reading the Harvey-who? look in Ballantine's expression, Savage explained, "Harvey Wahlberg, department psychologist, real oddball. Specializes in doing profiles on serial killers."

The reporter grinned comprehension. "Well, what about it, fellas?" he said. "Do I get the exclusive or not?"

Savage exchanged a split-second glance with Pete Pezzano. They'd worked together long enough to read each other's eyes. Both men turned simultaneously to the *Post* newsman and nodded.

THREE

In the late 1850s, the Hibernian working poor of New York City pooled their hard-earned pennies and nickels to acquire the entire square block of real estate that ran from Fiftieth to Fifty-first Streets between Fifth and Madison Avenues, and hired architect James Renwick—an Episcopal—to design them a splendid church. Some twenty years later—with time out for the Civil War—St. Patrick's Cathedral was completed. Twin spires were added to the Gothic Revival edifice in the late 1880s, making it the grandest Roman Catholic house of worship in the country—which it still is. St. Patrick's became the seat of the New York Archdiocese that includes ten southern counties of New York State. But ever since the first block was set in mortar, there has never been any question that St. Pat's was . . . of, by, and for, the New York Irish.

The surname of New York's first archbishop, and every archbishop and cardinal since, sounded as if it were randomly selected from a Dublin Dart Derby roster, or taken directly from an IRA roll call: John Hughes, John Cardinal McCloskey, Michael Corrigan, Cardinals Farley and Hayes, Francis Cardinal Spellman, Terence Cardinal Cooke, Edward Cardinal Egan. . . . It was, and is still, a closed shop.

Monsignor Albert Dunleavy, personal secretary to Cardinal Dennis Hammond, sat across from His Eminence in the warm study of the cardinal's official residence that is part and parcel of St. Patrick's Cathedral. It was almost nine, and their private regular Monday morning breakfast meeting was nearly over. Closely eyeing Hammond, Dunleavy saw a big man with thick shoulders erupting from a wide barrel chest. Big dark eyes, always inquisitive and calculating, suited his large head and broad nose, yet seemed mismatched with his small mouth and thin lips. Overhanging bushy eyebrows added the finishing touch to his full head of bristly, pure white hair that somehow never looked properly combed. The cardinal never left the residence without first donning the crimson skullcap, a zucchetto, or the three-cornered biretta to cover an abundance of cowlicks that sprouted everywhere.

After a quick review of the cardinal's proposed agenda for the coming week, and an exhaustive discussion of the Saturday shooting death of Father Thomas Gilhooley, Dunleavy decided to redirect the conversation.

"Your Eminence, the Vatican is demanding changes in the zero-tolerance sexual-abuse policy our American bishops have drafted. The Holy See is creating a joint commission with the Americans to work out the amendments."

"Does that come as a surprise to you, Albert?" Hammond said, his tone magisterial. He sipped at a steaming cup of tea, made a face, and quickly retrieved a sterling flask from his desk drawer. He uncapped it and poured liberally into the cup. "Do you not see why Rome is doing that?"

"Yes, their purpose seems quite clear," the monsignor replied. "May I be so bold?"

"Please," the cardinal said approvingly; then offered the flask to Dunleavy, who waved it off.

"I think the Vatican is concerned that the U.S. Conference of Catholic Bishops was allowing too many external forces to override internal control. . . ."

Hammond nodded. "Which is precisely the reason why the Vatican didn't want Cardinal Law to resign from his see in Boston years ago. They always considered him overvilified by the American media."

Dunleavy nodded back. "Law was the highest-ranking United States Church official to ever be run out of office as a result of scandal."

"But make no mistake about it," Hammond continued, again sipping his tea, this time without making a face. "They didn't accept Law's resignation based on public relations, Albert. No, no. They allowed his resignation only when it became clear that he'd been crippled in his ability to raise funds. The bottom line, of course, as always, is the dollar sign."

"We both know that Rome doesn't respond to public opinion polls, Your Eminence."

"Or to pressure," Hammond replied, slipping the sterling flask back into the drawer. "We've seen it time and again. They don't want to create an impression that they will cave in to pressures of any kind—especially from these lay organizations. Or that they would engage in damage control, like some government or corporate entity might."

"They fear a domino effect, Your Eminence," Dunleavy offered.

"True enough, Albert," Hammond said, as the phone on his desk began to ring. "What they fear most is too much laity control. They simply will not permit it."

"The liberal lay organizations are arguing that they only seek participation—"

"But Rome knows they're truly after a share of the power," Hammond interrupted, cutting Dunleavy off with the stop motion of an open palm. "Rome will forever suppress lay participation in Church governance. Excuse me. . . ." He picked up on the third ring.

Dunleavy sat patiently as the cardinal scribbled notations across a lined pad and uttered hushed grunts of understanding into his telephone.

In so many ways Hammond was truly a great man, Dunleavy thought. He was energetic and very likable, a wise and wily politician—an absolute must for his high-profile position—and a highly skilled administrator. Attendance at diocesan schools throughout the ten counties of the New York Archdiocese had increased modestly under his leadership, and the huge deficits that he'd inherited had been eased considerably. It was gratifying to be considered part of the cardinal's inner circle, a key element of his brain trust—especially in these trying times.

As the mantel clock above the study fireplace struck the hour, Hammond gently set the receiver down into its cradle and stared blankly at Dunleavy. His sudden pallor and sunken expression made the monsignor lean forward in alarm.

"Father Brodeur, that fine French-Canadian priest from OLPH on Fourteenth Street, has been shot and killed," Hammond stated in a monotone of disbelief. "His body was discovered a short while ago in a downtown construction site."

"Father Brodeur?" Dunleavy uttered in shock, blessing himself with the sign of the cross.

Snapping his index finger toward the telephone, Hammond added, "My source tells me the police department feels certain this crime was committed by the same person who killed Father Gilhooley on Saturday."

"Good Jesus, Mary, and Joseph. What . . . what is going on?" Dunleavy muttered, speaking more to himself than to the white-haired prelate.

"That's not all," Hammond said, leaning forward, pudgy hands clasped tightly together on his desktop. "It seems the *New York Post* has received a letter from somebody identifying himself as a soldier in the army of the Blessed Virgin. He alludes to the Third Secret and has declared a crusade against the 'serpents' of the Church."

"My God," Dunleavy echoed. "This . . . this monster thinks of priests as . . . serpents?"

"You've already been named as my official liaison with the police department, Albert. Now, with this latest development, I think it fair to say that they will be greatly intensifying their investigations. Therefore, from this point on, I think you should consider delegating some of your less critical responsibilities to others, and concentrate on dealing with the police . . . and their needs."

"I understand." Dunleavy, hanging on the cardinal's every word, gnawed gently at the rim of his lip.

Hammond sat back in his chair, gazed up to the ceiling, and exhaled heavily. "Mother Church is really being tested this time, Albert."

Measuring his words carefully, Dunleavy spoke. "We must walk a fine line here, Your Eminence. This murderous psychopath must absolutely be stopped. But I fear that if a police investigation—no matter how well intentioned—goes too far afield . . ."

Hammond raised his bushy brows for emphasis and tightened his intense gaze into Dunleavy's eyes. "Of course we must facilitate this investigation in every way possible. But we must use good judgment. We must be prudent."

"Yes, Your Eminence."

"The problem is, Albert," Hammond continued. "We just cannot allow the actions of a crazy man—no matter how horrendous those actions may be—to force us into exposing, shall we say, nonrelated information. . . . Nonrelated information that may damage the Church even more, especially now with His Holiness' visit merely a week away."

Monsignor Dunleavy nodded. It was clear that he and the cardinal were of a like mind in this matter.

The cardinal reopened his drawer, again withdrew his flask, and poured generously into his empty teacup. "We must do what is right," he said, flashing a look of complete resolve. "No damn scandals. Not in this archdiocese." He put the cup to his lips and downed the contents in three gulps.

The heady aroma of top-shelf Irish momentarily canceled out the decrepit mustiness of the airless book-lined room. "I understand, Your Eminence," Dunleavy said, struggling to accept his dicey task with more than tepid enthusiasm.

"I'll have Hans Peter drive you back over to the diocese office," Hammond directed. "I'm sure police investigators will be trying to contact you."

Dunleavy stood. "Yes, Your Eminence."

"Hans Peter will then bring you back here shortly before noon; we'll ride up to Gracie Mansion together for that luncheon."

Dunleavy gazed out the window. "I hope this snow lets up; it could get bad on the roads."

"Don't worry about that, Albert," Hammond said dismissively, as he slipped the sterling flask into his jacket pocket. "Hans Peter is expert at driving in heavy snow."

"I guess anyone born and raised in the Swiss Alps *should be* expert," Dunleavy commented. He bowed and turned to take his leave.

"Oh, Albert," Hammond called out just as the monsignor reached to open the study door. "One more thing. I've decided that when this terrible ordeal is behind us, and you've done a good job in the name of Mother Church—as I know you will—I intend to see you consecrated as bishop."

"Your Eminence . . ." Dunleavy uttered in total shock, never expecting to hear what he'd just heard; the words were unbelievable, all he had ever prayed for. It took many long seconds for him to regain enough composure to speak. "But, Your Eminence," he said, stammering, "is it not true that we are currently . . . somewhat out of favor with Rome?"

"In some ways, with some minds, yes. But you mustn't forget, Albert, that we do still have some strong allies, most notably within the Prefect of the Congregation for Bishops *and* the Section for Relations with States. How does Rochester sound to you?"

Quickly, Dunleavy crossed back to the desk and knelt

before the Prince of the Church. Taking Hammond's fleshy and veinless outstretched hand in his own, he planted a submissive kiss on the cardinal's huge sapphire ring.

"Thy will be done."

FOUR

With a silently sullen Jack Lindstrom riding shotgun, Thorn Savage slowly guided department auto number 7146 downtown on Second Avenue. Savage knew Jack had never been Mr. Personality. Charm just hadn't been built into his logical, rational, detail-oriented mind. But ever since his twin sister, Cheryl, had been one of the many who died that terrible September 11th morning, he had begun to change. Some time later his marriage started to disintegrate, causing him to evolve over a period of years into a somber, inward, almost antisocial wreck.

It had been a slow process, imperceptible at first, but a blanket of unhappiness now seemed to drape the man like a shroud. The wary, frightened frown of a crippled predator had replaced his once easy smile, and the muscles around his large jaw seemed locked and defiant. Jack was in deep trouble, drowning himself in booze and misery. He had eaten too much humble pie, and something had to be done before he wound up doing something stupid; like . . . maybe eating his gun. The time was right, Savage realized, for the heavy discussion he'd wanted to avoid.

"I know you've been living under a pile of pressure, Jack," Savage began. "It's been building on you for a long while. And I think the time has come to do something about easing it." Turning to face Lindstrom, he added, "Don't you?"

"Don't you think I'd like to ease out from under this mountain of bullshit?" Lindstrom replied, his voice a lifeless monotone, his bloodshot and watery eyes locked on the traffic ahead. "Don't you think I've tried?"

"I'm sure you have," Savage said evenly. "But sometimes . . . when things become too heavy, we can't lift the weight alone. Know what I'm saying?"

"Yeah, I know what you're saying," Lindstrom replied, still looking straight ahead. "You think I need a fucking shrink, don't you?"

Savage let the remark hang a moment, saying yes by saying nothing.

"Why am I like this?" Lindstrom asked, sounding exhausted. "Why am I always so frigging sensitive? Why have I always been so goddamned introverted . . . shy? Why couldn't I have been just a little bit more like fucking Richie Marcus?"

"Why would you want to be like Richie Marcus . . . or anybody else, for that matter?"

"That son of a bitch can stroll into a room full of strangers, and five minutes later *everybody* knows him— especially the women. They're all calling him by his first name and patting him on the back. I could walk into the same place and be there for a year, and nobody would know who the hell I am . . . *especially* the women."

"Everyone has his own strong points," Savage pointed out. "And you've got a whole lot of them, Jack."

"Well, attracting women isn't one of them," he mumbled. "Took me forever to find Joan years ago. And believe me, I *always* did the right thing by her. Still, it just wasn't enough."

"You'll meet somebody, Jack," Savage tried to reassure him. Besides being a subordinate, Lindstrom was a friend whose self-confidence had been trashed, and who, at the moment, had zero prospects. Desperation and loneliness were eating away at him.

"Look," Lindstrom said, "I know I haven't been myself lately. I know you think I've been hittin' the bottle a little too hard, and wallowing like some spineless shit in a tub of self-pity. . . ."

Again Savage chose not to respond.

"But I just can't turn myself in over at Psych Services. I've got to deal with this on my own terms. I'll come around, I promise."

"I don't think you can do it by yourself anymore, Jack."

"You don't know me very well, then."

"I know you well enough."

"Once Psych Services gets in the picture, my career won't be worth a goddamn. I'll be finished in this job; you know that."

"That's not true, Jack. Psych Services is totally confidential."

"Yeah, sure they are," he said, finally turning to face Savage. "The minute I tell them I'm depressed, they'll hand me a rubber gun and have me assigned to the Memo-Book Stapling Unit. No thanks. With all the other problems I have, I don't need some nerdy douche bag with a psych diploma fucking with my career. It's the only thing I got left."

"You're already fucking with your career, Jack."

"Give me a little more time, boss," Jack pleaded. "Honestly, I've been considering seeing a private shrink. But . . ."

"But what?"

"But it's a hundred and fifty bucks an hour, that's what; plus expensive prescriptions, which I'm sure there would be. If I'm going to keep word of my problems from The Job, I can't be using The Job's health and drug plans to cover treatment. I've got to go out of pocket. And right now . . ."

Savage understood Lindstrom's vicious-circle dilemma. A thread of an idea began to take shape in his mind.

"One more shot, boss," Lindstrom said faintly. "That's all I'm asking. Just one more shot. I'll get back on track. . . . I promise. Besides, my daughter's coming home from school for Christmas break. I'll get to see her on Christmas afternoon, take her out for dinner; spend some time with her. That'll help an awful lot."

Again Savage remained silent.

At Houston Street, they caught a solid red, which could cost them several minutes. Slowly, Savage eased the Crown Victoria into the spill-back-choked intersection, intimidating his way through the westbound bottleneck of horn-blowing taxis, trucks, and SUVs, forcing them, lane by lane, to make way and allow him through.

"Good on the right," Lindstrom uttered in a weary monotone, and Savage goosed the unmarked across Houston's clear eastbound lanes into Chrystie, and continued south past Roosevelt Park. With the first fat flakes of snow beginning to swirl, he clicked on the wipers to intermittent and made a left at Delancey, then another left into Allen Street. Near the mouth of a narrow alleyway that separated two partially gutted mirror-image apartment buildings—numbers 120 and 122—he parked the dark green sedan behind DeGennaro and Marcus' silver Taurus. Also on the scene were two radio cars from the Seventh, a Crime Scene van, and a transport vehicle from the medical examiner's office with a noticeably low right rear tire.

A dozen men—a demolition crew by dint of their hard hats and layered, tattered work clothes—were gathered randomly around a Dumpster set at the building line in front of 122. Some puffed cigarettes, others sipped from steaming foam cups, but none stood still against the biting cold. They were, no doubt, awaiting the crime scene to be cleared so they could get inside the buildings and start work for the day. An older man in his sixties, decked out in a cashmere topcoat and matching-brimmed hat, paced among them. Clearly agitated, he was chomping the bejesus out of a fat cigar.

Stepping from the vehicle, Savage glanced at the graffiti-scarred signs secured to the crumbling brick facades of the two buildings: FUTURE SITE OF THE CHAMONIX. 1-2-3 BEDROOM LUXURY CO-OP UNITS FROM THE MID $800s.

He silently thanked the apartment god for the good fortune of landing his rent-controlled one-bedroom over in the West Village years ago. Not as upscale as the Chamonix would be, but nobody's damn dump either. Besides, it was in the Sixth Precinct, a much better part of town.

Much of Manhattan's Lower East Side used to resemble Dresden after the intense allied bombing of WW II. Savage recalled that during the seventies, eighties, and into the early nineties, certain parts of the Seventh and Ninth Precincts looked like nothing more than war zones. For years, the areas had decayed into devastation, inhabited mostly by street corner pharmacologists, addict customers, and pathetic homeless. Starting in the midnineties, that all began to change. Most of the burned-out, half-demolished, nineteenth-century tenements were gobbled up by visionary investors and converted into luxury yuppie domiciles requiring hefty resources. This section of the Lower East Side, known as the Bowery, was now well into its renaissance. Who would have ever believed that the infamous wino-squeegee-guy capital of the world would one day be transformed into an exclusive got-rocks enclave?

"Jesus!" Lindstrom snarled. "Even if you had the mid-eight-hundreds for a lousy one-bedroom, they don't mention maintenance fees, which will probably run a grand or better a month for this place." He shook his balding head and muttered under his breath, "Where are people getting this kind of money?"

Savage shook his head in sympathy and flashed a what-can-you-do grimace as he closed the top button of his overcoat. "Stay out here and talk it up to these workmen, Jack," he said. "See if anybody knows anything." Savage then strode past the group of idle workers and entered the lengthy, debris-littered alleyway.

The snow had picked up momentum, now falling with a vengeance. Savage sensed that the temperature had dropped a few more degrees. He wondered if Ray had yet found his way home.

At Savage's approach, Richie Marcus nodded down at the still form at his feet. "Don't know who's colder right now, boss," he said, heavy breath vapors synchronized to his gruff words. "Me or the good padre here."

Dressed entirely in black, the dead priest was well shod in wing-tipped Bostonians, their outstretched heels and soles looked shoebox new—as if he'd been wearing them for the first time. Their topsides were highly polished. The neatly tied laces were the thin, waxy type. A green-faced Citizen quartz with a stainless band was strapped on the man's slender left wrist, and a signet ring of yellow metal adorned the third finger of his clenched left hand.

"We already have a positive identification, right?" Savage asked, watching snow quickly collect on the body. It was settling and gathering but not melting on the priest's bluing face. He'd been dead awhile. Falling flakes, like moths in wind-driven crazy flight, were being caught up in the web of the man's tightly curled dark hair.

"Yes," Diane DeGennaro said, thumbing through the dead man's black leather wallet. She looked up. "According to his I.D., *and* Sergeant Stabile, he's the Reverend Jean Brodeur." Diane nodded toward the female sergeant from the Seventh Precinct. The uniformed woman stood just opposite Thorn in the frozen huddle.

· "I knew him," Stabile said, her dark browns locking onto Savage's eyes. "He's one of the parish priests at OLPH up on East Fourteenth. I sometimes make early mass there before a Sunday day tour. He was a French Canadian, a very nice guy."

"OLPH?" Savage said.

"Our Lady of Perpetual Help." Sergeant Stabile was attractive, in her late-thirties, with a friendly demeanor, but Savage couldn't tell if she was built like Marla Maples or Rosie O'Donnell beneath the unflattering winter uniform. A Pistol Shot, a Meritorious, and two Excellent Police

Duty ribbons decorated the area above her gleaming sergeant's shield. Her eight-pointer with the golden chin strap was new, as were the chevrons on her sleeves. If the diminutive olive-skinned woman was wearing a ring, it was hidden beneath the gloved hands she alternately punched, one into the other.

"Ever see him other than up at OLPH?" Savage asked. "More precisely, have you ever seen him out and about down here in the Seventh?"

"No," Stabile replied, slowly shaking her head, her expression one of deep thought. "Can't say that I have."

"He had sixty-four dollars in his wallet," Diane said, "He also had a Visa card, an ATM card, driver's license . . . the usual."

"How old is he?" Savage asked.

"DOB on the license is June '49. Makes him . . . mid-fifties. Too damn young to die."

"Pockets?" Savage asked.

"Ring of keys, some small change," Diane replied. "And none of his pockets were turned inside out. Doesn't look like he was robbed."

The priest's body was supine, arms spread wide, collapsed backward onto a mound of jagged plaster-encrusted sections of splintered lath. Hazel eyes, dulled by death, were rolled partially back in his head and stared up at nothing. Dark bruising radiated out from a massive gunshot wound just above the bridge of a slender, well-formed nose. His unbuttoned black topcoat revealed a Roman collar at his neck. His plaster-smudged Homburg lay upside down several feet away on yet another pile of debris.

"Who found him and when?" Savage asked no one in particular.

"He was discovered by a couple of itinerant wine tasters about an hour ago," replied Ollie Beyeler from Crime Scene. The bug-eyed detective pointed to two homeless men who stood shivering just inside the doorless basement of 122. "Soon as they found him, they immediately flagged down a Seventh Precinct radio car."

"They told me they sometimes camp out in these under-renovation buildings," Richie Marcus said. "'Specially when it's this cold."

"And?" Savage prompted, expecting more.

"And," Marcus continued, "they'd just gotten themselves a coupla jugs somewhere up on Rivington and were diving into the basement of One-twenty to have a taste. They came upon the body as soon as they got to the back of the alley. Said they didn't see nobody else, though, and never heard the shot."

"So far," Diane DeGennaro added, "we've got no one who saw or heard anything."

"But," Ollie Beyeler said, opening a gloved palm to reveal a brass shell casing visible within a clear plastic envelope. "A forty-five, a Winchester, same as the two recovered from Blessed Sacrament Church the other day. How much you wanna bet they'll dig a full metal jacket out at autopsy?"

Savage nodded thoughtfully. The finding was good news in an evidentiary sense. But, he thought, it virtually locked in the frightening likelihood of a priest-hating serial killer on a rampage. The Soldier, he reluctantly concluded, was very much for real. He also wondered why Brodeur was shot only one time—in the head—unlike Gilhooley, who was also shot in the groin.

"Have we found a religious calling card?"

"Not on the body," Ollie replied. "But if one had been left, it might have blown away. And with this freakin' snow it might be all covered up by now."

"Can we figure all this went down before any of that demolition crew began showing up for work?" Savage asked, gesturing over his shoulder toward the milling group at the entrance to the alley.

"Yeah," Marcus answered. "The radio-car team that got

flagged down by Ernest and Julio said none of them workers was here yet."

"Get all of their names anyway, Jack," Savage said, turning to Lindstrom who had just joined the group. "Who knows? One of them might have seen something yesterday, or last week, for that matter, that could tie in." The bleary-eyed detective nodded, flipped to an open page in his notebook, and headed back out to the street.

"Excuse me," Ollie Beyeler said, motioning Richie Marcus to take a step back. Leaning over the dead priest, Beyeler focused his Nikon and quickly snapped a half-dozen shots of the bloody face.

Savage turned his attention to the medical examiner. The burly man in a snap-brim cap squatted beside the body that was quickly disappearing beneath a billow of white. "How long has he been dead, Doc?"

"Hard to tell, precisely," the ME replied, scrawling a signature on a blank toe tag pinched to a clipboard. Blinking away flakes that swirled wildly into his eyes, he looked up at Savage. "We've got a bit of rigor, and the belly-meat thermometer said ninety-five point four."

"A body loses one to one and a half degrees for every hour after death," Savage mumbled, doing a quick calculation. "So—"

"So," the ME interrupted, "allowing for this incredible cold, I'd say he died two, maybe two and a half hours ago." He raised the priest's semistiff left arm and glanced quickly at the green-faced Citizen. "Which would put probable time of death at about six thirty this a.m."

"What the hell was this guy—*this fully decked-out Roman Catholic priest, for crissakes*—doing in the back of this shit-filled alley at six-freakin'-thirty in the morning?" Richie Marcus said.

Savage searched his mind for some possible explanation. Surely the priest didn't have a paper route, and he certainly wasn't dressed for demolition work, and, Lord knew, there was probably plenty of wine to be had up at the rectory. Maybe he'd been called out for some purpose? If so, he was probably accosted on the street and forced into the alley at gunpoint, Savage reasoned.

"Anything else remarkable about the body?" Savage asked. "Any injury unrelated to gunshot? Bruises, cuts, that sort of thing?"

"Nothing apparent," the ME replied with an edge, seemingly irritated by the harsh working conditions. "We'll get a better look back at the shop."

Squinting against the swirling whiteout, Savage turned back to DeGennaro and Marcus. "Twenty minutes from now we'll all be up to our butts in white stuff. I'm gonna seal up the crime scene. I want you both to stay here and supervise barricading off the area. I want it preserved just in case we've gotta come back and look for a calling card when this shit finally melts."

"Then?" Marcus asked.

"Then both of you head up to Our Lady of Perpetual Help Church on East Fourteenth. Make certain it was where Reverend Jean Brodeur was assigned. Find out whatever you can. Get information on next of kin for notifications, and see if anyone there knows why this guy was out of the residence so early this morning."

"You mean like was he called out for something, like uh . . . I don't know," Marcus said, shrugging. "A wedding, a funeral . . . a bar mitzvah?" There was the impish Marcus grin.

Diane looked at Savage. "Are you going back up to the office?"

"No," Savage replied. "I'm heading up to the archdiocese headquarters. I want to personally sit down with that Monsignor Dunleavy. Gotta bring him up to date on Father Brodeur here and this. . . ." He handed Diane and Richie each a copy of the Soldier's letter.

"What about Jack?" Diane inquired. Her look was one of mild concern.

"I'll ask Sergeant Stabile if she'd be good enough to

taxi him over to the ME's office for us. I want that slug extracted ASAP and immediately hand delivered to Ballistics for comparison—he can take care of all that. In the meanwhile, ask those uniforms over there to give you and Richie a hand. I want to delineate as narrow a path as we can through this alley. Once it's established, make sure everybody steps in the same damn footprints."

"What do we do with Drunken Hines and his lice-ridden faithful companion?" Marcus growled, deadpan.

"Get them transported over to Bellevue," Savage said, glancing across to the pathetic pair of scratching and shivering winos. "Get them admitted, and get them warm. I want them fed, dried out, and deloused. We're gonna have to talk at some length with them, and I want the best, most lucid answers we can get. And," he added, "I don't want any of us scratching when we get done." He turned and nodded to the ME. "Let's close it up," he said.

A grateful smile spread across the ME's pudgy face. He nodded to his two assistants, one standing by with a body bag and the other who had just arrived with a wheeled gurney. "Let's move him out."

"Gonna be awhile, Doc," the gurney pusher said. "We done got us a flat. I radioed for another bus."

Shaking his head, Savage intruded on a testy conversation that was going on between the attractive Sergeant Stabile and the cashmere-coated cigar chomper he'd seen out front upon his arrival. She introduced the unsmiling man as Hy Wykoff, the building project's head contractor. The man's handshake could not have been more flaccid.

"Your precinct will have to provide a twenty-four-hour fixed post here to preserve the scene," Savage informed the sergeant. "One man in a radio car ought to do it. No one is to enter this alley—or either of these buildings—until we call the fixer off. Also, I've got a favor to ask of you. . . ."

Stabile readily agreed to transport Jack Lindstrom over to the ME's office.

"What about my demolition work?" Wykoff snapped

angrily, his glare intense as his eyes flashed back and forth between Savage and Stabile. The man's twenty-five-dollar cigar was nearly bitten to death. "I'm already behind schedule," he argued. "And that crew I've got standing around out there is looking to earn a goddamned day's pay."

"Now, Hy, let's you and me be reasonable," Sergeant Stabile said gently. "It's snowing like a son of a bitch. Come tomorrow, a team of huskies won't be able to get anywhere near this job; neither will your demolition crew."

"But . . . I've got—" Hy began to object, but was gently and firmly cut off.

"You have to understand, Hy," Stabile continued, "there is simply no possible way that Homicide can, or will, permit your men to work here today. If they did, important evidence in this case could be covered up, swept away, or totally destroyed. You wouldn't want that to happen, Hy, would you?" she murmured persuasively in a soft, sultry voice.

Savage remained silent, greatly impressed by rookie Sergeant Stabile's smooth style.

"What the hell am I supposed to do, then?" Wykoff whined, his hard shell obviously cracking. "Eat the day?"

Stabile slipped her arm into Wykoff's, turned him, and arm in arm began to slowly escort the perturbed man from the alley. "Listen to me, Hy," she pressed, "since there ain't a damn thing any of us can do about your crew getting into either of these buildings today . . . and since tomorrow is Christmas Eve anyhow . . . my best advice to you would be to cut your boys loose, pay 'em for the damn day, and come out of this whole thing looking like a real mensch." Stabile stole a dramatic look over her shoulder and winked coyly at Savage. "They'll love you for it. Whaddaya say?"

Frowning and frustrated, Hy shifted the gobbled cigar back and forth in his mouth like it was on rollers. Finally, he uttered a resigned, "Awright."

As Savage made his way back through the alley, he overheard the beginning of an exchange between Jack Lindstrom and Richie Marcus. He slowed his pace to listen.

"I wonder what the padre found when he got to the other side?" Marcus said.

"What do you mean?" Lindstrom asked.

"You know," Marcus went on. "Pearly gates? Harp music? St. Peter? That whole bit. Hey, wouldn't it be a real bitch if right now he was surrounded by seventy-two virgins doin' the dance of the seven veils? That'd be ironic, hah? Findin' out he'd put all his money on the wrong horse all these years." Marcus laughed.

"You oughtta know what that's like, Richie," Lindstrom said, needling the notorious gambler. "Putting all your money on the wrong horse."

"Yeah, well," Marcus snapped back. "At least I didn't wind up *marryin'* the wrong fuckin' horse."

Savage slowed his pace to a complete stop. The discussion was not headed in a good direction.

"Don't give me that bullshit, Marcus," Lindstrom shot back. "Seems I recall that *your* ex-wife walked out on you, too."

"Yeah, she walked awright," Marcus responded. "But I helped her pack her freakin' bags. I didn't kiss her ass and beg her to stick around. Besides, she left me for a doctor, for crissakes, an MD. Not for some good-for-nothin' fuckin' petty thief . . ."

It was go-time. Jack Lindstrom turned, squared off, and feinted a left jab as Marcus put up his dukes. Lindstrom quickly shifted his stance and swung, a right cross missing Marcus' chin by little more than a hair. Light on his feet and good with his hands, Marcus slipped the punch expertly, and had Lindstrom dead in his sights for a KO hook to the taller man's now unguarded jaw. Marcus, unquestionably the tougher of the two, did Lindstrom a big favor

by holding the punch, moving instead to restrain Lindstrom with a strong-arm clinch.

It took Savage, Diane DeGennaro, and a couple of
husky uniformed cops from the Seventh to safely separate
the wild-eyed Swede from the tough ex-marine.

Savage propelled Jack Lindstrom off to the side and
said firmly but quietly, "If you don't agree to do something
immediately about your problem, Jack, then you'll leave
me no choice but to refer you over to department Psych
Services."

"Don't do that, boss," Lindstrom begged. "That'd be a
mark on my record that would never come off."

Savage had decided to contact his old friend, Father
Vincent Rossi, a Jesuit with a doctorate in psychology.
Maybe Father Vinny could help steer Jack through this
mental minefield. Maintaining deep, no-nonsense eye contact with the troubled detective, Savage said, "I want you
to go talk to a friend of mine. If you do every damn thing
he says, I'll hold off."

Lindstrom dropped his head in wretched misery, then
looked up and nodded.

FIVE

Savage inched the Crown Victoria up First Avenue, passing the United Nations complex at a steady sixteen miles an hour. He no longer noticed the intermittent slap of ice-encrusted wipers, the roar of a defroster blowing at max, or, for that matter, the constant chatter coming over the police radio. Like a pinball, his thoughts caromed elsewhere, striking and quickly rebounding between butchered priests, the Soldier's poison-pen letter, and his old friend, Detective Jack Lindstrom, who was rapidly stripping his gears.

Steering cautiously, he maintained as much space as possible between himself and the other skidders and sliders attempting to navigate uptown, and wished he had chains on his back wheels for better traction. Auto number 7146 was his assigned department vehicle. Unlike most two-year-old department cars—marked or otherwise—the Ford had no dents or scrapes, and he was determined to keep it that way.

He was already a half hour into what should have been a mere ten-minute hop from the Allen Street murder scene up to the Roman Catholic Archdiocese offices in the high East Fifties, but Mother Nature had the city almost at a standstill. The storm-stymied late morning traffic was already bad, but Savage knew it was sure to get a lot worse before it got any better. If road conditions became too crazy by the end of the day, he'd leave the Crown Vic parked in the station house block and take the subway home. It was only two stops on the number 4, 5, or 6 train, with a one-stop change to the F over to West Fourth. Then it was a short two-block walk to his Sullivan Street apartment. He wondered if Ray would be there, or if the pizza slice he'd left down for him would at least show signs of having been gnawed. Sometimes—when Ray wasn't feeling quite up to snuff—he'd just pick at the cheese topping, but he never failed to knock off all the pepperoni slices. If the old tom wasn't there, he'd check for paw prints in the snow on the fire escape.

Careful not to give the car too much gas and wind up in a sideways skid, Savage slowly crested the slight incline at Fifty-sixth Street, and as he rolled through Fifty-seventh heard his cell phone ring. He passed Fifty-eighth and Fifty-ninth, and pulled into a bus stop beneath the stone arch of the Queensborough Bridge. One block ahead on his left, he could see a line of cars parked in front of the Catholic Archdiocese building entrance. Busy place, he thought, hoping a spot would open up by the time he finished taking the call; he was wearing an expensive pair of Allen Edmonds that were not designed to be used as snowshoes. He shifted into park and answered the phone on the fourth ring.

"Hello . . . *Thorn*?" The sultry yet resolute, feminine voice belonged to Maureen Gallo.

For many years, Maureen had been the only woman in his life, and twice they had even tried living together. But it hadn't worked. Outsiders looking in had always said they were "too much alike." Whatever the hell that meant. After they'd broken up the last time, he'd started seeing Gina McCormick. He hadn't heard from Maureen since she'd made her respectful appearance at Gina's funeral seven months and, he quickly calculated, twenty-one days ago.

"Maureen . . ." he said guardedly, not yet totally believing his ears.

"How have you been?" she asked softly.

"Been hanging in there," he responded, somehow warmed by her familiar and distinctive phone presence.

"Where are you?" she asked. "Can you talk?"

"I'm in my car at Fifty-ninth and First. I'm either going to get rammed by a bus or buried by a snow plow. . . . But I can talk."

"You're not too far from Neary's," Maureen said, a wistful quality riding on her words.

"It's right around the corner, a mere iceberg and a half away," he replied, intentionally casual, carefully avoiding any hint of wistfulness. Neary's Pub, on East Fifty-seventh, used to be one of their special places; it was where they had first met. "So," he said, "what have you been up to?"

"Well, since you asked, I took a jaunt down to Atlantic City with a few girlfriends over the weekend," she answered, then added with a chuckle, "I lost my shirt."

Her remark seemed to beg for a risqué, if not off-color, response—much like the one that had already leaped into his mind. A response he might normally have teased her with back in the days . . . back when. . . . He played it safe with a reply of neutral beige instead of racy blue. "I didn't know you were a gambler," he said.

"I'm not," she said defensively. "I just went along for something to do. Get outta Dodge; know what I'm saying? You know I'm no gambler, Thorn, any more than you are."

Maureen was right; he had never possessed the gambling instinct. He had absolutely no idea how to play craps, except knowing the numbers seven and eleven had some meaning in the game; exactly what, he did not know.

"You're not a card player," she said. "And I don't believe you've ever bet on a horse. And you're probably the only guy I know who's never been to Vegas."

"True enough," he acknowledged with a smile. "I don't like gambling my money; especially on odds set and controlled by somebody else."

"You'll never change," Maureen said. "I find it strange,

though, how you never question the odds when gambling life and limb."

"Huh?"

"Hell," she said. "You're a sky diver with over a thousand jumps. You've dived two times on the *Andrea Doria . . . that I'm aware of.* And I know that on more than one occasion you've bet the whole damn enchilada in a go-for-broke gunfight."

"Yeah," he replied thoughtfully. "But then *I* was making the odds."

She laughed. "You're as much a gambler as the worst of them, just in your own unique way."

Maureen's blasé comment about gambling triggered a fleeting notion: He could bet the ranch, and win, that more priests were soon going to die at the hands of a nut with a muffled cannon. Up ahead, he saw a dark blue Lexus pulling away from a spot directly in front of the archdiocese.

"I know you must be very busy, so I won't hold you," she continued, a dash of nervousness suddenly salting her voice. "And please don't think that what I'm about to ask is being disrespectful in any way of Gina's memory. I know how devastated you were when that terrible business happened, and—knowing how you hold things inside—probably still are."

"Unh," he grunted, fighting back the painful memories. "I've had better years."

"Well, it's Christmas," Maureen announced, putting on some Grade A–quality cheerfulness. "And it looks like it's actually going to be a white one at that. I was thinking that if you had no plans . . . and were going to spend Christmas Day alone . . . maybe you'd like to come to my place for dinner."

Her words were studied and smooth, almost scripted. They came quickly—not fast, just quickly—like a telemarketer gifted enough to complete the spiel before hearing the hang-up click. "I'd love to have you," she went on.

"Unhhh!"

"I could cook us a couple of those Scottish pasties you like so much. When was the last time you had one of them? You can't get them anywhere else; I'm probably the only person in New York with the damn recipe."

Caught totally flat-footed and at a true loss for words, Savage quickly thumb-nailed a Wint-O-Green Life Saver from a roll in his pocket. He had an open invitation for Christmas dinner with his sister, Emily, and her family, but . . . He popped the candy into his mouth.

"No pressure, Thorn," Maureen assured him. "Just a couple of old friends doing their best to help each other get through life."

"What time?" he asked quietly, not at all sure he was doing the right thing by acquiescing. He'd been here before. Maureen Gallo always knew just the right buttons to push to lure him back into her life. Trouble was, she just didn't know how to keep him once she got him. The appetizer was always great, he thought, but the entree . . .

"Why don't you get here around three," she said evenly, the telemarketer gone. "We'll eat at four."

"What should I bring?"

"All you've gotta bring is you."

Observing that the snowflakes were getting fatter and falling faster, John Wesley Krumenacker walked gingerly along the powder-covered sidewalk of Avenue B; he moved at the slow and steady breath-saving pace he'd become accustomed to in the last year. As he turned into East Seventh, he saw a Ninth Precinct radio car parked in front of his tenement. Two uniformed cops—a man and a woman—were out on the sidewalk among a cluster of loudly talking people gathered in front of the building. He recognized most of them as his neighbors. The cops were talking specifically to Alan Pitler, the elderly spastic from 1C. Curious about the excitement, he picked up his pace slightly and joined the very animated group.

Sidling up to Mrs. Brzazinski, the widowed busybody landlady from 1B, he asked, "What's going on?"

She pointed a bony nail-chewed finger at the rusty old chain that hung from the equally rusted wrought iron railing running alongside the stoop. Although the padlock was still locked and attached to it, the chain itself had been freshly hacksawed through.

"Some rotten son of a bitch and bastard has gone and swiped Mr. Pitler's three-wheeled bicycle," she snarled in one breath, shivering and crimping the collar of her coat against the chill. "The poor man needs that bike and basket to get around—shopping, the doctor. The guy can barely walk." Then, speaking in a hushed tone from the side of her crooked mouth, she added, "Poor bastard'll never be able to afford another one."

The beat-up adult-sized tricycle had been Alan Pitler's only known means of transportation for as long as John Wesley had lived at that address—four years. The neurologically challenged man would use it to pedal to the corner market, return with small bundles in the back basket, and chain it securely to the railing so it would be there for him next time. This was not a neighborhood where you left things of value—or of no value, for that matter—unsecured.

Finished taking their report, and with a cursory promise to keep an eye out for the stolen trike, the two cops climbed back into their cruiser and drove off. The group of neighbors quickly drifted back into the building. As Mrs. Brzazinski helped Mr. Pitler negotiate the snow-covered stoop, John Wesley saw tears in the fragile man's weary eyes.

Careful not to slip and fall, John Wesley Krumenacker slowly ascended the five snow-covered steps in front of the long-neglected Lower East Side tenement. He stopped momentarily at the top to catch his breath, then entered the building's outer hallway. After stomping the gathered snow off his spit shined U.S. Army jump boots—the very same pair he'd been issued at Fort Benning parachute-training school almost four decades ago—he turned a key in his mailbox to find the latest copies of *Reader's Digest*, *Smithsonian*, and *Natural History Magazine*. Quickly thumbing through the thick stack of envelopes, he saw that most bore return addresses that were a variation on a theme: Compassion Christian Child Sponsorship, Save the Children, Children of War, Children in Need, Children's Cancer Research Fund. . . . It was that time already, he realized; the third week of the month, when all the children's charities he supported sent out their monthly statements.

The remainder of this morning would be spent writing checks and draining what little was currently left in his account; his direct-deposited disability payment from Social Security wasn't due again until the first of the year. So what? he concluded with a mild sigh; he probably wouldn't even be here come the first. He stuffed the mail into the large patch pocket of his worn quilted parka and let himself into the building proper.

At the first apartment door on the right, 1A, he turned a separate key in each of two locks; then pushed against the aged door that dragged on galled hinges, letting himself into his cluttered room. He closed the metal door behind him and re-engaged the stout dead bolts from the inside.

Moving with shallow breaths matched to measured steps, Krumenacker crossed the buckled linoleum to the table against the far wall. It held his AirSep oxygen concentrator, his Underwood portable typewriter, and stacks of correspondence from dozens of children's welfare organizations and charity foundations. He slipped off the nylon tote that hung like a woman's purse from his narrow shoulder, set it on the table, and reached inside to close the valve on the D-size oxygen tank. His fingers unclipped the cannula from his nostrils and removed its snug-fitting umbilical from behind both ears, then gently massaged the deep impressions it left on both sides of his windburned face.

A quick glance into the small flaking mirror that hung cockeyed above the table reflected an unhappy snarl. The idea of needing such a lousy goddamned device just to be able to breathe was hateful. Shaking his head in disgust, he rolled and stored the tank-fed items into the bag and exchanged them for the AirSep cannula with its thirty-foot umbilical. He flipped the oxygen-making machine's switch to ON and breathed deeply. Home sweet home, he thought, rolling his eyes.

Krumenacker scanned the room's chalky green walls, whose only adornments were a palm-wrapped crucifix over his unmade sofa bed, a picture of dogs playing poker, and a plaque bearing the winged insignia of the 173rd Airborne Brigade that hung above his recliner. The place hadn't seen a lick of paint in decades, and the roaches that frequented the lopsided counter in the phone-booth-size kitchenette were sometimes bigger than the building's resident rats. The dump had water leaks, toilet backups, power failures; the list was endless. Sounded as if I'd just described myself, he thought. But the place was warm enough in the winter, and cheap. . . . He needed his money for other things.

John Wesley's mother had always liked a warm apartment too. He remembered hiking the long sixteen blocks home with icy fingers and numb ears and toes after serving mass as an altar boy at St. Benedict's up in Inwood. Mom's kitchen always smelled of fresh-baked cookies and steaming hot chocolate when he got home. He sighed; how simple life was in those days—before the horribly agonized death of his sainted mother . . . and the hateful years at St. Malachy's.

After exchanging his coat for a pilled green cardigan, he reached again into the nylon tote and carefully removed a Ziploc baggie that contained water and a single, very plump guppy. Charlie needed feeding.

He carried the baggie across to the four-drawer dresser that sat beneath the room's only window. The chest, made of flaking pressboard, was shimmed level at a legless corner by a stack of paperbacks, crime novels he'd read dozens of times. It supported a small television, a gilt-frame photograph of his mother taken before she fell ill, and a two-gallon fish tank.

"Is the vaunted commander of VC Company 308 ready for his rice ration?" John Wesley coughed his way through the words, temporarily clearing his throat of the constant phlegm.

The purplish-blue Southeast Asian exotic always expected his chow at ten thirty every morning. It was a ritual. John Wesley shook exactly two tiny pellets onto the surface of the crystal-clear water. One by one they sank, and Charlie quickly gulped one. Two Hikari pellets a day: any less and he would go hungry; any more and he might get sick.

The graceful betta rose to the surface, seemed to mouth hello, and dove once again to dine. J.W. smiled contentedly. He loved the damn fish. It was so nice to have trustworthy companionship again after all these years, he thought, even if it was a fish—and a gook fish at that.

After the crushing loss of his beloved mother, followed by his bumbling inability to head off poor Buffo's suicide, he had never again permitted a human being to enter his heart. Though he had known great loneliness in his life, it had been a small price to pay to avoid the pain of losing someone he loved, and the unbearable weight of additional self-loathing and guilt that would surely come by failing another friend.

And now he struggled with a different kind of self-loathing, a haunting thought he could not shake. He'd just killed the wrong man.

Savage left the sanctuary of the bridge underpass and drove the short half block to the First Avenue building housing the administrative offices of the New York Archdiocese. He pulled his department car into the spot vacated only mo-

ments ago by the Lexus, parking in front of a black Buick
sedan and behind a new gray Lincoln that was idling at the
curb. A miracle, he thought, or, at the very least, some small
degree of divine intervention. He tried remembering the last
time he'd found an open spot directly in front of anything,
anywhere in this city. Especially when the weather was bad.
He tossed the NYPD parking plate up on the dash and
stepped out into three inches of fresh powder.

The big Lincoln must have pulled up only moments earlier; the distinctive tracks of its wide Michelins were still
clearly outlined in the pristine snow. The chauffeur, a
blond Aryan type whom Savage figured to be somewhere
in his midforties, slouched behind the steering wheel while
flipping through a newspaper. A garish chunk of gold with
an almond-shaped red stone adorned the man's left pinkie;
funny, Savage thought, the guy didn't look Italian. One set
of size-nine footprints, impressed with the distinctive
badge of the Florsheim heel, led from the car's curbside
rear door directly into the main entrance of the archdiocese
offices.

Upon entering the building, Savage immediately picked
up on the strong aroma of burnt incense that seemed to per-
meate the entire interior. The offices smelled like the nave
of a church, which, he guessed, was fitting. He stepped to
the reception desk and was greeted there by a kind-looking
blue-haired lady.

"I'm Sergeant Savage from Manhattan South Homicide," he said in an appropriately hushed tone, discreetly
showing the elderly woman his gold shield. "I'm here to
speak with Monsignor Dunleavy."

"Oh, my, yes," the woman said. She rose slowly from
her chair, tapped gently on the office door immediately behind her, and let herself in. Her entrance interrupted a discussion between a lanky angular man in a tweed topcoat
and galoshes and a stern-looking woman in a drab business
suit and sensible shoes. After exchanging a few words with
the woman, Blue Hair returned to her desk.

"Angela, the monsignor's assistant, is busy right now," the receptionist informed him. "I've told her that you are here. If you wouldn't mind being patient for just a few moments, sir, she'll be right with you."

Savage smiled warmly and nodded to the old gal, who reminded him of his long-departed favorite aunt, his mother's older sister, May. Stepping aside from the reception desk, he was unbuttoning his coat just as the office door reopened and Angela escorted Tweed Coat toward the exit door; they were still in discussion. It was clear that the man was making a strong pitch for work schedule changes and pay increases for St. Patrick's organists.

Angela was a severely dressed and plain, unsmiling woman. She had a terminally pinched oval face, and her wiry salt-and-pepper hair was parted down the middle and pulled into a tight bun at the back of her head. The guy she was with was a fidgety Ichabod Crane type. Together, they looked something on the order of the grim figures in Grant Wood's *American Gothic*. When Tweed Coat finally left the building, Angela immediately turned her attention to Savage.

"I'm sure the monsignor will see you right away," she said tersely, with no preamble or outstretched hand. "Give me a second to let him know you are here."

Angela nodded curtly and stepped back into her well-lighted office. Savage saw her pick up a phone and punch in three digits. After a brief conversation, she returned and escorted him up a carpeted winding staircase to the second floor. Along the way, he picked up on a strange odor that seemed to compete with the aromatic scent of burnt incense, the ambient smell of the offices. Strangely, the sweet aroma was interspersed with something on the order of . . . *penicillin?* In the middle of the lengthy second-floor hallway, Pinch Face slammed on the brakes and rapped firmly on a gleaming mahogany door. A voice from inside said "Enter."

Monsignor Dunleavy's face seemed oddly small, a fair-

skinned oval surrounded by fine silver hair carefully
parted to one side. His deeply set Wedgwood blues were
icy cold, hyperalert, and radiated caution. He was dressed
in priestly black with the typical white square at his collar.
His long tunic—if that's what it was called—had tightly
spaced buttons of red satin running down the front, and all
the finished edges of the garment were outlined with
matching narrow red piping. He greeted Savage with a
ready smile, a firm handshake, and an offer of fresh coffee.

"Cream, half teaspoon of sugar," Savage replied readily,
still chilled from the bitter crime scene. Then, recalling the
few extra pounds he'd put on recently, he said, "Better yet,
hold the sugar."

"*Angela . . .* " the monsignor said, looking expectantly
at Pinch Face.

After the woman did an about-face and left the room, he
motioned Savage to an oversize lounge chair directly opposite his ornate walnut desk. The chair, artfully uphol-
stered with worn burgundy leather, was rich with hobnail
detailing. A deep crimson oval rug, richly paneled walls,
and high fretted ceilings evoked an air of Old World stately
refinement into the spacious room. How very ecclesiastic,
Savage thought. He unbuttoned the rest of his coat and sat.

"You just caught me, Sergeant," Dunleavy said, a little
too offhandedly. "As soon as my car gets here, I'm to pick
up Cardinal Hammond at his residence. The mayor has invited us to a luncheon at Gracie Mansion. The mayor and
the cardinal are very old and dear friends, you know."

Guy's gotta know the car's downstairs, Savage thought.
"I promise not to take too much of your time, sir," he said
respectfully.

Angela returned quickly with a steaming cup and
passed it silently to Savage from long-fingered bony
hands. Again he got a solid whiff of the peculiar odor that
was all about her. For just a second, he was back in his
high school chemistry lab, futzing with a fuzzy green cul-
ture in a petri dish.

"That will be all, Angela," the monsignor said. Fixing his gaze on her, he added, "Be sure and let me know the moment my car arrives."

The woman bowed slightly, turned on her heels, and left. She closed the office door tightly behind her.

"Angela is a fine person," Dunleavy offered with a knowing grin, obviously looking into Savage's head. "Very religious, very devoted. She's worked here in the archdiocese for many years. Don't know what we'd all do without her."

Savage nodded to Dunleavy, playfully thinking how Angela's vibes better fit those of an off-duty nun, a closet dominatrix, or a funeral director. Somehow he could see her all in leather, brandishing a riding crop or cat-o'-nine-tails. She just had that look. He remembered the nuns at St. Raymond's parochial school, which he'd attended as a child. Many of those nuns had that same air about them, and, he was convinced, had a genuine sadistic streak. More than once, some Little Sister of Mercy had slapped his face, pulled hair from his head, or whacked his knuckles with a rock-hard maple ruler until they bled.

Savage sipped at the coffee and detected a hint of hazelnut. It was good; Angela sure knew how to make a stand-up cup of java, but he missed the sugar.

"Looks like we're really in for it this time," Dunleavy said, turning to gaze out at the swirling storm through a pair of mullioned, leaded windows that framed a partial view of the storm-scrimmed north flank of the Queensborough Bridge.

His stance was wide and well planted on the doweled floorboards, and Savage noticed the distinctive round-toe Florsheims he was wearing were damp at the heels and soles. The priest stood in an almost military parade rest, with his small, soft hands clasped behind his back. The thumb of his right hand scrolled back and forth, visiting the tips of all his right-hand fingers. "Weatherman is predicting six to eight inches, with heavy drifting," he added, shaking his head.

"Afraid you're right, Monsignor," Savage replied. "But I'm sure we'll survive this one too."

"Outbound traffic on the bridge seems unusually heavy for late morning."

"Everybody's being cut loose early from their jobs," Savage suggested. "Otherwise, come this afternoon, nobody would ever get home in this stuff."

"Yes, I see," said the priest. He turned and looked at Savage. "How about you, Sergeant?" he asked intently. "Is the police department going to grant you an early excusal today?"

Maintaining steady eye contact, Savage announced abruptly. "I'm afraid that another priest has been shot and killed, sir."

"I'm aware of that," Dunleavy said, his stern expression morphing to one of pained acceptance. "I was notified of Father Brodeur's killing a little while ago. He was a fine priest." Dunleavy sat down heavily in the well-padded leather chair behind his desk. "Are there going to be more?" he asked.

Savage grimaced, but did not answer.

"Any advice?" Dunleavy said.

"Yes. Unless absolutely necessary, I would not go about in clerical garb, sir," Savage offered.

"You mean dress in mufti?"

"Until this psycho's caught . . . that's exactly what I mean."

Dunleavy nodded, his gaze focusing on something a million miles away. "Funny," he mused softly, "policemen don't get early excusals on snow days. . . . Do they?" he asked rhetorically.

"No sir, they don't."

"Firefighters don't get snow days either." Suddenly Dunleavy's piercing gaze locked on Savage like a laser.

"Cops and firemen are a very special breed, Sergeant, are they not?" he said.

Savage believed that to be true, but offered a noncommittal shrug in return.

"When a fire is raging in a building and everyone else is running out," the monsignor said, "firemen are running in. When some psychopath with a gun and a healthy supply of ammunition is in a building shooting up the place, guess who's running in?"

Savage nodded.

"That could explain why cops and firemen so readily back each other up when the proverbial you-know-what hits the blades of a wildly spinning fan, eh, Sergeant? Well, people who work for the Lord don't get snow-day excusals either." Dunleavy went on without waiting for a reply. His icy blue caution lights seemed to flash. "Working for God is a tough job. I'm sure you would agree that priests of the Church—much like policemen, on occasion—can be greatly misunderstood."

"How do you mean, sir?" Savage asked.

"Both need to maintain strong support within their respective communities to be effective. In that regard, policemen sometimes need to be . . . shall we say . . . *guarded* with certain information. We all know that policemen often employ the 'blue wall of silence' in order to protect their higher mission and the overall . . . *big* picture."

Savage wondered where the hell this was all going.

"The same is very much true for men of the cloth," Dunleavy affirmed. "Although we wear different uniforms, priests and cops can consider themselves very much brothers."

Savage didn't know if he bought into the monsignor's analogy of cops and priests; he would dissect that idea later. But one thing was certain—a far deeper meaning was floating somewhere just beneath the surface of the reaching comparison. The priest was trying to somehow enlist him. . . . In what he did not know, but . . . the holy man wanted something.

"If you don't mind my asking, sir," Savage said. "Who was it that notified you about Father Brodeur?"

"Is that important, Sergeant?" a wary Dunleavy replied too quickly, caution lights now beaming solidly. He reached across his desk to trigger his intercom. "Has my car arrived yet, Angela?"

"It just now pulled up, Monsignor," came her reply. "Hans Peter is waiting for you right out front. You're running late to pick up His Eminence."

Despite being mildly unsettled by the monsignor's nonanswer to his question, and the intercom theatrics about Hans Peter and the limo, Savage, in deference to the senior prelate, decided to let both matters slide.

"What can you tell me about the Third Secret, Monsignor?"

"Is that germane to this investigation?" Dunleavy asked, looking askance but not startled by the question.

"Possibly."

"Sergeant, within Catholicism—not necessarily within the Church proper—there are those who hold any number of myths to be true."

"Then . . . you consider the Third Secret a myth?"

"I didn't say that. . . ." Dunleavy replied defensively. "I merely meant that there will always be some who will carry the unexplained to extremes."

Will? Savage thought. "What could their justification for becoming extreme possibly be?"

"Some zealots say that the Church has seen a profound decrease in its devotion to the Blessed Virgin since 1960. From that they have extrapolated that a conspiracy must exist within the Church to conceal some horrendous information within the secret of Fatima. That's about the long and short of it."

As the priest rose from behind his desk and pulled a topcoat from a closet in the corner, Savage reached into his jacket and removed a copy of the letter from the Soldier. He unfolded it and held it up. "You need to read this before you leave, Monsignor."

Projecting an air of casually indifferent preoccupation, Savage sipped his now-cooled coffee, peripherally eye-balling the monsignor as the man set a pair of delicate wire rims to the tip of his small nose and began to read. The frosty, twinkling eyes moved rapidly over the page.

Savage was sure that the man had never seen the actual letter, but every instinct told him the priest already knew exactly what it said.

SIX

Richie Marcus parked the silver Taurus beneath the NO PARKING ANYTIME sign in front of the Our Lady of Perpetual Help parish house. He flipped the PD parking plate up on the dash and glanced over at his partner. "You ready?" he asked. Diane DeGennaro flashed him a sour look along with a barely perceptible nod. Richie knew she was still pissed off about the scrap he'd had with Jack Lindstrom, primarily, she had argued, because he'd provoked it—which, of course, was pure bullshit.

"Come on," he said, annoyed, shutting off the car's engine.

The detectives stepped from the small sedan and carefully negotiated the slippery sidewalk and half-dozen snow-mounded steps that led to the rectory's front door. They identified themselves to the small-boned elderly housekeeper who answered the bell. The woman wore a babushka that partially covered sparse hair and overshadowed a strange bluish mole in the middle of her wrinkled forehead. She said her name was Anya. Her English had a decidedly Eastern European flavor, Marcus noted. Romanian, perhaps.

"Is the pastor available, Anya?" Diane asked. "Or is there a priest in charge?"

"Father Flaherty is today here," the woman replied, unconsciously drying veiny work-gnarled hands against her apron as she let them into the vestibule. The eye-watering reek of full-strength Pine-Sol clung to her like a body stocking.

"He is pastor," she continued, "but is upstairs in bed . . . sick with flu." She shrugged her stooped shoulders apologetically.

"Are there any other priests available?" Marcus asked.

"No. Our parish has two priests only. Father Brodeur is not here, but should be very soon back." She welcomed them into the rectory proper with a sweep of a sinewy arm, closed the door behind them, and added, "But you can wait in room for sitting."

Agile in spite of a severe humpback, Anya ushered them down a long hall, into a large parlor.

"Would you be good enough to ask Father Flaherty to join us?" Marcus said. "I know it's an imposition to get him out of bed, but, ah . . . it is a matter of very great importance. We need to speak with him right away."

Curiosity and concern flashed alternately across the woman's lined and weathered face. "I will see," she replied slowly. Please to sit." She gestured to several overstuffed chairs and a brown leather sofa. She turned and was gone.

"Why the hell are you acting like this?" Marcus whispered to DeGennaro, biting off the words. "He was goosing me. . . . So I goosed him back. I didn't know he was gonna go off like a freakin' skyrocket."

"That's just it, Richie," Diane replied in a flat, hushed voice. "You damn well should have known."

"Guy can't take a joke, for God's sake," Richie persisted. "Takes himself too damn seriously, that's his freakin' problem."

"No. It's your problem for making the joke in the first place. You shouldn't have picked at that sore scab."

"How the hell am I supposed to know what's gonna rattle that jerk's freakin' cage?"

"I'm Father Flaherty," a weak tenor voice interrupted. A lean midsixties man entered the parlor, shuffling slowly in badly worn slippers. The six-footer's narrow shoulders looked almost bony beneath a loose-fitting plaid bathrobe. He had a large misaligned nose and his receding salt-and-pepper hair was tousled, as if he'd just climbed out of a bed. "May I be askin' what is so urgent, now?"

Freakin' League of Nations here, Richie thought; it had been the first syllable of *ur*gent that gave away the priest's mick brogue. "I'm Detective Marcus," he said, flipping his shield case open. "This is my partner, Detective DeGennaro. We understand that a Father Jean Brodeur is assigned here at this parish. Is that right?"

"Yes," the priest replied. "Is there something wrong?" His eyelids drooped and his unshaven ruddy face was drawn. He truly did look sick. Marcus decided not to get too close.

"When did you last see Father Brodeur?" Diane asked.

"About five thirty this marnin', it was. Why?"

"How come so early?" Marcus questioned. "Do you normally get up at that hour?"

"A phone call came in at about that time. A man requested that I go immediately to an address over on Allen Street to administer extreme unction—last rites—to an old woman who was dying at home."

"Did this caller give you his name?" Diane asked.

"Francisco, I think," Flaherty replied, squinting his eyes in concentration. "I'm really not sure."

"Did he give you the dying woman's name?" Marcus asked.

"A Mrs. dos Santos, I think he said her name was. The caller was emphatic that the poor woman had requested me personally. I was asked to hurry; there was very little time."

"And?" Marcus pressed.

"And, well, as you can see, I'm not feeling very well. I've been sick for days. And although I promised the caller that I would come, it became clear within a few minutes that I was still too sick. I awakened Father Brodeur and prevailed on him to go in my stead. Just what is this—"

"Do you have this Mrs. dos Santos' address, phone number, et cetera?" Marcus asked.

"It's all written down on a pad inside," the priest said, motioning listlessly with his thumb. "But the people had no telephone. The caller said he was using a pay phone on the corner. Just *what* is this all about, Detective?"

"I'm afraid we have some very bad news, sir," Diane said softly. "Father Brodeur is dead. He was found shot to death behind a building down on Allen Street several hours ago."

Father Flaherty gasped, went weak in the knees, and almost stumbled. Marcus and DeGennaro supported him and quickly steered him into the corner of the long leather sofa, where he collapsed. His face had gone ashen.

"Did they find the person who did it?" he finally asked.

"Not yet," Marcus said.

"Have you any idea why anybody would want to kill Father Brodeur?" Diane asked.

"Uh-uh," the quaking priest responded without hesitation. "Father Brodeur was a fine gentleman."

"Do you have any idea why somebody might have wanted to kill *you*?" Marcus inquired.

Flaherty shook his head, but wheels were clearly turning inside. "Do you think it was the same person who killed Father Gilhooley on Saturday?" he asked in a horrified croak, looking as if he really didn't want to hear the answer. The man's brogue was now very evident.

"Not absolutely certain of that yet, Padre," Marcus allowed. "But . . . it's probably a pretty fair bet."

"Saints preserve us," the priest blurted, quaking even more. "Sweet Jesus, give us strength."

"Did you happen to know Father Gilhooley?" Diane asked.

There was silence; the priest did not answer.

"Father?" Diane pressed.

"Huh?" Flaherty grunted, snapping out of deep thought. "Yes, Father Gilhooley. Yes, I did know him."

"How well did you know him?" Diane asked.

"I guess you could say I knew him fairly well. After all, we've both been priests in this town for a good long time."

"Do you have any idea why anyone would want to kill Father Gilhooley?" Marcus probed.

"No . . . no," Flaherty replied faintly.

There was no-no on Flaherty's lips, but Marcus thought he discerned a momentary yes-yes in the priest's oddly shifting eyes. If not a yes-yes, then it was at least a definite maybe.

"How long did you actually know Father Gilhooley?" Marcus asked.

"A rather long time."

"How long is rather long?" Marcus pried, continuing to work the Gilhooley connection. "Did you attend seminary together?"

"I can't talk anymore," the priest blurted suddenly. The lanky man stood up unsteadily in his loose-fitting robe and bolted for the bathroom off the parlor. Marcus heard him heave his guts.

SEVEN

When Savage returned to his Manhattan South office shortly after noon, he was surprised to find DeGennaro and Marcus already busy at their typewriters, putting together preliminary reports on the Father Brodeur killing. They followed him into the sergeants' room and stood by quietly as he dialed his upstairs neighbor, Mrs. Potamkin. It was a brief conversation. The feisty eighty-three-year-old woman had not seen Ray in several days, but would keep a sharp eye out for him. For some reason, Mrs. Potamkin absolutely adored the crusty, battle-scarred tom. She was his surrogate human.

"Was that the old lady on the third floor, above you?" Diane asked.

"Uh-huh," Savage responded.

"That old broad's a piece of work," Marcus growled. He sucked in a quick last drag of a Winston, then dropped the smoldering stub into an empty Sprite can he was carrying. "She seen the cat?"

"No," Savage answered. "But unless I miss my guess, as soon as we hung up she ran right for her long johns and galoshes. Despite the horrendous weather, she's probably going to conduct an all-out neighborhood canvass and search."

"They could use her over in Missing Persons," Diane said.

"How did it go over at Father Brodeur's church?" Savage asked.

Together, the detectives related a complete synopsis of their interview with Father Flaherty, the flu-stricken pastor of OLPH. Richie Marcus was unwavering in his belief that the priest needed to be reinterviewed . . . soon. The subtle clash of no-no words and yes-yes eyeballs was still nagging him.

"A check of the Mrs. dos Santos address to which Flaherty had been called earlier this morning—and to which Father Brodeur had responded in his place—turned out to be an empty lot not far from where Brodeur's body was discovered," Diane said.

"There are more than a couple of dos Santoses in the Manhattan phone directory," Marcus followed up. "I also called Rudy Caparo over at Postal Inspections. He found a few more with that surname residing in Manhattan."

"Is he going to check the other boroughs?" Savage asked.

"Oh yeah," Marcus replied, setting the smoky Sprite can on the file cabinet by the door. "But that's gonna take a few days. I also contacted a buddy of mine over at the Bureau of Vital Statistics. Any death certificates filed in that name—or anything close to it—within the five boroughs will be immediately flagged."

"Even though we now figure the dos Santos name to be bogus, we'll go ahead and touch all the bases on it until we know that for certain," Diane said.

Savage nodded.

"Detective DeGennaro," Eddie Brodigan called out from the wheel desk in the squad room. "Long distance—Montreal, Canada—on line twenty-three."

"Father Brodeur's next of kin lives up there," Diane said. "Montreal police are probably getting back to me on the notification I requested them to make. I'll take the call in the squad room." The first-grade detective snatched the Sprite-can-cum-ashtray from the file cabinet, eyed Richie coldly, and left the room.

Savage turned his attention to Marcus. "Did this Father

Flaherty think he could recognize the male voice from the phone call?"

"Wasn't sure. Besides being real sick, he said he was pretty groggy from sleep. Wasn't fully awake yet."

"Did he recall any peculiarities to the caller's voice? An accent, a lisp, masculine, effeminate . . . whatever?"

"Breathy," Marcus growled with a wheeze, flipping a fresh Winston between his lips and firing it up. "He said the voice was breathy. Like maybe the guy had been running."

"Or like maybe the guy was dumb enough to be a heavy smoker," Savage said flatly. "Any word from Jack Lindstrom yet?"

"Probably still standing by at Brodeur's postmortem," Marcus replied. "Waiting to courier the killing slugs over to Ballistics for comparison against those that offed Father Gilhooley." Cupping the lit cigarette with a sleight of hand worthy of Harry Blackstone, Marcus then added gruffly, "Which, we both know, is merely a freakin' formality at this point."

Savage grimaced his agreement. Marcus uttered a self-conscious snort and slipped quickly from the cramped office, a faint trail of blue smoke wafting from his right palm.

"What would I do without you, my little guerilla fighter?" John Wesley Krumenacker said, waving the baggie-packaged guppy just above Charlie's fishbowl. "And, for that matter, what would you do without me? Anybody else would have flushed your fancy ass a long time ago." His forced laugh ended in another rumbly cough.

With a stubby index finger, he raised a dust-caked slat of the blinds that hung crookedly at the window. Gray daylight filtered through the dirty pane. Outside on East Seventh, it was bitter cold; snow was still falling like crazy. Inside, though, it was hot as hell. The way he liked it in the winter: sweltering. Just like the doggiest days of the summer of '66 in the VC-infested HoBo Woods north of Cu Chi.

Winters were getting tougher for John Wesley. He had turned fifty-four two weeks ago. Ten years of toiling in the steel-dusted subway tunnels of the New York City Transit System, followed by another twenty years of body-shop work inhaling all kinds of paint thinners and chemicals and all that body-filler dust, coupled with a thirty-five-year, three-pack-a-day association with Commander Philip Morris had left him with a form of chronic obstructive pulmonary disease. It was now beyond the early stages, stealing away his breath. The medics at New York University Hospital had told him he was going down. Dying. They had said something in doctor-speak about damage to his ticker, but they couldn't, or wouldn't, tell him how much time he had. And that was okay. Hell, everybody dies.

But before he went, there remained a little bit more of God's work to be done. He had been given the holy task of inflicting the wrath of God on the sanctimonious holier-than-thou perverts and bullies who preached goodness, love, and mercy, then slipped into the sacristy to fondle and grope their altar boys. And worse. When Buffo died, the guilty bastards were protected by Mother Church. They still were, but a lot of that bullshit was going to stop. Retribution for past sins had already begun.

Sweat formed at his brow and upper lip; it was no good getting all worked up and going into bronchospasm. He still had much to do today. Krumenacker measured his breaths until he calmed down, then took a deep huff on his inhaler. From the corner of his eye he noticed Charlie, clearly agitated, churning his bowl into a spin cycle.

He held the clear bag containing the guppy against the fishbowl and cooed as if Charlie were a baby. "Look what J.W. got for his fancy-finned little sociopath."

The betta rose to the surface, his mouth opening and closing as if forming words.

"What's that?" John Wesley asked, scrunching his brow and cocking his head attentively. "You want to know if we're celebrating Tet?" A broad smile creased his face and he chuckled in mild derision. "No, no, no. But good old J.W.'s gone and bought a real nice Christmas present for you. Wasn't that nice of him?"

Charlie flashed back and forth in anticipation.

Krumenacker unzipped the bag and spilled its living contents into Charlie's tank. He watched for a moment, mesmerized, as the betta went to work on the sacrificial guppy. He hated to see the outclassed guppy suffer, but John Wesley Krumenacker fully understood the warrior need to kill.

"Sort of an ichthyo search and destroy, eh, Charlie?"

The sudden noisy flush of an upstairs toilet, accompanied by the simultaneous banging of water pipes inside the ancient walls, put an end to the one-way conversation.

He moved to the double-door wall cabinet above the dish-filled sink and did a quick food inventory. Except for an almost empty family-size box of Cheerios, a lone can of Franco-American Beef Gravy, and a half-used six-pack of ramen noodle soup, the cabinet's left side was totally bare. J.W. really preferred Lipton Noodle Soup above the Top Ramen brand. First of all, it had far less sodium for his high blood pressure—690 mg per serving, versus 910 mg—but Top Ramen was a damn sight cheaper. He made a mental note to pick up more Cheerios, ramen, and some Carnation Instant Breakfast, at least enough to last one more week.

The cabinet's right side contained his handgun collection—or what little remained of it. In the past six months, he'd sold off most of his guns, including his prized Dan Wesson .357; he'd needed the cash. He'd given the powerful .44 Ruger Magnum to Sister Lucia as a donation to the cause.

The bottom shelf on the right side was a hodgepodge of gun cleaning kits, spare holsters, and a variety of silicone-impregnated wiping rags. The middle shelf held several pair of shooting goggles and a variety of sound barriers; it also held the last two of his Smith & Wesson revolvers, both thirty-eights. The larger of the two was a Military and Police model with the heavy-duty four-inch barrel; he'd won a number of matches with that one. The other was an easily concealed five-shot snub-nose Chief; it was the older version with the rounded grip.

The top shelf held a neatly arranged assortment of handgun ammunition of every bore size, which ran the gamut from harmless theatrical blanks to custom-loaded fragmentation rounds offering maximum penetration. He'd inherited the blanks as part of a blind job-lot purchase years ago. He never had any use for them, but had never gotten around to tossing the damn things out. He saw that he still had a twenty-round carton of Hornady 180 grain magnums for the .44 Ruger he'd given away, and three fifty-round cartons of Winchester-Westerns for the thirty-eights. His supply of .45 caliber ammo was far more extensive. Stacked in one corner beside two boxes of Winchester Supreme 140 grain jacketed soft-points, were two hundred rounds of Winchester Supreme XST 230 grain hollowpoints. Stacked in the other corner were three hundred rounds of Winchester Cowboy Loads; they were flat-nose and excellent for target shooting and matches. He also had some Remington Golden Saber High Performance, a partial carton of Glaser Safety Slugs, and some WinClean 185 grain. John Wesley reached in and took the last remaining fifty-round box of .45 caliber Winchester full metal jackets, his old gun cleaning kit, and carried them to the shelf table. He set them beside his old Underwood.

The gnawing question of what could be done about the evil empire of priests had been a key element in his horrible nightmares. He hadn't slept an entire night in all his adult life. He had tried for years to run the whole damn business out of his thoughts, to cleanse his mind, to ease his psyche. He had tried all sorts of possible fixes; had been to half a dozen different shrinks and spent a small fortune on their useless couch treatment and worthless sugar-pill therapy.

Then six months ago, just after hearing his terminal prognosis from the pulmonary medics, the answers began falling into place. He had joined a support group for the sexually abused, and revealed his whole life story at the very first meeting he attended. He had gotten up in front of several dozen members and told of growing up in St. Malachy's, and the horrible sexual abuses committed on him and other boys by the priests there. He even told of Buffo's suicide, and then finished by telling of his tunnel rat years in 'Nam and of his numerous cold-blooded killings.

It was there, at the conclusion of that meeting, that Sister Lucia introduced herself. She so much resembled his mother—same coloring, same birdlike build . . . same passion to fulfill religious obligations, no matter how demanding they might be. They were also very much aligned in personality, both so difficult to ever please.

Sister Lucia—who had a direct line to the Blessed Mother—soon anointed him to help her carry out the cleansing of the Church. When he had doubted himself—felt too weak to fight—she had assured him that God's strength was made perfect in weakness. She cited Corinthians II 12:9. He had been chosen.

Thank you, God, he thought. In spite of my growing weakness, you have selected me once again to be an archangel, one of your warriors.

Suddenly excited just thinking about it, John Wesley began to gasp for air, and automatically reached for the inhaler. Within seconds, he was able to take several deep, ragged breaths. Then he belched loudly and began to choke. He quickly drew a glass of water and downed two cortisone tablets; they would soothe his ravaged air passageways. Again the nagging thought returned: He hated

himself for killing the wrong man. He would not make that
mistake again.

His breathing back under control, he sat down at the
shelf table. He reopened the oxygen bag's Velcro flap and
removed a silencer-lengthened .45 caliber automatic Colt
pistol. After this morning's mission—and before this afternoon's—the piece needed a wipe down and a reload.

J.W. and the gun were a matched set; together they'd
been to hell and back many times. With a supply sergeant's
complicity, he had appropriated the weapon from the U.S.
Army and successfully smuggled it out of 'Nam at the
conclusion of his tour. Hell, he'd earned it. Until last Saturday, it had been decades since the Colt had been fired
with prejudice but, just as in 'Nam, the hushed automatic
remained J.W.'s weapon of choice.

As he held the heavy gun up and ejected the magazine
clip from the butt, his phone rang. He put down the gun,
engaged the call, but did not speak.

"J.W., it's all right. It's me, Sister Lucia."

"Hello," he said, strengthened by her voice. "How do
you like this weather?"

"I don't," she snapped angrily. "And I don't like what
happened this morning."

"I'm sorry," he moaned. "It was my mistake. It was way
too late before I realized it wasn't Flaherty. He'd already
seen my face up close, heard my voice, seen the gun . . .
the whole bit. I had no choice. I had to sacrifice him to protect us for the rest of the work we have to do this week."

Long, long pause. "I understand," she finally said,
anger and disappointment still riding on her words. "Will
you be taking care of that other matter today?"

"I certainly plan to."

"Good. I'll come by this evening to pick up that little
thirty-eight you promised me. Also, I think it's time we
composed another letter to Mr. Ballantine at the *Post*.
We've got to keep these people all worked up."

"What time?" he asked.

"What difference? You going dancing?"

"Hardly," he said.

"Then I'll get there when I get there." He heard a click; the call was over.

He counted out four fresh rounds from the box of Winchesters and slid them into the ammo clip, topping it off. Later, when his second mission of the day was complete, he would come back to the apartment, clean the weapon, and write out some checks while he waited for Sister Lucia to come. He popped the full magazine back into the butt of the Colt and carefully placed the gun inside his oxygen bag.

His thoughts returned to the priest he had just killed, a priest with whom he had no quarrel. God would just have to understand. Closing his eyes and balling his fists, he exhaled an angry grunt.

A flash of movement in Charlie's tank caught his attention. The guppy's dorsal fin was partially shredded and one pectoral fin was entirely gone. Crippled, with no steering, it swam in a hopeless circle trying to delay the inevitable.

"War is hell," John Wesley murmured matter-of-factly.

After flipping through the *R*s in his Rolodex, Savage dialed the number for Father Vincent Rossi, his longtime Jesuit friend who resided at the rectory of St. Anthony's Church just below Houston Street. Clara, the rectory's housekeeper, answered the call and went in search of Father Vinny. A minute later, the line again came alive.

"This is Father Rossi."

"Father Vinny. Thorn Savage here."

"Thorn, my friend. How are things in the world's best police department?"

"No complaints. How goes it in your world? The *Big Boss* treatin' you good?"

"Tips and all, not bad," the priest said. Then, his tone changing, asked seriously, "I guess you guys are up to your eyeballs with the Father Gilhooley killing? That was just terrible. Any leads? Any suspects?"

"Not yet, Father. But I'm afraid this guy has struck again."

"What?"

"He shot and killed another priest down on Allen Street early this morning."

"What was his name?"

"A Father Jean Brodeur from Our Lady of Perpetual Help, over on Fourteenth. Did you know him?"

"Oh, my God!" Father Vinny moaned. "I didn't know Father Brodeur all that well, but . . . I've met him."

"I can't overstate this, Father. I'd be *very* heads-up if I were a cleric in this city. I can't tell you much more right now, except that this guy has declared open season on Roman Catholic priests."

"So you think it's the same person who killed Father Gilhooley?"

"No question."

"Jesus, Mary, and Joseph! What can I do? What should any priest do?"

"If you're called out someplace, make damn sure you know who it is you're talking to. Looks pretty certain that Father Brodeur was lured out on some pretext into an ambush."

"Yes, yes. That makes sense," Vinny agreed. "Dear God, this all has to happen only days before the Holy Father is due to visit us."

"Hate to switch gears so fast on you, Father, but while I've got you on the phone, I've got a problem. Thought maybe I could tap into your Ph.D. in psychology and get some of your wise counsel."

"About these murders?"

"No. Totally unrelated. Got a few minutes?"

"For you, Thorn . . . always."

Savage quickly brought Father Vinny up to speed on the troubled history of Jack Lindstrom, and the whys and wherefores—no matter how unfounded—of his refusal to utilize departmental psych services.

"I'm not being flippant here," Father Vinny said seriously. "But does this man have a sense of humor?"

"Used to. In fact, he used to have a damn good one. But I can't remember the last time I saw him smile, let alone actually belly laugh about something."

"How long has this been going on? A couple of weeks, a month?"

"A long time. I've watched it develop over the last few years."

"Under ordinary circumstances, I'd be very reluctant to offer any kind of opinion until I had a chance to interview the person," the priest said.

"I understand."

"But if what you're telling me is true, I would have to think it very likely that Detective Lindstrom is suffering from a severe clinical depression."

"What can be done? What do you recommend?"

"I'd be very happy to counsel Detective Lindstrom," the Jesuit said. "Both as a priest and as a psychologist. However, at this stage of the game, I think it more important that he immediately see a psychiatrist. He probably needs to get started on some meds and get started on them right away. I'm not an MD. I can't write prescriptions."

"Uh-huh."

"I realize the man's in no condition financially to seek help outside the department loop. But I have a good friend, Joel Horowitz. He's a top psychiatrist and a real NYPD buff. I'm sure that with very little persuasion, Joel will do me a favor and see Lindstrom pro bono. I'll set it up."

"Horowitz?" Savage repeated. "How ecumenical of you."

"He's a mensch, and he really knows his stuff."

True to his word, Father Vinny called back twenty minutes later. Everything had been arranged. Savage jotted down the particulars. Jack Lindstrom was to be at the Park

Avenue office of Dr. Joel Horowitz tomorrow morning at ten. And he was to be prompt.

At Thorn's invitation, Father Vinny agreed to meet for dinner at Forlini's that Thursday night. It would be Savage's treat, of course—always was. Father Vinny would surely go for the veal scaloppine—always did. Hanging up, Savage saw that he had an incoming call waiting on another line.

"This is Sergeant Savage."

"Good afternoon, Sergeant, I'm Detective Teddy Christman from the Boston, Massachusetts, PD, Homicide division."

"Glad it's your nickel," Savage said. How's the weather up in Beantown?"

"Beautiful day," Christman replied.

"Just wait!" Savage said, knowing the snow-dumping blizzard to be on a northeast track. "What can we do for you, Detective?"

"Well, actually, Sarge, I'm not sure. Maybe we can do something for each other."

"How's that?"

"According to my brother-in-law, who happens to be a New York City cop in the Seventh Precinct, two Catholic priests have been murdered in Manhattan within the last few days. Supposedly, one went down last Saturday, and now he's called me about another one from this morning."

"You heard right," Savage replied. "Did your brother-in-law give you my number?"

"No, I just went ahead and contacted your Detective Operations office. After I told them who I was and what I had, a Lieutenant Crowley referred me to you at Manhattan South Homicide. Said they were your cases."

"I'm listening."

"My brother-in-law described both those killings as having been 'particularly gruesome.' Is that so, and how?"

"Christman, is it?" Savage hesitated. "At this point

you're just a voice on the phone. You could be from the *National Enquirer*, for all I know."

"I understand, Sarge. Maybe you could fax the info to me. I'm trying to make a connection with one of my cases."

"You show me yours . . . and I'll show you mine," Savage said.

"Fair enough," Christman replied. "I've been working a homicide case for the last two weeks and getting nowhere fast."

"What was the date and time of the occurrence?"

"It went down at zero-zero hours on Tuesday morning, December tenth. The victim was a security guard at a high-dollar condominium complex over on our north side. You know, one of them potbellied uniforms in the entrance guardhouse who makes sure visitors have been invited before opening the gate."

"Gotcha."

"He was a white male in his sixties. Shot twice—once in the groin and once between the eyes."

"You're in the ballpark—you got my attention. Victim's name?" Savage asked, beginning to scratch the information boldly across a lined yellow pad.

"Grennan. Peter Grennan."

"Further 'script?"

"Five-ten, medium build, one-sixty, gray hair, brown eyes. Wore thick glasses; coworkers told us he was myopic. Can you believe that, a goddamned security guard, myopic? Jesus," Christman sneered. "Beyond that, he had no tattoos, no identifying marks. . . . How am I doing?"

"Keep going . . . DOB?"

"Eight, sixteen, thirty-seven."

"Any ballistics?"

"Both rounds recovered. Winchester Magnums, both fired from a forty-four. We make the weapon as a Ruger."

"That's a little off target, Teddy," Savage said. "But tell me more. Any witnesses?"

"Nope, no eyewitnesses. Several people claimed they heard what could have been two shots from their apartments, but it was late, after midnight. Grennan had just come on duty."

"Um-hmm. Go on."

"Victim was found about fifty feet away from his guard booth. Like I said, he'd been shot twice."

"Anything else?"

"Tossed onto the body was one of those religious prayer cards, you know, like the kind they give out at funeral parlors—a holy picture on the front, and a prayer on the back. They usually print in the decedent's name, date of birth, and date of death at the top."

"Oh, man," Savage moaned, feeling the hairs on the back of his neck spring to full attention. "Tell me, what size was that prayer card, what was the holy picture of, and what was the prayer printed on the back?"

"The card was two-and-a-half by four-and-a-quarter. The picture on the front depicted the crowned Lady of Fatima and three children kneeling before her. The prayer on the back was the Hail Mary."

"Jesus Christ almighty," Savage muttered. "Different weapon, but identical MO otherwise. We've got to exchange information. I'm gonna fax you a copy of the religious card we found on one of our victims; you fax me a copy of yours. Can you get it right out?"

"I'll do it," Christman said.

"I think we should also exchange ballistic reports. In case our forty-five shows up in Boston, or your forty-four shows up down here."

"Done."

"Anything else I might need to know?" Savage asked. "You may as well give me all you have."

"We don't know for sure that they really tie in, but we discovered some tire tracks near the scene. It appeared that whoever was driving that particular car had pulled off the road only a short distance from the guardhouse. Maybe it was the shooter; maybe it wasn't. The earth had been freshly turned there that day for a water main repair, so we got excellent impressions. We're still waiting to hear on the tire brand and size."

"I'll want that information also, as soon as you get it," Savage said. "Now, who do you show as Grennan's next of kin?"

"No one. Had none listed on his employment app."

"Any leads?"

"One of his coworkers said that Grennan took a bus down to New York last Thanksgiving. Supposedly, had an old spinster aunt there. Told everyone he was a New York guy, born and raised in the Bronx."

"Got any pictures of this guy?"

"I've got postmortem photos, and we also blew up the one from his employee I.D. badge."

"Send me everything you've got, Teddy. I'll send you everything we've got."

"Oh, and there's one other thing," Christman said. "It didn't mean very much at the time, but when we searched this guy's living quarters—a claustrophobic rented room— we turned up a lot of religious paraphernalia; crucifixes, statues of Christ, Bibles, Roman Catholic magazines, blah blah blah. One of the cops on the scene had quipped that the place looked like the cell of an off-duty monk."

"Do me a favor," Savage said. "Check with the Boston Archdiocese and see if this guy Grennan had ever been a priest up there. I'll do the same down here."

"Gotta tell you," Christman replied, "with all the bull-shit that's gone on with the Church up here in the past few years, those folks are hunkered down in total defense. They're battling about five hundred lawsuits and are a bit more than gun-shy about responding to questions from the police, or anybody."

"I hear you. I think I can relate."

"They're afraid to give out the time of day, for crissakes. But . . . I'll try."

EIGHT

It dawned on Hugh Quigley that he didn't even know what day it was as he turned the Cadillac into the narrow alley behind the Neptune Diner. Hell, how could he, working seven days a week, and every damn day just like the one before? Same shit . . . different day.

His life in these past few years had become so rutted, so damn predictable, it was hateful. Why not do something different for a change; go somewhere else for lunch besides the goddamned Neptune Diner? Try something new . . . pizza? Burger King? Kentucky Fried? Maybe give that new German joint over on Northern Boulevard a try. Being a complete creature of habit, he knew he wouldn't. But all that would soon change. Another week of this bullshit and the sale of his one-man private car service would be finalized, and he would have all the ready cash necessary to move on.

The twelve-, sometimes fifteen-hour marathons of fighting merciless city traffic, and the endless kowtowing to onerous jerks that couldn't—or wouldn't—buy or drive their own automobiles would be finished. No more toting lead-filled luggage and kissing lead-filled miserable butts. But best of all, he could then escape the damnable New York winter weather and close on that one-bedroom condo in West Fort Lauderdale. Maybe he'd even take up golf. He was never much for athletics, but hell, he wasn't looking to join the PGA. Quigley watched as giant flakes of white swirled all around the car. Miserable stuff, snow; he'd come to absolutely despise it.

The buyer of his business, a Greek guy from Astoria, had wanted to wait until after the first of the year to close on the deal. He didn't want to have any tax connection or burden for the few remaining days of the current year. A Greek worried about paying taxes; now, that was a laugh. If anybody knew how to bury money from a mostly cash business, it was a Greek. That's probably why they owned so many diners throughout the northeast. *C'est la vie*, Quigley thought. He was just glad he was able to sell the business to somebody—anybody—and get most of his asking price.

Quigley idled the big sedan to the lot's deepest corner, near the kitchen door and right next to the overflowing Dumpster where no one else was yet parked. He always parked as far away from other cars as possible. The car was his tool, how he earned his living; he had to keep it looking nice, especially now with a sale pending. But sometimes, no matter how many precautions he took, some thoughtless bastard with a twenty-year-old, smoke-belching, beat-up piece of shit would squeeze into the space next to his immaculate black Fleetwood and fling the door open wide. . . . *Ahh,* he thought, just another frustration that would soon be history.

He grabbed the newspaper from the front seat, locked the car, and walked through the quickly gathering snow to the diner's front entrance. Once inside, he gently stomped the white powder from his shoes while nodding to Aristedes, the always-flashy owner who had a thing for light gray sharkskin suits and muted blue silk ties. Ari was topping off the toothpick dispenser at the cash register counter. Proudly displayed across the entire mirrored wall behind the silver-haired man was a collection of autographed eight-by-ten glossies. The most prominent of which showed Ari posed with the late Telly Savalas, Ari standing with local newsman Ernie Anastos, and a once dark-haired Ari shaking hands with Michael Dukakis. It was a regular Greco Wall-of-Fame. Ambling to the center of the long counter, Quigley smelled the beef barley soup in the air. Today was Tuesday, he suddenly remembered. Tuesday was always beef barley day at the Neptune.

"Good afternoon, Mr. Hugh," George, the mustachioed Greek behind the counter said as Quigley sat down on his usual stool. "Beef barley today . . . your favorite."

"Umh . . . yeah. I'll have a bowl of that, and give me a grilled cheese and bacon to go with it. Make sure the bacon's crisp." George nodded and disappeared into the kitchen.

"That your fancy Cadillac parked out there?" The question came from an odd-looking man who had seated himself on the next stool. Quigley put the guy in his fifties—albeit hard fifties. He carried a nylon shoulder tote and wore oxygen-supply tubes clipped into his pointy nose.

"Yes, it is," Quigley replied, wondering how the man had actually seen the car, considering he'd parked it in the back.

"Are you for hire?" the strange man asked, then turned and went into a brief coughing spell.

"Yes. That's the idea," Quigley responded with a warm grin. "Have I seen you here before?"

"I just started coming here a few days ago."

"I have lunch here most every day," Quigley volunteered. He then recalled seeing the guy in the diner the day before and, if he wasn't mistaken, the day before that. Hell, he was certainly memorable enough.

"Every day . . . is that so?"

"Hey, what can I tell you?" Quigley said with a shrug. "The food's good, and the prices aren't bad."

"That's exactly what I thought," the man said agreeably. "Listen, I need to get to downtown Manhattan right away. Can I hire you?"

"Now?"

"Yes, now. It's most urgent."

"I'm afraid not." Quigley glanced at his watch. "I have a pickup at Kennedy Airport in forty-five minutes. Besides, with the storm and all, once I got into Manhattan, I'd have a real tough time getting back out. You do understand?"

"I guess so," the man replied. He had a look of great disappointment on his face. "It's worth a hundred bucks. . . ."

"Can't do it," Quigley said, shaking his head. He turned on his stool and pointed to the el that ran right past the diner on Thirty-first Street. "If I were you, I'd grab the N train. It will get you downtown quicker than I can, and you'll have ninety-eight bucks change."

"Do you have a card?" the man asked. "I don't drive anymore, and I hate using taxicabs or the subway. By the way, I'm Mr. St. Michel."

"I'm Hugh Quigley, of Allied Cars," Quigley replied, handing over a business card.

"Cars? Plural?" the man said, scanning the card. "If I call for service, I'm not going to get somebody else, am I? He lowered his voice. "You know, some dot head . . . or Jamaican? I wouldn't like that."

"Nope, Mr. St. Michel. I'm it."

"Good, good; very good," the man whispered, rising. "You'll definitely be hearing from me. I need a good car service."

George appeared from the kitchen and placed a low, wide bowl of beef barley in front of Hugh Quigley. The odd little man with the oxygen tubes and shoulder bag had disappeared as quickly as he had come. Quigley opened his newspaper to page one. The cops still had no leads as to who had killed his old friend, Tommy Gilhooley. He pursed his lips tightly, shook his head, and crumbled a package of Saltines into the steaming soup.

Tomorrow would be Wednesday, he reminded himself; chicken noodle.

*   *   *

It was a given throughout the NYPD that Chief of Detectives Ray Wilson never liked being caught short for answers about the progress of ongoing high-profile investigations within his bureau. When queried by the police commissioner, the mayor, or the media, Wilson wanted his office to be as up-to-the-minute on those big cases as the detectives in the field who were actually working them. Not that he would ever prematurely reveal anything confidential to the media—or anyone else, for that matter. Decades of police experience had taught him how to make those distinctions and how to navigate around sticky questions without pissing anybody off or seeming evasive. That was just one facet of Wilson's style and what made him such a damn good Chief of D.

"Tell me something good on the priest thing, for crissakes," Wilson said, storming into the cramped sergeants' room and pulling the door tightly closed behind him. "I've got the goddamned commissioner *and* the mayor's office calling me every hour on it. Besides that, there's a legion of snow-stranded, coffee-wired press loitering in the lobby of One PP wanting more information."

"Wish I could, boss," Savage replied, not surprised by Wilson's late Monday-afternoon visit. It was only minutes after Jack Lindstrom had returned with the preliminary autopsy report on Father Brodeur and the positive slug comparison report from Ballistics. The timing was incredible. Chief Wilson, Savage was certain, had some power of perception beyond the five senses. "But this thing's getting legs."

"Shit. Don't tell me that," the tall, distinguished black man murmured, wrapping a large right hand around his smooth brow. His thumb and middle finger massaged both temples. "I'm starting to get one of those murderous migraines—haven't had one in months."

Unable to tell the dapper chief anything positive, Savage simply offered a mute grimace. He also noticed that his old friend was beginning to gray at the temples. Wilson was now in his late fifties and his job was a killer, one that allowed no time-outs.

"Okay," the chief said, seemingly resigned to the next round of bad news. "Let's have it." He opened his camel-colored topcoat and sat half-assed at the edge of Bill Lakis' desk.

Savage explained the fresh ballistics report confirming that all of the rounds removed from Brodeur and Gilhooley were fired from the same Colt .45.

"No surprise there, right?" Wilson said with a shrug.

"No surprise."

"Well, we can feed that little nugget to the boys down in the lobby of One PP. Maybe then they'll venture home."

"You don't really believe that, do you, boss?" Savage asked with a laugh.

"No. Not with the goddamned pope comin' here next week, I don't."

"Word is you're forming a task force, Chief."

"Had to. This guy's a bona fide serial killer. I've plucked a total of twenty-five detectives and bosses from commands in Manhattan, the Bronx, Queens, and Brooklyn. Although you'll be sharing all your information back and forth with each other, I want you and your team to stay independent. Theirs will be a parallel investigation. They'll work out of One PP, and report directly to me through Ops."

"Who's running it?"

"Terry McCauley. The whip from the Sixth Squad."

Savage nodded. "McCauley's a good man."

"Yeah, McCauley's a good man," Wilson agreed. "But there ain't gonna be any goddamned world beaters in the twenty-five detectives I'm gonna get. You know the game. As a squad boss, you've played it yourself. Downtown forms a detective task force and sends out a requirement to *X* amount of squads to supply *X* amount of men from their already overworked office. . . . Who do you think they're gonna give up?"

"Not their superstars," Savage replied with a broad grin.

"Got that right," the chief went on. "They give up their squad malingerer, their drunk, their problem child, the guy who couldn't find his ass with both hands. . . ."

Savage knew the chief was right, but hey, that's how the game had always been played. Since squad bosses were held strictly accountable for their clearance rates, they really couldn't be expected to periodically volunteer away those people who keep their ship afloat.

" . . . Right now, all they'll be doing is canvassing anyway," Wilson continued, his expression one of mild exasperation. "Shit, until we get something, that's all they can do."

Savage nodded understandingly, then revealed the conversation he'd had with Boston Detective Teddy Christman a few hours earlier, and his strong sense that the three-week-old, out-of-state case Christman was carrying would ultimately wind up connected to the killer of the two priests in New York City.

"You sure you're not being a little premature on those assertions?" Wilson asked in a hopeful tone. "Boston is a good piece down the road, you know. Like, two hundred miles."

"Maybe, boss," Savage responded, "but every instinct tells me otherwise."

"What else are your instincts telling you?"

"I don't believe these victims were selected at random. Aside from two of them being priests, I think there's another dynamic at work here."

"Something else that connects them to this wacko?" Wilson asked.

"Yes. If we're going to find this guy, we've got to find that additional common denominator."

"I know we're talking about two different guns, but is Boston getting all their ballistic information down to us?"

"Already got it. It was faxed directly to Davy Ramirez at our ballistics unit."

"I hope to Christ you're wrong on this, Thornton," Wilson said. "But I need to know your reasoning on everything," Wilson pressed. "Give it to me point by point."

In one easy motion, Savage reclined into a comfortable half-slouch and rested his right ankle atop his left knee. Like a computer in defragment mode, his mind quickly discarded all extraneous and redundant data and chronologically organized the known facts that had prompted his conclusions.

"Gilhooley and Brodeur, both priests, both killed with the same weapon. They were each shot once between the eyes, and Gilhooley was also shot in the groin area. In the case up in Boston, the victim, Peter Grennan—a security guard and devout Roman Catholic—was also shot once in the groin and once between the eyes."

"And the weapon used to kill Grennan was a forty-four," Wilson inserted. "That is not the same gun that killed Gilhooley and Brodeur."

"Right. But Gilhooley and Grennan each had a prayer card left at the scene."

"With you so far," Wilson said. "Go on."

"In all three cases, there were no eyewitnesses. And in all three cases, no one reported hearing shots."

"Could mean a silenced weapon in all three."

Savage nodded.

"What else?"

"Gilhooley . . . Grennan," Savage intoned. "Both mid-sixties, both very strong Irish names."

"So what?" Wilson responded, turning up both palms. "There are a lot of Irish in New York and Boston. Besides, Brodeur sure sounds like a Frog to me, and he was only in his fifties."

"Yes," Savage agreed. "But we're sure he was not the intended target. A Father Killian Flaherty, another Irish priest, was. Brodeur wound up being there in Flaherty's place. It was a damn fluke."

"Now I suppose you're gonna tell me this guy Flaherty is in his midsixties, right?"

"Sixty-five."

"Shit. Has Flaherty been interviewed?"

"Somewhat," Savage replied. "But the guy's pretty sick and doesn't have much to say. We'll be getting back to him in another day or two."

"Anything else?" Wilson finally asked after a lengthy silence.

"The final piece of the equation, boss," Savage responded. "And we don't have it yet."

"How about this Monsignor Dunleavy at the archdiocese?" Wilson said. "Have you been in touch with him?"

"Met with him this morning."

"Does he know about this Boston gig . . . and the similar prayer card?"

"No, not yet. Wanted to run it by you first. I didn't want him being more in the know than you are."

"I appreciate that," the chief replied. With an ominous laugh, he added, "Watch yourself with that guy, Thornton. I've already had the pleasure of speaking to Dunleavy twice since Saturday. I got the impression the man is a pit bull in priest's clothing."

"Un-huh," Savage agreed. "A cunning pit bull. Before I left his office, I asked him to provide us with the diocesan records pertaining to Gilhooley and Brodeur, and when I call him later, I'm going to add a request for the same on Flaherty. I also intend to ask him whether Peter Grennan was ever a priest locally."

"How did he take your request about Gilhooley and Brodeur?"

"Said he'd get right to work on it. His words were coated with enthusiasm, but—"

"But what?" Wilson interrupted. He leaned forward, his smooth brow now furrowed.

"He told me to give him a day or two."

"Think he's pulling your chain? Buying time? Why would he do that?"

"Don't know. He said that with Christmas Eve and Christmas Day activities within the Church being so hectic, he'd be short of staff. . . ."

"Sounds reasonable."

"Umm, maybe," Savage said. "But after I left his office this morning, I pulled around the corner and watched him get into the back of a limo and drive off. A limo, I'm certain, he knew was out there all the time, but he had acted—purely for my benefit—as if he didn't."

"Why would he do that?"

"I think it was an escape card. When he got tired of me, he played it."

"Cardinal Hammond personally assured me, and the police commissioner, of one hundred percent cooperation," Wilson proclaimed, folding his arms across his chest. "Said we could have anything we wanted. That Dunleavy would handle everything. He's Hammond's go-to man."

"We'll see." Savage shrugged.

"But meanwhile we've got to keep Dunleavy very much up-to-date. He's the direct link to Cardinal Hammond, who in turn is pressuring the PC. And guess whose private parts the PC has got clamped in a vise?"

"I read you, boss. I don't mind keeping him up-to-date, but I get the strange sense that so far he's been one full step ahead of me."

"How do you mean?"

"Not sure," Savage said. "I couldn't swear to it, but . . ." Out of the corner of his eye, he noticed Jack Lindstrom hovering at the office door. "Just a second, Chief." He motioned the detective in.

"We've received a fax of that prayer card from Boston," Lindstrom announced. "Identical to the one we found on Father Gilhooley."

Wilson stood. "Guess I better give that one to the press right away."

"May as well," Savage agreed. "You gotta figure it's going to make the Boston papers tomorrow."

"Keep me informed, Thornton." The chief of detectives abruptly ended the conversation, and with long steps breezed through the squad room and left the office. Savage turned to Lindstrom, who was casually scanning Marcus' DD-5.

"So, Jack. You look a little better. How you feeling?" he asked.

"Ehh," Lindstrom uttered with an abbreviated shrug. "I bummed some aspirins over at the ME's. I guess I'm feeling better than Father Brodeur . . . but," he added with a weak smile, "not much."

Savage offered a half-grin in response. He opened the center drawer of his desk, looking for some Wint-O-Greens; there were none. He wondered if he still had some in the glove compartment of his department car.

"Sorry about this morning, boss," Lindstrom said, placing Marcus' reports back on Savage's desk. "I lost it. What can I say? My sangfroid sucks, and my *gemeinschaft* and *gesellschaft* have gone down the shit shaft. But I've spoken to Richie. . . . I think we're straight." He smiled slightly.

Relieved, Savage nodded and said, "Good." He held out the scrap of paper bearing the time and place of Lindstrom's morning appointment with Dr. Joel Horowitz. Lindstrom took it, read it, and slipped it into his pocket.

"It's on the arm," Savage said in a muted tone. "Don't be late; he's coming in just to see you."

"Thanks, boss," Lindstrom said sheepishly. "I saw from Richie's five that the Soldier's letter and the prayer card has already been sent down to Latent."

"Uh-huh. And as soon as they're done lifting any prints, it's going right over to Forensics. We need to know more about our boy's typewriter. Manufacturer, model, any identifying peculiarities of its imprint, that sort of thing."

"You Catholic?" Lindstrom suddenly inquired.

"Nonpracticing, but a Catholic," Savage replied, unfazed by the typical Lindstrom left-field query. Never devout, Savage hadn't so much as set foot into a church since Gina's funeral mass. Before that it had been more than twenty years ago, when his wife and daughter had died. He got all the religion he needed from the NYPD. "Why do you want to know?" he asked.

"Just curious. Even though I'm a Protestant, I've been studying the workings of the Catholic Church since I was a kid. It has always fascinated me."

"Jack," Savage said, "you've studied the workings of *everything* since you were a kid."

Lindstrom smiled appreciatively and went on. "I probably know more about Roman Church history than most. But I'm wondering what the average Catholic lay person thinks about all the scandals within the Church these past few years."

"I'm not the average," Savage replied, "so I'd probably be the wrong one to ask."

"Mind if I speak openly?" Lindstrom said, narrowing his gaze under his scrunched, rubbery brow.

"Go ahead," Savage replied, pleased that Lindstrom was expressing interest in something other than himself.

The detective spun Billy Lakis' chair and sat. Savage noted the characteristic intensity that had been missing for some time. "There is so much going on in the Roman Catholic Church right now. They have so damn many issues to deal with."

Savage nodded, not asking what those issues might be. Jack, he was certain, was about to tell him. He shifted in his seat and got more comfortable; he might be there awhile.

"Did you know that there is a thriving gay subculture within the Roman Catholic priesthood, being fed by the increasing number of homosexuals entering seminary? Some studies put it at over twenty-five percent."

"Didn't know that," Savage replied, though not surprised.

"Did you know that the age of the average priest is nearing sixty, and the number of priests ninety and older will soon be greater than those thirty-five and under?"

"Didn't know that either," Savage said, thinking the statistic quite remarkable, and impressed by Jack's broad knowledge on so many topics. "Well, then," he said, just for the sake of conversation, "it seems this upheaval within the Church was inevitable."

"Oh yes, definitely. Part of the reason is because a modern, highly educated, well-informed and nonsuperstitious society will no longer respond to presumptuous dogma, especially from a church scandalized by endemic hypocrisy." Lindstrom was on a roll.

Whoo! Savage thought, a bit too heavy for me, and we're going to be all day if he really gets started. Needing to cut the sensitive Lindstrom off without insulting him, he cleared his throat and looked at his watch.

Lindstrom, taking the hint, stood and turned to leave. "Oh, another thing," he said, glancing back to Savage. "In Richie's five . . . the one where Father Flaherty stated he was called out early this morning by a guy named Francisco to give last rites to a Mrs. dos Santos."

"Uh-huh," Savage grunted slowly, anticipating a Lindstrom pearl of wisdom.

"In his letter to Ballantine, the Soldier referred to the three peasant children involved in the Miracle at Fatima," Lindstrom said flatly.

"That's right."

"Francisco was the name of the little boy. Dos Santos was the surname of the eldest of the two girls. I think she was nine at the time. Her full name was Lucia dos Santos. She went on to become a nun. Do you believe in miracles, Sarge?"

"Don't know," Savage said truthfully. "Do you?"

"You know what Einstein said: 'There are only two ways to live your life. One is as though nothing is a miracle. The other is as if everything is.' "

NINE

The rap on the door was loud. Impatient. John Wesley pressed his face against the peephole and looked out into the dimly lit hallway. Even in the poor light, he could see the high-mounded blond locks poking from the front of a tightly pulled kerchief. It was Sister Lucia in her Dolly Parton wig, which, he thought, looked ridiculous on her. One by one, he undid the series of locks and dead bolts.

"Good Lord," she snapped, pushing her way into the apartment as soon as the door was cracked. "Can you make it any darker out there. . . . Or any hotter in here?" She moved immediately to the table and placed her handbag down beside the typewriter and the oxygen pump.

"I wanted to get adjusted to hell," he replied, shuffling to his recliner while repositioning the nose cannula.

She undid the knot of her kerchief, folded and put it in her pocket. "You're not going to hell, John Wesley. You're going straight up. . . . You know that. The Blessed Mother has given a promise."

"Just hedging my bets," he said, slowly easing his wiry frame into the chair.

"Tell me about Quigley," she said excitedly.

"It didn't go off."

"*What?!* What do you mean, it didn't *go off?*"

"Just what I said, dammit. It didn't go off."

"Will you please tell me why?" she enunciated, rocking her wig-covered head back and forth to emphasize the cadence of her words. He noted that her voice and expressions were just like his mother's used to be whenever she became infuriated.

"Because of the damn storm, that's why. Blame the weather."

"Didn't he show up?"

"Oh, he showed up at the diner right on schedule," Krumenacker responded tersely. "You can set your watch by the son of a bitch. But I was unable to hire him. For one thing, he was already booked. And because of the storm, he didn't want to get stuck in the Manhattan traffic mess."

"Well, that's just great." Sister Lucia groaned, knitting her arms tightly across her narrow chest. "Now that makes *two* who have slipped away on us today."

Krumenacker pulled Quigley's business card from his sweater pocket and held it up. "I'm going to book him for Sunday. He won't get away." Fatigue washed over him; he laid his head back in the chair and closed his eyes.

"Do you feel all right?" she asked, changing her tone suddenly. "You look a little peaked."

"I'm okay," he lied. The aches in his joints and the general blahs had him very down. He hoped it wasn't the onset of a flu bug. "Do you want some tea?" he asked.

"No, not now," she answered, pulling off her coat and draping it across his bed. She turned and looked him square in the eyes. "I still don't believe how you could have mistaken Father Brodeur for Father Flaherty," she said. "We've got our work cut out for us just to get those who need to be taken care of . . . without wasting time on those who don't."

"I know," he responded sheepishly. "But like I told you, he'd already seen my face, air tubes and all. . . . And the gun—"

"Did you at least leave one of our cards?" Sister Lucia interrupted.

"No, I didn't. And I didn't shoot him between the legs either. But if I gave him a bye altogether, the cops would know what to be looking for on Christmas Eve and New

Year's Day. Speaking of which, have you made the necessary arrangements?" He'd spoken too many words at once; he gasped lightly and measured his breaths.

"Of course," she replied tersely. "Father Darwin Clapp will be there with bells on, and so will we. The moron went right for the bait."

"God, I've waited a long time to get even with that bastard."

"You're absolutely sure he's the one?" she asked, her gaze squinted into tight focus.

"Positive. I told you. Several nights before Buffo killed himself, Clapp had whipped him like a dog for some made-up reason. I don't remember what it was, but I'll never forget Buffo sobbing the whole damn night in the cot next to mine. He kept begging me to help him run away."

"Did he ever talk about me?" Lucia asked quietly, sitting down at the small table and resting her slender hands in her lap.

"He often spoke of an older sister—I don't recall Lucia being her name, though—and every time he mentioned her, he cried."

"Lucia was the name I took when entering the convent. It is not my given name."

John Wesley stared at her, waiting, expecting to hear her real given name. It was not forthcoming.

"Well, anyway, he must have loved you dearly. He told me all about how you guys got separated when your parents died."

Sister Lucia opened her bag and removed a tissue. "I went to live with an aunt who only had room for me. I knew little Emilio had been placed in St. Malachy's Home. . . . " She dabbed at her eyes, then blew her nose. "We were sure he would be safe there." For an instant, pain twisted her pale face. "Dear God, were we wrong."

"Everybody was wrong," Krumenacker mumbled.

"When he died, I was only fifteen. My aunt told me it was from pneumonia—she believed the lie too. Years later, long after I had taken my vows and entered the convent, I found out that he'd actually killed himself."

"Yeah, but you didn't know why. . . ."

"Not then," Lucia replied. "It was much later when I found out it had been because he was being abused by those disgusting priests and brothers over there. That's also when I left the convent and first got active in the movement."

Krumenacker stood and walked to the kitchenette; he lit a fire under the kettle.

"This Father Clapp . . . he walks with a gimp?" Sister Lucia asked.

"Yeah. Supposedly, one leg had some kind of birth defect. Always used a cane."

"Shouldn't be too hard to spot."

"I'd know him anywhere," Krumenacker uttered through tightly clenched teeth.

"There will be a lot of priests and nuns there that night."

"Don't worry, he'll stand out like a sore thumb. And then he'll be ours."

"He'd better be ours," she snapped. "Christmas Eve will be our last chance to settle our score with him. After that comes one more, and then the big one. . . ." The fragment of a smile played at her thin lips. "And then we're through."

Krumenacker nodded, rinsing a cup. He dropped his next-to-last Lipton tea bag into it. "Are you absolutely sure that the big one needs to be done?" he asked.

"Are you doubting me?" she said, gazing down her nose at him. "Are you doubting our Blessed Mother?"

"I know firsthand that Gilhooley and the rest of those bastard priests all deserve to rot in hell. Believe me, I know all the evil they've done, and who they did that evil to. But the pope . . . ?"

"He is the Antichrist, J.W.," she snarled unequivocally, slamming her open hand down on the tabletop. "The current one, the most recent in a succession of Antichrists who

have taken over our holy Church," she raged on. "Our
Lady of Fatima warned us of this. How many times have I
told you that it's absolutely necessary to remove this rotten
cancer before it metastasizes any further into the bowels of
beloved Mother Church?" Sister Lucia bowed her head
mournfully and made the sign of the cross on her breast.

Krumenacker could see her lips moving in murmured
prayer. He concluded at that moment that she really was
wacko . . . gone way 'round the bend . . . *bowels?* And he
wondered if he'd made a terrible mistake in joining forces
with her in the first place. "It's going to be almost impossible to get close enough to do it," he said.

"I've told you not to worry about that," she said firmly.
"Between the two of us, at least one of us will get close
enough. I know if you can't, I certainly will. By the way,
do you have that other gun ready for me—the .38 revolver?"

"Yes," he said, nodding. "Remind me to give it to you
before you leave. But getting back to next Tuesday, there
will be no possibility for escape afterward," he said. "The
place will be crawling with cops."

"We will almost certainly die accomplishing it," she
replied coolly. "But who cares? You're dying anyhow. Besides, we're going right to heaven. We will be martyrs for
Our Lady." A faraway look appeared in her eyes. "Who
knows? Some day, maybe hundreds of years from now, we
may even be consecrated as saints." She bowed her head
and blessed herself again.

"But he's not one of those pedophiles who beat and de-
filed me or your kid brother," Krumenacker argued. "He's
the pope, for God's sake."

"Don't start that garbage now, J.W.," she snapped back,
wagging a long index finger. "We discussed this, planned
it, and you agreed to it, right from the very beginning."

"I know, but—"

"You know, *but?* J.W., are you that naive to think that
we're alone in this?" she snarled derisively. Though she

kept her tone muted, it barely concealed a volcanic anger verging on catastrophic eruption. "There are a lot of people," she continued, "some in *unbelievably* high places, who have come together to play a role in this affair. They are sticking their necks way out, and they're totally depending on us. We are to be the martyrs of this glorious cause."

"What's their stake in all this?" he asked.

"The same stake the German generals had when conspiring to eliminate Hitler. They had no motives of self-aggrandizement; they were doing it for the sake of the fatherland and the German people. It was a higher cause. It was valorous and brave."

"We both had a personal stake in taking care of all these priests. . . ."

"Yes. And it was our plan to get them out of the way first, because if we did the pope first, we'd never be able to do them afterward. J.W.," Sister Lucia pressed, "don't go getting weak in the knees on me now."

"That was our plan, all right," Krumenacker quietly agreed, feeling reconvinced. He then went into a coughing spasm. Hacking for thirty full seconds, he finally spit a glob of greenish-yellow sputum into a trash-swollen Hefty bag propped in the corner of the kitchen.

"Don't you ever put your garbage out?" she asked. "Seems that same bag has been there since I know you."

"It's not quite full yet," he replied, half in jest. "Hell, I gotta get my money's worth. Besides, there ain't no damn chicken bones in there smelling up the joint."

Sister Lucia turned away with a disgusted look on her face.

"I think it's very unwise for me to try to carry the forty-five into St. Patrick's on Christmas Eve," he said. "The place is always flooded with cops. This year, you can bet there'll be even more."

"What are you suggesting?"

"We plant it inside, in the same place we intend to plant

it the night before the pope comes. Anyway, it will be a good test. The cops surely won't be frisking or searching people as they leave the cathedral after midnight Mass, but I bet you they'll be doing it when they arrive."

"Good," Sister Lucia said, nodding agreeably while reaching for her purse. "Give it to me now. I'll bring it with me tonight and plant it first thing in the morning."

Krumenacker removed the pistol from his oxygen tote and laid it on the table beside her.

"Where's that thirty-eight you promised to let me have?" she asked.

Krumenacker stepped to the kitchen cabinet and removed the fully loaded Smith & Wesson snub-nose. He laid it on the table beside the forty-five.

"Here," she said, dragging a rubber clown mask from the purse and tossing it at him. "Get rid of this thing. I don't think I'm going to need it anymore." She slipped both guns into the bag and closed it. "Now come, sit, we have to type another letter. But I want this one to be better; a whole lot better. Let all these rotten bastards know what's coming down the pike."

TEN

Vatican City

Pasquale Cardinal Damiani stopped to rest at the top step of the grand staircase that opened onto the broad second-floor corridor; he'd been in too much of a hurry since leaving his residence and had climbed the long flight of stairs too rapidly. Making matters worse, he patted the pocket sewn into his cloak and realized he'd forgotten to bring his little tin of nitro. During normal hours he would have ridden the elevator up the one flight, but it was just past midnight in Rome and, at that hour, no operator was on duty in the old-fashioned elevators of the Curia Romana. He noted how the usually bustling area was deep in repose, dimly lit and strangely quiet.

Catching his breath, Damiani realized that in only ten days he would be celebrating his third anniversary as Cardinal-Secretary of the Roman Curia; the Vatican rank comparable to that of the U.S. Secretary of State. Who would have ever thought that the timid peasant boy from Padua, with buckteeth and prominent ears, would one day rise to such a station? As the senior curia functionary and the closest official collaborator with the Holy Father, he was charged with implementing the policies of the reigning pontiff. He was also the link between the pontiff and the papal court, the body of congregations and offices that assist the pope in the government and administration of the Church.

During his tenure, Damiani had witnessed the upsurge

in tensions between the younger liberal and older conservative factions within the Holy See. He had watched the Church in America decline into near extremis. The College of Cardinals—once a bastion of conservative mentality and a staunch proponent of traditional church dogma, rules, and traditions—was now home to many liberal thinkers who wanted theological change. Crises all, he thought, but nothing to compare to this latest threat.

Sufficiently rested, Damiani quickly adjusted the red zucchetto atop his balding head and stepped forcefully along the lengthy corridor. His slippers fell silently on the inlaid and highly polished marble floor as he moved past a collection of seventeenth-century Renaissance artwork and tapestries that lined the ancient walls. The only sound was the crisp rustle of the scarlet taffeta lining of his mantle echoing within the barrel-vaulted gallery.

Damiani turned abruptly at the midway point of the hall into an arched alcove and pushed through a set of heavy doors into a small antechamber. Another set of matching doors, thickly padded and inlaid with rich red leather, led into the soundproof chamber used as an informal Curia Romana conference room. James Cardinal Remlinger, Emil Cardinal Deliberto, and Colonel George Olmstead were already present.

Remlinger headed the Section for Relations with States; the arm of the curia that dealt with outside civil governments, political authorities, and international diplomacy. Seated opposite Remlinger was Colonel Olmstead, commander of the Swiss Guards. Olmstead was a single man who had dedicated his life to his career. Known for a penchant for fine wine, it was suspected that he also had quite an eye for the ladies during his off-hours. When Damiani took his usual place at the head of the conference table, Cardinal Deliberto, prefect of the Congregation for the Doctrine of the Faith—founded by Pope Innocent III in the thirteenth century as a safeguard against heretical movements—sat down beside Remlinger.

"Please forgive my summoning you at this very late hour," Damiani began, glancing back and forth at the three men. "But something has come up, and we must act quickly and make some major decisions."

"What could possibly be the matter, Cardinal-Secretary?" Cardinal Remlinger asked. Austrian by birth, the sixty-eight-year-old Remlinger was a tall man; he was broad at the shoulders and exhibited a strong athletic quality. His face seemed always frozen in a preoccupied frown.

"I was awakened an hour ago by an urgent phone call from the papal nuncio to the United States," Damiani replied. "As we were already aware, he reported that a New York City parish priest was murdered—shot to death execution style—inside a Manhattan church last Saturday, December twenty-first."

"Yes," Cardinal Remlinger uttered, "that was terrible. God rest his soul." Deliberto and Olmstead nodded in solemn agreement; Deliberto crossed himself.

"I won't go into the details now," Damiani continued, "however, he reports that a second priest has now been killed in New York City in virtually the same manner— shot to death like a dog on the streets of Manhattan. The nuncio also has information that the New York City Police Department is in possession of a letter, purportedly written by the person or persons who takes responsibility for both these vicious acts."

"Do we know the contents of that letter?" Olmstead asked.

"It claims that the Church is full of 'serpents', and that it needs a cleansing from"—Damiani raised his pale eyebrows to emphasize his next words—*"top to bottom."* Looking at both Cardinals Remlinger and Deliberto, he added, "It also makes considerable mention of the Third Secret."

Deliberto frowned and cradled his ample chin in his hand.

Colonel Olmstead looked agitated. "The Holy Father is

scheduled to visit New York City on New Year's Eve," he
said tersely. "He is to celebrate the Eucharist in a special
Mass that afternoon at St. Patrick's Cathedral. . . . Right in
the heart of Manhattan."

Damiani nodded grimly.

"Unless the killers are apprehended before the Holy Father leaves Rome," Olmstead announced, "it is my duty as
commander of papal security to argue against his making
the trip."

"Is there not security in place for this visit?" the intense
Remlinger asked.

"Of course," Olmstead replied. "Plans were finalized
months ago. But there is never a good defense against a
madman."

"Agreed," Damiani stated flatly. "What do you have in
place?"

"Most of our three squads of Swiss Guards will be making the trip. They will be dressed in civilian clothing much
like that of the American Secret Service. And they will
carry concealed automatic weapons. There is a very tight
itinerary and a limited agenda. The New York City Police
Department will have thousands of officers on duty for the
entire period of the Holy Father's stay, which is scheduled
for one overnight only. They will also provide all motorcade escorts."

Damiani leaned forward. "What are your thoughts, Cardinal Deliberto?" he asked.

"The Holy Father must make the trip as scheduled," Deliberto responded decisively. "For the Holy Father not to
do so," he continued, "would give credence to those who
argue that the Church hierarchy fears the contents of the
Third Secret."

"With all due respect, Your Eminence," Olmstead broke
in, bristling. He faced Deliberto. "To hell with what those
people—or their heretical organizations—think."

"We should be very much worried about what they

think, Colonel," Deliberto fired back. "The Church in the United States is crumbling."

"But we're talking about putting the life of the Holy Father at great risk," Olmstead argued hotly.

This time Damiani interrupted. "What is your position, Cardinal Remlinger?" he asked, making tight eye contact with his first assistant.

The staid Austrian leaned back in his chair and crossed his arms. "It is my opinion that the Holy Father should not be discouraged from making this trip," Remlinger replied brusquely. "And I am sure I would be speaking for several others if the Curia were to be polled."

"Can you be more specific, James?" Damiani sensed an opportunity opening up.

"I know I speak for the prefect of the Congregation for Bishops, and the prefect for Causes of Saints."

Damiani nodded. He had thought as much. Remlinger might have just inadvertently unmasked a few more deeply hidden insurgents of the liberal cabal.

"I am meeting with the Holy Father at seven a.m.," Damiani said, "and will inform him of the situation. You may be assured that I will relay all your carefully considered opinions on this matter. But I will also tell him that I concur with the commander of the Swiss Guards. This trip to New York City absolutely must be canceled."

As Savage had predicted, the three-week-old killing of a myopic, senior citizen security guard up in Boston and its clear connection—via weapon and perpetrator MO—with the Manhattan killings of Fathers Gilhooley and Brodeur was the lead story of the Christmas Eve editions of the three New York dailies. He had no doubt that the same was being reported in Beantown. Jesus, he thought, wait till they get a load of Thursday's *Post,* with the Soldier's letter. The only positive in the whole damn mess was that newspaper circulation in both cities was probably up.

For sure, the cases were going nowhere fast, the main

problem being the complete lack of witnesses. The secondary problem, as he saw it, was the inaccessibility to Church personnel records. Also, Latent had discovered nothing in the way of usable evidence on the Soldier's letter. The only discernable prints on it or the envelope belonged to *Post* reporter Joe Ballantine and the copy boy, Timmy Chaney. The letter and envelope had now been forwarded over to Forensics. They would try to determine the typewriter's make and model and identify any peculiar signature it might have. They had also removed the envelope's saliva-activated sealed edge, so it could be run for DNA.

The shooter would have to make a mistake to give Homicide at least a thread to get the tips of their fingers on. Which hopefully would lead to a string they could pull, and then maybe a line with which to reel him in. Savage wasn't holding his breath on this one, though.

At one thirty, just as he was heading for his fifth cup of coffee, his desk phone rang.

"Thorn, Father Vinny here."

"Yes, Vinny. Good to hear from you. What's doin'?"

"Is Jack Lindstrom back in the office?"

"Yes, he is. I can see him from where I'm sitting."

"Did he mention to you how his appointment with Joel Horowitz went?"

"Said he liked Horowitz, and it went very well. I thank you for the steer. Jack told me he started him on some kind of antidepressant. Zoloft?"

"Yes, I know," the priest replied. "I've already spoken with Joel."

"Your friend, Dr. Horowitz, provided Jack with a freebee supply of physician samples. Wants to see him again in two days, and then every seven days thereafter for the next month."

"Good," Vinny said. "Joel is going to keep a close eye on him in the coming weeks. You need to also. This can be a dangerous period."

"Why is that?"

"Zoloft, Prozac, any of that whole spectrum of antidepressants, when first administered, might actually elevate a person to a plateau where they feel good enough to hurt themselves."

"Does Horowitz think Jack's that far gone?" Savage asked.

"He didn't say that. I'm thinking Joel just wants to play it safe; cover his butt. You know. At any rate, he wants to know if there's any way you can take Lindstrom's guns away till he gets safely beyond that stage."

Savage exhaled hard; the request might have sounded easy to a doctor or a priest, but to a cop it was heavy—about as heavy as it could get.

"In Jack Lindstrom's case, it is *gun*, singular," Savage said. "He's one of the few guys I know who doesn't even own an off-duty. Jack doesn't like guns; probably wouldn't even wear one on the job if he weren't made to. But he still is not going to like giving it up."

"Sorry, Thorn, but I think Joel is absolutely correct. It's the right thing to do," Vinny said. "And you're certain he has no other guns? He's not a hunter? Maybe he keeps a rifle or shotgun at home?"

"What? Shoot Bambi?"

"I getcha," Father Vinny said.

"It's probably a holdover from his pacifist hippie days back in the late sixties," Savage said. "He's really a gentle person." The thought crossed Savage's mind that he wouldn't shoot Bambi either. He was more into the two-legged variety of game, armed game that could shoot back. "Does Horowitz want me to give Jack some time off?" he asked.

"Not necessarily. Continuing to work might help keep Jack's mind occupied with things other than his own troubles. But Horowitz said he'd leave that call up to you."

Savage pondered Vinny's sage words of warning and agreed to pull Lindstrom's gun. Maybe it would be done unofficially, but it would be done. After hanging up, he called Lindstrom into the office and told him to close the door.

"Your doc wants me to take your gun," he said with no preamble.

Lindstrom's bland expression seemed to freeze. The long seconds of uncomfortable silence that followed were broken only by the annoying constant buzz of the fluorescent ceiling fixture. "Is that a must?" Lindstrom finally muttered.

"No, Jack," Savage replied. "I'm not going to make you. The decision to give it up is yours."

"On the record . . . or off?" Lindstrom asked quietly. His eyes were those of a cornered injured cat, his rubbery brow twisting into a frustrated frown.

"Keep your nose clean, Jack. . . . Stay out of trouble. . . . Do exactly what your doctor wants, and it'll stay off the record. I'll keep the piece here in my locker. Keep your jacket on and buttoned, and no one else will know about it. You fuck up, I'll have no choice . . . we go public."

"Anything else?"

"Till you get your gun back, you're restricted to the office working the phone. I don't want you out on the street unarmed. Do you want to take some time off?"

"No," Lindstrom replied unequivocally. "How long is this going to go on?"

"For as long as it takes."

Monsignor Albert Dunleavy sat expressionless in the backseat of the dark gray Lincoln, his deeply set, startling blue eyes staring blindly out at snow-blanketed Second Avenue. It was four thirty in the afternoon on Christmas Eve, and there was much on his mind.

"You will be making a left turn at Fourteenth Street," he said, snapping from his deep thought. He leaned forward and exchanged a momentary glance with Hans Peter via the rearview mirror. "The church of Our Lady of Perpetual Help is two blocks up on the right-hand side." As soon as Dunleavy had spoken the words, he realized that the driver needed no directions. Hans Peter knew the precise location of every parish building in the archdiocese—and the quickest route to get there—probably much better than he.

The fastidiously groomed Swiss immigrant at the wheel today was the archdiocese's best chauffeur. Hans Peter was not only an excellent driver, but also a wonderful confidant and an impartial sounding board—the latter being an invaluable asset that Dunleavy treasured. Most importantly, Hans Peter was the epitome of discretion. The man had not even raised an eyebrow when Dunleavy appeared from his residence dressed in casual street clothes—an infrequent occurrence, indeed. Dunleavy wished he could have dressed more formally today, but the police safety recommendation had been to travel in mufti as much as possible. . . . To say nothing of the damn weather.

Dunleavy's informal visit to the small church was one of archdiocese protocol. Speaking on behalf of His Eminence, Cardinal Hammond, he was to express condolences to the bedridden Father Killian Flaherty on the terrible murder of Father Brodeur, and to assure the pastor of any archdiocese support he might need in the coming months.

As the sedan turned east on Fourteenth Street, Dunleavy slipped back into deep thought. The Holy Roman Church, the ship that had carried him since childhood—and to which he had devoted every moment of his life ever since—was foundering beneath him, very much in danger of sinking into unrecoverable depths.

Civil lawsuits were pouring in all over the country. Wave upon wave of people—thousands—encouraged and supported by organizations like the Survivors Network of Those Abused by Priests were coming out of the woodwork, alleging all sorts of abuses going back decades, for God's sake. The backing of these organizations allowed the individual complainants in these actions to enjoy a sense of safety in numbers. And inside the courtroom, the one-two punch of representation by high-powered attorneys and the court's civil discovery process was a killer.

By analyzing the myriad alternatives, Dunleavy was attempting to hack a path through the ever thickening complexities and problems that had grown up around Mother Church during his lifetime—first surrounding her, then enveloping her, now strangling the very life from her. He had to save her, somehow defend her. Use any means necessary to keep her afloat—all for the higher good, of course—until he drew his last breath.

Suddenly, the Lincoln's back door swung open and Hans Peter was standing there, offering his arm for support. They were parked in front of the OLPH rectory. "Careful on those stairs, Monsignor," the chauffeur said, nodding toward the few stone steps that led to the rectory's main entrance. "They look slippery."

Dunleavy was warmly dressed in reindeer-skin mukluks, cuffed and pleated wool slacks, and a fur-collar bomber jacket bearing the insignia patch of the 380th Bomb Wing. "Guess I'd never be mistaken for a cleric in this getup, eh, Hans Peter?" he said, laughing self-consciously.

"You do look somewhat different, Monsignor," the chauffeur agreed.

"It actually feels good to wear plain everyday clothes for a change," Dunleavy said. "This leather jacket was a gift from members of the 380th when I left my post as their chaplain at Plattsburgh Air Force Base, twenty-five years ago. I haven't worn it in years."

"It is a handsome jacket, Monsignor."

Anya, the rectory housekeeper, did not immediately recognize Dunleavy in his noncleric casual clothing when she answered the parish house door. After he finally convinced her of his identity, Dunleavy was given admittance.

"Please, pardon me, Monsignor," she said, embarrassed, bowing her head and clasping her hands in supplication.

"But with terrible thing happened to poor Father Brodeur . . . and Father Gilhooley . . . we are all so afraid. . . ."

"I understand completely," he assured her. "You're wise to be very careful of who you allow inside." He blessed Anya with the sign of the cross, then strode right by her into the pastor's office. "Ask Father Flaherty to join me," he said, unzipping his jacket.

Anya bowed again and turned away. Her long apron flapping with each step, she quickly disappeared down the long narrow hall. A minute later, a pale and agitated Father Flaherty, dressed in sweats and slippers, scuffed into the office and pulled the door tightly closed behind him.

"Pardon my appearance, Monsignor," he said tensely, extending his hand.

"And pardon mine," Dunleavy replied, then announced, "His Eminence, Cardinal Hammond, wishes to extend his deepest sympathies to you and the members of your parish on the tragic loss of Father Jean Brodeur."

"Umh," Flaherty grunted, nodding in disinterested acknowledgement. "That's very good of His Eminence." Sitting down heavily in one of the two leather chairs that faced the large mahogany desk, he then said straight out, "You need to hear my confession, Monsignor. And you need to hear it right now."

"Why me and not your usual confessor, Father?" Dunleavy asked. "I have never heard your confession before."

"My usual confessor is dead," Flaherty responded soberly. "He was murdered a few days ago. . . . "

Dunleavy acknowledged with a nod.

"Two more reasons," Flaherty continued. "First, and most importantly, I wish to deliver myself from the guilt of mortal sin, and thereby save myself from its eternal punishment."

"Secondly?"

"You, in particular, Monsignor, need to know what I am about to tell you. Although you will then have the burden of this knowledge, you, as my confessor . . . will be bound to the inviolable secrecy of the confessional. Even by the weight of man's law you will be unable to ever repeat or reveal it to anyone. But you may find the burden to be great."

Dunleavy sat down slowly in the chair behind the desk. It was clear that the pastor was seriously troubled by a problem of considerable magnitude. "Please, Father," he said softly, making the sign of the cross, "proceed with your confession. God will ease your mind and soul."

"Father Thomas Gilhooley and I met many years ago, as young priests, when we both worked at St. Malachy's Home for Boys," Father Flaherty began. "During that period, sexual abuses of the younger boys by some of the staff—with the wink-wink knowledge of the rector in charge—was rampant. Regrettably, both Gilhooley and I were active participants."

Dunleavy's eyes grew wide. He fought to keep an unshakable priestly demeanor, but it wasn't easy.

"How many years ago was this?" he asked.

"Way back in the sixties," Flaherty responded in a mournful monotone, wringing his clasped hands. "After the suicide death of one boy, it was all hushed up. The rector at the time simply arranged to have those of us involved transferred out to other assignments; most, like Gilhooley and I, went to parishes."

"Have you never confessed this before to relieve your soul?" Dunleavy asked.

"No, Monsignor," Flaherty said in a barely discernable whisper. His ruddy face twisted violently as he fought to hold back tears. "I have always been too damn ashamed."

"What brings you to confess it now, Father? To me?"

"The murder of Father Thomas Gilhooley had something to do with those horrible days at St. Malachy's."

"What makes you so sure?"

"Whoever killed Tom Gilhooley intended to kill me too; Father Brodeur died instead." A tear traced down Flaherty's florid face. He wiped it away with the back of his hand as another quickly formed.

Dunleavy's mind was racing at full gallop. He wondered what to say, wondered where to go from here.

"Was that the only time you ever engaged in any such conduct?" he finally asked.

"It was," Flaherty responded firmly. "But tomorrow, I am to be interviewed by detectives about Father Brodeur's murder. And as a result, I am on the horns of a great dilemma."

"And what might that dilemma be?" Dunleavy asked, thinking he knew the answer.

"Do I tell them everything I know? As I should?"

Dunleavy weighed his response carefully. "If you go public, you will be incriminating yourself, and possibly others, to crimes long in the past," he stated finally. "And you all will bear the consequences, legal and otherwise. To say nothing of the devastating effect such revelations would have on the Church in general, and this archdiocese in particular. Are you prepared for that?"

"For those of us who actually did the wrong, so be it." Flaherty said resignedly. "My dilemma . . . my concern . . . is that it could go somewhat higher."

"Higher?"

"The rector of St. Malachy's Home for Boys in those days, the one who simply transferred us to other assignments while knowing full well our transgressions, was none other than the current archbishop of New York."

"His Eminence, Cardinal Hammond?" Dunleavy blurted.

Flaherty exhaled explosively, as if a dam had broken somewhere, and nodded in the affirmative.

"What am I to do, Monsignor? If I lie to the police tomorrow, His Eminence's reputation will be spared, but other priests may die as a result. Therefore, I am damned if I do . . . and damned if I don't."

The man was damned for eternity no matter what he

chose to do, Dunleavy thought. The tortured soul needed some form of hope at this moment, but . . .

"Cardinal Hammond must not be destroyed," Dunleavy said, after a long pause to consider his course. He stared intently into Flaherty's watering eyes. "In the name of Jesus and for the good of the Church, man," he pressed emphatically, "I urge you to find another way."

The wind had really picked up in the last twenty minutes. The intermittent gusts swirled the finely powdered snow into miniwhirlwinds and dragged them—like frozen dust devils—along the elevated platform of the White Plains Metro North station. Shivering from the bitter cold, Father Darwin Clapp leaned on his Blackthorn, snugged up the woolen scarf at his neck, and looked at his watch. The 4:05 to New York City was two minutes late. He should have stayed in the heated platform house, and he would have, if he'd been duly recognized, instead of just flat-out ignored by the small group of people inside. They were his parishioners, dammit, and he knew every one of their faces. They, no doubt, were also heading in early to attend midnight Mass at St. Patrick's. But did they say hello? No. When he'd first entered the station, their eyes seemed to glaze over and they acted as if they didn't see him. As if he were invisible. Hell, he thought, it might be heated in the platform house, but the atmosphere was colder in there than outside at the track edge.

Why the archdiocese had specifically invited him—out of all the other priests from St. Cecilia's—to attend tonight's Mass was still a mystery. He would have guessed that Father Coniglio would have gotten that call. After all, Coniglio was far more popular, not only with the parishioners but with the archdiocese as well. Coniglio would have been recognized by the snobby group, no question, and probably invited to join them. When you got right down to it, Coniglio was a real ass kisser, a glad-handing politician. Clapp had to concede it was very nice of the archdiocese to finally consider him for a change.

The 4:05 pulled in at 4:13, and Father Clapp prepared to board the third car from the front. Out of the corner of his eye, he watched as the animated group of parishioners left the platform house and walked back to car number 5.

Sighing, he boarded the train and limped to a seat beneath a heat vent. The warming air was a godsend.

"If you don't mind my saying so, Monsignor, you look terribly upset," Hans Peter said, veering carefully around a double-parked taxicab and turning uptown at Third Avenue. "Is everything all right with Father Flaherty at OLPH?"

"I suppose," Dunleavy responded pensively, dismissing the chauffeur's query. "It's just that we've all been under a great deal of pressure lately." It was now clear that even his practiced calm could not belie the perfect storm that was raging within his mind and soul. He still could not believe what he'd heard from Flaherty only minutes ago. What to do?

"Our beloved church is under siege, Monsignor," Hans Peter said bitterly. "She is becoming swallowed up in a jungle of scandal."

"Unh," Dunleavy grunted. Hans Peter's analogy was right on. Dunleavy understood but would never admit, publicly or privately, that the seeds of that jungle had been planted long ago. Fed and nurtured over many centuries with arrogance and hubris and tended, in recent decades, by an institution-wide shell game of shifting problem clerics from parish to parish and diocese to diocese, the entangling jungle had finally blossomed and completely taken over.

"It's true that the Church has been badly scarred by scandal," Dunleavy said, his voice a somber monotone. "But scars alone do not kill. What will kill is the feeding frenzy of multibillion-dollar litigation being brought by salivating, money-mongering, opportunist lawyers who are bleeding the Church to death."

Foul jackals all, he thought bitterly; they hide behind a high-flown mask of unselfish concern for others, when in fact what they really care about is themselves and how they could retire for life like kings on a one-third contingency share of just one such case.

"Terrible," Hans Peter murmured, slowly accelerating the big Lincoln through Twenty-third Street on the green. "They care nothing for the two-thousand-year-old-institution whose life's blood they are siphoning away. Talk about thirty pieces of silver . . . those god-awful lawsuits will bring ruin to every major diocese in the United States within ten years."

Shakespeare was right, Dunleavy thought. *First, kill all the lawyers.* What next? he pondered, wringing age-spotted hands in his lap. Learn from history's examples, Albert. Stand up, help slay the dragon, do what has to be done in the name of the Lord. *If only Judas had eschewed the thirty pieces of silver. If only Brutus had stood with Caesar.*

And now the broth had thickened even further. His Eminence, Cardinal Hammond, had promised him the bishop's miter. But if Hammond was caught up in a scandal, tarnished by the sins of others committed a long time ago, he could be expelled from his see or forced to retire. And with the cardinal would go his own dream of a bishopric. That must not be allowed to happen. He *needed* to be made bishop. Not for vanity . . . not for ego . . . and certainly not for selfish ambition; but to gain the power required to help effect drastic changes of the Church from within. As a middle-ranking soldier in an army, one could hardly bring about much in the way of change. As a general in that army, however, one could do much more. His rise to bishop—and perhaps, one day, his elevation to cardinal—was imperative. Hammond had to be protected at any cost. . . . Even the sacrifice of a few priests.

"Are you going back to the office, Monsignor, or are

you going back to your residence?" Hans Peter asked as the Lincoln neared Forty-second Street.

Dunleavy allowed many seconds to pass before responding, as an idea began to formulate in his mind. "Stay on Third," he finally said decisively. "When we get to Forty-fifth, make a left. I'll point out where to stop." Hans Peter nodded, and set the turn signal.

"I will be picking up a gift for a friend," Dunleavy volunteered. "When we get back to the archdiocese, just bring the package up to my office and leave it. I'll take care of it from that point."

At Forty-fifth the Lincoln turned and crept westbound. Near the corner of Lexington it pulled to the curb and Dunleavy climbed nimbly from the rear seat. Treading carefully on the slippery sidewalk, he entered the showroom of Warshawski & Washburn Office Equipment.

"Can I help you, sir?" The eager sales clerk who greeted him was a tall man in his late twenties wearing an ill-fitting tweed suit; his lapel label identified him as Bob. Bob was one of those guys who not only encroached on space, but also created too much saliva when he talked, and, Dunleavy could tell, he liked to talk too much.

"I need to see something in a paper shredder."

If only Nixon—or some stand-up aide within his inner circle—would have destroyed those damning tapes before they'd been subpoenaed . . . and before anyone really knew they even existed . . .

"You've come to the right place, sir," Bob said cheerily, offering a wide, wet smile. "We've got an Aurora model paper shredder on sale today. Only thirty-nine ninety-nine."

Dunleavy took a half step back. He didn't mind Bob's wind, but he couldn't stand the rain. And the man's breath smelled as if he'd had a garlic hero for lunch.

"Does it make those long stringy cuts, or does it make confetti?" he asked.

"Uh, no sir. That particular model only offers a vertical cut. However, as we move up the line of qual—"

"What's the *best* one you carry, Bob?"

"If you're looking for increased security, sir, that would be the Fellowes model PS80. It's kind of industrial strength, if you get my meaning. That baby not only cross-cuts into minute confetti, but chews up staples and small paper clips as well. . . . *And*," Bob added with a sly wink, "if the lady of the house is an inveterate shopper, credit cards. The PS80 is two hundred bucks. But for today only we're offering an instant twenty-dollar rebate. The unit will take ten sheets per pass and has a one-year parts and lab—"

"I'll take it. But only if you can gift wrap it for me."

Bob smiled wetly again and led the way to the nearby sales counter. "No problem, Mr. . . . ?"

"Hogan. Charles Hogan."

"Would you prefer the Christmas tree wrapping paper, Mr. Hogan? Or the green-and-red stripe?"

"The Christmas tree stuff will do fine."

"Will that be check or charge?"

"That, sir, will be cash."

ELEVEN

Midnight Mass at St. Patrick's was not only a religious event of grand proportion, but also a New York City happening. John Wesley knew this year would be no exception. The bitter cold and continuing snowfall had done little to discourage the hundreds of faithful who found their way to Fifth Avenue and Fiftieth Street. They streamed into St. Patrick's Cathedral as her bells pealed out their joyous Christmas Eve summons. The carillon reverberated through the steep-sided canyons of Midtown, its glorious hallelujah reaching north to the snow-buried footpaths of Central Park, the tenement rooftops of the West Side neighborhood called Clinton—also known as Hell's Kitchen—and the high-rise terraces of the fashionable East Side that some still called Turtle Bay.

Krumenacker gazed wistfully at the ice-draped Gothic Revival structure from the opposite side of Fifth Avenue. Megawatt kliegs, their intense brightness softened into a muted glow by the windblown maelstrom of falling snow, looked to the heavens and bathed the imposing edifice with a halo both mystical and hallowed. The cathedral's twin spires—each with a cross of Christ as a finial—twisted up into the night sky. It reminded him of the crystal abbey in a fairy tale his mother had once read to him. Mother had often read to him at bedtime when he was very young—maybe four or five. Afterward, she would hum Brahms' Lullaby until he closed his eyes and drifted off into secure, peaceful sleep.

John Wesley had been to St. Pat's before on many Christmas Eves. People of all faiths traveled from all over the globe just to attend the midnight Mass. Christians of every denomination would come. Jews, Muslims, and agnostics would be in attendance, and probably more than a few heathens and pagans·as well. Besides those just there to see, there would also be a large contingent of those simply wishing to *be* seen. Celebrities, politicians, the rich and famous, the powerful and well connected—those who always seemed to get seated in the best up-front pews.

And then there would be the clerics, dozens and dozens of priests and nuns from parishes all over the city. Tonight he was interested in seeing only one. The one he knew would be there. The one he had not laid eyes on in many decades. Brother Clapp, the son of a bitch with the bum right leg. The "Prince of Darkness," the child-beating bully who had once held the title "Dean of Discipline" while working his way through holy orders at Saint Malachy's Home for Boys.

John Wesley recalled the brutal sting of Clapp's whipping stick on his bare ass. He recalled having cried the first time, but thereafter he'd always taken his beatings in stoic silence. There were other boys, smaller and younger boys, who were so fearful of being sent to see Brother Clapp, that they sometimes "settled out of court" with the brothers or priests they had supposedly offended. The smaller, weaker ones like poor little Buffo, whom Clapp used to beat unmercifully, had little choice; numbing fear made their decisions for them. But tonight, they all would be avenged.

Krumenacker carefully measured his breaths as he slowly crossed Fifth Avenue. He could tell he was running a temperature, and the fever was quickly burning up what was left of his strength. He passed seemingly unnoticed through the outer phalanx of white-gloved uniformed policemen that ringed the church. Most of them were young, he observed, rosy-cheeked eager rookies no doubt. The senior men in the police department could probably wrangle Christmas Eve off to be home with their families, and those who couldn't were probably sipping coffee and eating doughnuts in a nice warm radio car. Not unlike Army RHIP, he concluded, where *rank has its privilege.*

As he neared the five steps that led to the huge central door, he sensed great weakness coming on. He looked to see if Sister Lucia was standing where they agreed to meet. He did not see her. Where could she be? If she didn't show up, or if for some reason they couldn't find each other in the incredible crowd, the whole night would be a damn waste—since she had the gun—and that bastard Clapp would get in the wind. Maybe she was waiting just inside the door to shelter from the cold, he reasoned, trying to calm his concerns.

Suddenly, he felt a strong hand on his shoulder and a man's voice broke into his thoughts. "Excuse me, sir."

Krumenacker spun to face one of the white-gloved cops he'd just passed. The uniformed man was big, six feet or better, and his oversize dark eyes had a no-nonsense glare. His name tag read REGEL. Officer Regel was accompanied by a shorter, stocky woman cop. She too emitted a no-nonsense aura; Krumenacker didn't catch her name.

"Yes, officer?" he stammered.

"Are you here to attend tonight's service, sir?" Regel asked. His overgrown eyebrows arched seriously beneath the brim of his police cap.

"Why . . . yes," Krumenacker replied, shivering with a sudden feeling of chill. He was very sick and needed to sit down soon and rest. He struggled to breathe deeply but found it impossible.

"I'm sorry to bother you, sir," the cop said, his big browns now studying the cannula in Krumenacker's nose. His eyes then traced the route of the plastic tubing that looped Krumenacker's ears and ran to the nylon tote that hung from his shoulder. "But I have to see what you have in that bag."

"What do you mean . . . what I have in the—" A long, rumbling cough prevented him from finishing the sentence.

"No one is permitted in the church this evening carrying any packages," the woman cop said. She had a snotty, tough-broad edge to her voice.

John Wesley's pulse was now in full gallop. His blood pressure was probably sky-high. If he didn't calm down soon, he'd go into bronchospasm. He shivered again.

"What are you so nervous about, sir?" Regel asked.

Krumenacker fought for self-control as he struggled to breathe. "I'm not nervous. . . . I'm sick. This is my oxygen supply," he said, gasping. "Can't you see that?"

"We can see that," Regel replied. "But what else do you have in that bag?"

"Good Jesus," John Wesley said angrily. "Why are you bothering me? Can't you see I'm not a well man?"

"Why don't you let us take a quick look in that bag, mister," the lady cop said. "Then you can be on your way. We'll even escort you to a nice seat inside. How's that?"

Krumenacker hesitated, trying to think clearly. Half in anger, half in the immediate need to get inside the warm church and rest, he pulled the nylon tote defensively under his arm and turned away.

Regel stopped him cold. As the big cop restrained him, the lady cop tore open the Velcro flap on the Oxy Tote. Shining a flashlight beam into it, she quickly groped around inside with her gloved hand. In moments, the search was over.

"Nothing in here but a small oxygen tank, Tommy," she said, "and a few vials of medication."

As John Wesley collapsed slowly to his knees, Police Officer Regel, Tommy, kept him from falling completely.

"St. Pat's detail, post five, to Central, K," the lady cop said into her portable radio. "Have a bus respond to the front of the church. We have a man down—serious breathing problems. Put a rush on it, Central."

Lying there, semiconscious and freezing, surrounded by police and curious onlookers, John Wesley realized that tonight's mission would have to be aborted. He hoped Sister Lucia—wherever the hell she was—would understand. There came a gentle, warm hand on his brow. He opened his eyes to see her there beside him. She was nodding reassuringly.

"Don't worry sir," she said. "*Everything* will be all right. . . . *Everything* will be taken care of."

J.W. forced a weak grin of relief and felt himself fade into unconsciousness.

•   •   •

> *O holy child of Bethlehem, descend to us we pray*
> *Cast out our sin and enter in, be born in us today.*
> *We hear the Christmas angels, the great glad tidings tell,*
> *O come to us, abide with us, Our Lord, Emmanuel.*

While the St. Patrick's choir in the gallery above the narthex and beneath the magnificent Rose Window sang their way through the fourth verse of "O Little Town of Bethlehem," Father Darwin Clapp buttoned up his overcoat, snugged his woolen scarf tightly at the collar, and, seeing an opening, slipped into the nave's central aisle that was packed with celebrants slowly inching their way from the awesome cathedral. The Christmas Eve Mass—the Angels' Mass—had been a moving experience, he thought. He was especially impressed with Cardinal Hammond's homily, which had focused on the true meaning of Christmas: "*Populus, qui ambulabat in tenebris, vidit lucem magnam*—The people who walked in darkness have seen a great light." He would remember those words; he would incorporate them into his homily when serving Christmas Day Mass up at St. Cecilia's.

When he reached the great bronze doors of the West

Portal, Clapp stood off to the side and blew his nose for what seemed like the hundredth time in the last hour. He didn't know what it was—the flu maybe, or just a bad cold—but he was coming down with something. He pocketed the sodden handkerchief, pulled on his gloves, and watched as the exiting crowd broke down into smaller groups. Mostly couples, they peeled off and filtered through a legion of uniformed police before going their many separate ways along brightly lit Fifth Avenue. He also saw that sometime during the Mass, the storm that had dumped close to a foot of powder on Manhattan's sidewalks in the last day and a half had finally let up.

The city was special tonight, he thought; it was pure and clean and white—nicer than he'd seen it in years. Finally ready to trek the nine blocks back down to Grand Central, he took a deep breath of the cold night air, leaned heavily against his Blackthorn walking stick, and began limping south.

As he passed the broad display windows of Saks department store, Father Clapp stopped to marvel at the incredibly lifelike scenes depicted within. Mannequins in haughty poses lazed there, dressed in some of the most expensive apparel of the day. They all looked so real. And just like real people, their frozen gazes fixed on everything but him. Even to mannequins he was invisible.

Ever since he was a child, he had always felt as if he had his nose pressed against the window of life, never a real participant, merely a frustrated, if not alien, onlooker.

He caught a glimpse of his own reflection in the glass and sighed. The image that looked back was that of a lonely and lame old man. His thoughts were suddenly interrupted by the sound of a loose snow chain slapping at the fender of an icicle-laden radio car that cruised slowly by. He hadn't seen snow chains in years. He moved on.

Clapp gazed across Fifth Avenue into Rockefeller Center. The plaza was occupied with dozens of bigger-than-life brilliantly lighted angels all heralding Christ's arrival on long, golden trumpets. Beyond the plaza, he could see the giant tree with its countless lights. Every building along Fifth Avenue was handsomely decorated for the Yule as well. The night air was still bitterly cold, but as crystal clear as a newly blown Waterford goblet. Interesting, he thought, how much sharper things seemed to look on bitter cold nights such as this; how much redder the red traffic lights were, and how much greener the green ones appeared. It was like looking at the world through freshly cleaned spectacles. How he missed living in the city; Westchester County was so . . . *ehh*. He sneezed again and wiped his nose.

At Forty-fifth Street, Father Clapp turned and walked east, amazed to see how quickly the city had dealt with the major snowfall. Most of the sidewalks had already been shoveled, and beeping snowplows were everywhere in the side streets and avenues. By tomorrow morning it would be business as usual in Manhattan. Passing between Madison and Vanderbilt Avenues, he saw that McHugh's, a nice bar opposite the Roosevelt, was still open; perhaps a little snort might help ease his cold. The last Metro North wouldn't be leaving Grand Central until 1:30. That would get him back up to St. Cecilia's rectory no later than 2:30, which would still allow him adequate sleep to be ready to serve tomorrow's Christmas Day Mass. Hell, he remembered the days when he could serve all the morning Masses after having no sleep, but that was when he was much younger. Things change; the body changes. Father Coniglio, who liked to get up with the birds, was already scheduled to take care of the dawn Mass. Well, then, he thought eagerly, let's get to it.

Clapp let himself into the dimly lit saloon and sat at the end of the long bar, which was still fairly crowded considering it was late on Christmas Eve. He leaned his walking stick against the wall beside him, removed his gloves, and opened his coat; the place was warm, for which he was very thankful.

"What'll it be, sir?" the horse-faced bartender asked, setting a cocktail napkin neatly before him on the polished mahogany.

"Cutty and soda—make it a double," Clapp said. As the barman stepped away to mix the drink, Clapp felt a sneeze coming on. He snatched up the little bar napkin and let go violently. After wiping his nose and pocketing the now balled-up wad of paper, he felt a light tap on his shoulder. He turned to see a fair-looking woman who had just entered the bar. She was undoing a scarf. Once uncovered, he saw that her blond hair was nicely groomed and rather long; it also seemed fake. She did not look at all familiar. He caught no scent of perfume, but did detect a faint aroma of something . . . *musty*.

"Pardon me," she asked softly, an amazed look on her taut face. "But aren't you Father Clapp from St. Cecilia's Church in White Plains?"

"Why, yes . . ." he said, making it a point to smile. He felt elated. He shook her hand, grateful that someone had actually recognized him.

"I knew it was you," she said, undoing the two top buttons of her coat. "I just came from midnight Mass at St. Patrick's. I thought I saw you there."

"Oh yes," he responded. "I had a special invitation from the archdiocese." The barman set the scotch and soda before him on the bar, then looked toward the woman. She ordered a glass of dry red.

"I hope I'm not bothering you, Father," she said dolefully. "But I thought I might have one glass of wine here before calling it a night. It's sort of a ritual. My husband, Harry, and I always stopped here after midnight Mass every year. I lost him six months ago."

"I'm so sorry," he offered with a sympathetic nod.

"It all happened so quickly," she said. "Heart attack. He passed away in White Plains Hospital. He was buried from St. Cecilia's. Father Coniglio did the service. Oh, Father Coniglio was so-o-o nice."

"Yes, he is nice," Clapp agreed. "A fine man. A wonderful priest."

"Are you taking Metro North back to White Plains tonight, Father?" she asked, reaching for the wine that the bartender set down before her.

"I'm taking the one thirty train," he replied. "Why don't we ride back together? Then you could tell me more about Harry."

The lady smiled broadly, and the tensed shoulders beneath her coat seemed to relax at his invitation.

"Oh, that is so nice of you to offer, Father," she said, "but I'm staying in the city tonight. I've taken a room at the Roosevelt. I'm meeting a group of friends in the morning."

"I see," Clapp said, trying to conceal the not unexpected disappointment. He raised his drink in toast. "Well, then, Merry Christmas to you, Mrs. . . . ?"

"Mrs. dos Santos," she replied, raising her glass to meet his. "My friends call me Lucia."

"Merry Christmas to you, Mrs. dos Santos . . . Lucia."

"And a very Merry Christmas to you, Father Clapp. And may you have many more."

TWELVE

When the nightstand phone rang at three o'clock on Christmas morning, Savage stirred but fought against waking. For openers, the call would louse up the deposit he was hoping to make in his seriously overdrawn sleep account, but more importantly, it would cut short the very lifelike dream he was having of his late wife and daughter.

In the dream, Jenny was about five, or six maybe—she was missing one of her front baby teeth. Her little feet were bare, and she had on those pink flannel Barbie pajamas she used to love so much. A look of wonderment lit her angel face as she shrieked with little-girl excitement at the mountain of presents Santa had left beneath a tinsel-draped tree on some Christmas morning long past. All the gifts were wrapped in shiny red paper, tied with pretty green bows and shiny red ribbons, and the tree was lit up like Times Square.

The dream was so real he could almost smell balsam . . . and rich brewing coffee . . . and bacon too—he even heard its distinctive sizzle as it fried in some offscreen pan. And Joanne, of course, looked beautiful; dark eyes shining. She wore a soft robe over her lean size six, and had those dumb fuzzy slippers on her feet. The twinkling lights of the tree played off the sheen of her healthy hair; it was tied up with a green velvet band—just the way she used to wear it. On the telephone's second ring, the screen went black.

Savage threw back the covers and sat naked at the edge of the bed, rubbing the heels of his palms into bone-dry and weary eye sockets that couldn't seem to get enough massage. He answered the badly timed call on the third ring, guessing it would be from Detective Operations. It was. He hoped it didn't involve another dead priest. It did.

After a slapdash electric-razor shave, a quick hot shower to get his heart started, and a failed check to see if Ray had come home, he let himself into the kitchen and downed several ginkgo biloba, two vitamin C tablets, and a 60 mg capsule of coenzyme Q-10 with a tall glass of pulpless OJ. He glanced at the big calendar pinned beside the fridge; it was December 25th. Hell of a way to start Christmas Day, he thought. Oh well . . . let the games begin.

He clipped his holstered .38 Smith & Wesson Chief into his waistline, pulled on his topcoat, and let himself out of the second-floor apartment. It was incredibly cold outdoors. As he walked up Sullivan Street to his car, he thought about the dream of Jenny and Joanne with the nagging sense of tragedy and loss he had never gotten over. And never would.

For Thorn, still groggy, his caffeine-deprived, ten-minute ride up to Midtown from the Village was surreal. Thorn couldn't recall ever seeing the city so quiet and still, so bereft of animation, so bereft of . . . life. Nothing seemed to be moving. He saw no bread trucks along the way, no *Daily News, Times*, or *Post* delivery wagons . . . not one single taxicab; he didn't even see a pigeon, for crissakes. But, he reminded himself, pulling beneath the terraced viaduct that connects Park Avenue on the Vanderbilt Avenue side of Grand Central Terminal, it was still not quite four a.m. on a bitterly cold snow-covered Christmas Day. It wouldn't be long—an hour maybe—and the city would once again be wide awake.

He parked beside an idling morgue wagon and wondered why he hadn't chosen to become a CPA or a dentist or a center fielder for the Mets, someone who never got called out at this ungodly hour. But he knew why he'd become a cop in this city. He loved The Job, and he loved New York. There was truly no place else on earth he would rather be. This, for better or worse, was his life.

Savage stepped from his car and nodded to Diane De-Gennaro, who was taking notes from a couple of Midtown South uniformed cops. She broke away from the huddle and, slipping the notepad into her coat pocket, joined him.

"He was found by that cabbie," she said, pointing to a young man shivering beside a yellow taxi parked near a Dumpster at the far end of the viaduct. He was tall and lanky with a long ponytail and a ski-slope nose. Richie Marcus and Ollie Beyeler were squatting next to the lifeless body of Father Darwin Clapp, searching through his pockets. Savage and DeGennaro walked in that direction.

"Cabbie states that he had pulled in there to relieve himself behind the Dumpster," she continued.

"How many times was the victim shot, and where was he hit?"

"He's got one between his eyes, Sarge," Diane said, "and, just like the Gilhooley case, another one below the belt line, close to his privates."

"We got a Hail Mary prayer card?" Savage asked.

"Oh yeah."

Arriving at the Dumpster, Savage looked down at the lifeless body and exhaled hard. This guy, the Soldier, or whoever the hell he was, was truly a son of a bitch.

"Let's get him rolled over, Richie," Ollie said. "Gotta get into the back pockets. And if you don't mind, let's see if we can't hurry this up, for crissakes. I was out late last night bowling; I got my freakin' in-laws and their hyperactive brats coming over to the house this morning. *And* I'm freezing my balls off."

"Bowling?" Marcus sneered in disbelief. "On freakin' Christmas Eve? That's funny, you don't look Polish." Richie then gently rolled the priest's body over on its side; the blood that had puddled into a halo around his head had coagulated into a red gel. Nearly frozen, it stretched from his head to the asphalt like saltwater taffy. Marcus held the body in that position as Beyeler quickly checked the victim's rear pockets. They were empty. Beyeler nodded and Richie eased his hold, allowing the priest to flop back into his original supine position.

"What have we got for property?" Savage asked.

"Fifty-seven dollars, an old-fashioned Benrus, a pair of bifocals, a ring of keys, and a Metro North train ticket." Marcus replied.

"That dark wooden cane was laying a few feet away, just under the Dumpster," Beyeler added, pointing it out.

"That's a walking stick, not a cane," Marcus corrected. "A Blackthorn. My uncle used to use one."

"Well, excuse me," Beyeler said haughtily. Ollie was surely in a bad mood this morning, and he was never much for being corrected anyhow.

"Tell me about the train ticket," Savage said.

"It's a ten-dollar Metro North round-tripper from White Plains," Marcus answered. "It's been canceled for the trip down."

"What have you got in the plastic bag?" Savage asked Beyeler, who was zipping it closed.

Ollie held up the clear evidence envelope. "What we got here is a filled-to-capacity snotty handkerchief and a crumbled napkin." Beyeler sneezed twice in rapid succession. "Guy must have had the same cold I'm getting."

"What's in the napkin?" Savage asked.

"Snot," Beyeler replied. "What else?"

"Open it up and see," Savage said. "I know you're cold," he teased, "I know your in-laws and their brats are coming, but I never knew you to be lazy."

Ollie gave Savage a queer look, removed the balled up wad of paper from the evidence bag, and gingerly unraveled it.

"That's a cocktail napkin from McHugh's," Marcus pointed out. "It's printed with McHugh's name and his shamrock logo."

"Jack McHugh's place is right around the corner, right?" Savage said.

"Forty-fifth, Madison to Vanderbilt," Marcus confirmed.

"Boy, you knew that answer right away," Ollie said, chuckling. "What is it, one of the many saloons you're known to frequent?"

After shooting a barely discernable nervous glance at Diane, Marcus responded, "Never been in the establishment."

"Don't give me that," Beyeler snorted, suppressing a grin. "There ain't a barkeep in this town who hasn't served you up a beer."

"I don't normally drink beer," Marcus replied disdainfully. "On those very rare occasions when I'm out and about, I happen to drink Dewar's Scotch on the rocks, with a nice twist of lemon. Beer is for barbecues, backyards, and boring bisexual bowling bozos."

Ollie's face twisted up. He snapped the surgical gloves from his hands and flipped them angrily into the Dumpster. "Yeah, well," he shot back, "it has to be something that's killing off your freakin' brain cells, Marcus."

"Screw you, Ollie," Marcus growled at the Crime Scene tech. He flashed a coy wink and an impish grin to Savage and Diane.

"For sure nobody's at McHugh's at this hour," Savage said, talking to himself.

"Won't be nobody there till sometime in the morning," Marcus agreed. "If at all. It *is* Christmas Day, you know."

"You and Diane get on that," Savage said. "If, in fact, they're closed for Christmas Day, check the licensed premise file at Midtown South, get a contact name. Find out who was working the bar last night. This guy shouldn't be too difficult to remember . . . a nose-blowing priest with a Blackthorn walking stick."

*   *   *

It was just before 8 a.m. when Diane DeGennaro reached past Richie Marcus and pushed the bell button to apartment 1F at 34-02 Ninety-fourth Street in Jackson Heights, Queens. The initial response was violent barking, indicating that a very large and very nasty canine existed within. Diane looked over at Richie, who was shaking his head. Richie never liked dogs, especially big nasty ones. Seconds later, they heard a gruff male voice from inside.

"You the detectives?" the voice asked.

"Yes, sir," Diane responded. She held her gold shield up to the door's peephole.

"Give me a minute," the voice said. "I gotta put the dog away."

"Freakin' dogs," Marcus grumbled under his breath. Diane chuckled to herself; she liked dogs.

The frantic barking inside the apartment finally subsided. The detectives were met at the door by a tall and unshaven dark-eyed man with equine features and eyebrows long overdue for a serious pruning. His distended belly was bursting through a soiled terry robe, and he wore unlaced high-top sneakers with no socks. The place smelled like a puppy dog Motel 6 before the morning housekeeper visit. The dog could still be heard whining and scratching at a closed door somewhere in the apartment's interior.

"Are you Walt Wallis?" Diane asked.

"That's me," the man replied. He spoke out of the side of his mouth like a bookmaker, or an old-time plainclothesman. "Jack McHugh called a while ago and told me to expect you. Sorry you hadda wait till I put the dog away. The freakin' neighborhood ain't what it used to be . . . if you know what I'm sayin'? C'mon in." Wallis led them into a narrow kitchen and sat himself at a table by the window. "Care for some coffee?" he asked, pointing to a dented pot atop a grimy stove.

"No, thanks," Marcus grumbled. Diane saw that Richie was making an eye sweep of the filthy kitchen. She hoped he wouldn't be sick. Richie couldn't tolerate filth in a kitchen, especially when accompanied by the aroma of rain-soaked dog and the offstage stench of its fetid leavings.

"It's our understanding that you were working the bar at Jack McHugh's place last night," Diane said. "That right?"

"That's right. Been working for Jack McHugh for sixteen years now."

"What time did you close up shop?" she asked.

"It was Christmas Eve, so we closed early. . . . At two. By the way," he added kindly, "Merry Christmas to you both."

"Merry Christmas," Diane and Marcus replied in unison.

"Do you remember seeing, or serving drinks to, a man in his sixties, dressed all in black, sometime late last night?" Diane asked, intentionally abbreviating the victim's description, hoping it would be enough to trigger the bartender's recall. It was always preferable not to put words in a witness's mouth.

Wallis shrugged.

"Better put," Marcus interjected, filling in the rest of the blanks, "do you recall a Catholic priest in his sixties coming into your joint? He might have been carrying a walking stick."

"A Blackthorn," Wallis replied, nodding with a smile. "Sure do. Came in before one; double Cutty and soda. Tried to keep his Roman collar concealed beneath a scarf. Guess he didn't want no one knowin' there was a priest in the joint."

"Was he alone?" Marcus followed up.

"Was when he came in."

"How long did he stay?" Diane asked.

"Not long. Long enough to knock off his drink. Twenty, twenty-five minutes at the most, I'd say."

"Did he leave alone?" Marcus asked.

"Nope. A woman he'd been talking to left at the same

time. But I got the sense they were going their separate ways."

"Why do you think that?" Diane asked.

"When they got up, they shook hands and said good-bye."

Diane exchanged a quick questioning glance with Richie.

"Now, there's a reason," Marcus muttered jokingly.

"Could you describe the woman?" Diane followed up.

"Tall, slim, decent-looking—dry red drinker—probably in her mid-to-late forties. They walked out together at around one . . . maybe one fifteen. I overheard her say she was staying at the Roosevelt. Seemed like they knew one another; old friends maybe. They were really yukking it up there for a while."

"Was this woman already in the place when the priest got there, or did she come in after he did?" Diane asked.

"She came in a minute or so after he did."

"What else do you remember?" Diane probed. "Hair, makeup, clothes, et cetera?"

"Looked kinda nice. Blond hair—"

"Straight? Curly? Real? Dyed?" Diane interrupted.

"Wavy," Wallis said, "and lots of it. Looked like one of them damn country western singers. Don't know if it was dyed. I'd say she was a bit much on the makeup, too. Money."

"How do you know money?" Marcus asked.

"Expensive-looking clothes," Wallis said with a shrug. "And she was carrying a big leather bag. I think it was a Gucci. I ain't gotta tell you what them things cost—unless it was a knockoff. You sure you don't want some coffee?"

"Would you be able to recognize this woman if you saw her again?" Diane asked.

"I think I could. . . . Hey, I'm in this business so long that I associate a face, and sometimes even a voice, with a particular drink. Like if I saw her again, I'd think . . . dry red . . ."

"Do you recall if anyone else—a man maybe—came in and left the bar right around the same time?" Marcus asked.

"People were comin' and goin' all night, Detective," Wallis said with a shake of his head. "Lots of people left at about that time. It was nearing closing."

"Anybody in particular stand out?" Diane queried.

"Like how?" Wallis responded; the overgrown eyebrows scrunched in question over a pair of bloodshot eyeballs.

"Like did anybody else in the joint seem to be paying any particular attention to the priest?" Marcus said.

"Besides the woman?" Wallis replied contemplatively. "Nah. Just the usual boozers payin' strict attention to their drinks." The bartender then tightened his gaze on Richie Marcus. "Don't I know you from somewhere?" he said.

"I don't think so," Marcus replied.

Suddenly Wallis' face lit up. "I know! Dewar's on the rocks—twist of lemon. Tall glass, extra ice."

Marcus sucked an incisor, snorted, and glanced sheepishly at Diane. From a back bedroom, the dog again began to bark.

Savage had checked out of the medical examiner's office and gotten back to his Manhattan South desk at 8 a.m., by which time several things had been firmly established. It was now known that Father Darwin Clapp had been assigned to St. Cecilia's Roman Catholic Church up in White Plains, and had traveled by Metro North train to Manhattan for midnight Mass at St. Patrick's the evening before. It was also known that he was shot with .45 caliber slugs, the same type of round used to kill all the other priests. Ballistics testing to see if they were fired from the same gun would have to wait until tomorrow morning. There was, however, little doubt about that certainty. The ME had put Clapp's time of death at between 1:00 and 2:00 a.m., and had also determined that the priest had a blood-alcohol level of .08—

about two strong drinks' worth. If the priest had not consumed any sauce before attending midnight Mass, he might have stopped for a few quick ones at McHugh's joint before heading to Grand Central for the last outgoing train on the Harlem Line, which had pulled out on track 25—on time—at one thirty.

The very next thing on the to-do list was talk to McHugh's late-night bartender, who Jack McHugh himself had identified as Walt Wallis. Wallis lived in Jackson Heights, in Queens. Marcus and DeGennaro were probably already there interviewing him. Their Christmas Day was certainly being screwed up, but . . . such was The Job.

Needing to speak again with Monsignor Dunleavy, Savage picked up the phone and dialed the archdiocese. The call was answered by the severe, pinch-face secretary. He sensed a strange tingling in his knuckles and had thoughts of moldy bread.

"The monsignor is unavailable at this time," the deadpan Angela abruptly informed him.

"Where is he?" Savage asked. "It's urgent that I speak with him ASAP."

"The monsignor is at the cardinal's residence. He is there to have Christmas morning breakfast with His Eminence *and* the mayor. They are also going over the plans for the pope's visit next Tuesday. The monsignor left word that he is not to be disturbed."

"This is a police matter of considerable importance, ma'am," Savage said firmly. "I would not unnecessarily disturb the monsignor, but I'm certain he would wish to be apprised immediately of what has taken place."

"If you are referring to the terrible thing that happened this morning to Father . . . *Clapp,* was it?"

"Clapp. Father Darwin Clapp," Savage inserted, wondering how in the hell Angela could possibly know what had occurred, or to whom. News of the priest's killing may have already flashed on the radio, but pending notifications to Clapp's next of kin, his actual name had not yet been released to the media—or to anybody else.

"Yes, Father Clapp," she repeated somberly. "I can tell you, the monsignor and His Eminence are already well aware of that tragedy. However," she said, her tone changing to one of unadorned dismissiveness, "I will give the monsignor the message that you've called. I'm sure he'll get back to you within a reasonable time."

"Well, that would be real nice," Savage responded, unable to control the impatient edge to his voice. "But I want to speak with him *right now!* Either give me the number where he can be reached or call him and tell him to call me right back."

"I do not *tell* the monsignor what to *do,* Officer," Angela shot back in that all too familiar, condescending and scolding tone. I am here merely to convey messages to him. Do you understand?"

Savage visualized the forbidding woman slapping her gloved palm with a ruler—or maybe a riding crop. "I understand, ma'am," he replied in a voice edged with steel. "Believe me, I understand more that you know. But I advise you to do as I say, or I will be knocking on the cardinal's door in ten minutes. Do *you* understand?" He hung up and bit pensively at his lower lip. He would wait ten minutes for the monsignor's return phone call. No call, and he'd be on his way to Madison Avenue and East Fiftieth.

Thorn walked slowly into the squad room to make a pot of coffee, hoping there was some unspoiled half-and-half left in the refrigerator. It appeared that Dunleavy was one up on him again. How? Savage had no idea. But he did know that he and the pit bull cleric were going to have to tangle, if not today, then very soon. He felt it in his bones.

THIRTEEN

Savage rarely took a hand in brewing the office coffee; with all the caffeine hounds working there, he rarely had to. But it was early on Christmas morning and he was the only soul in the office. If he wanted coffee, he'd have to make it himself. Normally, one side of the dual-burner Newco in the corner of the squad room was on a perpetual perk. Any coffeemaker unfortunate enough to be purchased for use in a police facility never got any time-outs. And forget decaf—*nobody* drank decaf.

He brought the least grimy of the glass coffeepots into the washroom and gave it a much-needed scrubbing, which did nothing to remove the dark stains that made it almost opaque. After filling the water reservoir and loading the basket with a premeasured filter pack of Maxwell House, he hit the ON switch for the left burner, but nothing happened. Recalling the secret procedure for the cranky machine, he jiggled the toggle a half-dozen times until the red BREW light finally came on.

At that same instant, Sergeant Jules Unger, the Team 2 boss, arrived. Julie had volunteered to cover the office for Christmas Day. It was a mutual; Savage had covered Julie for Yom Kippur back in October.

"Isn't that considerate!" Unger said with a wide grin, as he unwound his scarf. "Sergeant Savage coming in to make coffee for me on this bitter cold Christmas morning." He leaned over the wheel desk and signed himself into the command log. "What's a nice clean-cut goy boy like you doing in a place like this on such a high holy day?"

"No rest for the weary," Savage replied. "We had another priest go down early this morning."

"Oy!" Unger said, his jovial tone gone.

Savage gave Julie a quick thumbnail of the events up to that point, including his decision to go after the archdiocese with subpoenas if Dunleavy stalled any further in providing the records he wanted. When the coffee finished brewing, they each filled a mug and retreated to their desks in the sergeants' room.

I wonder how this is all going to play out?" Unger mused. "You remember the monstrous sex-abuse case that nearly bankrupted the Boston Archdiocese? The one that forced that cardinal . . . Law, I think his name was, to resign a while back?"

"Of course," Savage replied, sipping gingerly at the lava-hot brew.

"The judge in that case had to order the Boston Archdiocese to release some eleven thousand documents, involving sixty-five priests, that they wanted to keep private."

"That's right, but as I recall, those records contained devastating evidence of widespread *sexual abuses* by those priests, and the subsequent outrageous cover-ups by the Boston Archdiocese," Savage said. "It's no wonder they didn't want to give them up."

Unger sipped at his steaming coffee and fixed a steady, knowing gaze on Thorn, but said nothing.

"Look, Julie," Savage said, "I know what you're thinking. The *'Believe me, I know'* line in the Soldier's letter seems to spell it all out."

"Far as I'm concerned, it don't leave much to the imagination," Julie said. "Just the way he phrased things, this Soldier character comes off like a really pissed-off victim of priestly sexual abuse."

"That may well be true," Savage acknowledged. "But

we can't conclude anything at this point. He could turn out to be some wacko self-deputized avenger for those who *have been* sexually abused. We're really working in the dark until we can get a look at the personnel records for all these DOAs."

"What exactly are you looking for?"

"We need to know when they became priests, the seminaries they attended, parish assignments down through the years, and then we can look for a connection."

Unger nodded. "And see what else turns up under those rocks," he said ominously.

"This is Homicide—not Public Morals. We're certainly not digging for any dirt, and I hope to Christ we don't trip over any. This case is mucked up enough."

Unger shrugged. "It may eventually take you there, Thorn. You know that. But don't go thinking for a minute that only priests can get caught up in these kinds of scandals. Last year, we had a rabbi over in Woodmere convicted of the same shit. He's now doing jail time."

Savage exhaled hard. "If sexual abuse, pedophilia, homosexuality, or even failure to pay parking summonses are the common denominator here, then so be it," he said. "We'll cross those bridges if and when we come to them. But meanwhile, we have to move forward and remain open to any possible answers."

Unger set his coffee mug down on the desktop. "Let me ask you something," he said, coming across like a counseling uncle. "If you go pushing for a handful of subpoenas to release Church records—records which may inadvertently start an avalanche of scandal within this archdiocese, *the New York Archdiocese, I remind you*—do you really think the department is going to stand behind you one hundred percent? You may just be stickin' your shlong into a guillotine. If you haven't noticed, Irish Catholics still run this shop, you know."

Savage mulled his friend's thoughts in silence.

"Besides," Julie went on, "the archdiocese will immediately resist any court-ordered demands."

"On what basis?" Savage asked.

"They'll make First Amendment arguments to block the release of Church files. Their lawyers will cite violation of constitutionally guaranteed separation of church and state. They'll tie your subpoenas up for weeks—maybe forever. What's to be gained?"

"Those same arguments failed in Boston and Louisville," Savage noted.

"True enough," Unger said. He drained his coffee mug, and added, "but those very same arguments are still pending elsewhere."

The phone on Savage's desk rang, and Julie glanced meaningfully at Thorn, then picked up the morning paper and headed for the washroom. Gulping the rest of his java, Savage steeled himself before picking up the receiver.

"Sergeant Savage, please." Monsignor Dunleavy's voice on the line was clear, the pronunciation crisp and resonant.

"This is Sergeant Savage," he replied, then wasted no time in applying the salve approach. "Let me start by saying that I'm very sorry to have had to disturb you this way sir, but—"

"And damn well you should be, *Sergeant!*" Dunleavy broke in. "You were disrespectful to my assistant, and pulled me away from an important meeting with His Eminence . . . *and* the mayor. Just what is so all-fired important?"

Savage felt his fight-or-flight valve opening decidedly on the fight side. "You lost another priest this morning, Monsignor," he said flatly. "Isn't that reason enough?"

"Don't take that tone with me, mister," Dunleavy shot back. "I'll put in a call to Commissioner Johnson, and you will be off the case before I finish my bacon and eggs."

"Listen to me, Monsignor," Savage said, his tone soft, like velvet-covered steel, "and listen very closely. You can take your threats and stick them where the sun never shines, do you understand? I know you possess the power to do what you say, but I guarantee that pulling strings will only raise the stakes on this case considerably. No one really wants that. I've tried to be respectful to you, and I've overextended my patience with you because of who you are and what you represent. I've been waiting for those personnel records, and have cut you slack I would have denied anybody else. That's *my* fault, but now there are two more dead priests. I'm not waiting any longer. I want those records I've already requested, *plus* any records having to do with Father Darwin Clapp. I want them by nine o'clock tomorrow morning or I'm going for subpoenas. And if I have to take that very drastic step in order to have the Church help me find a priest killer, you know that the first people who will get wind of it will be the press." He stopped only to take a breath.

"How dare you threaten me?" Dunleavy hissed, the ice-coated syllables registering just above absolute zero. "How dare you impugn my integrity, and in so doing impugn the integrity of His Eminence and this entire institution? Just who do you think you are? I have the mayor of this city sitting in the next room . . . not twenty feet away."

"You do what you have to do, Monsignor," Savage declared firmly. "Then I'll do what I have to do."

There was a protracted silence, but through the dead air, Savage could hear the gears in Dunleavy's head churning. He also thought he heard the sound of a guillotine blade being honed.

He had rolled the dice on this one, but Dunleavy's quiescence before hanging up had spoken volumes. For the moment, at least, the man was on the ropes. Not that this was over—not by any means. Dunleavy was just off somewhere licking his wounds and considering strategy. He'd be back. But for the first time, Savage knew he was at least even with the shrewd priest.

*   *   *

Wiped out by fatigue and malaise, and racked by grinding anxiety tearing away at his guts, Jack Lindstrom sat in a daze waiting for the green at 108th Street and Sixty-ninth Road in Queens. It was clear that the head pills he'd gotten from Horowitz had yet to work. He hadn't slept again last night. Truth was, he'd forgotten what a real night's sleep was actually like.

The pressures of his life were redlining. His mind flitted constantly between his unwanted divorce from Joan, the accompanying visions of her exchanging bodily fluids with some borderline low-life, and the memory of his twin sister being squashed to nothingness within the compressed rubble of the South Tower of the World Trade Center. They never did find her body, or any part of it that could be buried.

How he hated those rag-head Arab pieces of shit. It was unbelievable how eighteen assholes with a bargain-basement investment in one-way airline tickets and a few cheesy box knives had forever altered the course of the entire fucking world. And here he was, unable to halt the continuing downward slide of his own miserable existence.

The light finally broke green and, as he accelerated his car through the intersection, he noticed the odometer rolling over to 166,000 miles. The old Civic was plain tired and ready for the scrap heap—just like him. Lindstrom knew he had all but lost his ability to cope, and worse, even to care. Indifference was a terrible thing. The answer, of course, was a woman. He needed one in his life; he always had. He needed someone to come home to, someone who truly cared about him. But that was wishful thinking. Joan had been the only woman in all his life. He'd never find another. From now on, his life was in the hands of God.

Last night, lying there, sleepless for hours, sometimes crying uncontrollably . . . he had had bad thoughts again . . . real bad. He had gone well beyond redline. If his gun had been home in his nightstand instead of in Savage's locker, he knew he would have used it.

At Jewel Avenue he made a left turn, and then a right on 110th Street.

He tried to convince himself he should be happy; he was on his way to pick up his daughter, Cheryl, and her premed boyfriend, Dave Pafko, and take them out for Christmas Day dinner. They'd come down from school for the holidays, staying with his ex-wife, and were leaving in the morning to drive up to Binghamton to spend the remainder of the break with his folks. He hadn't seen Cheryl since September, although they spoke on the phone at least twice a week. For many months, she had been the only thing in the world that had kept him alive. But now it seemed even that might no longer do it.

Cheryl was being coy, but perceptive Dad sensed something in the air with the kids. Ideas of marriage, he suspected. David was a starting guard on Villanova's football team, on his way to becoming a plastic surgeon. His wonderful daughter had chosen wisely; he just hoped they'd wait until after graduation.

At Seventieth Road, Lindstrom slowed down and began to look for the kids; they had said they'd wait outside for him, which spared him from having to run into his sleazy replacement. As he neared his ex-wife's apartment building, he saw two men exchanging blows in a rip-roaring, slip-sliding fistfight on the sidewalk. Grappling, they bounced off the hood of a parked car and rolled into the middle of the street, still pummeling each other. He slammed on the brakes and skidded to an angled stop, narrowly missing the embattled pair.

He recognized one of the men as David Pafko. Standing off to the side he saw Cheryl, hands clasped to her head, panic written all over her face. Lindstrom slammed the Honda into park and jumped from his car. Approaching the melee, he realized the other combatant was Joan's scumbag boyfriend. There was no longer any question of whose side he was on.

Grabbing Sid Fordham by the collar, Lindstrom tried to pull the two apart. It was like trying to separate two warring male polar bears on an ice floe. This was not a maybe fight. . . . It was a real knockdown, drag-out, hammer-the-shit-outta-the-other-guy rumble, and it was clear that David was racking up some heavy points. Suddenly, Lindstrom took a hard right to the jaw from Joan's bloodied pal.

Something in his head snapped. It was as if somebody had thrown a switch. Instantly, he had the strength of ten, and for the first time in his life, he discovered what it was like to want to really lay a hurtin' on somebody. Adrenaline coursed through him like a shot of hot heroin. Lindstrom planted his right foot as well as he could in the snow and threw a merciless roundhouse that landed solidly against Fordham's square jaw. Mr. Scumbag's eyes crossed and he reeled backward, colliding with and denting the faded front fender of Lindstrom's idling Civic.

With police sirens sounding in the distance—but getting closer by the second—and Joanie's shithead boyfriend now shouting curses and threats, Lindstrom pulled David Pafko and Cheryl off to the side and, in no uncertain terms, directed them to immediately get lost. God, he felt good.

Savage squinted involuntarily, his cool gray eyes assaulted by the glare of midafternoon sun reflecting back from a world of total white as he emerged from his Greenwich Village apartment house. He considered a quick trot back upstairs to fetch a pair of sunglasses, and then decided to tough it out. His eyes would soon adjust.

Although the ambient temperature was hovering somewhere in the high teens, the lack of any windchill factor and the strong rays from the warm sunshine made it a beautiful Christmas Day.

As he ambled along the snow-packed Sullivan Street

sidewalk, cradling a gift-wrapped bottle of Bardolino in the crook of his left arm, his glance darted into every nook and cranny and scanned beneath every car parked along the curb. His ears were perked too, listening intently, straining to detect even the most remote meow or faint whine of feline distress. There was not even one discernable paw print in the snow. Pasted on every light pole were LOST CAT signs that described Ray in detail, with Mrs. P's phone number in bold lettering. The old girl was really on the case. But he was beginning to fear that time, and Ray's ninth—if not his fiftieth—life, might have run out. At Houston Street, he crossed against sparse holiday traffic and continued walking south, seriously bummed. He tried to think of things other than his lost buddy, murdered priests, the clock running on a papal visit to New York, and a belligerent monsignor.

It was only a ten-minute trek to Maureen's place, and he pondered whether it had been a subconscious desire to see her or his lust for pasty that had motivated him to accept her Christmas Day dinner invitation. It was—he tried assuring himself—the lure of the pasty.

Meat pasties were either Scottish or Cornish in origin; Savage had never found out for sure which. All he knew was the simple recipe went back generations on his father's side, to Nanny Nye, his feisty Scottish great-grandmother who had operated a prizefighters' training gym near Coney Island back in the teens and twenties. She was a rip, he'd been told, every bit as tough as the questionable mugs who hung out there.

Pasties were nothing more than cubed pieces of round steak draped over a mound of diced potato and strip of suet. Wrapped in a piecrust, the ingredients were baked until the beef juices seeped down through the potatoes and caramelized into the bottom crust. When made softball size, they were a filling energy supplier for Highlander husbands who toted them around in their coat pockets until the lunch whistle blew. When made half a football

size, it was a dinner feast. They were, for some, an ac-
quired taste. Too dry, many would say. Thorn Savage had
been raised on them; to him they were manna from
heaven. And, best of all, they contained no veggies. He
hated veggies; never ate them.

More than once, when strung out and needing a pasty
fix, Savage had actually attempted to create one himself.
He would buy the ingredients and do the dicing and cub-
ing. To that point, all would go well. The creation of the
piecrust shell, though, was a skill simply not in his play-
book. He always wound up with wads of dough stuck all
over his fingers and countertop, and yet another schlock-
coated rolling pin chucked angrily into the trash. Those
ill-fated attempts were usually followed by a hasty phone
call to Angelo's on Eighth Street. He'd end up with pizza
for dinner, and Ray would feast on neatly cubed raw round
steak.

Then came Maureen Gallo, a firm believer in the phi-
losophy that the way to a man's heart was through his
stomach. Among other things, Maureen possessed the divine knowledge of how to roll dough. For Thorn's sake,
she became a pasty maestro despite not being wild about
the dish or even cooking in general. No question about it,
there was more than a hint of truth to the old adage.

Maureen kept a meticulous one-bedroom apartment
immediately above her SoHo art gallery on Spring Street,
just off Wooster; only six blocks from Savage's place on
Sullivan Street. As he crossed Thompson at Prince, it occurred to him that almost two years had passed since he
had last taken this walk. That had been a break-up night
for them—for the zillionth time—after a six-year love affair that had seen more ups and downs than the Empire
State Building's elevators.

So much had happened in those two years, he thought,
as he turned south and then crossed West Broadway on a
diagonal. Gina McCormick had happened during that
time. And during that time, Gina had died violently. He

was certain if Gina had never met him . . . she would still be alive. She had died in a monstrous act of revenge against him—because he was a cop, because he was doing his job. It was a nail-studded cross he would bear for the rest of his life.

At Spring Street, he walked east to the first door just past Wooster. He checked his watch; three o'clock on the dot. He rang the buzzer and nervously cleared his throat. Maureen answered the door looking casual in a holiday pullover dotted with tiny reindeer in red Santa hats, and sexy in snug-fitting deep blue velvet slacks. Eighteen karats dangled at her ears, neck, and wrists. Except for a restrained "Merry Christmas," neither seemed able to find immediate words. During the next few seconds—in what seemed to him only a mildly abridged eternity—their gazes locked. All that had once been between them was there in her face. He checked a sudden impulse to take her full in his arms. Their embrace had always been so natural and satisfying; in that respect, at least, they were always a perfect fit.

"Come in, Thorn," she finally said, stepping back into the heated vestibule. She hugged him lightly, and he kissed her politely on the cheek. He smelled the Giorgio.

"You look beautiful . . . as always . . . Mo," he said, a self-conscious stumble affecting his voice; he was momentarily lost in her deep-set blue-green grays that were easily her most outstanding facial feature. There were movie stars who would kill to have those eyes.

"Thank you," Maureen said with a barely perceptible nod. Her intense gaze never left his eyes. "You look pretty darn good yourself." Flashing, for just an instant, a killer seductive smile, she softly added, "I'm so glad you're here."

Without another word, she took him firmly by the hand and led him up the long flight of squeaky stairs to the second-floor landing, then through the foyer into the living room of her familiar, cozy apartment.

He breathed deeply. The tree's strong balsam scent mixed with the aroma of baking pasties conjured up thoughts of Christmases long past. Christmas the way it used to be. It smelled like . . . home.

Savage took a slow, appreciative gaze around the large, comfortably furnished room. A beautifully decorated Christmas tree stood in the far corner, looking as if every light, ornament, and strand of tinsel had been placed on it by the premier window-display team from Lord & Taylor. The linen-covered table in her small dining room was intimately set for two. He also recognized her finest china and silver. The flickering flames from two tall candles reflected and danced in the crystal stemware and wine goblets. He was flattered that she'd go to such lengths for him. Vintage Maureen, he thought. Everything in the place was perfection.

He handed her the bottle of Bardolino, the dry red Italian wine she'd introduced him to so long ago, then removed his jacket and hung it on the hall tree that still stood in the foyer. He unhooked his cell phone from his belt and placed it into the jacket's side pocket.

"Great minds think alike," she said, peeking beneath the bottle's gift wrapping. "I have some already chilling in the fridge. Care for a glass now?"

"Yes," he said, agreeably. "That'd be great." It felt strange actually having some time off, to be with someone other than another cop or a district attorney . . . or a medical examiner.

"Be right back," she said.

Thorn watched her as she moved toward the small kitchen. He couldn't help but notice; Maureen still had a great ass.

In moments she returned to the living room, carrying two brimming goblets of their favorite wine. They clicked glasses and sipped.

"Glad you could come," she repeated, her face flushed from the heat of the oven.

"So am I," he admitted with a slight nod. His trepidations about spending the afternoon with Maureen were beginning to ease. It might turn out to be a nice day after all.

"So, how's my boy Ray doing?" Maureen said, motioning him to the green sofa. She sat across from him, legs curled beneath her on a purple club chair. "Did you get him something he'd like for Christmas, like a six-pack of beer? Or did you get him something more practical, something he could really use?"

"Besides a new left ear and an attitude adjustment, what could *he* possibly use?"

"I was thinking the latter," she said, grinning coyly. "A Dale Carnegie course, perhaps. You know, *How to Win Friends and Influence People . . .*"

Savage laughed hollowly. Maureen had often alluded to Ray's notorious disdain and cold indifference to most two-legged vertebrates—which was not to say that he wasn't absolutely correct in most cases. More often than not, Savage found himself agreeing wholeheartedly with Ray's critical assessments of primate genus *Homo.* Although she considered Ray a complete curmudgeon, Savage knew that Maureen loved the crazy cat. . . . And Ray liked her.

"I'm afraid Ray's gone missing on me," Savage said. "He went AWOL three days ago."

Maureen frowned with real concern. She set her wineglass on the lamp table beside her. "Not in this horrible weather. Do you think he's all right?"

"Don't know, but he's pulled this stunt before; once for a whole week. That's when I took him to the vet and had that I.D. chip implanted in his neck."

"If anything ever happened to that cat, I don't know what you'd do," Maureen said. A pained look clouded her lovely face. "You guys have been roommates for a long time. I know you must miss him."

"I don't miss him drinking my beer," Savage said with

a half-grin. "But I've gotta confess, I do miss the haughtiness and scintillating conversation."

"Most people would think you're kidding," Maureen said with a loud laugh.

"I'm sure he'll turn up, though," Savage added with a not-so-sure grimace. An awkward pause ensued.

"Looks like the NYPD is going to have its hands full in the next couple of days," Maureen said, shifting gears, again reaching for her glass. "What with the pope coming and all . . ."

"That's putting it kind of mildly."

"And I bet you're right in the thick of the mix," she said offhandedly, teasing but probing. "Right?" She took a sip of the red.

Savage shrugged and stalled for time by taking another sip of the Bardolino. He really didn't want to go down that road, which history had taught him could be littered with land mines. This kind of discussion about his job, which always began innocently enough, invariably wound up in a full-blown battle of wills and dropped a curtain of frostiness between them.

She must have read his mind. Quickly shifting gears again, she put down her glass, uncurled her legs, and crossed to the sofa. She sat next to him and gently slipped her hand into his. "I've missed you," she said quietly.

He shrugged lightly and said nothing, wishing he knew the right words. For sure he was feeling something, but wished he wasn't. Dammit, what he really wished for was to know his own mind.

Maureen leaned closer, holding her gaze. With the fingers of her free hand she stroked his hair, just like she used to. It felt good. Then she brought her lips to his.

It was all he could stand. Like no other woman he'd ever known, Maureen had always possessed the ability to seduce him at a moment's notice, anytime—day or night. He shifted to put his arm around her. He wanted to kiss her deeply, passionately. . . . He couldn't believe what he was doing; he had to tell her that. As he opened his mouth to speak, the cell phone he'd left in his jacket pocket began to ring. He didn't miss the oh-no expression that fell immediately across Maureen's pretty face. Shaking his head in disbelief, trying to gather composure, he crossed to the foyer and pulled the Nokia from the pocket.

"Thorn Savage?" The guarded voice on the line was that of Detective Don Stewart. Savage and Stewart had been comrades-in-arms years ago, working the most dangerous areas of the city in civilian clothes when both were assigned to the now extinct Street Crime Unit. Stewart was presently a second-grader in the 112 Squad out in Forest Hills.

"Donny," Thorn said, his tone even, trying to conceal the fractured passion he was feeling and the puzzlement of why Don Stewart would be contacting him on this of all days. He hoped he was not about to hear that another priest had been executed somewhere out in Queens. "What's doing, buddy?"

"Sorry to fuck up your Christmas Day, but one of your boys—a Detective John Lindstrom—is being held here for investigation of an assault. The complainant wants to press charges."

Savage grimaced and exhaled hard. "Tell me more," he said. His eyes followed Maureen abstractly as she set the goblets of chilled wine on the dining table. She had been down this road many times before during their previous relationship, and every movement reflected her resentment.

"Guy's name is Sid Fordham. Claims to have had his lights punched out by an off-duty detective by the name of John Lindstrom. When I called Lindstrom in, he told me he worked for you at Manhattan South Homicide. That's why I decided to call you first."

"Gonna tell ya right off the bat, Donny, that doesn't sound like Jack Lindstrom. Who is this guy Fordham?"

"Says he's Lindstrom's ex-wife's boyfriend. And if it

wasn't Lindstrom who punched this guy's lights out, I can tell you this: Whoever did it did a damn good job."

"Jesus. He lookin' that bad?"

"He's black and blue, got a few stitches over a half-closed right eye, and generally looks like he got carted away from a Rangers-Islanders bench-clearing brawl. By the book, Jack's facing assault two—a felony. With a little poetic license, we might be able to dumb it down to assault three, class A misdemeanor."

"Fordham absolutely wants to press?"

"Oh yeah. Big time. The way I read it, he wants Lindstrom's fucking job."

"Is Jack there?"

"Yeah, I got him in a separate room. I don't know how you want to handle this, Thorn, but my boss is getting nervous. You know the rules. An allegation of serious misconduct against a member of the department requires us to immediately notify IAB. So far, he hasn't, but he's way out on a limb. I've been holding him off on making the notification. . . . But I don't know how much longer I can."

Savage nodded, fully understanding the squad boss' situation. The man was certainly holding the bag, but he was doing it for Don Stewart, a real stand-up guy.

"What has Lindstrom said?"

"So far, he's not saying anything."

"Can we make this go away?" Savage asked.

"If this guy recants, we can," Stewart replied quietly.

"Give me forty-five minutes," Savage said, trying to conceal his annoyance. He repocketed the tiny phone and slipped the jacket from the hall tree hook.

"Gotta go, don't you?" Maureen asked.

"Uh-huh," he murmured, wishing mightily that he didn't have to.

"Some things never change, do they?" Maureen said, an edge evident in her voice.

"It's a friend," he replied softly, hoping she would understand. He knew otherwise; she had always hated the demands of his job.

"It's always something." After a long, deep breath, Maureen picked up the wineglasses and retreated to the kitchen. He heard her click off the stove.

FOURTEEN

It was four twenty by the time Savage arrived at the 112 Precinct on Yellowstone Boulevard in Forest Hills. He parked in the enclosed side lot, entered the building by the rear door near the gas pumps, and took the back stairs up to the squad room. Detective Don Stewart greeted him and brought him to a back office where Jack Lindstrom sat stoically. The first thing Savage noted was the absence of any marks on Lindstrom.

"Jack," Savage opened. "What the hell is going on?"

Expressionless, Lindstrom looked up and shrugged. "Prick got what he deserved, Thorn," he said in a monotone.

"I'm guessing he probably did," Savage agreed. "But do you know where this may leave you?"

"Out in the cold."

"Don't you care?" Savage asked. "If this guy presses, your ass is grass."

Lindstrom turned up his palms and offered a defeated "Who gives a fuck? My ass is grass anyway."

"Where did this all supposedly happen?" Savage asked, turning to Stewart.

"According to this guy Fordham, it all went down right in front of Jack's ex-wife's place, over on Seventieth Road and One Hundred Tenth Street. Two minutes from here."

"That true, Jack?" Savage asked.

Lindstrom nodded. "I guess."

"You guess?" Savage said, struggling to keep his tone

from elevating. "What the fuck do you mean, you guess? Did it happen there or didn't it?"

"Yes."

"Did you beat this guy up, Jack?" Savage pried. "'Cause you ain't got a fuckin' mark on you. This bullshit is just not your style. You hiding something?"

Lindstrom looked away.

Sid Fordham was nobody's Wally Watercress, and he was certainly nobody's punching bag. The man was just under six feet, and Savage placed him at a sturdy one-ninety. He had strong shoulders, big hands, and a many-times-broken nose. Mr. Fordham also had a big fucking attitude. Small wonder that his schnozz had probably seen more icepacks down through the years than a tenth-ranked welterweight. Although this probably wasn't the first beating Fordham had taken in his life, it was clear to Savage that the man was not at all used to losing when he put up his dukes. It was also clear that there was no possible way Jack Lindstrom could have done that amount of damage—not to this guy.

"I know exactly what's going on here," Fordham began. "This guy's a cop, so you guys are gonna gang up on me to protect his fucking ass. Am I right?"

"That's not at all true, sir," Savage replied calmly. "But before we go any further, I must ask you to tell me—in your own words—exactly what took place."

"I already told everything—*in my own fucking words*—to that black guy. What's his name—Stewart? You mean I gotta tell it all fucking over again to you?"

"I would really appreciate that," Savage said evenly.

There had to be a great deal more to this, Savage thought as he drove quickly over to Joan Lindstrom's place. The whole damn thing was wrong. He didn't know how or why, but he knew with every cell in his body that Fordham was full of shit. What he didn't understand was Lindstrom's reluctance to defend himself against the man's charges. Fortunately, Sergeant Jerry McQueen—Donny Stewart's boss—had granted an additional forty-five minutes' grace before notifying IAB; time was of the essence.

"Sid is lying," Joan said emphatically, stepping aside to allow Savage to enter the apartment. "Though I can't tell you the whole story, Jack did *not* beat him up." She motioned Savage to a club chair in the corner of the living room.

"I'm afraid you're going to *have* to tell me the whole story, Joan," Savage pressed. "Sid, Mr. Fordham, is pushing to have Jack arrested and charged with assault. The day will no doubt come when we can prove his innocence in a courtroom, but the damage will have already been done."

Nervously licking her lips, Joan Lindstrom sat on the edge of the sofa opposite, her knitted hands tucked tightly in her lap. Reluctance riding on every word, she described the events leading up to the fight.

"This all started because Sid and I have been having some problems," she said just above a whisper. "I broke it off with him a few days ago. He didn't want the relationship to end. . . . But I'd simply had enough."

"And?"

"And," she went on, "Cheryl came home from college last night to spend some of the holidays. She was going to stay here with me but also visit with her father."

"Uh-huh."

"Cheryl had asked permission to bring along her boyfriend for the stay."

"What's his name?"

"David . . . David Pafko. He's a terrific young man," Joan volunteered. "Very intelligent, very respectful . . . so I approved."

"Are Cheryl and her boyfriend still here?" Savage asked, looking around the neat apartment.

Joan Lindstrom shook her head. "They left for Binghamton about an hour ago. Jack called and said it would be best for them to head out."

"Does David Pafko go to the same school as Cheryl?"

"Yes. He's a premed senior. And he's at the top of his class."

"Is he a big, strong kid, Joan?"

Joan nodded grimly. "Yes, he plays on Villanova's football team. Thorn," she added with a plea in her voice. "In the past months, I've come to find out that Sid Fordham is devious and cunning and a bully. Please, David was only trying to protect me."

"And Jack is only trying to protect David."

Ten minutes later, with Detective Don Stewart at his side, Savage revisited Sid Fordham in the privacy of a meeting room on the second floor. Arms folded tightly across his wide chest, an angry smirk still twisting his swollen face, Fordham slouched arrogantly in a folding chair at the head of the room's conference table.

"I'm going to give you the facts of life here, Fordham," Savage began.

"You're gonna give *me* the facts of life?" Fordham shot back. "How about givin' your fuckin' buddy, Jack Lindstrom, the facts of life? He's the one who needs them."

"Here's the deal," Savage continued. "Detective Stewart here is going to give you a pen and a piece of paper. You will then write down a little statement about how you were mistaken that Jack Lindstrom assaulted you, and then you will walk out of here. This whole matter will die. No hits, no runs, no errors, no men left on."

"Why should I do that?" Fordham snarled.

"So you can go home and lick your wounds, just like the scummy jackal that you are."

"You must be out of your fuckin'—"

"If, on the other hand," Savage continued, "you should decide to stick with this fictitious bullshit story you've created, a cross-complaint of assault will be lodged against you. Beyond that, you will also be charged with trespass and making an apparently false statement in the first degree—a felony, Mr. Fordham."

"A *felony*?" Fordham protested, sitting bolt upright in the creaking metal chair.

"Article Two-ten-forty, New York State Penal Law," Detective Don Stewart chimed in. "Making a false statement becomes a felony when the statement is made with the intent to mislead a public servant in the performance of his official functions. I'm the public servant, you have definitely tried to mislead me, and I'm definitely pissed off."

"Yeah, well, I didn't assault nobody," Fordham protested. "You fuckin' cops are all alike."

"I got a college kid downstairs," Savage said, bending the truth, "who says he walked in on a loud argument between you and Joan Lindstrom at Joan Lindstrom's house."

"Is that a fact?" Fordham sneered. He cleared his throat nervously.

"He said that when Mrs. Lindstrom directed you to leave, you refused—which, by the way, accounts for the trespass. When he tried to intervene and calm things down, you pushed him. Now we're getting to the assault. This thing spilled out into the street and became a whole lot uglier. You and the kid wound up rolling around on the sidewalk for a minute or two, while he did a damn nice job of rearranging your ugly puss. That's when Jack Lindstrom arrived on the scene. We have statements from Jack's ex-wife and his daughter that Jack simply broke the fight up, nothing more, nothing less."

"Yeah . . . what else they tell you?"

"They said you made a few angry threats, got in your car, and raced off. You obviously went and got your face stitched up, brooded about your licking, and came up with a plan—a moronic plan . . . but a plan nonetheless," Savage continued. "An hour later, you came strolling in here claiming you got this beating from Jack Lindstrom, which is a total fucking lie."

"And why would I do that, smart guy?"

"Because rejection is hard to swallow and there's no wrath like an asshole scorned. You knew perfectly well that you'd never have a chance of reconciling with Joan if you made the complaint against her daughter's boyfriend. But your mongrel instincts figured out if you went for Jack, Jack would simply have no choice but to stay quiet and take all the weight for the kid. Aspiring surgeons can't have assault on their records."

Savage leaned his knuckles on the tabletop and got right into Fordham's face. "Jack would lose his fucking job, ergo, Joan would go begging without her alimony payments, and you could play the hero to the rescue."

Fordham smirked and looked away.

"Now, if you don't want to do jail time for this little fairy tale you cooked up, you'd better start writing."

Nostrils flaring, Fordham bit nervously at his swollen lip. His eyes shifted from Stewart's implacable face to Thorn's and back. "All right," he finally snarled. "Give me the fuckin' pen."

FIFTEEN

Savage was forty minutes early for work when he signed into Manhattan South at eight twenty on Thursday morning—he had something really important to take care of before the frenetic police rodeo got fully underway for the day. Someone in the office—probably the slinky, dark-eyed, and miniskirted Miss Ponce—had already revved up the coffeemaker. He poured himself a mug, flipped his Visa card onto his desk, picked up the phone, and dialed.

"Gramercy Florists."

"Good morning," he said. "I'd like you to deliver a dozen roses—yellow, if you've got 'em—down to an address on Spring Street."

"We just happen to have some very lovely long-stems on hand right now," the gentle male voice said. "They're absolutely beautiful. Delivered—with tax—the total would come to eighty-six ninety."

"All right," Savage said, then gave Maureen's name and address, followed by his credit card information.

"What would you like the card to say, sir?"

"Say this: 'Sorry about yesterday, but I really had no choice. Did you save the pasties? Sometimes they can be even better when reheated.'"

"Pasties?"

"Yes, pasties. P-A-S-T-I-E-S. Sign the card, 'Thorn.'"

Savage hung up the phone, slipped the Visa card back into his wallet, and quickly unwrapped the still-warm buttered poppy seed bagel he'd picked up on the way in. He had just taken the first bite when his phone rang. He knew it was the call he'd been expecting; the one he knew beyond any question would be coming. He picked up.

"Thornton," Chief of Detectives Ray Wilson said, beginning cheerily enough.

"Good morning, Chief," Savage replied warily. Wilson almost always used the formal *Thornton* when irked or pissed off.

"Something told me I'd catch you at the office early," Wilson said, his cheery tone already showing signs of faltering. "I suppose you might have some idea of why I'm calling?"

"I might have some idea," Savage replied, resigned to a blast. He dug a floss pick from his desk drawer and quietly dislodged a poppy seed wedged between a recently capped incisor and a canine. Due at the dentist's again in two weeks for his quarterly, he made a mental note to cancel and push the appointment back a month.

"Monsignor Dunleavy called me a little while ago," Wilson said flatly. The four-star chief cleared his throat. "We had a very nice, very cordial, very constructive discussion."

"Good."

"The monsignor told me that he is putting together a complete package for you. It will contain the records you want, the records, I'm given to understand, that you and he had occasion to *discuss* sometime yesterday."

"Terrific."

"He said he's sending a chauffeur over to your office around noontime to drop them off. He also went on to apologize for any delay in getting these records to us, but the delays were unavoidable."

"Glad to hear it," Savage said, still waiting for the other shoe to drop.

"During my very pleasant discussion with the good monsignor, however, I gleaned—by reading between the lines of his thinly veiled allusions—that perhaps you had roughed him up a bit yesterday. Did I interpret that correctly, Thornton?"

"Yessir, you did," Savage replied respectfully. "And, yessir . . . I did."

"I see," Wilson purred, seeming to strain to stay composed. "Of course, you realize that had this come down to me through channels . . . by way of either the PC, or the mayor . . ."

"I'd be getting my uniforms out of mothballs."

"That about says it. But why do you think Dunleavy is complying with your demands, and at the same time taking an oblique unofficial shot at you?"

"He's coming up with those records only to shortstop my threatened use of subpoenas, boss. Sorry to sound like a doubting Thomas, but I'll believe I have those records when I actually see them. As far as the oblique shot, he's hoping to Christ that you on your own—without the muscle of the PC or the mayor—will send me packing and put someone more, shall we say . . . flexible on the case. He doesn't want to bring the PC or the mayor into the act, or lodge any kind of official complaint to you because he fears I will make that backfire on him and really open up a can of worms."

"You've gotta know you're flirting with disaster for both of us, Thornton. Dunleavy made it abundantly clear that should there be a next time around, he will go right to the top. The Catholic Church in this town is powerful beyond belief. We'll both be pressing our fucking uniforms."

"I'm aware of that possibility, boss. But if it does come down to that, I'll take all the weight."

"Well, I do believe that you'd take a bullet for me, Thornton," Wilson said with an ironic snicker. "But you know full well how these things always go. We'd both be standing against the wall with blindfolds and cigarettes."

Despite the sardonic truth of the chief's words, Savage grinned as a humorous twist on a line from *The Treasure of the Sierra Madre*, one of his favorite old Bogart movies, suddenly popped into his head. *Blindfolds? We don't need no stink-keen blindfolds. . . .*

"Manhattan South Homicide, Detective Lindstrom."

"This is Harvey Wahlberg, Detective. I'm calling about the psychological profile work I've been doing on this priest killer. Is the CO around?"

"Sorry, Harvey. Both Lieutenant Pezzano and Sergeant Savage have stepped out of the office."

"When will they be back?"

"My guess? I'd say in about half an hour. I think they went to grab some lunch. Have you guys come up with anything on our boy yet?"

"Certainly, I have," Wahlberg replied tartly. "Of course," he added in his customary scholarly opinionated air, "I'm preparing a full written report, but I thought I'd hit the high spots with Pete Pezzano or Thorn Savage so they'd know what's heading their way."

"Good," Lindstrom said, reaching for a fresh notepad. "If you don't mind, I'll be very happy to take it down and pass it along."

"Okay," Wahlberg began. "I figure this guy is fairly intelligent, probably uneducated, but smart. I place his IQ into the high one-twenties. He lives alone and was probably never married, or he's at least divorced. No children. He's angry at the world in general, and the Catholic Church in particular. He either didn't like his father or didn't have one, and is big time hung up on his mother figure."

"Do you think maybe priests in some way represent a failed father figure to this guy?" Lindstrom asked.

"Perhaps," Wahlberg drawled thoughtfully. "But I'd really be speculating there. He either hated his father to an extent that makes him hate priests or he hates priests to the extent that he came to hate his father."

"Or maybe he just naturally hates them both, hah?"

Lindstrom said, rolling his eyes at Harvey's cover-all-the-bases bullshit.

"Beyond that," the psychologist continued, "I also suspect that he's a sexually inadequate loner, probably no siblings, who may be suffering emotionally from posttraumatic stress disorder. Even more likely, suffering physically, possibly in serious failing health."

"Is he Capricorn or Aquarius?" Lindstrom asked, hoping for a chuckle from the dry-balls Mr. Superego. None came.

"I also believe that he is ex-military."

"Uh-huh," Lindstrom uttered, still taking notes. "Our office has already got a team working that angle. Now, aside from the letter writer actually identifying himself as the Soldier, what else strengthens your conclusion that he is military?"

"*Ex*-military!" Wahlberg corrected impatiently.

"Ex-military," Lindstrom repeated, again rolling his eyes, thinking that Harvey Wallbanger was an insufferable asshole. But an insufferable asshole who sometimes came up with really good shit.

"His writing contained more than a hint of military-style speak and phraseology, like the use of *twenty-one, December,* and *our orders have been cut.* He even specifies the word *army.*"

"Gotcha. What do you think he did in the service?"

"Not sure. He types . . . maybe he worked in a military office, perhaps as a clerical assistant to a ranking superior."

"What about the possibility of him being a former paratrooper? An airborne Ranger, Green Beret, Navy Seal . . . that sort of thing."

"Where you getting that idea?"

"The guy is an expert marksman and cool as they come. He also referred to himself in the letter as a grunt. More precisely, he stated, '*Nowadays* I am merely a grunt.' The *nowadays* makes me think he at one time was airborne."

"*Grunt?*" Wahlberg said. "What the hell is a grunt?"

Schmuck doesn't even know what a friggin' grunt is, Lindstrom thought. "It's a derogatory term sometimes used by airborne soldiers—paratroopers—when referring to lowly infantrymen."

Wahlberg cleared his throat.

"Have you figured an age for this guy?" Lindstrom asked, flipping a page on his lined pad.

"I figure he was active military back during Operation Desert Storm. Therefore, I'd have to put him in his early, possibly late thirties."

"Wrong," Lindstrom said flatly.

"What?"

"Gotta tell ya, Harvey. I can go along with a lot of what you've been saying except his age and the time period he was in the military."

"Well, *excuuuse* me!"

Lindstrom thought he heard the department's profile guru choke in disbelief at his temerity to question *and* offer an opinion. "I think this guy is fucked up from some real nasty, grisly battles; like the kind in Vietnam. Which might put him in his mid-to-late fifties."

"That so, Doctor Lindstrom?" Wahlberg said sarcastically. "If grisly battle is what you base your hypothesis on, then why not World War II, which could make this guy a hunched-over octogenarian?"

"Different ball game," Lindstrom countered calmly. "We sent millions of everyday butchers, bakers, and candlestick makers into deadly combat situations in World War II, and we didn't have boatloads of wackos like John Wayne Gacy coming back. They did their job extremely well, came home, and now we're calling them the greatest generation."

"What's so different about Vietnam, for crissakes? War is war."

"Vietnam veterans are a very different story, Harvey. It was a far nastier situation than WW II or Kuwait or Iraq. Fifty thousand GIs got slaughtered in unbelievable ways by men, women, and even children who did not wear uniforms. And at the same time, many Vietnamese who didn't wear uniforms were killed. A lot of survivors of Vietnam had injuries that were not just physical, but emotional."

"Well, yes, to some extent that's true, of course, but—"

"You've got to believe that the likelihood of being haunted by all the killing is greatly increased when the carnage is hard to justify. When soldiers kill reflexively—when military training has effectively undermined their moral autonomy—they morally deliberate their actions only after the fact. If they can't justify what they have done, they often suffer guilt and psychological trauma."

There was a long silence before Harvey Wallbanger finally uttered, "You don't say?"

"I do say."

"So why Vietnam and not the Gulf War, *Lindstrom*?"

"Stress inoculation."

"What?"

"Operant conditioning—you know what that is, Harvey. It's the single most powerful and reliable behavior-modification process yet discovered by the field of psychology."

"How does it apply here?"

"Modern soldiers are trained differently," Lindstrom replied. "That training prepares and equips them in a manner to succeed after war."

"Just what is so freaking new about military training?"

"Recruits learn SERE: survival, evasion, resistance, and escape. They go through drills designed to raise their threshold for staying calm. It doesn't mean that they're immune to later stress, but it takes a lot more to rattle them than an old-time draftee."

"And just where did you learn all this?"

"*New York Times.*"

It was half past seven when Savage parked in front of the Manhattan Criminal Courts building at 100 Centre Street.

Leaning into a flesh-numbing bitter wind, he quick-walked one block east to Forlini's, at 93 Baxter. He let himself into the restaurant's warm entry foyer and checked his topcoat and scarf.

His favorite Italian dining spot was right on the cusp of Chinatown and Little Italy and, even on a Thursday evening, both dining rooms—front and rear—were already at noisy capacity. Stepping into the adjacent taproom, he found it also mobbed with those content to do cocktails while awaiting a table. He was glad he'd called ahead and made a reservation—not that he ever minded killing time at the bar. Billy Salvato, Forlini's evening bartender, was an old acquaintance. A graduate of Iona and the Culinary Institute of America, *and* the "third best gin player on the East Coast," Billy was an encyclopedia on Yankee baseball lore, a topic on which they often tested one another's knowledge. Also an excellent tennis player and hopeless Green Bay Packer fan—Savage forgave him the latter—Billy poured a good drink and wasn't at all afraid to let the Forlini family buy one or two every now and then. As he edged his way into the crowded lounge, Savage finally caught the busy mixologist's eye.

"Father Vinny is already here," the diminutive but sturdy Billy called out, deftly curling a long-stemmed maraschino into somebody's Manhattan. "He's in the back. . . . Just sent him a drink."

Savage nodded, smiled warmly to his friend, and continued working his way through the well-dressed, talkative throng.

"Hey, Thorn," Billy called out over the din. "Gene Woodling, left field, early fifties—what was his uniform number?"

"Fourteen," Savage hollered confidently without looking back. "Yankees wound up trading him to Baltimore. Ended his career on the '62 Mets." Leaving the bar area, he moved past the kitchen's swinging doors and allowed himself a deep breath of the seductive, saliva-inducing aromas that were wafting out. He entered the rear dining room through a side hall.

There, dressed in casual mufti, the half-Italian, half-Scottish Jesuit was seated in a side booth, pondering the cognac-filled snifter set on the cloth-covered table before him.

"Courvoisier?" Savage asked rhetorically, sliding into the booth's opposite side.

"How long have you known me?" Father Vinny asked, narrowing his gaze playfully and jutting out his dimpled chin. Half standing, he clamped both his hands warmly around Savage's large extended mitt.

"A millennium . . . maybe two. Somewhere there-abouts," Savage replied, unfolding the starched linen napkin and pulling it down onto his lap.

Growing up in the Bronx, they had been first-string teammates on the Cardinal Hayes High School basketball squad. Savage was the pure athlete, Vinny less so, but a shrewd finesse player nonetheless. After both had graduated from Fordham University with honors, Vinny heard the calling and surprised everyone who knew him by entering seminary. Savage had heard his own calling and, like his father before him and younger brother behind him, pursued *his* brand of holy orders at the NYPD Police Academy. Unlike Vinny's, Thorn's decision came as no surprise to anyone, especially his father, who on more than one occasion had remarked that Thorn had been a policeman since he was an embryo.

"Ever known me to drink any other brand?" Vinny asked.

Savage smiled. "I once saw you put a fair-size dent in a bottle of Rémy. I see you're working in plain clothes this evening."

"Got that right," Vinny *hrumph*ed. Nibbling his narrow lip, he peeked quickly over both shoulders, then added in a whisper, "Like you said, no point walking around wearing a bull's-eye. Even though I've got my reservations all set, I'm not quite ready to check into that big resort in the sky."

"That former fisherman still the desk clerk there?"

"Oh yeah!" Vinny's face lit with a devilish grin. "Peter's still there. And your papers had better be in order, or he'll send you packin'. No suite, no harp lessons, no nothing." Vinny quickly shifted gears. "My friend, Joel Horowitz, told me he met with your detective Jack Lindstrom again today."

"That's good. We're all very concerned about Jack. He's obviously under a great deal of pressure."

"Did you pull his gun the other day?"

"Yes."

"Any resistance?"

Savage shrugged. "He wasn't happy about it. But he understood."

"Is he working?" Vinny asked.

"Yes," Savage replied, opting not to mention yesterday's events out in Queens. "Really can't afford to go without him. The guy is my detail man, my maven of minutiae."

"Good. It's probably best he stays busy."

"Cocktail, Sergeant?" Rico, one of several waiters who'd been working at Forlini's for decades, broke into the conversation.

"Extra-dry Stoli martini, straight up with a twist," Savage responded. "Tell Billy it's for me. He'll know." The attentive waiter nodded and spun on his heels.

"Martini?" Vinny said, raising an eyebrow. "Good thing I didn't order for you. On a cold night like this, I would have guessed Rusty Nail."

"I'm in a martini state of mind tonight," Savage said, grimacing.

"Who wouldn't be, if they were in your shoes?" Father Vinny said. "That letter from the Soldier published in today's *Post* was a policeman's nightmare. From a priest's standpoint, it was disturbing for me to see the references it contained about the Third Secret."

"What's the story there? Is there any substance to this Third Secret business he spoke of?" Savage asked. "Is that business all for real?"

Vinny nodded, but did not speak.

"You know, I remember hearing as a kid that the pope had some kind of secret letter from the Virgin Mary which was supposedly given to him by one of the children of Fátima. I also remember hearing that he was supposed to read it to the world in 1960. What's the Church's stance on all this? Is it considered some sort of borderline myth?"

"Not totally. The Catholic Church pronounced the Fátima apparitions as worthy of belief in October 1930. But in February of 1960, the Vatican issued a simple press release that the Third Secret of Fátima would not be revealed."

"Did it give any reason?"

"It said that although recognizing the Fátima apparitions, the Church did not wish to take the responsibility of guaranteeing the veracity of the words that the three shepherd children said that the Virgin Mary had addressed to them."

"So what could be this guy's beef?"

"Problem is that a segment of the Church, which includes lay people, priests, bishops, and even some closeted cardinals, are staunch Marianists. They have problems with the Vatican's stand on this issue. Very profound problems."

"Like what?"

"The more extreme elements of this Church segment— the lunatic fringe, some might call them—now identify the pope as the Antichrist. They argue vehemently that the reason this letter has been hidden away is because it will reveal just that."

"Sounds very heavy."

"It is," Vinny said firmly. He looked away and seemed

to choose his next words carefully. "It is, because the lunatic fringe of any organization can be cause for great concern. Does the name Mehmet Ali Agca ring a bell?"

Savage thought for a moment. "Can't say that it does. Though it sounds very much like a guy who might take flying lessons without wanting to learn how to land."

"The three peasant children of Fátima first encountered the Blessed Mother on May 13, 1917. . . . "

"Right. I was told that the other day."

"Well, sixty-four years later to the day, May 13, 1981, Mehmet Ali Agca, a Turkish assassin, shot Pope John Paul the Second during an open-air papal audience in St. Peter's Square."

"Just coincidence?"

"Maybe. But since the odds were 364 to 1, there are those in this fringe group who see a correlation, especially since Agca has supposedly been quoted as saying the pope *is* the Antichrist, and that he was only doing what God had told him to."

"Wasn't this guy Agca a Muslim?"

"Yes," Father Vinny replied, "but the loony fringe will hang their hat on anything. Do you guys have any idea who this nut the Soldier could be?"

"Our profiler's written report just came through about an hour ago. It makes him as someone with a military background in Vietnam. Probably Green Beret type, airborne at the very least." Savage then related the entirety of Harvey Wallbanger's lengthy profile.

"Hmm," Father Vinny uttered thoughtfully. He took a tentative sip of brandy.

"Salud," Savage offered.

"But there's gotta be an untold number of ex-military out there. Zillions maybe. How do you expect to home in on this one guy?"

"We're contacting the VA. See if they're treating anyone at their health facilities within a fifty-mile radius that might fit our profile."

"Former airborne, midfifties, seriously ill, never married, no dependants, no siblings . . . that sort of thing?"

"Right. Then we'll try to narrow it down even further, to people trained in the use of Colt forty-fives . . . *silenced* Colt forty-fives, that is. It's thin, I know. But we've gotta start somewhere."

"Sounds like a long, slow process, Thorn," Father Vinny said. "But that alone can't be what's bugging you."

"It's not."

"What is, then?" Vinny's face flashed into a question mark.

"You've seen the papers. You've seen how we've been able to connect our cases with that one up in Boston."

Vinny nodded. "Looked like real good police work to me. What's the problem?"

"I'm being jerked around by *your* bosses."

"My bosses?"

"The archdiocese in general . . . Monsignor Dunleavy in particular."

"You for real?" The priest's always expressive face scrunched into a look of puzzlement. "How do you mean?"

"This Monsignor Dunleavy is giving me a real good, real smooth, stroke job. But I've been jerked off by better. I've been after him to supply us with some records. . . . "

"What kind of records?"

"Employment records, I guess you'd call them; personnel records, assignment records, employee evaluations . . . whatever they're called in your organization. I want to know as much as I can about the dead priests' Church backgrounds."

"And you're not getting them?" Vinny asked as Rico reappeared and placed a double martini before Savage, the widemouthed, stemmed glass opaque with frost.

"Not really," Savage replied. He held out his drink in toast, then sipped. "Dunleavy gave us what appears to be a complete personnel record for Father Jean Brodeur. At least it seems to be complete. It showed the seminary he attended, his date of ordination, and all the parish assignments he's had. But Brodeur had only been a priest for sixteen years."

"So what's the problem?" Vinny asked.

"The records the archdiocese sent us this afternoon for Fathers Gilhooley and Clapp are totally disorganized and incomplete. They give us some early information, seminaries they attended as young men, dates of ordination—that sort of thing. But not much beyond that."

Expressionless, Vinny sipped again at his brandy.

"Also," Savage continued, "they've yet to give me anything on Father Flaherty."

"Tell me about Father Clapp's early information."

"He grew up in Staten Island, went to Catholic Schools, and as a young man went to study with the Christian Brothers in Barrytown, New York. He continued his education at Manhattan College and Middlebury College. He did graduate work at the Catholic University of America—Phi Beta Kappa."

"Sounds like a brilliant guy," Vinny said.

"Yeah, he sounds like a brilliant guy all right," Savage replied. "But he might have been a brilliant guy with a head full of problems."

"And Father Flaherty from OLPH. Has anyone from your office ever questioned him about his entire Church background?"

Savage nodded and sipped his martini again. "We've tried, but each time he's claimed to be too sick to speak to us. The flu. He's supposed to be better now. Two of my detectives have an appointment with him first thing tomorrow morning."

"How did the archdiocese explain the gaps in Gilhooley's and Clapp's personnel records?"

"Said that in years past, archdiocese record keeping was spotty, if not downright sloppy. They're pushing the blame off onto earlier hierarchies. But worst of all, they tell me they've not found any record of Peter Grennan—the Boston victim—ever having been a priest in this or any other arch-diocese. I have a problem with that."

"Well, then maybe Grennan never was a priest."

Savage shrugged. "Maybe." A from-the-gut hunch was screaming at him that Grennan had been a priest, but he wasn't ready to argue the point. He took another hit of the Stoli.

"You know," Vinny said in a moderated tone, leaning forward, "the Church has been hammered for years now with all these god-awful pedophile scandals and sexual abuse allegations, most of which, I'm ashamed to say, are probably true."

"I know that," Savage responded sympathetically. "And I'm figuring that Dunleavy and His Eminence, the cardinal, would like nothing more than for this whole murderous affair to end. They've got enough damn problems."

"You've got that right," Vinny agreed. "And don't think for a minute that those problems aren't being compounded exponentially by the pope's scheduled visit this week. That visit is a real big deal for them, especially Cardinal Hammond. If that visit were to get screwed up or canceled because of scandals, murder, or mayhem, he'd be left with a lot more than egg on his face."

"Vinny . . ." Savage said, leaning across the table to whisper his words, "they're dragging their feet, trying to exercise some sort of privilege. Maybe they're thinking that we can collar this Soldier schmuck soon and close the case, obviating the need for them to open any of their deep, dark personnel archives." He paused for a second, then went in with the hook. "Do you know anyone on the inside who might have access to those records? Without them, our investigation is sucking wind. And frankly, I don't want to have to subpoena them."

"Why not?"

"Politics. The mayor is tight with the cardinal; they go way back. Beyond that, Police Commissioner Johnson is also a devout Catholic. Back when he was a lieutenant, he was the head of the department's Holy Name Society."

"So?"

"So. If we press hard and go after the archdiocese with subpoenas for these records, all manner of things might happen. Good heads are going to roll. Most notably that of the Chief of Detectives, Ray Wilson . . . and yours truly."

"How can that be? Your job is civil service." Vinny sipped at his brandy, a puzzled frown on his face.

"My civil service rank is safe, but with the stroke of a pen I can wind up as a patrol sergeant in the outer reaches of Staten Island. As far as Chief Wilson goes, any rank above captain is an appointment, no longer civil service. One serves at the pleasure of the police commissioner. And the police commissioner serves at the pleasure of . . ."

Vinny nodded his head. "The mayor . . . I get you."

"Obviously, the archdiocese does not want anybody— especially a police agency—rooting around inside *their* files. They don't want another Boston debacle down here. They might have things floating around in those records that they'd like to keep buried. Things that may very well have no connection to this investigation, but could hurt them anyway."

"They'd very much like to win this battle but not lose the damn war," Father Vinny muttered.

"Exactly. Believe me when I tell you, Vinny, I do truly sympathize with their thinking here. They're trying to protect the *Hornet*. They want to be able to cherry-pick what we can see. But if we're gonna break this case in good time, we absolutely need more than they're giving us."

Father Vinny sat back in the plush booth, slowly rolling the near-empty snifter back and forth between open palms. "You're asking me to do an end around on my superiors— the Church hierarchy. His Eminence, the cardinal, for God's sake."

Savage offered a hopeful grimace but remained silent.

"It's unthinkable, Thorn," Father Vinny said apologetically. "It would be an act in total violation of my vows. I simply cannot do it. I'm sorry."

"I understand your ethical dilemma, Father," Savage said. "But any delay in this guy's capture is going to mean the possibility of more priests dying."

"Then it must be God's will."

"You don't believe that, Vinny."

The Jesuit drained his glass. "I'm going with the veal scaloppine and I'm betting you're going to have the frutta di mare. . . ." He held up his empty snifter and motioned for the waiter.

Savage was steamed, but he knew the discussion was closed.

SIXTEEN

The hot shower relaxed and soothed Father Killian Flaherty's aching bones. The alternating fits of fever and chills were gone and, aside from some lingering malaise, he again felt almost human . . . physically. If only he could make his head right, but he knew that could never be.

Whenever pressured or faced with a particularly difficult or disagreeable task, a steaming shower beforehand always seemed to help. Bathing in sudsy warmth had always given him an inner sense of serenity and security. The sensation was heaven-sent, he thought, as the needles of hot water beat against his narrow back and long stringy body. He was built just like his father and his two brothers had been—bless all their dearly departed souls.

Warmth was the most wonderful thing. He had known very little of it as a child growing up in Castlebar, County Mayo. For sure, there was little of the emotional kind from his parents. Killian was the oldest of six children—three boys and three girls—and mother always had the remainder of the sibling brood to see to; raising them as best she could was a full-time job for the poor, saintly woman. She had their arses and noses to continually wipe, their few pieces of threadbare clothing to scrub with lye in the old wooden tub while trying to keep track of her whiskey-witted and woefully wrongheaded husband.

Dermot Flaherty, his pugnacious father, had spent half his short life bellied up to the bar and the other half split between sleeping it off and beating the bejesus out of Killian or Killian's frail mother. The man preferred using the lash, but when too stinko to find where the children had hidden the cursed thing, he used his closed fists; he twice broke Killian's nose, and once his jaw. Dermot Flaherty's liver gave out early, thank God, for if it hadn't, Killian probably wouldn't have made it through his teens.

Nights could be cold in Ireland's northwest, and there was no thermostat to push up to eighty to warm you in your bed, only the body heat from your equally freezing siblings. There was no such thing as hot showers and baths. There was no plumbing . . . no shower stall, no bathtub, and no hot water. He remembered actually praying for warmth in those days. Wishing for it, craving it, as other children looked forward to sweets. He recalled thinking if ever he managed to find security in life, the most basic thing he would always provide himself with was warmth; a warm, comfortable bed at night—one he needn't share unless he wished to—and plenty of hot running water day and night. Becoming a priest of the Roman Catholic Church had virtually guaranteed those basics . . . and more.

Seemed hard to believe that fifty-three years had raced by since his parents and five siblings said good-bye to County Mayo and traveled freighter-belly steerage to the blessed United States of America. He was only eleven then. He'd had his first hot shower in New York City, in their first tenement apartment up on Willis Avenue in the Bronx. It was grand, he recalled.

Lathering for the third time, Father Flaherty then stood stoop shouldered within the torrent, again allowing the hot water to rinse him clean. He was feeling much better now; even the body aches were easing. The miserable flu that had plagued him during the week had finally passed. He'd been able to make only a brief appearance at Father Brodeur's funeral Mass yesterday. At least he'd had the chance to bless the coffin before it started its long journey up to Montreal. Brodeur was to be interred in a family plot there between his mother and father. My God, the poor man, he thought. I know he died standing in my shoes.

Flaherty turned off the faucets, stepped from the shower, and sawed a thick towel briskly across his bony shoulders. As he shaved away a day's growth of gray-red beard stubble, he heard a rustling outside the bathroom door; Anya, no doubt. The housekeeper was hanging his freshly pressed black suit and delivering his newest white collar, as he'd requested. Anya, poor thing, was a good soul. He strapped his old Gruen to his slender wrist. Gazing through its yellowed and scratched crystal, he saw it was ten minutes before nine. The police detectives would arrive to question him in forty minutes. There was still time to prepare.

Father Flaherty slowly and methodically dressed in the clothes Anya had carefully laid out for him. The trouser creases were sharp as a razor; the woman could work wonders with a steam iron. He sat down heavily on his bed, slipped into his shoes and laced them, then picked up the telephone. For the second time this morning, he dialed the number written across a piece of scrap paper on his nightstand. After three rings, the same woman's voice answered. It wasn't Hugh; it was some damn answering service. Frustrated, he blew out hard through pursed lips. Again he hung up without saying anything.

After checking his collar alignment in the medicine cabinet mirror, Flaherty went immediately downstairs and passed quickly through the rectory into the small sacristy. He entered the church proper via the door behind the altar, genuflected before the Eucharist, and crossed to the Blessed Mother's side, where he lit two candles: one in memory of his own sainted mother, and one for poor Father Brodeur. Tears welled in his eyes as he knelt, bowed his head, and prayed for forgiveness for that which he had done in life. . . . And that which he was about to do.

When finished, he checked his watch again; it was ten past nine. He had to hurry now; the detectives might arrive

at any minute. He looked slowly around the nave before returning to the sacristy. There among all the colorful vest-
ments he'd worn to celebrate countless Masses at OLPH,
he made a slapdash noose from several belts, wound it
tightly around his neck, and hung himself from the iron
pole in the vestment closet.

When men want to die, they hang themselves, or stick the
business end of a six-shooter into their mouth, or step in
front of a barreling downtown express or off a thirty-story
ledge. Women are generally neater. When they decide to
shuffle off this mortal coil, they take gas, swallow a hundred
pills, or slice open their wrists while lounging comfortably
in a warm bath surrounded by Calgon bubbles. However,
they too sometimes do the thirty-story leap. Savage had no
actual numbers or stats to support the grim theory; it was
simply anecdotal on his part after decades in the NYPD.
What an all-encompassing training ground The Job was for
the darker realities of life, he thought. What a broadener.
He'd often said that when he came on The Job he was only
twenty-one, and six months later he was thirty-five. Now,
looking on in silence as Crime Scene did their obligatory
photo shoot of Father Killian Flaherty's purple face and lifeless body that hung like a sack of potatoes from a convenient closet pole, Savage wondered if he didn't feel like a
hundred.

"Well, now we got us another priest dead," Richie Marcus said. Uttering the observation in his version of a
hushed tone, his rasp was still that of a Harley chopper, albeit a distant one. He popped a Winston between his lips,
fired up his lighter, and inhaled deeply. "But at least he
didn't die like the others." He exhaled the smoke down the
front of his jacket.

"Maybe he wasn't the recipient of a couple of neatly
placed slugs delivered by some homicidal hump who calls
himself the Soldier," Savage responded, "but he's gonna be

stretched out on ice, sporting an ME's toe tag just the same."

"There must be at least a dozen reporters sitting outside, waiting for a statement," Marcus said. "Of course, the question of the day is gonna be, Do we deem this suicide somehow related to the other priest killings? And how will this latest death affect the pope's New Year's Eve visit?"

"It's going to be the town's lead story no matter what we call it," Savage replied.

Savage had always wondered at suicide scenes what prompted such irreversible action. What happens to the mind? Surely something does. Entranced in thought, he unconsciously peeled away the annoyingly tough to open bubble of cellophane from an individual Wint-O-Green. He'd have to go back to buying the rolls.

He didn't know how Father Flaherty's suicide related to the killings of the other priests, but his every sense told him that it did. That Flaherty had resorted to the taking of his own life this morning—mere moments before being leaned on for tough answers to hard questions by Detectives Marcus and DeGennaro—spoke volumes; but what were those volumes saying? He popped the candy into his mouth just as the chief of detectives walked into the sacristy.

Ray Wilson took a long, deliberative look at the body hanging in the vestment closet, then turned to Savage. "Any note?" he asked.

"Nothing down here, boss," Savage quickly replied. "But Detective DeGennaro is upstairs. She's searching his living quarters."

"Unh," Wilson uttered, his normally relaxed face showing signs of strain. "The PC has tripled his Rolaids consumption, and the fuckin' mayor's verging on cerebral hemorrhage. All he can see is his hard-earned and well-deserved reputation of being the great no-nonsense law-and-order guy who made the city safe once again, going right down the political dumperoo. . . ."

Savage nodded.

"Especially," the chief went on, "if the friggin' Vatican decides to pull the plug on the pope's New Year's Eve gig, because of concerns for his safety. If that happens, the city will take years to live it down." The chief took a breath and looked tightly into Savage's eyes. "Have we got any sense at all of why this guy decided to do the choke?"

Savage shook his head, wondering what could have been the force that drove this priest to self-destruct? Had it been some unbearable guilt for past deeds? Had it been a fear of discovery of those deeds, and the shame or disgrace he would suffer with their revelation to the world, his family, friends, and parishioners? Maybe Father Flaherty's suicide had nothing at all to do with guilt. Maybe he was sick. Suffering from some terminal and increasingly terrible malady. Autopsy might reveal that.

"One thing is for certain, Chief," he said. "Nobody does *anything* in this world without a reason, whether that reason is as real as a pink slip from George Steinbrenner or just flat out imagined like the phantom stalker lurking over a paranoid's shoulder."

Diane DeGennaro appeared in the sacristy just as two strongbacks from the ME's office were undoing the belt noose and muscling Father Flaherty's stringy form into a waiting body bag. She acknowledged Wilson's presence with a respectful "Good morning, Chief."

"Anything?" Savage asked hopefully.

"No note," Diane replied, shaking her head.

Savage and the chief exchanged quick glances of dismay.

"The room's so small and spartan, it didn't take long to go through it all," she said.

"Any *Playboy* or *Penthouse* in his sock drawer?" Marcus inquired, flashing his eyebrows suggestively.

Diane ignored the remark. Chief Wilson simply *ahem*ed.

"I did find these, however," she added, holding up a

piece of scrap paper bearing a hastily scrawled telephone number, and a dog-eared address book. "Found the phone number on his nightstand next to the telephone, and the address book among a bunch of old papers inside a dusty valise that was stashed underneath his bed."

"Did you dial the number?" Marcus asked.

"Turned out to be just an answering service for a limousine company," she replied, checking her notes. "Allied Cars."

"What about the address book—any familiar names in there?" Savage asked. "Gilhooley . . . Clapp?"

"No such luck," Diane replied. "But look here." She opened the book to the *G* page and pointed to an almost illegible penciled-in phone number and street address for a Barbara Grennan on Belmont Avenue in the Bronx.

"Maybe this Barbara Grennan has some connection to the Boston victim?" Marcus piped in. "Peter Grennan."

"My thoughts exactly," Diane replied, "But it gives an old 212 area code. The Bronx has been 718 for fifteen years or more. Right?"

"Get with Patti Capwell over at Telephone Security," Savage directed. "Find out if the number's still active. If not, have her trace to see if she can find a forwarding number anywhere in their system."

"As far as I'm concerned, if this Barbara Grennan is related to the Boston victim," Chief Wilson said, "your hypothesis of all these priests being somehow connected will be totally borne out."

"Yeah," Savage murmured, pulling on his left earlobe. "But then where the hell do we go from there?"

SEVENTEEN

Seated at the edge of his bed, clad only in a wrinkled and backless St. Clare's Hospital johnny coat, John Wesley Krumenacker gazed dully out at the rapidly darkening New York City winter afternoon. Through the windows of his semiprivate second-story room, he watched the headlights of Ninth Avenue traffic moving in hectic spasms. He felt like shit, but that was still better than yesterday, and a damn sight better than the night before when they had to pick his ass up off the sidewalk outside of the cathedral.

Gotta get outta this place, he thought, unconsciously fingering the hospital I.D. band that had been put too tightly on his hairy, skinny wrist. He couldn't wait to get home and cut the damn thing off. Gotta get home . . . Charlie needs feeding. And I gotta get over to St. Pat's and make sure the damn piece has been put back where it's supposed to be.

"Now take a deep breath and hold it," Dr. Stordahl said. The pulmonary specialist pressed a stethoscope below Krumenacker's left shoulder blade.

J.W. carefully inhaled a shallow breath and fought to keep from breaking out in a hacking cough. The stethoscope was cold against his naked back. The doctor kept moving it around among several locations—it never got any warmer.

"What's the verdict, Doc?" Krumenacker asked. "Am I ready to challenge the four-minute mile?" *Cough, cough.* "Get saddled up for the Tour d'France?"

The doctor didn't respond. He pulled down the front of the wrinkled robe and placed the stethoscope against Krumenacker's hyperexpanded chest.

"I need to get out of here, Doc."

"There's no way I can recommend signing you out of here, Mr. Krumenacker," the doctor finally said, folding the stethoscope into the big side pocket of his white lab coat.

"Look, Doc. I've been here since they . . . wheeled me in on Christmas Eve, for God's sake. I'm feeling better . . . honest. I got a life, ya know." *Cough, cough.*

"And if you want to keep it, you should probably stay here for another week. . . . Or perhaps longer, for that matter," Dr. Stordahl replied, the gravity of his words accentuated by his alert and piercing eyes. "You are not a well man."

"Hey," Krumenacker said, forcing a wry smile. "I've got me a real big shindig to go to . . . on New Year's Eve, Doc." Winking, he added, "You wouldn't want me to miss out on that, would you?"

"You check yourself out of here, as you've been making noises that you're intending to do, and you might just not make New Year's Eve, Mr. Krumenacker. I kid you not."

"Why stay?" Krumenacker asked, returning the tight eye contact with the physician. "Hell, there's not a damn thing you can do for me."

"We can continue to monitor and medicate."

Monitor this, Krumenacker thought.

"The acute respiratory infection that brought you here in the first place is still not totally under control. We also need to improve your blood gases. Your CO_2 is very high."

"What else?"

"As soon as you're better, I'm putting you down for a flu shot. For people with your condition, it's a must, especially this time of year. I don't believe your system could handle any further infection."

"You gonna cure me?"

"Mr. Krumenacker, COPD is a chronic disease for which there is no cure. There are two varieties: emphysema and chronic bronchitis. You have a good mix of both. And I'm afraid that yours has become rather well advanced."

"So what am I supposed to do?" Krumenacker asked with a shrug of his bony shoulders.

"Remain on your supplemental oxygen—oxygen that your body badly needs to carry on basic functions. And continue taking the antibiotics."

"It's not gonna fix anything, though . . . right?"

"It can't repair your damaged lungs, Mr. Krumenacker. But it can stop the overproduction of red blood cells. Too many red blood cells thicken the blood and slow its circulation."

"I know that, Doc. Now tell me something I don't know, and maybe I'll stick around." *Cough.* "Otherwise, I am freakin' outta here."

Dr. Robert Stordahl looked over at the assisting floor nurse, shook his head, and spoke. "Have him sign the standard release, then get him his clothes. There's no way we can help him if he refuses to help himself."

Savage and the crew had left the Father Flaherty suicide scene and arrived back at Manhattan South by noon. By four o'clock, Telephone Security had declared the Barbara Grennan phone listing no longer active, disconnected back in '01 with no forwarding. But Marcus and DeGennaro were now on their way to the old Bronx address anyhow . . . just in case. At four thirty, Savage took a call from Lou Jacobs at Forensics.

"Got some pretty solid determinations on the Soldier's letter," Jacobs began.

"Great," Savage replied. He pushed aside a stack of DD-5s and reached for a notepad. "Shoot."

"According to our resident typewriter maven, the letter

was typed on an old Underwood Model 5A manual, not an electric."

"How old?"

"The Model 5 itself goes all the way back to the teens, you know, those old Front Page–era black upright table models. But this particular version is what is known as a modern Model 5. 1960s, '70s . . . thereabouts."

"How do we know it was an Underwood?"

"Microscopic comparison of the type style."

"And how do we know it was a manual?"

"On a manual, some letters get struck harder than others. On an electric, the strike pressure is always the same."

"Makes sense."

"The machine is very well used—if not abused—and has plenty of identifiable characteristics and imperfections."

"Such as?" Savage asked.

"We'll start with the uppercase *T*. It appears a number of times within the body of the letter. In each appearance it has a score mark running east to west entirely through the center of its upper right-side serif. The left-side serif at the bottom of the lowercase *L* has a slight chip at the leading edge. Also, the lowercase *A* seems to always land high. There are a number of other identifiers, but they'll all be spelled out in detail in our report. I'm also sending you enlarged photos of all these exemplars. Mind you, any one or two of these flaws could possibly be found on other typewriters of this type and manufacture, but the odds on all of these flaws appearing on any other machine other than this one would be as astronomical as a DNA match."

"Gotcha. What else can you tell me?"

"The ribbon color is black, and the ribbon itself is pretty well used up."

"What about the paper?" Savage asked. "Any peculiarities there? It was pretty yellowed, as I recall."

"Quite yellowed," Jacobs agreed. "Which means it's at least a quarter of a century old, for crissakes."

"How can you tell?"

"By the mere fact that it had turned yellow."

"Explain."

"Up until the late seventies or early eighties at the latest, all paper manufacturers used a rosin-alum sizing process that contained acid."

"Sizing?"

"A process that prevents stationery from acting like a blotter. Unsized paper would suck in the ink and allow it to radiate out, and the writing or type would be blurry and illegible."

"I see."

"Anyway, since then, all manufacturers have moved to an acid-free process."

"Acid-free paper doesn't yellow?"

"Nope," Jacobs said unequivocally. "You can leave modern stationery out in the sun for a whole damn year and it won't yellow a bit. And just to make sure we'd be giving you the proper skinny on your paper, we snipped a small piece from the letter and checked the pH. It read 5.9."

"Okay. So the stationery's quite old," Savage said. "Anything else?"

"Manufactured by Hammermill Paper Company, Erie, Pennsylvania."

"How can you tell?"

"The paper's branded with their name, watermarks, and production coding."

"Can the production coding or watermarks tell us anything else?"

"Doubt it can really tell us anything we need to know," Jacobs responded. "It's just a sheet of old paper. Anyway, I believe Hammermill was taken over by International Paper years ago."

"Can you fax me all the info on the watermarks and production coding?"

"I'll do that right now."

"Thanks, Lou." Savage took his notes and went immediately to the office computer in the squad room. He went online and typed in HAMMERMILL PAPER. They had a Web site with a link to International Paper. They also had a phone listing for a department they called Consumer Response Service Center. Savage returned to his office and dialed.

"International Paper, this is Joan Zalonis."

It turned out that Joan Zalonis, Product Specialist, had been with the Hammermill Paper Company for many years before they were taken over by International in 1987. She also turned out to be a warehouse of knowledge about their products, and was very eager to help.

"Tell me about watermarks," Savage said.

"Stationery from the Hammermill Paper Company was some of the most widely used watermarked brands in the country," she replied.

"If I were to fax you exemplars of codes and watermarks we've found on a sheet of Hammermill paper, is it conceivable that you could further identify it somehow?"

"It might take some doing," she said, "but I guess it's possible. Hammermill created probably hundreds of private watermarks for customers over the years. I'm sure they're recorded somewhere."

"Think you could find them?"

"I don't believe *I* could find them, but I do know who probably could."

"I have a world of faith in you, Ms. Zalonis," Savage said, laying on the charm. "Let me have your fax information; I'll have that stuff out to you within the hour."

EIGHTEEN

Diane DeGennaro slowly backed the silver Taurus into a tight spot in front of Margarita's Full-Service, a bodega on Crescent Avenue, in what some called the East Fordham section of the Bronx. The building that she and Richie Marcus were looking for was just around the corner on Belmont Avenue.

"Boy, has this neighborhood changed since I was last here," Marcus said, his eyes clicking back and forth in a one-eighty scan of the avenue. "It's no freakin' wonder that Barbara *Grennan's* phone listing was long disconnected."

"Used to be a lot more mixed," Diane agreed, pulling the gearshift lever up into park. She shut down the motor and slipped the portable radio into her pocketbook. "I counted five Mexican restaurants in the last block and a half."

"I counted a hundred Mexicans in the last fifty feet," Marcus grunted. "Did you know that Dion and the Belmonts came right from this neighborhood?" he added, lifting his square chin toward the Belmont Avenue street sign as they stepped from the car.

"Didn't know that," Diane responded, looking up at the sign. "But now that you tell me, it makes perfect sense. I always knew they were from the Bronx."

"They were Italian kids that started out here as a street corner doo-wop group. But hey," Richie said, resignedly throwing open his palms, "that was a lot of damn years ago. Seems like in another life."

"So maybe now we'll run into a street-corner mariachi band," Diane joked. She looked at Richie and realized he hadn't been listening; he was off in another world.

"Dion and the Belmonts were my favorites back in them days," Marcus sailed on nostalgically. " 'Teenager in Love', 'Runaround Sue' . . ."

" 'No One Knows'," Diane interjected.

" 'The Wanderer'," Richie added.

"My favorite was 'Where or When.' "

"Yeah," Richie said, nodding enthusiastically. " 'Where or When'; that was good, too."

"You know, Arthur Avenue's only a few blocks away, and it's still heavy Italian," Diane said. "When we get done here, why don't we take a quick run over there? We could pick up some of that Pecorino cheese you like, and there's no place to get better Italian sausage."

Marcus seconded the notion with a broad smile. Always thinking of his belly, Diane thought. Richie loved to eat, and he especially liked when she cooked Italian.

The surnames taped to the mailboxes in the narrow vestibule of the old five-story walk-up looked like the who's who of Guadalupe, Guadalajara, and Ciudad Juárez. But mixed in among all the Rodriguezes, Lopezes, and Moraleses was a lone B. Grennan in apartment 5C. Marcus and DeGennaro exchanged looks of mild disbelief.

"Figures it'd be on the freakin' top floor, though, right?" Marcus growled.

"C'mon," Diane teased, "it'll do you some good. You're just too used to working in Midtown, where every building has an elevator."

They entered the tenement's dimly lit interior and began ascending the badly dished marble treads of the winding staircase. A severely deaf person must have been wrapped up in a Spanish-language TV game show in one of the apartments on the second floor, and somebody on the third floor was cooking up something really nasty for dinner.

"Boiled cabbage?" Richie asked, scrunching up his nose at the strong odor.

"Not sure," Diane responded, taking the steps with ease. At the fourth-floor landing, Richie rested briefly before continuing. When they reached the fifth floor, they found the Grennan apartment at the end of the hall.

Diane twice rang the buzzer on the 5C door; Richie rapped three times. There was no answer.

"What do you think?" Diane said.

"I think she's probably DOA in there." Richie coughed the words, wide-eyed and still huffing and puffing from the climb. "Those freakin' stairs would kill Tensing Norgay."

"Have another cigarette, Rich," Diane scoffed, then added, "Maybe she works. It's just now five o'clock."

Wounded by the dig, Richie let go with a middle-finger glare, then rapped on the door of the opposite apartment, 5D. A dark-eyed young woman in a tank top and low-cut jeans eventually answered. Rosita was Mexican, stacked, and spoke in broken English. That was Diane's cue to do the talking.

Rosita said that Barbara Grennan was a "very old" and white-haired "gringo señorita" who worked days in one of the many Laundromats somewhere over on Tremont Avenue, she didn't know which one. She further described the woman as always wearing a knee-length green coat and red plaid scarf, and stated that she always got home at about six.

"We'll come back in an hour, no?" Diane suggested.

"We'll come back in forty-five minutes, park right out front, and catch her downstairs before she comes up," Richie replied. "I ain't climbing those freakin' stairs again."

Diane pointed to her watch. "We've got a little time to do that shopping."

Richie smiled.

*   *   *

The meter had just clicked to four dollars when the taxi pulled to a stop inside Fiftieth Street, between Fifth and Madison Avenues. John Wesley Krumenacker reached forward and handed the driver a crisp twenty.

"Leave the meter running," he said. "I shouldn't be more than a few minutes."

Gauging his every move, expending as little oxygen as possible, Krumenacker let himself from the cab's backseat and walked slowly up the stone steps, through the south transept doors, into St. Patrick's Cathedral.

It was a typical Friday afternoon, and the church interior was crowded with gawking tourists, who moved slowly when they moved and spoke in reverential, hushed tones when they spoke. John Wesley crossed to the main altar and hesitated near the marble pulpit fronting it. Searching for any indication of plainclothes or uniformed security within the nave, he slowly turned a three-sixty, carefully scanning the entire crowd; he discerned none. He continued past the altars of St. Andrew and St. Therese of Lisieux, then passed the Pietà that was three times larger than the Michelangelo Pietà in St. Peter's Basilica in Rome. At the Lady Chapel, he knelt, blessed himself, and murmured a prayer.

"Dear Mother of God in heaven. Don't really know why I was chosen by you, but you must allow me enough time . . . and give me enough strength to do the task. I need just a few more days of breath. Then it will be done, and Satan will lose his grip on the throat of our beloved Church. Then I will be free to come home to you; home to my place that you have set aside for me in paradise. This I pray in your blessed name."

He made the sign of the cross, stood, and retraced his steps back to the altar of St. Andrew. There he knelt before an ornate bronze stand that supported a bank of votive candles; he lit one. Head bowed as if in prayer, he slowly reached beneath the stand. The gun was there, precisely where Sister Lucia had left it, totally hidden from anyone's view within the blind metal recess that had once served as an offering repository. It would be there next Tuesday afternoon too, safely planted and available for the moment of truth when the pope himself would be seated at the main altar, a mere twenty-five feet away. J.W. wished he could feel as strongly about killing the pope as he did about icing the goddamned priests. What if Sister Lucia was wrong about the pope? Believing that things always have a way of working out, he blessed himself and slowly made his way back to the south transept exit.

Outside on Fiftieth, he climbed back into the waiting taxicab. "Take me to Mallory's Bicycle Shop," he said, noting that the cab's meter had run up to ten dollars. "It's on the corner of Fourth Street and First Avenue."

Seated behind the wheel of the idling unmarked opposite B. Grennan's Belmont Avenue address, Diane slipped the cell phone back into her pocket. She glanced over at Richie Marcus, who was monkeying with the dashboard heater controls.

"Boss gave us overtime carte blanche," Diane said. "We're to stay here all night if necessary. He wants this woman interviewed, no matter what."

"What's he up to?" Marcus asked.

"He's calling it a day. Getting ready to sign out now. He said he's gonna bring the entire case folder and those puny archdiocese records home with him; gonna study them all over again later tonight. But first, he's heading over to P. J.'s for a few cold ones. Said we're welcome to join him if we get done here in time."

Marcus nodded and took a second generous bite of Italian pastry.

"Can't you wait?" Diane said. "I bought those for dessert at home."

Marcus grinned impishly and kept right on chewing.

At precisely five minutes to six, an older woman matching Rosita's description of Barbara Grennan came into view beneath the corner streetlamp at Belmont and Crescent. Wearing a long green coat and a red plaid scarf draped over thinning snow-white hair, the woman was hunched somewhat from age, but moved sprightly along the snow-patched sidewalk. When she turned to let herself into the staked-out building, Marcus quickly rewrapped what was left of the piece of pastry he'd been sampling, and Diane pulled the keys from the car's ignition switch.

"Wipe that cannoli cream off your mouth, Rich," Diane said, as they half trotted across the street. When they entered the building vestibule, the woman was shuffling through several pieces of mail from the 5C mailbox.

"'Scuse me, ma'am," Diane said in a gentle tone, holding her detective shield out for the woman to see clearly. "I'm Detective DeGennaro from Manhattan South." Nodding her head toward Richie, she said, "This is my partner, Detective Marcus. Would you mind giving us a few moments of your time?"

The old woman glanced up warily through moist blue eyes. They were rimmed in red and looked tired from a long and difficult day. Diane also decided they were dull and murky from a long and difficult life.

"Are you Barbara Grennan?" Diane asked.

The woman frowned defensively and nodded. "What is the problem?" Her low voice was froggy and timid.

Diane removed the enlarged, employee-I.D. photograph of the Boston victim, Peter Grennan, from a manila envelope.

"I'd like you to look at this picture and tell us if you know this person."

Barbara Grennan placed a pair of rimless spectacles on the tip of her pug nose. "That's my nephew," she replied instantly. "My brother's only son, Peter Grennan. What's wrong? What has he done? Is he all right?"

"You look very tired," Diane said. Despite knowing that Richie would probably freak, she added, "Would you mind if we came up to your apartment and talked for a little while?" She heard Richie mumbling under his breath as they headed for the killer stairs.

P. J. Clarke's has stood at the northeast corner of Third Avenue and Fifty-fifth Street for more than one hundred and twenty years. In New York City history, as well as in booze-dom lore, it is an unquestioned landmark. For seventy years it sat in the soot-dripping and light-stealing shadow of the Third Avenue El; until the day in 1955 when the city finally tore the damn thing down.

Dwarfed today by neighboring skyscrapers, it had undergone a refurbishing of sorts a few years ago; they made the back dining room a bit more "upscale"—and the burgers a bit more pricey—but the tinwork ceilings were still peeling, the mammoth prehistoric urinals were still filled with blocks of ice, and Frankie McBride, Thorn's longtime buddy, was still the head bartender after forty-plus years of service. Despite some minor changes, it was still P. J. Clarke's saloon, and it was still Savage's favorite spot to unwind on a Friday evening after a particularly nutsy day, and this had been a particularly nutsy week. He got there at six forty-five.

Because his instinctive internal GPS was always fully engaged—some would call it police paranoia; cops called it self-preservation—Savage covered his back by situating himself on the stool against the wall at the front end of the long bar. The location gave him a good view of everyone who came and left, everything that was going on in the place, and since it was right at the front window, also allowed him to keep an eyeball on the rest of the world as it hustled by on busy Third Avenue.

It was through that very window on a hot summer evening a few years ago that he'd watched two gun-toting stickup men bolt from the high-dollar florist shop across the way. They had dodged through traffic at a full-felony gallop, crossed Third Avenue on a diagonal, and headed— he later learned—for the getaway car they'd earlier stashed on East Fifty-sixth. Savage had politely excused himself from the conversation he'd been having with a brunette looker and let himself out of P. J.'s front door just as the two gunmen were about to streak by. Casually, he tracked the pair in his peripheral vision and placed himself directly in their path. Waiting until the absolute last second, he braced himself and thrust out two elbow-locked straight arms as each opted to go around him on either side. The poor bastards never knew what hit them. He turned the two dazed and broken-nosed dopes over to the Seventeenth Precinct Anti-Crime team that rolled up several minutes later, and was back inside P. J.'s before his beer lost its foam. And, more importantly, before the looker was discovered by anyone else.

"And what'll be your pleasure this fine Friday night, Thornton, me lad?" Frankie McBride's robot-sounding esophageal voice burped from the hole in his trachea behind his black bow tie. Sans a larynx but cancer-free now for thirteen years, the seventy-three-year-old Frankie swabbed the bar top and set down a fresh coaster.

"Let's go with a Rusty," Savage replied decisively, reaching across the wide bar to clasp his old friend's hand. "When the hell are you going to retire, Frankie?" he teased. "Crissakes, you must have more money than God."

"Yeah, right!" Frankie replied, his thin-lipped mouth twisting in sarcasm. "If I'd taken the test for the cops fifty years ago like I should have, I'd already be retired thirty." He leaned his form across the bar and whispered as best he could, "Ain't no pension plans in saloon work, buddy. You work till you die. We get too soon old, and too goddamned late smart."

"You'd have made a good cop, Frankie," Savage said.

"Not so sure about that," the silver-haired man replied thoughtfully, turning away for a second to offer a quick friendly nod to an incoming group of Friday night revelers. "I'm afraid I'd have fallen prey to at least two of them damn three Bs."

Savage grinned broadly. "Booze, bucks, and broads; the three police-career enders. Which two would it have been, Frank?"

"The broads, for sure," Frankie said with a big smile and a wink. "And it woulda been real close between them other two. Let me go make your drink."

"And can you arrange to hold a table for three in the back room? I'm sort of expecting company."

The bartender shrugged. "Can't hold one on a Friday night. But as soon as you're ready, I'll see you get the very next available."

With quick, short steps, Frankie waddled stiffly away in his jerking side-to-side strut. His strange walk was because of hip arthritis and the iron-board flat feet he'd earned after a lifetime of treading the boards, serving up stupid juice to the thirsty masses. Little beady eyes, black slacks and a bow tie, and a formal white shirt also created the image of a venerable emperor penguin. Savage watched as Frankie pointed him out to the pretty dining-room hostess and instructed her about the table; she was nodding. She must be new, he thought; he didn't recognize her.

P. J.'s on a Friday evening was always a zoo. The fact that today was the Friday between the major holidays of Christmas and New Year's seemed to make it even more so. Thirsty suits from the surrounding corporate bastions were pouring in two and three at a time. Within ten minutes, there wasn't a seat to be had at the bar—it was already two deep and counting.

"Your table's arranged," Frankie said, returning with the Rusty Nail. "Now, tell me, what the hell's going on with this priest thing?"

Savage offered his friend an exasperated shrug in response. "There's not a whole lot to tell," he said, slowly stirring the cocktail. "So far we've got nuthin', and this son of a bitch is going to be real tough to find."

"Tougher than normal?" Frankie asked, narrowing his gaze. "Why's that?"

"Guys like this—serial killers—are usually just everyday schmucks, same as anybody else in most respects, except for their lethal tendencies. Hell," Savage said, flipping his right hand dismissively, "son of a bitch could be sitting in here right now sucking down a Watney's and not feeling an ounce of guilt; maybe looking forward to his kid's soccer game tomorrow afternoon or his niece's piano recital on Sunday. His neighbors think him a little eccentric or weird, but probably also believe he's the salt of the earth. As a rule, except for a parking ticket or three, these guys usually don't have any police record. They vote. They're not mobbed up. They don't hang around in pool halls with the usual suspects. . . . In many ways, they're everyman." Savage raised the glass, took a tentative first sip, and added, "Yeah, this guy's gonna be tough."

Frankie leaned closer, looked left and right, and whispered as best he could, "Everybody's speculatin' there's a fifty-fifty chance it has something to do with degenerate sex. Little boys . . . that kinda thing."

"You know the fifty-fifty rule, right, Frankie?" Savage answered. "Any time you have a fifty-fifty chance of getting something right, there's a ninety percent probability you'll get it wrong."

"By the way," Frankie said at full volume, once again standing upright. "An old friend of yours was in here last week asking about you."

"Oh?" Savage replied. He took a deeper, fuller sip of his drink. "Who?"

"Maur-reen," Frankie intoned, his shrublike eyebrows waggling over expressive Gaelic blues.

"No kidding?" Savage said.

"She was with some girlfriend of hers. Said they were in the neighborhood and decided to come in for a drink. Can't bullshit me; she came in here looking for you. I always liked Maureen."

"I know that," Savage acknowledged. Looking up, he noticed Diane DeGennaro and Richie Marcus enter the saloon and begin working their way over to where he was seated. Diane ordered a Baileys, and Marcus went with the Watney's Red Barrel.

"Any word on Ray?" Marcus asked.

"No," Savage uttered with a grimace, shaking his head.

Frankie was back in a flash with the beer and Baileys; he shot Savage a good-luck wink—all the drinks were on the arm. "Table's ready," he said. "I told them to put some nosh out for you."

Thorn left a ten-spot on the bar, and the three headed for the back room.

"Ready for this?" Diane said excitedly, as soon as she'd sat down. Without giving Savage so much as a half a beat to answer, she went right on. "The B. Grennan in Father Flaherty's telephone book turns out to be the spinster aunt of one Peter Grennan."

"*The* Peter Grennan?" Savage asked. "The security guard victim up in Boston?"

"One and the same," Marcus broke in. "She I.D.'d him immediately from the photos we brought along."

"*Awright!*" Savage drawled. "Could she say why Father Flaherty had her name and phone number jotted down in his old address book?"

"She knew Father Flaherty. Years ago, Flaherty was a friend of her nephew, Peter Grennan. She sometimes would have them both over to her place for dinner."

"Did she say how her nephew was connected to Flaherty?" Savage asked.

"That's the best part," Diane said with a wide grin. "Peter Grennan was at one time a Roman Catholic priest."

Savage pumped a short jab into the air, then pulled in his shoulder as a busboy leaned past him and set down a bowl of peanuts on the center of the table.

"According to the old lady, Grennan started out as a Christian Brother," Marcus said. "He did some teaching in a couple of different schools while he was studying for holy orders. And by the way," he *hrumph*ed sarcastically,

"I don't wanna be calling Mon-*signor* Dunleavy a fat-assed liar, but every one of them schools Grennan taught at was within the New York Archdiocese."

"But," Diane quickly added, "the old lady was absolutely certain her nephew had only befriended Flaherty when both were working at St. Malachy's, a Catholic home for boys up near Van Cortlandt Park."

Savage sipped at his Dewar's and Drambuie. "Had she ever heard of Father Gilhooley or Father Clapp?"

"Said Gilhooley sounded a little familiar," Diane replied. "But she really wasn't sure. Couldn't remember, it was just so many years ago."

"Didn't that Monsignor Dunleavy hump tell you that the archdiocese had no record of a Peter Grennan ever being a priest in the New York area?" Marcus said.

Savage nodded, fuming inside. "Did she say why or when Grennan left the priesthood?"

"Yeah," Marcus responded. "Said he left some time back in the midseventies, but she didn't know why. Said he would never tell her."

"And she had no idea he was dead?" Savage asked.

"No idea," Diane answered. "Hadn't heard a word from him in six or eight years. Had absolutely no idea where the hell he was all that time. Often wondered if he was still alive. She was surprised to hear that he'd wound up in Boston working as a security guard. We gave her as much information as we could, including Detective Christman's name and phone number. She's gonna call up there and arrange to have the body shipped back here for burial."

Savage leaned back in his chair and massaged the stiffness in his neck. After dinner and dessert he would go home and restudy the case folder. He would focus on the priests' employment records—sketchy as they were. His gut instinct, and decades of experience, told him there was something missing. The case was still terribly fragmented, no question, but finally some pieces appeared to be falling into place.

"You grew up in a Catholic orphanage, Richie, right?" Savage queried gently.

"Yeah," Marcus replied, nodding soberly. "Me and my brother both."

"Were priests running it?" Savage asked.

"Oh yeah!" Marcus said firmly, grabbing a fistful of peanuts. He cleared his throat, and added, "There were some lay people there, but the joint was run by Catholic priests and brothers."

"Richie and his brother got placed there when Richie was ten and his brother, Kenny, was twelve," Diane inserted, telling Savage what he already knew.

"Now comes a sensitive question," Savage began, staring at Marcus. "When you were—"

"When I was in the orphanage," Marcus broke in, sparing Savage from completing the question. "You wanna know did I ever get molested by any of the priests?"

Savage sipped at his cocktail and held his gaze.

"No," Marcus said flatly. "And if you ask Kenny, he'll tell you the same thing. Neither one of us were ever even approached—even obliquely—by anybody, priests or lay, for any of that nonsense."

"Did that kind of stuff go on there?" Savage asked.

"Don't know. It just never went on with me or my brother." He popped some peanuts into his mouth, chewed, and washed them down with a gulp of Watney's. "Fact is, we both hated living there—couldn't wait to get out. But looking back after all these years, we've come to realize that they actually treated us very good. Where the hell else would we have gone?"

"How long were you in?" Savage asked.

"I joined the marines when I was sixteen."

"Six years is a long time," Savage offered sympathetically. "I remember that your mother died about ten years ago. Since she was alive in those years, how did you and Kenny wind up in a home?"

"A pencil box," Marcus said with a blasé what-can-you-do grimace and shrug.

"Pardon?"

"A pencil box," Marcus repeated, raising the mug to his lips and taking another long gulp.

"You won't believe this story," Diane inserted, shooting a quick glance at Savage and shaking her head. Turning to Marcus, she said, "Tell him the story, Rich."

"My old man was rarely around when Kenny and me was growing up," Marcus began. "Booze. He drank us into the freakin' poorhouse. Eventually, he stopped coming around altogether. Don't know what ever became of him."

"So, you were still living with your mother?" Savage said.

"Yeah. It was in early September," Marcus continued. "Right around Labor Day. School was about to begin. I was about to start the fourth grade, I think it was."

Savage shifted his glance momentarily to Diane. "Wait till you hear this," she said.

"I asked my mother for money to get school supplies," Marcus went on in his blunt-instrument voice. "I needed to have a composition book and some pencils—you know. She wasn't at all happy about it, but she gave me a dollar and told me to bring her back fifty cents change. Mind you now, we was *real* poor." He took another sip of his beer, put the mug down, then raised it again, taking several more. "When I got to the store, I picked up the least expensive composition book I could find—I think it probably only had ten freakin' pages in it—and a couple of number two pencils. When I went to the cash register to pay for them, I saw these pencil boxes; you know, they were the plastic ones you could see through. They had that pencil sharpener built right on to a sliding top that was a twelve-inch ruler."

Savage nodded. He remembered those pencil boxes. "They came in all different colors, right?" he said, reaching for a peanut.

"Yeah, right. I liked the blue ones," Marcus replied with an ironic chuckle. "But if I bought one, I'd be a nickel over. Which meant I could only bring home forty-five cents. But hey, fuck it; I bought the damn thing. When I got home, my mother went totally ballistic. I thought she was gonna kill me. The very next day, she dragged Kenny and me into some courtroom and turned us over to the state. Told them she didn't want us anymore. We wound up in St. John's Home. She then went on to drink and party the rest of her life away. Bitch."

"So you think your mother actually put you in a home because you spent a nickel too much?" Savage asked gently, wanting some more insight into his old compadre.

Marcus rolled his eyes, shrugged, and turned away as if looking for a waiter. Savage exchanged a heavy glance with Diane. She shrugged also and gently shook her head. Savage took a deep breath.

"Did you ever see her again?" Savage asked.

"Nope," Marcus offered, raising the frosty mug of Watney's ale to his lips and taking a long pull. Swallowing with relish and smacking his lips, he smiled broadly over at Savage. "Uh oh," he said, with a forced smile that belied the sad look in his eyes. "They're goin' down real good tonight."

As a waiter set three menus on the table before them, Marcus held up his empty mug, pointed to Diane's glass and Savage's half-finished Rusty Nail, and said in his Harley-chopper growl, "Do us again."

NINETEEN

Savage didn't even attempt to find a parking spot near his Greenwich Village apartment. By eight o'clock, he reasoned, there probably wasn't a spot to be had there anyway. Parking on Sullivan Street between Houston and Bleecker on a Friday night required vast knowledge in legerdemain, a talent for juggling, and the timing of a Swiss stopwatch— all of which would have absolutely zero value without the most important element: phenomenal luck. One had to be pulling through the block at the very instant someone else was pulling out. A second early was too early; a second late was too late. If by some lapse, you passed a spot and had to go around the block, forget it. Even if you floorboarded it, the spot would be gone on your return. There were no second chances on Sullivan Street.

Not feeling particularly lucky that evening, and deciding to walk off some of P. J. Clarke's sixteen-ounce New York strip, double-baked potato, and rich chocolate layer cake, he parked instead beneath the NO PARKING ANYTIME sign directly in front of St. Anthony's School over on Mac-Dougal Street. Father Vinny wouldn't mind. He flipped the PD parking permit onto the dashboard and stepped out into the bracing night air, which brought on thoughts of Vermont and a long-overdue ski trip. He decided if he could ever put a couple of days together, he'd head up to Stratton or Killington . . . maybe even Gray Rocks in the Laurentians. He might even ask Maureen if she'd like to come along. . . . Maybe not.

Buttoned up against the cold, he waited for the fast-moving traffic to pass, then quickly crossed Houston and turned onto Sullivan. He let himself into the unlocked vestibule of number 184, checked his mailbox, and found it crammed. Along with the latest editions of *AARP* and *Hemming's Motor News* was a statement from Visa, a glossy ad flyer touting the benefits of Viagra, and a Have You Seen Me. Savage wondered if they had Have You Seen Me ads for cats. He visualized Ray's scarred and whiskered face staring back at him from a milk carton. Also in the mix of mail was a yellow Hallmark envelope addressed to him in Maureen Gallo's unmistakable hand. Inside the envelope was a handwritten note thanking him for the dozen roses he'd sent her. The attached postscript was vintage up-front Maureen. It read:

> Yes, I did save the pasties. How does New Year's Day sound? Give me a call. And by the way, you are absolutely right. Pasties, like so many *other* things in this world, can often be very much better when reheated. . . .

Savage slipped his key into the lock of the inner door and climbed the stairs to his second-floor flat. He was anxious to see if Ray was there—though not holding out much hope. He couldn't wait to strip off his suit and tie, kick off his heavy brogues, and slouch like a lazy bum on his big comfortable sofa. In his own space he could reread the entire case uninterrupted. Plus, the Rangers were playing the Bruins at the Garden tonight. A win would lift the Broadway Blues back into a tie for the last playoff spot.

Ray's food and water bowls were still full. As he'd done first thing the last several nights when he arrived home, Savage grabbed his flashlight and immediately went to his bedroom window, the one that contained Ray's swinging cat door. He lifted the lower sash fully and felt the bitter night air blast into the warm apartment. Methodically, he worked the light beam back and forth across the snow-covered iron-slat landing of his fire escape. Not one cat print; not one print of any kind. He leaned out farther and shone the light downward to the rickety rose trellis that was Ray's access to the fire escape. It was still safely in place. He hissed an expletive and lowered the sash.

Ten minutes later, dressed in sweatpants and a Yankees tee, Savage was back in the living room. He dropped the case folder and a fresh legal pad on the sofa table in front of his old chesterfield and settled into his usual corner of the couch. He tore open a box of Better Cheddars, clicked on the lamp to its highest setting, and turned on the hockey game with the volume on low. It was eight ten when he set his half-glasses on the tip of his nose and started reading and scribbling notes.

By the time he scrutinized the last piece of paper and laid his pen down, the hockey game was late in the third period and the Rangers were getting their asses kicked again, down by an embarrassing 5-1 with a minute and a half to go. Half the box of Better Cheddars was history, and he'd still been unable to find any connection between Gilhooley and Clapp. There was nothing clear-cut, yet something nagged him. Somewhere within the scramble of papers, someplace within the educational and training records, parish assignments, and personnel evaluations, lay an answer. He knew it; he just couldn't put his finger on it. What had he failed to see? Had he read right past something? Jesus, he'd read through the stuff twice.

It had been a long day after a long week, and Savage was dog tired. Before dropping into bed, he checked out the fire escape one more time. No luck. Bummed, he killed the lights.

At three thirty he sat up with a start, awakened by a priority message coming in from his subconscious. Flipping on lights as he moved, he stumbled naked from his bedroom back into the living room. He was right. He knew he was right. He could feel it. Again he pored through the pile of papers, this time paying strict attention to any and all dates appearing anywhere on every archdiocese document provided by Dunleavy.

There it was. Or better stated, there it wasn't. Each priest's records contained a similar gap in time. Not one piece of paper in Clapp's folder bore a date between February 1964 and July 1968. Gilhooley's was blank between December '60 and July '66. Savage unconsciously nibbled another cheese cracker, certain the connection, if any, must lie somewhere within that specific time frame of forty years ago.

The Rangers had slipped backward in the NHL standings, but the NYPD investigation into the killings of Catholic priests might have just inched ahead. It was not what the stack of documents contained that was moving the investigation forward. . . . It was what they did not contain that he suspected would show the way.

Returning to the bedroom, he re-eyeballed the fire escape, then climbed back into bed. But still something nagged at him. How interesting that Gilhooley and Clapp's records had a big hole from the 1960s, right about the time of Peter Grennan's relationship with Father Flaherty, when, according to Grennan's biddy aunt up in the Bronx, both were priests working at St. Malachy's Home for Boys. A smile eased its way across his face. The thread had just turned into a string.

He rolled over, repositioned his lumpy pillow, and slipped immediately into a deep and satisfying sleep.

TWENTY

SOLDIER WRITES HOME AGAIN

The flippant headline of the morning *Post* in Savage's lap announced in bold type that the deadly game was still on. The entire contents of the Soldier's second letter to reporter Joe Ballantine was reprinted on page two, and reading it left no doubt that not only was the game still *fully* on, but that the stakes had been greatly raised. In the Soldier's words, not only would more "evil" priests soon die in the name of the Blessed Virgin and the Third Secret of Fatima but, as Thorn had feared, they also included a not-so-thinly-veiled threat against the "Antichrist pope." But there was something queer about letter two, something different. He read it five times, at speed, and then more slowly. He compared it over and over again to a copy of the first letter. Something wasn't ringing true.

Savage spread the newspaper out on his desk, sipped at his unusually tart coffee—Brodigan must have made it this morning—and quick scanned through the rest of the newspaper. The weatherman was predicting continued cold temperatures with a chance of more snow in the coming days. The Dow was up, math scores in city schools were down while the teachers' union was threatening a walkout, and the Giants needed a win tomorrow against Dallas to stay alive in the NFC East. The world keeps moving right along, he thought.

There was a small item on page four with a byline from

Pensacola, Florida. A Catholic priest had resigned there after admitting he molested a boy thirty-four years ago. The cleric, now seventy-four, had been a priest for forty-two years and worked at St. Michael's Catholic Church for twenty-five of those years. Savage grimaced and shook his head; he folded the paper and put it away in his desk.

At eight fifteen, Jack Lindstrom let himself into the sergeants' room looking bright eyed, clean shaven, and rested. His outdated gray Penney's suit was pressed and he was wearing a new tie sans pills, pulls, and gravy stains. Savage also noted the troubled frown that had slowly become Jack's full-time expression, though still discernible, was less wary, and the muscles around his chin and ample jaw seemed far less tight.

"Nice tie, Jack," Savage commented, catching a whiff of Old Spice so strong he could almost taste it. He hadn't smelled that stuff in years.

"Got it from my daughter for Christmas," Lindstrom replied, beaming proudly. He fluttered the fingers of both hands through the tie, ruffling it à la Oliver Hardy. "De la Renta, pure silk—you like?"

"I like."

"I thought I saw Joe Ballantine leaving as I came in," Lindstrom said, sitting himself down in Billy Lakis' swivel chair. The man's cordovan wing tips—though somewhat in need of new heels–were freshly shined.

"He swung by to drop this off," Savage replied. He handed Lindstrom the clear plastic evidence envelope containing the Soldier's second poison-pen letter. The detective quickly read it.

"Boy," Lindstrom said, laying the envelope back on Savage's desk, "this son of a bitch is totally gonzo. I see it's been typed on the same yellowed paper. I guess it's safe to say that this is not the work of some wacko copycat wanting a few minutes of vicarious notoriety."

"Not so sure of that," Savage grunted. "I'm wondering if the same guy actually wrote it."

Lindstrom held the envelope up to the light and scrutinized its contents. Mumbling to himself, he added, "Same uppercase *T* . . . same lowercase *L* . . . and same high-striking letter *A*. Gotta be the same guy. Why do you think different?"

"I don't know," Savage replied, leaning back in his chair and shaking his head. "This letter just sounds different somehow. . . . a slightly different voice, different meter—know what I mean?"

"I thought it sounded pretty similar," Lindstrom said. "But maybe you've got a better ear for that."

"How are you feeling today, Jack?" Savage inquired.

"Better. I'm almost afraid to say it, but I think maybe those pills are kicking in."

Savage nodded, noting that Lindstrom's voice seemed to have regained some of its former timbre.

"Just got off the phone with some lady mucky-muck over at the Veteran's Administration office," Lindstrom said. "A Lorelei DeKohning. Told her who I was and generally what it was we were looking for. You know, as per Harvey Wallbanger's profile. I asked if there was any way she could help us out with researching their medical records."

"And?"

"And wouldn't you know? She told me that she's got two brothers on The Job, one in Brooklyn North Narcotics and the other one a lieutenant out in the One-ten. Suggested that I come over with a list of all the specific parameters; said she'd be happy to assist us by running some searches through their active medical files. Without a name it doesn't promise much, but . . ." Lindstrom wore a hopeful look on his face, like a child waiting for permission to go outside and play. "I wouldn't be out of the office long . . . just an hour or two to get her launched."

"So?"

"So," Lindstrom whispered, with a wide-eyed shrug.

"When you took my gun, you told me that I'm restricted to the office. . . ."

Always so damn totally literal, Savage thought. "What I meant was," he said evenly, "I didn't want you out on the street in any *enforcement* capacity while not armed. . . ."

Lindstrom smiled in relief.

"I don't have to tell you, Jack, as far as the PC and the mayor—and all the other powers that be—are concerned, this is no longer an open-ended investigation. Unless it is soon decided otherwise, the pope of the Catholic Church is going to be in town in three days," Savage said. "And the powers want this Soldier lunatic in irons before he gets here. If not, there's gonna be hell to pay. Maybe literally. So, in that regard, we're pretty close to running out of time."

"I understand," Lindstrom replied. "Not to take us off the hook or anything, but isn't the department arranging super-duper heavy security for this visit? Hell, we could just surround the man in a cocoon of cops."

"Don't forget, Jack, the night of his visit is New Year's Eve. Half the damn department is already booked to be on OT in Times Square till two o'clock in the morning. That cuts down greatly on the amount of warm bodies that'll be available earlier in the day."

Lindstrom nodded. "And if the pope so much as stubs his toe while he's here, we'll never hear the end of it."

"You got it," Savage said. "Now, getting back to the VA. Even if this DeKohning woman can compile a list of vets within a fifty-mile radius who fit Harvey Wallbanger's medical criteria—Vietnam vets who are seriously ill—it may number in the many hundreds."

"You suggesting we cut down the radius?"

"For now, we'll have to. For starters, have her limit her search to residents of the five boroughs. We can always expand it after New Year's. Besides," Savage said, tearing open a new roll of Wint-O-Greens, "even if Wallbanger is right about this guy being a seriously ill Vietnam vet, it does not necessarily follow that he'd be seeking medical attention from the Veterans Administration. Hell, most vets I know would opt for private care."

"I explained our time and other constraints to her," Lindstrom assured. "She seemed to fully realize our situation and is very eager to help. And she also seems to know her business."

"Well, good. Go over there and get her launched, and get back here as soon as you can. At the very first instant that you consider this angle a dead end, though, we drop it and move on. *Capisce?*"

"Gotcha," Lindstrom said. He rose and closed the office door. This was now to be a private discussion. "I don't know how to thank you for untangling that fucked-up mess the other day," he said.

"Don't worry about it."

"If you didn't show up there and take care of business, at the very least I'd have an IAB cloud over my head right now. At worst, I might have been collared."

"Don't worry about it."

"I had to protect the kid. . . . You understand that, right? He's probably gonna be my son-in-law. His whole beautiful future—and my daughter's—could have been fucked up because of a bullshit arrest that he wouldn't have deserved."

"I read you, Jack. I really do." Two raps came to the office door, and Eddie Brodigan stuck his head in.

"Pick up on twenty-three, boss," the wheelman said. "A Joan Zalonis from International Paper."

Lindstrom handed Savage a Post-it square. "That's the number at the VA where I'll be at, in case you need me."

"Before you disappear," Savage said, popping a Wint-O-Green, "round up Marcus and DeGennaro and have them stand by. We're gonna have a meeting in Lieutenant Pezzano's office in ten minutes."

Lindstrom smiled, clicked his heels, and snapped a smart salute as Savage reached for the phone.

"Good morning, Ms. Zalonis. Very good to hear from you. Do they actually make you guys work on Saturday up there in Erie, Pennsylvania?"

"Good morning to you, Sergeant," the lady responded. "And no, I'm off today. But I think we've managed to come up with something interesting on that watermark exemplar you faxed us last night."

"Terrific." Savage flipped to a fresh page on his legal pad.

"I told you I knew just the person to go to, and I must say, I certainly wasn't wrong. Herbie Kleiman is *the man*, I wanna tell you. He worked all last night on it. Nobody, and I mean nobody, but Herbie could have possibly dug this information out of our archives. But then again, he's been with the company for over five decades. His grandfather was here in 1898 when the company was founded, for God's sake."

"You're keeping me in suspense, Joan," Savage said.

"Sorry," she replied with a slight chuckle. "I just find this all so exciting."

"What does the watermark tell us?" Savage asked.

"Well, I don't know how much it's going to help, but here goes. That particular piece of paper was part of a two-hundred-ream order we supplied back in January 1976. The purchaser was the New York City Transit Authority. Their billing address was Jay Street in Brooklyn, New York."

"You're sure on this?"

"No," Zalonis replied. "*I'm* not sure. . . . But Herbie Kleiman is. And if he says it's so, you can take it to the bank."

"Thank you, Ms. Zalonis. I really appreciate all your efforts. Oh, and uh . . . do thank Mr. Kleiman."

"I know you're all probably asking yourselves why I invited you here this morning," Savage opened with a half-grin, tightly closing the door to Pete Pezzano's office.

Detectives Marcus, DeGennaro, and Lindstrom sat in a semicircle facing Pete Pezzano, who was seated behind his desk.

"Ray came home?" Diane asked hopefully.

"Nah," Savage said, ruefully shaking his head. " 'Fraid not." He handed each one present a copy of a work sheet he'd prepared. It was a distillation of the archdiocese records he'd pored over the night before.

"Somebody gave ya five tickets to the Super Bowl, and you've decided to take us all with you," Marcus remarked, flipping a fresh Winston between his lips.

"Actually, I was only able to get four, and I was hoping you'd volunteer to stay home," Savage replied, noticing that Pete Pezzano had flashed Marcus the fisheye. Marcus immediately removed the as yet unlit cigarette from his face, snorted self-consciously, and gingerly returned the weed to its pack. Petey didn't allow smoking in his office; he didn't care if you were a goddamned chief.

"Thanks to Richie and Diane's efforts in the Bronx yesterday," Savage began, "I think we've made a breakthrough in the case."

"Don't mention it, boss," Marcus growled playfully, holding out his hands in a stop motion. "We was just doin' our job. Know what I mean?" Diane and Pete Pezzano both seemed amused by the typical Marcus venture into levity. Jack Lindstrom cleared his throat.

"Looks like Gilhooley and Brodeur went to the same seminary," Diane said, looking up from the page on her lap. "St. Joseph's, up in Yonkers."

"True enough," Savage acknowledged. "But if you'll notice, not during the same time period. Gilhooley had already graduated and was ordained by 1959. Brodeur attended many years later."

"What about Father Clapp?" Pezzano asked.

"He attended St. Bernard's up in Rochester," Savage replied.

"Hmm. These records show they never shared any parish assignments," Pezzano said.

"Correct," Savage replied. "But I found something interesting in Gilhooley's and Clapp's file folders. A similarity that goes back forty years."

"And what is that?" Pezzano asked.

"A gap of information from the early to mid-1960s. Neither file contains any significant information about those years, certainly no assignment information. I'm betting that is when all our dead priests—with the probable exception of Father Brodeur—shared their connection."

"That's the same years that Peter Grennan was a priest," Marcus pointed out.

"And the same years that he was buddy-buddy with Father Flaherty," Diane chimed in. "According to his aunt up in the Bronx, it was during those years that they both worked at St. Malachy's Home for Boys up in North Riverdale."

"Exactly," Savage agreed. "And that's where I believe the connection lies. If I'm right, then I think at least in Gilhooley's and Flaherty's cases, their archdiocese records have been intentionally purged of that information."

"What do you think they're trying to hide?" Pezzano asked, drumming the eraser end of a pencil on his desktop. "Something really heavy?"

"Looks like it," Savage responded.

"Okay," Pezzano said. "What's the plan?"

"As soon as we're done here, Jack's going to head over to the VA," Savage said. "He's found a sympathetic ear over there. If we sift their medical files, maybe we can get some names."

"What about Richie and me?" Diane asked. "Do you have something in mind for us?"

Savage quickly related his earlier conversation with Joan Zalonis up at International Paper. "I want you to pay a preliminary visit to the administrative offices of the

Transit Authority. Lay some groundwork over there. Make a connection we can tap into if and when we need to."

"Maybe we can get a printout of current and former employees—that sort of thing," Marcus said. "People who were working there back around '76."

"That list would look like the New York Telephone Directory, for crissakes," Jack Lindstrom observed, his light hazel eyes intense and beginning to reflect some of their former inquisitiveness.

"We're aware of that, Jack," Marcus replied with an aggravated edge. "But we're still at the wide end of the funnel on this case. Gotta start somewhere." Obviously irked, he shot a millisecond glance at DeGennaro, then, again facing Lindstrom, added, "By the way, what Woolworth's did you find that antique aftershave in? Or did somebody give it to you for your thirteenth birthday?"

"At least I don't smell like a gin mill ashtray."

Marcus chewed at the inside of his cheek and again glanced over at DeGennaro. This time, she glared back.

"What's on your agenda?" Pezzano asked, making tight eye contact with Savage.

"St. Malachy's Home for Boys still exists, so I'm going to take a little jaunt up there," Savage replied. "It's imperative that we get a list of all the staff who worked there during the sixties and, even more importantly, a list of all the boys who were processed through there during those years."

"You thinking that the Soldier could be a graduate of St. Malachy's?" Pezzano said.

"Why not?" Savage replied. "Our perp profile puts him at the right age. As far as I'm concerned, it's the most logical direction to look in at this time."

"I agree," Pezzano stated. "But the minute you announce yourself and your purpose up there, they're gonna clam up. You know that, right? Once they know that the information you're seeking is tied into this goddamned case, they're not gonna give you anything without an approval from the archdiocese."

"I'm going to try and catch them cold, maybe finesse them somehow," Savage said.

"What do we tell Downtown?" Pezzano asked.

"For the moment . . . we tell *them* nothing," Savage said. "Let's just keep them on hold for the time being."

"You thinking Downtown could be the source of Dunleavy's miraculous knowledge of our every move?"

"Either that or he's got himself a crystal ball," Savage said. "My sense is this: If we don't tell Downtown, then Downtown can't possibly alert the archdiocese. And the archdiocese can't preempt us up at St. Malachy's, if they haven't already done so."

"Let's just suppose for a minute that we've already been preempted up there," Pezzano said, laying the work sheet down on his desk blotter.

"I don't think we have," Savage said.

"For the sake of argument, what if they have gotten to St. Malachy's?" Pezzano pressed.

"Then we go to court and get an order."

"Then we're right back into the damn subpoena tank," Pezzano groused.

"Maybe so," Savage agreed. "But this is the only thing we've got so far. There's too much potential for more dead priests.

"And now the very strong likelihood of an attempt being made on the pope's life this Tuesday," Pezzano mumbled.

"We're running out of time, boss," Savage said. "We've got to play the card."

"What about our nine o'clock update to Lieutenant Wonderful over at Operations?" Pezzano asked.

"I'll take care of that," Savage said, glancing at his watch.

When the meeting ended at exactly 9:00 a.m., Savage

returned to the sergeants' room, picked up the phone, and dialed headquarters.

"Lieutenant Crowley, Chief of Detectives office."

"Loo, good morning. Thorn Savage, Manhattan South. How you doin' this morning?"

"Another fucking goose egg this morning, hah Savage?" Crowley asked in his inimitable please-punch-me tone.

"'Fraid so, Loo," Savage responded, oozing regret. "We've got absolutely *nothing* to report."

The Vatican

"It is settled," Cardinal-Secretary Damiani stated to the assembled. "Despite my strong recommendations to the contrary, the Holy Father will not permit the cancellation of his announced trip to New York City."

Cardinal Remlinger sat expressionless, as did Cardinal Deliberto. Colonel George Olmstead flashed a worried glance to Damiani without speaking.

"We discussed it at great length," Damiani continued, "and he has made his decision. And that decision is final."

"Certainly the Holy Father has been made aware of the fact that there are now four dead priests in New York," Olmstead blurted, his tone a mixture of raw anger and stark disbelief. "Three dead by gunshot, and one by suicide."

"This is the Holy Father's decision," Remlinger pointed out brusquely. "His will cannot be questioned."

The commander of the Swiss Guards slid his chair back angrily, stood, and paced about the room. "There is a raging maniac in that city, who randomly murders priests and intends to kill the pope. What more must happen to prove that intent beyond any question? Does anyone here doubt what I am saying?"

The three cardinals sat stone-faced.

"And," Olmstead went on, "I for one do not believe this person is acting alone."

"You sense a conspiracy, George?" Deliberto asked dismissively.

"This 'Soldier' character has announced that he is part of an army," Olmstead shot back. "Which I interpret to mean that many more could be involved." He made intense momentary eye contact with each cardinal, and added, "And not necessarily from outside of the Church, but from within as well; possibly from quite high within."

"What are you saying, Colonel?" Cardinal Remlinger asked.

"I suspect there may be some snakes in the grass at the Vatican," Olmstead replied.

"Those are serious words," Remlinger said angrily. "Do you have any evidence to support such a statement? Or are you merely hypothesizing?"

"I have no firm evidence at this time, Cardinal Remlinger," Olmstead answered, looking intently at the man. "I have some strong suspicions, but no evidence as yet. Unfortunately, the pope is due in New York in less than seventy-two hours, hardly enough time to investigate. However, upon our return, I intend to investigate with great vigor."

Cardinals Deliberto and Remlinger remained expressionless and silent. Cardinal Damiani spoke softly. "The Holy Father sees America as a lost sheep that has wandered far from the flock. He feels he must go in search of this sheep . . . find it . . . and bring it back safely into the fold."

"And while he searches for this errant sheep, the pontiff may wind up right in this maniac's crosshairs." Olmstead shook his head in disbelief. "This is pure madness."

"Yes," Damiani replied, still softly. "What you say may be absolutely true, Colonel. But the Holy Father has decided not to allow these terrible acts to discourage him from tending his flock. He knows that the entire world is watching, waiting to see if the Vicar of Christ caves in to fear. Under no conditions will he permit that to happen. The honor of the Church has been terribly wounded these past years. The Holy Father's strength can go a long way toward healing those wounds—"

"If he lives!" Olmstead shouted.

Remlinger raised an eyebrow. "I would not worry about the Holy Father," he said coldly. "He fully comprehends the potential for danger to him that lurks everywhere in the world, not just in New York."

"He is not the strong man he once was," Olmstead interjected, "physically or . . . mentally."

Cardinal Damiani shook his head. "He is as weak and frail as I have ever seen him, but his will is iron. He will not be discouraged." Turning his full attention to Colonel Olmstead, the Cardinal-Secretary then added, "The Holy Father is going; there is no argument. What I want you to do is be certain that absolutely everything will be done to improve or tighten up the security plans that have already been laid out."

"I understand, Cardinal-Secretary," Olmstead replied stiffly, with a slight bow.

"Do you see any specific weakness at all in the existing plan? Any problems with the itinerary, travel arrangements?" Remlinger asked Olmstead.

"Under the circumstances," Olmstead replied, "I am growing increasingly concerned that the pontiff is to travel by motorcade from Kennedy Airport into midtown Manhattan."

"Sit down and tell me of your concerns, Colonel," Damiani said, gesturing to Olmstead's usual place.

"It is a distance of many highway miles that involves passing under countless overpasses and using either bridges or tunnels," Olmstead began, slipping into his chair and dropping his plan folder on the conference table before him.

"So?" Remlinger queried. "Will the motorcade not be escorted by the local police, as well as our Swiss Guards?"

"Yes, of course," Olmstead answered, nodding emphatically. "But despite the heavy security promised to us by the Port Authority and New York City Police Department, there is absolutely no way that every potential hazard could be covered. Even if we had an army."

"You are suggesting?" Damiani inquired.

"Allow the announced plan of the motorcade from Kennedy to remain publicized. But upon arrival we use three helicopters, each identical in markings, two of which would be decoys. The pontiff could be flown right from the tarmac at Kennedy International directly to the East Sixtieth Street heliport, bypassing all those bridges and overpasses where he would be most vulnerable. Then all that would remain would be a short motorcade to St. Patrick's Cathedral: a distance—as the crow flies—of just over one mile."

Damiani, Remlinger, and Deliberto exchanged glances and agreeing nods.

"Then you must begin to make the necessary arrangements," Cardinal Damiani said.

"Yes, Cardinal-Secretary," Olmstead replied. "There is little time left, but I will do everything I can." The Swiss Guard Commander gathered up his folder and slid his chair back from the conference table.

It had appeared that the meeting was concluded until Cardinal Remlinger settled them all back in their chairs with a loud, forced "Ahem." Concentrating, he propped his elbow on the chair's arm, rested his square chin atop his thumb, and tapped pensively at the tip of his nose with his index finger.

"Your thoughts, James?" Damiani said.

"It occurs to me that perhaps Colonel Olmstead should go to New York in advance, several days before the pontiff is scheduled to arrive."

"To what end?" Damiani asked.

"He could work directly with the New York Police Department in setting up the entire security. Thereby ensuring it will be most to his liking."

"What do you think, Colonel?" Damiani said. "Would such a plan be beneficial, even in the slightest way?"

"It is customary for me to be at the right hand of the pontiff whenever he travels," Olmstead said thoughtfully. "But these are not ordinary circumstances. Therefore, yes," he said firmly, "I agree that it is a good plan."

"For maximum security," Remlinger added, "I think perhaps the Colonel should travel to New York by commercial airline. Beyond that, it might also be wise for him to travel under an assumed name."

"Why an assumed name?" Damiani inquired.

"Added security," Remlinger replied. "In case some sort of conspiracy is at work, as the Colonel fears, we must take every precaution with our moves. Once the Colonel is in New York, he should reveal his true identity only to the New York City Police."

"What of the upper levels of the archdiocese?" Deliberto asked. "At the very least, should we not inform Cardinal Hammond?"

Remlinger shook his head. "No. I don't think it necessary that Hammond be notified. Let us keep the circle small."

"With all due respect, Cardinal Remlinger, if I were to travel under an assumed name as you suggest, I would need unquestioned documentation in order to get through customs at New York." Olmstead turned out his palms in question. "Where would I get such documentation at this late stage?"

"Must I remind you that I head the Section for Relations with States, whose purview includes all Vatican dealings with outside civil governments, political authorities, and international diplomacy?"

Olmstead nodded.

"Fear not, Colonel," Remlinger continued, his tenor firm, his face locked in that ever present frown. "My staff will see to that documentation. And while they are at it, they will also make all of your travel arrangements."

TWENTY-ONE

When Jack Lindstrom arrived at the Varick Street offices of the Manhattan Veterans' Center, he discovered that his recently made acquaintance, Lorelei DeKohning, was a mild-mannered, prim divorcée in her midforties. At first glance, he suspected that she might be really pretty; he just had to look a little longer and deeper to see it. She wore her brown hair straight and short, her unflattering skirt pleated and long, and she sorely needed a surgical road crew to flatten out the horrific speed bump that loused up the bridge of her otherwise small nose. A little glamour wouldn't hurt either. Lindstrom tried to visualize her with a flash of gold at her neck and ears, a different hairstyle, and a little makeup. He was right; she was basically very pretty. And she had great eyes; medium gray and haunting. And true to her word, she was eager to set right to work cross-referencing and downloading a virtual mountain of medical files. Lindstrom could tell by her general demeanor that Lorelei DeKohning was very efficient. . . . He liked that quality in a person.

"Sounds like you're looking for a needle in a haystack, Detective," she said, ushering him into her small seventh-floor office with ammonia-and-squeegee-starved windows that looked out in the direction of an ever congested Canal Street.

"We're used to looking for a needle in a haystack," he responded with a friendly grin. "Problem with this needle is we don't even know which haystack to start looking in, and we're working very much against the clock."

"Well, as far as VA records are concerned, we carry them within a number of different divisions," Ms. DeKohning said. "But since you feel that your man may turn up in a medical-related sense, I suggest we look first in the Health Benefits and Services haystack."

"What other divisions are there?"

"We have Vocational Rehab and Employment Services, Compensation and Pension Benefits, Education, Board of Veteran's Appeals . . . and more."

Lindstrom noticed a framed photo on DeKohning's desk. It was of a young man in a dress navy officer's uniform. "That your boy?" he asked.

"Yes," she acknowledged with a loving smile. "That's my son, Roy."

"Good-looking young man," Lindstrom commented. "He a sailor?"

"That picture was taken at Annapolis. Immediately after graduation, he went for flight training down at Pensacola. Right now he's with an air wing stationed outside Norfolk."

"N.A.S. Oceana?"

"Exactly. Are you familiar with Naval Air Station Oceana?"

"Spent a few years there," Lindstrom said. "I wasn't a flyer, but I was attached to an air wing there. I was an airedale."

"An airedale?"

"We worked the flight deck on aircraft carriers. I was a bomb loader."

Lorelei DeKohning's eyes grew wide. "That sounds awfully dangerous."

"Not if you don't drop anything."

Lorelei DeKohning smiled. "It's going to be a pleasure to help you, Detective," she said.

"Please, Lorelei. Call me Jack."

"Okay," she said with an even bigger smile. "Let's get to work . . . Jack."

*   *   *

As Diane DeGennaro steered the silver Taurus off the southbound FDR Drive onto the Brooklyn Bridge approach, Richie Marcus circled *Klimactic Katy,* the five horse in the sixth at Santa Anita.

"Got me a guaranteed winner for today," he announced confidently.

"That so?" Diane responded sarcastically. "Every time you find yourself a 'guaranteed winner' we wind up not going out to eat for a few weeks."

"Klimactic Katy," he continued, unfazed. "A three-year-old. Been watching her move steadily up in company for months. Been carefully studying her, analyzing her every performance. She's ready."

Nobody handicapped like Richie Marcus, he thought. Most betters only played hunches, which, of course, was a fool's game. There was absolutely no question in his mind that Klimactic Katy was now at her peak and unbeatable. So sure of it, he decided he'd go ten times. Glancing quickly at his watch, he calculated that, thanks to the coast-to-coast time difference, he still had several hours to get posted with his book. Confident of his choice, he folded the *Daily Racing Form* in his lap, and looked out to gaze at the classic span's stone Gothic towers.

"Savage's favorite bridge in all the world," he grunted flatly.

"Really?" Diane replied, carefully merging into the Brooklyn-bound traffic.

"Every time I've crossed it with him, he never fails to tell me. Like maybe I forgot, or sumpthin'. Jeez, he must really like this damn bridge."

"I think it's everybody's favorite bridge," Diane said. "Don't you?"

"You got a favorite bridge?" Richie asked in mild disbelief, feeling suddenly animated.

"Of course."

"You gonna tell me?" Richie pressed. "Or are you gonna leave me wandering in deep, dark suspense?"

"I guess this is my favorite bridge too," Diane answered. "Then the Verrazano." Taking her eyes off the road for a split second, she turned toward Richie. "What's your favorite bridge?" she asked.

Richie thought for a long moment and realized that he had never considered such a thing. He had favorite bars, favorite foods, and favorite pastimes like fishing, gambling, and pinball, but . . . *favorite bridges?* "I guess I'd have to go with the Pulaski Skyway," he ad-libbed in an unsure growl. He then snorted, shrugged, and quickly reburied his face in the *Racing Form.*

"The what?" Diane rolled her eyes. "Next to the Williamsburg, it's gotta be the ugliest damn bridge in the world. What do you find to be so great about the Pulaski Skyway?"

"I just like it," Marcus said in a tone that signaled end of conversation.

Rechecking the Santa Anita sixth, he saw that the four horse was named Bridge of Sighs. He'd never heard of the three-year-old, but was swept up by a strong hunch. He quickly scratched out *Klimactic Katy* and drew a bold circle around *Bridge of Sighs.* It was a freakin' lock.

Having crossed the East River, Diane ignored the Cadman Plaza exit that led to the back end of Brooklyn Heights and the BQE, and stayed with the straight-through traffic onto Adams Street into downtown Brooklyn. At Tillary, she hung a left. Two minutes later, they parked in front of 370 Jay Street and entered the administrative offices of the New York City Transit Authority.

Harold Borgen, that day's supervisor in the agency's personnel division, was a smiley, likable, soft-spoken type who probably weighed in at near four hundred pounds. His short legs seemed an afterthought beneath the bulk of his mammoth torso, giving him the appearance of a hastily drawn caricature, and his black loafers looked squashed and way too small to support the top-heavy load. He reminded Marcus of the Pillsbury Doughboy after getting whacked by a rolling pin.

"Of course," Borgen opened, leading the two detectives into a large, well-lit room filled with computers. "Virtually everything we have in the way of employee records—going back many years—has now been totally computerized. And if I hit the right button, I can print out countless thousands of names. Surely you can be more specific?"

"About the only thing we can tell you is that he may have been employed by the TA sometime back in the late seventies, after doing a stint in the military," Diane said.

"And may still be employed by the Transit Authority," Borgen suggested with raised brows over incredibly large and round bright blue eyes.

"And may still be," Diane agreed.

"Limiting a search to only those with military service on their records would surely cut down the numbers," Borgen said. "But do you have any idea of what this guy did for us? What department he might have worked in? That would narrow it down much more."

"You mean like motorman . . . or token-booth clerk?" Marcus inquired.

"You mean train operator or station agent?" Borgen corrected.

"Uh . . . right," Marcus replied with a mild grimace. "We really don't know what he did. The thought is, perhaps he worked in some clerical capacity. Truth is, we're not even certain that our man ever worked for the TA. Gotta admit, it's just a very outside shot."

"Hmm," Borgen uttered unhappily, leading them from the computer room into an office-lined hallway. For a morbidly obese man, he moved very well. At the end of the hall, he turned into a small cubicle. "Without a name, or a social security number, or a tax I.D. number, or an employee number, we're kinda dead in the water, Detectives. Don't you know, we're all nothing but numbers in this old world anymore." The man shrugged beefy well-padded shoulders that looked like they could burst through his shirt at any moment. "Wish I could give you better news."

Marcus looked over at DeGennaro. "Looks like we gotta hope the boss can get us something up in Riverdale." Turning back to Borgen, he asked, "If we were to get you a list of names . . . say, maybe a few hundred, how long would it take to run them?"

"If the damn computers aren't down—which they often are—not terribly long. You get me a few hundred names and it will probably take me several hours to confirm if anybody by those names ever worked for us. You get me names *and* numbers, not only can I tell you if that person ever worked for us, I can tell you when he was hired and, if he's no longer with us, I can tell you when and why he was fired, quit, resigned, or retired."

"If he's no longer an employee," Diane asked, "would your records give a last known address?"

"Sure."

"And if he's retired and collecting a pension," Marcus followed up, "your records would then indicate a current address."

"You bet."

The detectives thanked Borgen and returned to their car. Wordlessly, they recrossed the Brooklyn Bridge and headed uptown. When Diane steered off the Drive at Twenty-third Street, she finally broke the silence.

"We've worked a lot of investigations in our time," she said. "And in some of those investigations—mostly the very important ones, mind you—we've had to chase down some pretty thin leads." She turned, faced Marcus, and added fretfully, "But as far as thin leads go, I think this case definitely takes the cake."

Marcus nodded; he felt her frustration. "I wish we had more, too," he said calmingly. "But we don't. So like the boss says, we gotta keep pullin' on the strings we do got."

"Our guy *may* have been in the military," she went on. "Our guy *may* have worked for the Transit Authority. Shit!

For that matter, *our guy* may have been a frigging astronaut, for crissakes, or a goddamned chimney sweep. . . ."

"Ehh, what are you gonna do?" Marcus shrugged. "Sometimes you get the bear. . . . Sometimes the bear gets you. So, where do you wanna go to eat?"

TWENTY-TWO

Thankful for the light Saturday morning traffic, Savage took a slow ride uptown on the well-plowed, -sanded, and -salted FDR Drive. At the very top of Manhattan Island, he crossed the Harlem River into the Bronx and continued north on Broadway through Kingsbridge, into the Fieldston section where Broadway also becomes Route 9. He passed Manhattan College on his left, then went under the Henry Hudson Parkway.

St. Malachy's turned out to be a low-slung, two-story white brick building situated at the end of a winding driveway just off Broadway; not at all what Savage expected to find. It just looked too new, too modern. Surrounded by huge winter-bare maples, oaks, and sycamores, the building sat atop a knoll overlooking Van Cortlandt Park in North Riverdale, a stone's throw from the City line—next stop, Westchester County and Yonkers. Savage hadn't been in this section of the Bronx in many years. Like most other areas of the city, it still looked very much the same as it might have forty years ago. But he knew this St. Malachy's building could not have been here forty years ago.

He parked the Ford in a spot opposite the front of the building, and was immediately approached by a teenage boy in a faded and ill-fitting hooded sweatshirt who had been shoveling snow from a narrow footpath that led down to Broadway.

"Can't park there, man," the kid said boldly, just as Savage stepped from the car. The kid looked cold; his cheeks were windburned and cherry red. His nose was running like a river. There was no joy on this boy's face.

"Okay," Savage replied. "Where *can* I park?"

"Visitors' parking." The kid pointed to an area alongside the building. "The curb bumpers are marked, but you can't see them right now. They're all still covered with snow. I ain't got there yet."

Savage nodded his understanding and slid back behind the wheel.

"You're a cop," the tough-sounding kid said, "aincha?" He wiped his runny nose with the cuff of the sweatshirt.

"And you're a snow-removal engineer," Savage replied with a good-natured grin. "With a side gig of parking lot attendant."

"Yeah, well one day I wanna be a cop too," the erstwhile Bowery boy said, leaning on the shovel handle. "Either that or a fireman."

"That so?" Savage indulged him. "Why's that?"

"They're good jobs. And I could be doin' sumpthin' good."

"How old are you?" Savage asked.

"Seventeen and a half."

"Stay outta trouble, keep your nose clean—no pun intended—and maybe someday you will."

"How much you guys make?" the teenager asked brazenly.

"If I told you, I'd have to kill you." The kid smiled widely. Savage noted that a set of braces could do wonders for his mouthful of badly aligned Chiclets. "What's your name?" he asked.

"Todd. Todd Dalton."

"How long have you been here, Todd?" Savage asked.

"Too fuckin' long," the kid murmured; then speaking up, added, "Since I was eight."

"They treat you good?"

The kid's shrug was noncommittal. He wiped his runny nose again.

"That's nine and a half years," Savage said. "A long time."

"Yeah, well . . ."

"Who's the record holder for time here, now?" Savage asked.

"You mean a kid . . . or one of the staff?"

"Whoever."

"Cyril."

"Cyril?"

"The head cook. Been here forever. Don't know how he freakin' stands it."

"You take care of yourself, Todd," Savage advised with a wink as he started the engine.

"Yeah, you too," Todd replied. He shivered, turned, and headed back toward the sloping footpath. The kid wasn't wearing boots, and his low-cut shoes were sopping wet.

Savage parked the Ford in the visitors' section and entered the building through a double set of heavy glass doors that opened into a large sitting area. The space had a number of typical waiting-room chairs and several chrome-legged black vinyl sofas, flanked by low tables of chrome and glass, which were covered with magazines. Despite its ample size, the room seemed somehow cluttered. Although he saw no one, he heard laughter and adult voices emanating from behind the far wall that had a reception window of opaque glass; it was a slider, and it was closed. There was also a call bell—one of those shiny, round, hotel-desk plunger types. Making no attempt to announce himself, Savage quietly took the opportunity to peruse the dozens of large framed photographs that lined three of the big room's four walls.

One of the long walls was covered with pictures of priests, with their names and the years they served at the orphanage printed boldly beneath. Savage saw that none of the murdered priests' photos were among them. But he also noted that of those priests shown, none had served during the 1960s.

On the opposite long wall were dozens of pictures of St. Malachy's sports teams from years gone by, with ranks of athletic-uniformed boys flanked by their adult coaches and other staff. Some of the photos had printed legends identifying everyone in them. Some did not. The letters *SM* adorned all the boys' baseball caps and basketball jerseys. Some of the more recent photos were in color; the older ones—the ones from the fifties—were in fading black-and-white; some were even cracked with age. None—not even one—of the photos was representative of anything from the 1960s. There was that goddamned gap again.

The largest photo monopolized the short end wall and showed an austere-looking, parapeted, four-story building. The structure reminded Savage of 1313 Mockingbird Lane; the street address of TV's *Munsters*. He felt a chill in his spine, and thought how fortunate he was to have been raised in a warm, loving home by his own loving parents; orphanage life must be hell.

"That's what St. Malachy's once looked like," a voice from over his shoulder said. The tone was soft and feminine. He turned to see a tall, attractive brunette approaching from the reception area. About fifty, she was in great shape. As she neared, he read her name tag: ANNIE TALBOT.

"Yes, I know," he lied. "I remember it from many years ago."

"Oh," she said, cocking her head. "You were a resident?"

"No, no," he replied with real feeling. "I was never a resident." He discerned the I-know-you're-a-cop look written all over Annie Talbot's pretty face. He had to go with it. "I used to play baseball in the CYO . . . the Catholic Youth Organization. We played against St. Malachy's from time to time," he lied. "They usually beat us." He chuckled casually and reached out his hand, wondering where that line of bullshit had come from. "I'm Sergeant Thornton, NYPD," he said, intentionally omitting his last name, "and you're Annie Talbot."

"Yes," the woman replied. She smiled warmly yet somehow defensively as she took his hand. "What is it we can do for you, Sergeant?" she asked. "Are you here to visit or inquire about one of our residents?"

"No," he said. "I need some information, but not about a current resident. Tell me," he said, turning and pointing to the picture of the Victorian haunted house, "whatever became of the old place?"

"Burned to the ground about eight years ago. It was a firetrap, in unbelievably bad condition. Fortunately, no one was killed or seriously hurt, but we lost everything."

"Everything?"

"Well, every record . . . every scrap of paper . . . It was just terrible. We had to start all over again. St. Malachy's has a great history, I'll have you know. But the record of it went up in smoke that awful day."

"You mean if I wanted to trace an old chum that grew up here during, say . . . the sixties?"

"You couldn't. Every last one of those resident rosters was lost."

"Well, wouldn't the archdiocese have copies, backups?" he asked, putting on his best benign-surprised look.

"Back in those days, St. Malachy's was totally self-contained. The archdiocese apparently never saw any need to maintain duplicate files. Of course, since the fire, things have changed."

"Of course."

How convenient, he thought, wordlessly turning to again face the wall-covering collection of team photos.

Right away, Annie Talbot seemed to pick up on what he was thinking. "Many of the pictures you're looking at survived only because the photographer still had copies and negatives," she volunteered, heading off the obvious next question.

"I see," he said, nibbling the inside of his cheek. "How long have you been here, Ms. Talbot?" he asked.

"Fifteen years." Then she asked again, "What is it we can do for you, sir?"

He hated to jerk the lady around, but he was willing to bet that she was ready, willing, and able to jerk him around with rehearsed answers. Too damn much was at stake, he thought as he quickly manufactured a cover story. "I'm with the PAL." he started. "The Police Athletic League."

"How nice." The tenseness he had read in her shoulders seemed to relax slightly.

"We have a terrific young man—twelve years old—who plays on one of our basketball teams. The boy's been raised in a single-parent household since he was born. Unfortunately, his mother is now terminally ill, and he has no other family to turn to. . . . "

"Oh, that's so sad. So he will need to be placed. . . . "

"Precisely. A number of us on the staff at the PAL have banded together to look out for his welfare when the time comes."

"He's a very lucky young man to have such concerned support, Sergeant . . . *Thornton,* was it?"

"Uhh, yes."

"What is the young man's name?" she asked.

"O'Hara," Savage replied, using the most Irish sounding name he could quickly conjure up. "Bobby O'Hara."

"May I ask why you have selected St. Malachy's?"

"Actually, we haven't made any decision as yet. Several other places are also under consideration."

"I see. Come with me," Annie Talbot said. "I'll give you a quick tour of our facility. Then we can sit down and discuss the application and entry process. I'm sure with the backing of the PAL, however, there will be no problem getting the young man accepted here. That is, of course, should you decide—"

"Is the facility still overseen by Christian Brothers and Catholic priests?" Savage asked suddenly.

"No longer," she replied tersely, moving quickly down a long main corridor.

"And why is that?"

"Although St. Malachy's still comes under the umbrella of the New York Archdiocese, it is now completely administered by lay people. Unfortunately, as I'm sure you know, the Church is having great difficulty in keeping at least one ordained priest at every parish. There are actually parishes within the city now that have no priest. It's a shame."

"Could I see the kitchen?" Savage asked.

Annie Talbot glanced over with momentary surprise at the request.

"Just want to see if it's clean," he said.

At the end of the corridor, Talbot swung open the door to a noisy, cafeteria-size kitchen. Stainless steel and aluminum glistened from everywhere. Savage quickly counted six very busy-looking adult men and women, and two equally busy-looking young boys. One boy was walloping pots at a huge double sink, and the second was running a string mop across a spill on the orange quarry-tile floor. Plates were banging, steam was steaming, and a wide-shouldered gray-haired black man, dressed in starched kitchen whites, seemed to be conducting the madness.

"Things are very hectic in here right now," Annie Talbot said, glancing at her watch. "Lunch begins in thirty-five minutes."

A loudspeaker suddenly crackled. *"Ms. Talbot, please come to admin. Ms. Annie Talbot, please come to admin."*

"Come, Sergeant," she said, turning to leave the kitchen.

"Do you think I could trouble the kitchen staff for a cup of coffee?" Savage asked, mashing his hands together. "It was cold as hell out there, and—"

"Why, certainly. *Yoo-hoo,* Cyril," she called to the black man. "Do you have a moment? I'd like you to meet somebody."

Cyril's handshake was as firm as his mahogany eyes were coolly penetrating. And yes, he did have fresh coffee.

"Cyril, would you be good enough to entertain Sergeant Thornton here for a few minutes?" Talbot said. "It seems something has come up in the office." She glanced at Savage apologetically. "I'll be right back," she said, then disappeared quickly through the kitchen's swinging doors.

Cyril handed Savage a thick china cup and matching saucer. "Decaf or regular?" he asked, sounding annoyed.

"High test," Savage replied, holding up the heavy cup as the kitchen boss poured from a Proctor Silex pot. "Terrific institution, St. Malachy's," he said. "How long have you been here, Cyril?"

"Started here as kitchen help forty-some years ago. Just what brings you here, Sergeant?" Cyril asked, his tone now mildly suspicious.

"Just looking the place over. We have a young man we may wish to place here."

Cyril locked eyes. "That a fact?" he said, disbelief riding high on his words.

"You thinkin' I might be here for some other reason?" Savage asked. He took a careful sip of the steaming brew while maintaining tight eye contact.

"I thought that was a possibility," Cyril said, glancing away self-consciously. "We just don't see police officers here that much."

"That a fact?" Savage said, trying to hold Cyril's evasive glance. The man was spooked, defensive. And unless Savage missed his guess, sweet Annie Talbot was now frantically dialing the diocese for guidance on how to deal with the surprise police visit. "You been reading the newspapers lately? Listening to TV?" Savage asked, making his move on perhaps the only person in the building who could really help him.

"I read the papers."

"Does the name Father Thomas Gilhooley or Father Darwin Clapp somehow ring a bell with you?"

Long pause. "Not really," the man finally said with a soft shrug, still avoiding Savage's eyes.

"Of course they sound familiar," Savage pressed. "They were both murdered within the last week—you know that—and both used to work here at St. Malachy's back in the sixties, isn't that right, Cyril?"

Cyril made a face and shrugged, then snapped an order at the kid with the mop. Turning back to Savage, he said, "I gotta get to work. Gotta get lunch up in ten minutes."

"According to my watch, you still have thirty minutes."

Cyril stood, stone-faced.

"Can I take your silence as a yes?" Savage asked.

"All right, so maybe I knew them."

"They worked here?"

"Yeah."

"So did a priest by the name of Father Peter Grennan. Am I right?"

"Yes."

"And another priest by the name of Killian Flaherty."

"Uh-huh."

"They all worked here about the same time, midsixties."

"Yeah."

"They're *all* dead now," Savage said, leaning into Cyril's face. "Three murdered, one suicide. And it all comes back to good old St. Malachy's Home for Boys, doesn't it?"

Cyril remained mute, but dew was forming above his thick upper lip.

"Talk to me, Cyril," Savage murmured softly, pressing him.

The black man's eyes flashed nervously toward the kitchen door. "This is my job," he whispered strongly. "The only damn one I've ever had. I can't afford to go losing it; I'm too damn old to be thinkin' about looking for a new one. Y'unnerstan' what I'm talkin' about . . . *Sergeant*?"

Savage empathized. Cyril was clearly stuck between the proverbial rock and the hard place, but people were dying and he could hold the key to the riddle. "You gotta talk to me, Cyril. We can do this one of two ways. . . ."

"Not here. Not now." The big man wiped away a bead of sweat that raced down his puffy face.

"It's gonna have to be now."

"You want something from me, it's gotta be on my terms."

"Okay. Where and when? And it better be soon."

"I get out of here right after dinner," the man stammered nervously. "Say, six thirty by the Van Cortlandt Mansion and Museum."

The kitchen IN door swung open and Annie Talbot made a forceful reappearance. Savage noted the concerned look she flashed toward Cyril.

"Well," she said, "shall we be moving on, Sergeant? There's so much more to show you."

"Good coffee, Cyril. Thanks," Savage said, placing the half-empty cup on a stainless counter.

"Don't mention it."

The remainder of the tour was a pas de deux of playacting. Savage continued to play his role, and so did Annie Talbot. At the conclusion of the tour, Savage revisited the gallery of pictures in the waiting room off the lobby. The photographer's imprimatur at the lower left corner of one of the baseball team shots from the late fifties, and another from the early seventies, read J. C. COMBES, WHITE PLAINS ROAD."

Savage soon discovered that J. C. Combes, photographer, was no longer at the White Plains Road address. The sign in the window announced a recent move to Baychester Avenue, in the Wakefield section. When Savage got there, he found that it was no longer simply J. C. Combes. It was now J. C. COMBES AND SON PHOTOGRAPHIC ASSOCIATES, SPECIALIZING IN PRECIOUS MOMENTS IN TIME FOR OVER SEVENTY YEARS. Well, la-de-dah, he thought, letting himself into the spotlessly clean, brand-new studio.

John C. Combes—junior—was a wavy-haired gent somewhere in his sixth decade of life. Very tall, thin, and heavily wrinkled, his extreme gauntness was accentuated by the relative prominence of large facial features. A peculiar sort, he wore a floppy nineteenth-century-style black bow tie over a loose-fitting, ruffled white shirt. He had a large mole on his right cheek, and Savage visualized him with chin whiskers, a stovepipe hat, and his right arm tucked beneath his left lapel. Mr. Combes bore some resemblance to the dude on the five-dollar bill. He also turned out to be a very gentle, friendly, accommodating man.

"It's been many years since we did any work for St. Malachy's," Combes said. "Probably the last thing we did was back somewhere in the eighties. Which type photos are you looking for?"

"What I'd really like are individual head shots of each and every kid who was a resident there during the sixties, along with a name to go with the picture."

"Yearbook type?"

"That'd make my day," Savage said.

"We don't have any. The orphanage never sprung for individual portraits. The diocese used to pressure my old man to donate his time and material to do it, but . . ."

"How about their athletic-team portraits?" Savage asked. "More specifically, those wide-angle shots that identified everybody in them; you know, left to right, seated, first row, second row . . . Is it possible you have any on file from that long ago?"

"Not sure," J. C. Combes Jr. replied, his brows scrunched in a pondering frown. "I haven't been anywhere near those files for years."

"Look," Savage pressed. "I know without question that your company did those type photos for the orphanage during the fifties and seventies—I've actually seen some of them—but what about the period in the middle? The 1960s?"

"My old man did all of St. Malachy's work back in those years. If he took the damn pictures, then I assure you we will have negatives of them."

"Terrific."

"Pop was from the old school; never threw any photo work away. He kept impeccable records. Today, most photographers purge their negative files every five years. I'm just like he was; I keep them forever. When do you need this stuff?"

"Now."

The ectomorph's eyes popped wide. "Look," he said apologetically, "we just moved our entire operation into this location a week ago. I've got seventy years' worth of work packed in boxes in the back room. Then, when I find it—if I find it—I've got to scan the negatives on a computer or print them up in the darkroom; either way, that's going to take at least several more hours. The best I can hope to do for you would be tomorrow sometime, and that's really pushing it."

"Here's my card," Savage said. "Call me at that number as soon as they're ready. Someone will come right over to pick them up." As he left the photo shop, strains of "The Battle Hymn of the Republic" played in his head.

Darkness had set in more than an hour ago, and the temperature in the Bronx had fallen at least ten degrees. Savage figured it was now somewhere in the midteens. Despite the cold, he waited patiently outside of 7146, his back against the driver's door and his arms folded across his chest. He wondered if Ray had made it home yet; he also wondered if the scruffy tom was even still alive. He wondered too if Maureen was ever going to reinvite him to dinner. The thought of her home-cooked pasties made him hungry. He dug a Wint-O-Green from his pocket, popped it into his mouth, and let it dissolve slowly, savoring it. Damn, it was cold.

At six thirty, a faded red Oldsmobile sedan with lots of

minor body damage along its entire left side drove into the parking lot of the Van Cortlandt Mansion and Museum. The car pulled into the spot right next to his and shut down, silencing its noisy exhaust. Still dressed in his kitchen whites beneath a blue quilted ski parka, Cyril the cook stepped out. He was chewing on the stub of an unlit cigar. He wasn't smiling.

"All right, I'm here," he said, without preamble. "What is it you want to know?"

"What happened at St. Malachy's back in the sixties?" Savage said, uncrossing his arms and standing tall. He looked deeply into Cyril's large eyes; they reflected resistance.

"Whaddaya mean?"

"I mean, it's becoming abundantly clear to me that something catastrophic, something the archdiocese is going very much out of their way to conceal, occurred at St. Malachy's sometime in the mid-1960s. I want to know what it was."

"What makes you think I would know whatever you're talkin' about?" the big man asked, chewing nervously on the half-smoked stogie.

"Because I know you do."

"How do you know?"

"I read it all over your face, Cyril. I watched you sweat."

Cyril's glance fell away as he removed the cigar from his mouth. He bit nervously at his thick lower lip. "It all happened a long time ago," he said. "Why can't we just leave it rest?"

"It all happened a long time ago, all right, but whatever it was is back with a vengeance. That's why we can't let it rest."

The cook dug a plastic lighter out of his jacket pocket and put a flame to the cigar stub. He inhaled deeply, then exhaled hard. His bulging brown eyes looked back at Savage.

"A kid died. Killed his self."

"Okay. Tell me more."

"There been a rumor goin' around here for years that the kid was gang-raped by some of the priests one night. Next day he took a dive from the fucking rooftop."

"Un-huh. When did this happen?"

"Sixty four. October."

"You sound awfully sure of that."

"Yankees was playing St. Louis in the World Series," Cyril said with no hesitation. "So happens, the day the kid died, Gibson had come off two days' rest and kicked the Yankees' ass in game seven."

"What was the kid's name?"

"Don't remember. Honest to God, I don't." Cyril squinted in thought. "It was a long, unusual-sounding name."

"Irish, Polish, Italian?"

"I don't remember."

"All right," Savage said. "If it was suicide, there'll be a police record of it."

"There ain't no damn record," Cyril replied with a get-real snicker. "The archdiocese got one of their stooge doctors to certify that the kid died from pneumonia. The whole thing was totally hushed up. They even managed to keep it out of the press." Cyril took the cigar from his mouth, turned away, and spit a fleck of tobacco onto the asphalt.

"How'd they get away with that?"

"The very long arm of the archdiocese in them days, you might say."

"How come you and others have stayed quiet all these years?"

"Where would be our proof?" Cyril argued. "An MD certified the cause of death, and the kid's body was immediately cremated—which in them days was against Church rules. No way nobody was gonna stand up to the Church. Not in this damn town. Not in them damn days."

"What about my four priests?" Savage asked. "Grennan, Flaherty, Gilhooley, and Clapp? To the best of your knowledge, were they all involved in the rumored gang rape of this kid?"

"I'm not sure," Cyril said, looking down and shaking his head. "But two weeks after all this shit happened, they all got their asses transferred out of St. Malachy's. You know, one went here, one went there—not fired, mind you—just *fuckin' transferred*."

"Jesus."

"Jesus ain't got a goddamned thing to do with it," Cyril offered, a grimace straining his big brown face. "Men. Just men who sometimes *think* they're freakin' Jesus." He spit another fleck to the ground.

Savage stared deeply into the aging cook's eyes. He saw something lurking there. "I've got a strong feeling you've got more to tell me," he said.

"You're very perceptive, Sergeant," Cyril replied, flicking the smoked-to-death cigar butt into the thick hedgerow that edged the parking lot.

"Let's have it."

"Unless he's already dead by natural causes, there's one more priest out there."

This was music to Savage's ears. "Please tell me exactly how you know that."

"Because there was five priests immediately transferred, not just four."

"What was the fifth guy's name?"

"Quigley. Father Hugh Quigley. I remember him bein' probably the nicest one of the bunch. Last I heard, he was out of the priesthood, though. Doin' odd jobs."

"Odd jobs like what?"

"First I heard he was doing some interior house painting. Then he was working at the Waldorf, as what I don't know. Last I heard he was driving a damn cab."

"A yellow cab?"

"Nah. He started his own one-man operation. Bought

his self a used limousine. He don't cruise for no fares, he just goes out on private calls."

"A *limo* service, you say?" Savage intoned thoughtfully, piqued by the revelation. "This limo service, has it got a name?"

"I'm sure it does. . . . But I'll be damned if I know what it is."

Recalling the phone number of Allied Cars found by Diane DeGennaro on Father Flaherty's nightstand, Savage wondered if there could possibly be some connection. Something told him there was. There had to be; it just felt right.

Savage gave Cyril his card, got back in his car, and put the heater on high. So far, all the leads in this case had led only to mounds of paperwork and a lot of wheel spinning. But this lead was different; this lead revolved around a possibly still-warm body who had been at the center of things—someone with answers.

The string was getting stronger and stronger.

TWENTY-THREE

The Sunday afternoon traffic on the Grand Central Parkway was light to moderate as Hugh Quigley guided the highly polished sedan past the Flushing Meadows site of New York's two World's Fairs. He hadn't gone to the one in '39; hell, he was only a toddler then. But he did get to visit the 1964–65 exposition several times.

"Peace Through Understanding" had been the high-flown motto of that World's Fair. What a laugh, he thought. In all the intervening years, the hapless human race couldn't seem to find either. People all over the globe were still fighting and dying; Jew versus Muslim, Catholic versus Protestant, Shiite versus Sunni, Hindu versus Sikh, and more; all in the name of God, or Jesus, or Allah, or Buddha, or some fucking water buffalo. And to think, I was once a man of the cloth. He sighed deeply, squirmed in his seat, and took a long, studied glance in his rearview mirror.

He'd attended the World's Fair with Tommy Gilhooley in '64 when it first opened, but terrible rainstorms had ruined their day. In '65 he'd gone with Killian Flaherty. He remembered they'd taken the subway out to Flushing. That had been a beautiful day; he was young, fit, and healthy, without a care in the world. Now Tommy Gilhooley had been shot to death right in his own church, and Killian had taken his own life. The two deaths by themselves could have been coincidence, but when Darwin Clapp was murdered outside Grand Central Terminal, and shortly thereafter the news of Peter Grennan's slaying in Boston was reported . . . well. Somehow, the killing of that Father Brodeur down in Lower Manhattan didn't fit into the equation.

"I never cease to be amazed by the Unisphere," the lone woman passenger in the backseat said. Mrs. Farace, a longtime regular customer, was looking out the window at the 900,000-pound, 140-foot-high globe of the world that had been built by U.S. Steel and had been the centerpiece of the last fair.

"Me too," Quigley said tersely. He didn't want to offend the attractive widow by sounding disinterested, but he was busy studying every image reflected in his rear- and side-view mirrors.

"It's one of the few things that still remains, you know," she continued. "Most everything else has been torn down, or, like the poor New York State Pavilion, fallen pretty much into a terrible state of ruin. That Landmarks Preservation Commission is just a joke, that's what it is. A bunch of goddamned *stunads*."

"Yeah, right . . . *stunads!*" Quigley repeated, not really knowing the true meaning of the Italian slang, although he suspected it meant something on the order of asshole.

"Did you know the Unisphere's size was designed to show what the earth would actually look like from six thousand miles in space?" she asked.

"That right?" he mumbled in a preoccupied monotone. He was dying to turn the radio on to hear the latest news. It might even help shut the woman up.

"Are you all right, Hugh?" Mrs. Farace asked bluntly.

"Yes, I'm fine," he replied, again squirming in his seat. "Why do you ask?"

"Well, you just don't seem to be your usual talkative self today, that's all. And that sigh you let out a minute ago was straight from hell."

"Maybe you're right, ma'am," he admitted. "Maybe I

am a little under the weather today." If she only knew, he thought.

As Shea Stadium came into view, he checked his watch; it was ten minutes after one. Mrs. Farace had a two fifty flight to Florida and needed an hour and a half check-in time at LaGuardia; he'd have her there in plenty of time. His next call wasn't until two o'clock, a round tripper from Long Island City to Middle Village and back—a cemetery run. The fare was a first-time client, and Quigley wanted to make a good first impression by being punctual.

"I just cannot wait to get myself into that warm Florida sun," the persistent passenger said. "I've had just about as much winter as I can stand."

I know how you feel, he thought. "We've still got three more months of winter to go, Mrs. F," he replied. "How long do you intend to be away?"

"Not long enough," the woman said in disgust. "I should be back around the fifteenth of February. I'll call you about a week ahead and let you know what time my return flight will be arriving."

"Very good, ma'am." Quigley declined to mention the pending sale of the business, just in case it didn't go through, although he didn't want to even think about that as a possibility.

The Cadillac cruised past the World's Fair Marina at the foot of Flushing Bay and exited the parkway at LaGuardia Airport. Quigley pulled to a stop at the U.S. Airways departure terminal, stepped around, and opened the rear door for his fare, then lifted her three pieces of luggage from the trunk and set them on the sidewalk before a waiting sky-cap. She handed him a twenty for the fifteen-dollar ride and told him to keep the change.

"Enjoy your trip, Mrs. Farace," he said, pinching the brim of his black cap. Preoccupied with getting her proper baggage checks, the woman ignored him. Disgruntled, he got back behind the wheel and drove off. At the red light at

Ninety-fourth Street and Astoria Boulevard, he picked up his cell phone and dialed his answering service.

"Allied Cars."

"Hey, Deborah, Hugh Quigley here. Any calls?"

"Nothing, Mr. Quigley. The only call we've had all day was that two o'clock Long Island City–to–St. John's Cemetery, which we already booked."

"Thank God," Quigley said. "If you get any more calls, tell them I'm booked for the day. Flip the work over to Charlie Greenspan, if he wants it. Don't even try to reach me; I'm really beat. After the two o'clock run, I'm heading home to crash. What was that fare's name again?"

"St. Michel."

The light went green, and Quigley goosed the gas. He had an hour to kill; time enough to get a quick grilled cheese and soup. It was Sunday, probably chicken and rice at the Neptune Diner. Then he'd head to Long Island City. The fare to Middle Village and back would surely kill off the rest of his day, especially if they dillydallied around at a couple of different grave sites like most people tended to do. He hoped they wouldn't; he was tired, worn out after several sleepless nights. His heart raced as he glanced again at the headline of the Sunday *Post* on the seat next to him.

NEW LETTER FROM THE SOLDIER
DEAD PRIEST TALLY NOW STANDS AT FIVE.

Of the five dead priests, he'd known four—three of them intimately. This whole damn Soldier thing had become too much of a fucking coincidence, he thought, shaking his head and exhaling hard. Whoever this Soldier son of a bitch was, Quigley knew he was on his god-awful hit list. He could feel it. Ever since reading about Darwin Clapp getting killed on Christmas morning, he'd begun to imagine booted footsteps coming up behind him. His clammy hands wrung the Cadillac's leather-wrapped steering wheel as he quickly checked the mirrors again. Turning the radio on, he tuned it to WINS for any late-breaking news; maybe they'd caught that Soldier bastard. He closed his eyes for just a moment and prayed.

Another week and he'd be out of this city for good, safe in his own condo in Fort Lauderdale. God, he couldn't wait, but for the next five days, he'd be sure to have eyes in the back of his head.

First thing Sunday morning, Savage had assigned Jack Lindstrom to the Allied Cars question and its possible connection to onetime St. Malachy's priest Hugh Quigley. It might be a long shot, but they were well overdue for a break. Lindstrom, appearing far more focused than he had been of late, went right to work like a pit bull sinking its teeth into the mailman's argyles. By one fifteen the detective was back in the sergeants' room with all kinds of answers.

"Taxicab and Limousine says that Allied Cars is licensed to and operated by one Hugh Quigley," Lindstrom said, a sly smile slipping across his face.

Savage pushed away from his desk, rose, and leaned out of the cramped office's doorway. He called to Marcus and DeGennaro, who were at their desks in the squad room. "Richie . . . Diane . . . Got a minute?"

"It's a one-man operation," Lindstrom continued, as the two other detectives joined the huddle. "Probably works right out of his residence. Turns out that the phone number Diane found on Flaherty's nightstand the morning of his suicide is, in fact, Quigley's business line."

"When I dialed it that day I got a woman's voice at Allied Cars' answering service," Diane said. "Since Flaherty's death was clearly a suicide, I didn't think much of it. It was basically just a cab company phone number."

"I just called them too," Lindstrom announced. "The woman I spoke with identified the name of the company as Metropolitan Answering Service, Steinway Street in Astoria. On the outside shot that Quigley could be the Soldier,

I made no reference to him or Allied Cars. I didn't want to raise him up."

"How about a residence line?" Savage asked.

"Went through our good friend Patti Capwell over at Telephone Security. Told her this was top priority. She got right on it and got his unlisted residence line and his home address. He lives out in Maspeth."

Lindstrom handed his neatly transcribed notes to Savage. Savage turned them immediately over to Richie Marcus. "You and Diane get right out there. Hook up with Emergency Service for backup, squat on his residence, find him, and let's get him in here."

"Backup? Are you really thinking it's possible that this guy Quigley could be the Soldier?" Marcus asked.

"Why not?" Diane piped in. "He is the only one of the five St. Malachy's fallen angels who's still standing."

"Maybe they were all subscribers to a tontine," Lindstrom offered, glancing at—and bait casting—Marcus.

"A *what?*" Marcus asked; his ruggedly handsome face was distorted into a clueless question mark.

"An annuity scheme," Lindstrom explained condescendingly, "in which subscribers share a common fund with the benefit of survivorship, the survivors' shares being increased as the subscribers die, until the whole goes to the last survivor. It's sort of a *thinking man's* form of gambling. . . ."

Probably wondering whether or not he was being put on, Marcus glared blankly at Lindstrom. After a long second and a dismissive sneer, he turned back to Savage. "And what if Quigley is not the Soldier?"

"Then he might be living on borrowed time," Savage replied.

"If that's the case," Marcus said, "maybe we should go through his answering service, have them contact him, and alert him to come on in on his own ASAP."

Savage grimaced and sat back down at his desk. "Harvey Wallbanger's profile notwithstanding, we cannot say with absolute certainty that Quigley is not the Soldier. We can't; we just don't know enough yet. That's why I want the backup when you go for Quigley. Better to have and not need than to need and not have."

"Hell, he does fit right into the puzzle, though," Marcus acknowledged. "He could be the Soldier, or he could be the Soldier's next goddamned victim. He's pretty much got to be one or the other."

"Good bet, hah, Richie?" Lindstrom uttered, rolling his eyes. Turning to Savage, he continued. "If Quigley's not the Soldier, and if he hasn't been living in a cave for the past week with no radio, TV, or newspapers, you'd think he'd have come forward looking for protection by now."

"Yeah. But if he did that," Savage responded. "He'd almost have to open the nasty St. Malachy's can of worms that's been on the shelf for forty-some years."

"Thereby implicating himself in that whole goddamned mess," Diane inserted.

"Afraid old Father Quigley's pretty much got himself locked in between the rock and the hard place," Lindstrom mused.

"We'll have to play it both ways," Savage declared. "Jack and I will head right out to the answering service in Astoria and get whatever information we can." He turned to Marcus and DeGennaro. "Get over to Quigley's residence. Have an Emergency Service truck 10-85 you there for backup. If Quigley's at home, fine; bring him in. If he's not there, reach me immediately on my cell phone. We'll decide then what the next step will be."

"Sergeant Savage," Eddie Brodigan called out from the wheel. "Pick up on twenty-three. It's some guy by the name of J. C. Combes. He said you were expecting his call."

"Stand by, Jack," Savage said to Lindstrom, as Marcus and DeGennaro left the room and headed for their coats. "Possible change of plans. Instead of going with me to As-

toria, you may have to take a quick ride up to the Bronx instead." He reached for the phone.

"Sorry I didn't get back to you sooner, as promised,"
J. C. Combes said apologetically. "But I had to work well
into the night just to locate the damn negatives. Wouldn't
you know, the boxes I finally found them in were completely mismarked. I'll have you know that's not at all like
me."

"How did we do?" Savage asked.

"I think we did very well. I think you'll be pleased. I've
got thirty-seven portrait-size photographs of various St.
Malachy's athletic teams from 1961 to 1970. On top of
that, I also came across a half-dozen photos of the St.
Malachy's debating teams of that era."

"Names?" Savage intoned hopefully.

"We've got all kinds of names, Sergeant. Most all of the
portraits included a list of those appearing in the photo and
their position within the pose. I told you my old man was
a detail freak."

"God bless him," Savage said. "It's clear that J. C.
Combes and Co. does very exceptional work." Half in jest,
he added, "I'll be sure to spread the word to all my friends
and family."

"Give me another half hour and I'll have everything
ready for you to pick up. . . ."

"I've got a man on the way now." Savage nodded to
Jack Lindstrom, who was already buttoning his topcoat.

At precisely two p.m., Hugh Quigley brought the big
Cadillac to a stop in front of the Queens Bridge Houses on
Forty-first Street, just off Vernon Boulevard, and collected
his Middle Village fare. They were, to say the least, a
strange-looking pair. Aside from an outrageous long blond
wig that just didn't suit her at all, the woman was a real
plain Jane. No makeup, no nothing. The man—Mr. St.
Michel—didn't look well; he was pale, very pale, and he
had those skinny oxygen tubes connected to his hooked

beak of a nose. It was then that Quigley recognized Mr. St. Michel. He was that odd little man he'd been running into lately at the Neptune Diner; the one who offered him a C-note to drive him into Manhattan the day of the snowstorm.

"I'm sorry," the woman said straight off. "We misinformed your office when we booked you earlier today. We had said we wanted to go to St. John's Cemetery over in Middle Village. Our mistake; we really need to go to St. Raymond's Cemetery up in the Bronx. Is that going to be a problem for you?"

"Not at all, ma'am," Quigley replied, forcing good humor. Annoyed by the much longer trip, he wondered how stupid people like these managed to get through life.

"Do you know the location of St. Raymond's Cemetery?" the woman said. "It's up in the Bronx, just over the Whitestone Bridge."

"Are you going to the new St. Raymond's or the old St. Raymond's?" Quigley asked, expecting that they probably wouldn't know.

"The old one."

"I'm acquainted with it, ma'am," Quigley replied courteously. He laughed to himself. If only they knew how many burials he'd officiated at there when he was in the priesthood.

"Well, that's where we're going," she snapped. "We're going to visit the grave of an old acquaintance of my husband's."

"Will you be visiting just one grave, ma'am?" he asked.

"Just one."

"I see, ma'am," Quigley said, delighted but not showing it. "Sort of a Christmas visit, I suppose."

"Yes. That's exactly what it is," she replied with an ironic chuckle. "A surprise Christmas visit."

TWENTY-FOUR

Before heading out of the Manhattan South office to go knock on Hugh Quigley's door in Queens County, Detectives DeGennaro and Marcus contacted the Emergency Service Unit and arranged for backup. They agreed to meet an ESS team at Herbie's Shell on Sixty-ninth Street in Maspeth, not far from the Quigley residence. Emergency Service cops were the ones who scaled bridge cables to rescue would-be jumpers, or crawled under jacked-up subway cars to fetch the gruesome bits and pieces of "train jobs." They were also the department SWAT unit; the first in when some asshole with a death wish and an AK-47 was barricaded and "not coming out alive." Emergency Service was easily the toughest job in The Job, requiring the biggest and brassiest balls. They *really* earned their pay, Diane thought.

When they arrived at the busy gas station at 1400 hours, Sergeant Phil Penkowski and his three-man flakjacketed crew from Truck 10 were already there, standing by. Despite the years, a few additional pounds, and a thick black mustache, Diane immediately recognized Penkowski; she'd gone through the academy with him years ago. She recalled his putting more than one romantic hit on her there. Still married then, albeit very unhappily, she'd declined. But she had thought about it.

"*Diane,*" Sergeant Penkowski said, beaming as he strutted over to the Taurus. He leaned his broad-shouldered bulk right into her open passenger's-side window. "How've you been? Saw in the orders you made first grade a few years ago. Congratulations." He reached into the car and shook her hand, maintaining the physical connection a few beats longer than necessary.

"Thanks, Phil," she replied amiably, pulling her hand back into her lap. "I see you made boss. That's great." Aiming her left thumb at Richie, she added, "Like you to meet my very *longtime* partner, Richie Marcus."

Penkowski grunted a cursory acknowledgement of Richie's presence, but his large, deep-set brown eyes never left hers.

"Sure has been a while, Di," the sergeant schmoozed, overly friendly, overly familiar, and obviously not picking up on her emphasized *longtime* cue.

"Yeah," she replied casually, her gears spinning, concentrating on how best to handle the apparently still-horny Penkowski before Richie got the wrong idea. But unless she missed her guess, her longtime partner—both on and off The Job—had already gotten the wrong idea.

"The guy's residence is the third one off the corner in the sixty-seven-hundred block of Clinton Avenue, number 67-06," Richie announced firmly, an edge slowly emerging in his voice. "Whaddaya say we get this show on the road, eh?"

"Relax," Penkowski said dismissively. "Just taking a minute to renew a *very special* old acquaintance here."

Marcus cleared his throat and sucked noisily on an incisor.

Despite the heater being full on, Diane felt the ambient temperature inside the car drop about fifty degrees, and it had nothing to do with the December chill filtering in through her wide-open window. The frosty feeling now gathering inside the car was a recurring phenomenon. Whenever Richie's fear of rivalry or his jealousy gland opened, everything around him rimed over.

"Not too sure of what we're going to find there, Sarge," Diane said evenly to the Emergency Service boss, who had a rack of ribbons above his gold shield. "This guy might not even be home."

"We did a real quick ride-by; didn't see much sign of life," Marcus growled.

Without even looking at Marcus, Penkowski answered him with a curt "We'll find out." Then, addressing Diane in a lighthearted, devil-may-care tone, he added, "I understand we're here to find either a former Catholic priest who now drives a limo or a former Catholic priest who now drives a limo and likes to shoot people."

"That's about it," Marcus spoke up, the surly edge on his tough-guy Brooklyn growl now honed for battle. "The latter is a very outside possibility, but if we're wrong, this guy is pretty handy with a forty-five."

Diane could see the carotid in Richie's thick neck pulsing.

"That's okay. That's why you invited us along," Penkowski asserted cockily, giving Marcus a derisive stare. "When we make the approach, I want you to go with two of my guys and immediately cover any rear exits. You got that . . . *Marcus?*"

"Yeah . . . I got it."

Glancing warmly at Diane, Penkowski continued, "When we get there, you come with me and my extra man; we'll take the front door." After skipping only a half-beat, he added, "So, I heard you got divorced."

"Oh, that was a long time ago," she replied demurely, doing her best to remain friendly but in no way encouraging. She needed this guy's hard-hitting attention right now like she needed impetigo. "But I've been involved with—"

"Not for nuthin', Sarge," Marcus growled, slapping the car's gearshift lever into drive. "But if you're backin' us up, whaddaya say—let's do it, okay?" Marcus inched the car forward, leaving the startled superior officer no choice but to stand away.

"Asshole's either arrogant or stupid," Marcus snarled, talking to himself. "No," he amended, "that freakin' dildo is both!"

"Richie!" Diane hissed through gritted teeth, as the car continued to roll. "Stop acting like a goddamned jerk." Turning away, she called out the window to Penkowski, "There's no limo parked there right now, Sarge; either in front of the location or in the side driveway. If it's not in the garage in back, this could very well be a dry run."

"And," Marcus called out, just a hair short of insubordinate, "we got no warrant, so we're not here to kick in any fuckin' doors if we don't get no answer. *Capisce?*"

"All right, let's get this over with," Penkowski announced, somewhere between startled and annoyed. Pointing a thick index finger at Diane, he added, "I'll give you a call sometime and we'll go have a drink." Then, looking at Marcus, he said, "Okay, we'll follow you."

"Damn right, you'll follow me," Marcus sneered under his breath, pulling out onto Sixty-ninth Street. Several moments later, the big Emergency Service diesel rig, with its crew of four, fell in behind.

Here it comes, Diane thought, as Marcus snorted and cleared his throat nervously. He adjusted the rearview, reset the heater controls, and shifted around, antsy as a dog with fleas.

"Never knew you had a thing for freakin' Polacks," he finally blurted, steering the Taurus into the Clinton Avenue turn at a speed greater than he should have been traveling.

Diane rolled her eyes. "You're just having a bad day, Rich," she said evenly, despite her aggravation. She'd been here before; this jealousy business would just have to blow over. It always did, but right now she wanted to give him a poke.

Having overheard him on the phone with his bookmaker that morning, she couldn't resist setting the hook. "I'm sure you'd be in a better mood if you'd stayed with Klimactic Katy yesterday instead of switching off to that fugitive from a glue factory. What was its name—Bridge of Sighs?"

Marcus turned, glared icily at her, and bit down on his

upper lip. "Long time no see, *Di*," he mimicked. "Heard you got divorced, *Di*. We'll go have a drink, *Di*."

"Shut up, Richie."

"Wanna sit on my face, Di?"

With the peculiar-looking and oddly nontalkative couple in the backseat, Hugh Quigley ran Twenty-first Street from Long Island City into Astoria, where he picked up the entrance to the Triborough Bridge. Traffic was very light to moderate, thank goodness; the aftereffects and icy remnants of last week's storm were still keeping people, especially the annoying Sunday drivers and out-of-towners who never knew where the hell they were going, off the highways. Quigley crossed the main span and had just paid the four-dollar toll when his cell phone began to ring. He eyeballed the calling number. It was the damn answering service. Dammit, he thought, as they crossed the Bronx Kills span, he had specifically told that jerky woman not to bother calling him again today. But she never listened. Quigley clicked the ringer off and dropped the cell phone back onto the seat.

He drove eastbound on the Bruckner Expressway while his passengers sat in stiff and stony silence, which suited him just fine. He often tried to make small talk with his fares, but not today; there was just too much bullshit bouncing around inside his head. He sensed something, or someone, stalking him, a constant presence hovering nearby, waiting for the right moment to strike—to do what, he did not want to know. He felt it in his bones and in the back of his neck; it was either paranoia or ESP. Quigley swallowed dryly, studying his rear- and side-view mirrors. Then, one at a time, he wiped his sweaty open palms along the top of his trouser legs, but the dewy dampness immediately returned.

Quigley had never believed in extrasensory perception or telepathy or clairvoyance. It was all just a bunch of hokum generated by soothsayers, sages, and ball-gazing gypsies. But then, he'd never experienced anything like this all-consuming feeling of dread.

Seven minutes later, he steered off the Bruckner onto East Tremont Avenue and brought the bulky Cadillac through the open gates of St. Raymond's Roman Catholic Cemetery.

Mr. St. Michel spoke at last. "Make a right at the second cut and follow that road all the way around to where it ends. I'll tell you where to stop."

Quigley nodded and slowly followed the narrow and circuitous lane as it wound its way past thousands of headstones. Much like the traffic on the highways, there were very few visitors at St. Raymond's today, and none at all within view when they reached the cemetery's westernmost edge. Just beyond the fence, he could see traffic moving on the Hutchinson River Parkway.

"Pull over right here," the man in back directed. Quigley pulled to the side of the narrow lane and stopped.

"Shut the engine off, and hand me the keys," the woman said firmly.

"Excuse me?" Quigley uttered in disbelief. He turned in his seat to stare into the muzzle of a huge pistol in the man's gloved right hand.

Fear raced up his spine and out to every extremity; his toes, his fingers.

"Do exactly what she tells you," the man said in his breathy voice.

Quigley turned off the car's motor. Hands shaking almost uncontrollably, he dropped the ring of keys into the woman's outstretched gloved hand. "What do you want from me?" he asked, his voice quavering.

"We've brought you here to discuss the current sorry state of the Roman Catholic Church, and how it has been sullied by the acts of some of its priests," she said. "You know, like those degenerates Father Gilhooley, Father Grennan, Father Flaherty, Father Clapp . . ."

"They have all been dispatched for the Lord's judgment," the man said. "Now it's time for you to face your maker and answer for your sins."

The statement hit Quigley like a barreling crosstown bus. He thought he might wet himself; he fought to control the sphincter of his bladder.

"What is this?" He choked out the question, knowing damn well what it was but praying to God that he was wrong . . . or dreaming.

"Do you know who I am?" the man said softly, then let out a series of dry coughs.

"No . . . I—I don't know," Quigley lied. He had no doubt that he was looking at the Soldier. "Who . . . who are you?" he asked, stumbling over the words. His breaths were coming shallow and short; he was near hyperventilating.

"Father Gilhooley remembered me," the man said. "Well, not at first, actually"—*cough—cough*—"but during our brief conversation in his confessional, recognition did finally set in."

"You killed Father Gilhooley?" Quigley said.

"*We* killed Father Gilhooley," the woman interjected coldly. "I must tell you that he did not die very well. It wasn't a pretty picture."

"Are you afraid to die, Mr. Quigley?" the man with the pistol said. "Or perhaps I should be calling you *Father* Quigley? Would you like that better? Would that be more appropriate?"

"To be more specific, Father *Hugh* Quigley from St. Malachy's Home for Boys," the woman snarled.

"*Why?*" Quigley managed to utter, his heart pounding in his chest, his mouth gone cottony. "Why are you doing this?" He felt a tear race down his cheek.

The man and woman looked back and forth at one another, as if deciding what to say or do. Finally, the man spoke, his tone an unforgiving blast of incredulity.

"You want to know *why?*" he said.

"Calm down, John Wesley. We've got time," the

woman piped in, patting the man's knee reassuringly. Facing Quigley, she added, "And you're going to listen, Father Quigley, because"—her eyes narrowed with malignant satisfaction—"what the hell else can you do?"

John Wesley . . . John Wesley. It sounded so familiar. Hugh Quigley's mind streaked off in fifty directions trying to place the name, and at the same time searching for some means to save himself. Should he run for it? He could, but he could never outrun a bullet. Should he fight? The man was weak; the woman was . . . a woman, but there was the gun. Always the gun, held in the hand of a man who clearly knew how to use it. Bolting would not work. Force would not work. Finesse . . . maybe.

The architecture of the Archie Bunker–style, two-family attached house on Clinton Avenue was typical for this part of Queens. Diane could see it was much in need of attention. The pink-painted clapboards on the Quigley half were peeling, the front steps needed a brick or three, and the iron fence around the postage-stamp-size front lawn was rusted, cockeyed, and ugly. A barely visible sign hanging from the gate read BEWARE OF DOG.

"A fucking dog," Marcus chuckled, parking the Taurus at the curb directly opposite the subject house. "Isn't that nice? I'm glad good old Sergeant Kielbasa Brain is going in first. Let him deal with some freakin' stupid pit bull. Hell, who knows, they're probably even related."

Ignoring Richie's remarks, Diane let herself out of the car and undid the snap on her holster. "Once it's determined we're not going to get an answer at the front door, I'll come around back and we'll check the garage," she said.

They were all just goin' through the motions, Diane thought. She knew this guy, Quigley, wasn't home. She quickly crossed the street and took a position beside Phil Penkowski at the front door. When Richie and the two

Emergency Service cops were in position, covering the back door, she rang the bell and knocked.

Five minutes later, it was confirmed. No one, not even the pit bull—if one existed—was around. A check of the garage revealed no car either. After trying mightily—but failing—to get Diane DeGennaro's home phone number, Sergeant Phil Penkowski and his boys said good-bye and headed off for a late lunch.

"Better let the boss know that plan A is DOA," Marcus said drolly, as they got back into their auto.

At the instant Diane pulled the cell phone from her purse, it began to ring.

"Diane, Thorn Savage here. Our boy Quigley wasn't home, was he?"

"'Fraid not, boss," she replied. "You want us to hang out and wait?"

"Don't bother," Savage said. "I'm at the offices of Metropolitan Answering Service. According to them, he's currently on a run to St. John's Cemetery in Middle Village."

"I know where that is," Diane said. "Right off Woodhaven Boulevard."

"Good. I want you to take a run over there as quickly as you can. We've been trying for the last ten minutes to get through to him on his phone," Savage said, "but no answer. The woman here says this is his last run for the day."

"We might be able to catch him there before he takes a fade," Diane said.

"Right. I've already alerted the One-oh-four. They've dispatched a few sector cars over there to squat on the exits."

"Gotcha," Diane said, gesturing for Marcus to get the car rolling. "We're on our way."

"One more thing," Savage said. "This answering service maintains a complete log of all Quigley's fares. According to their records, Quigley was on a fare to Bridgeport, Connecticut, on the afternoon that Father Gilhooley was shot."

"Sort of takes him out of the Soldier spotlight," Diane said. "Right?"

"Pretty much."

Richie remained icily silent as they sped, lights and siren blaring, south on Sixty-ninth Street and headed east on Metropolitan Avenue. He was still pissed off big time. This flap about Penkowski wasn't over, Diane thought, not by a long shot.

Aviation Unit Number 3 circled at an altitude of one thousand feet above St. John's Roman Catholic Cemetery in Middle Village, Queens. With its bird's-eye view, the helicopter radioed the location of every black sedan or limousine-type vehicle it could see down to 104 Precinct sectors Eddie and George. They in turn checked out plate numbers, looking for the one registered to Allied Cars. It wasn't there.

John Wesley Krumenacker slowly related the story of his abuse at St. Malachy's to a sobbing Hugh Quigley.

"But I only did it once, twice maybe," Quigley sniveled. "It disgusted me."

"That's like saying you were just a little pregnant," Sister Lucia interjected.

"The others, they did it all the time," he cried. "I wasn't at all like they were. I swear to God, I never meant to hurt anybody."

"God?" Sister Lucia snarled. "How dare you invoke the name of God?"

"Please hear me!" Quigley pleaded. "I left the priesthood on my own, right after leaving St. Malachy's. What I had done was so vile, and I had violated my oaths—my holy orders. *Please!*" he begged, his small hands kneading the top of the seat back. "I've paid for those terrible acts a thousand times in my life. I've never known a peaceful day or a decent night's sleep since."

"Neither have I, Quigley," Krumenacker said evenly,

his voice just above whisper. "I went off to Vietnam and became a murder machine. I enjoyed killing. I became a monster, all because of you and those other bastards." He began gasping and went into a wild coughing fit.

"Do you remember Buffo?" Sister Lucia said tersely, speaking over John Wesley's tubercular hack. "His actual name was Buffolino. Emilio Buffolino."

"Yes, I do," Quigley quickly replied. "I'll tell you everything. I won't lie to you, but please, *please* don't shoot me. Little Buffo was a terrific kid. I remember the day he killed himself. How could I forget? It was terrible. His death made me realize what monsters we'd become. That day changed my whole life."

"It changed my whole life too," Sister Lucia sneered. "My name is Angelina Buffolino. Yes," she added at Quigley's sharp reaction, "Emilio's older sister. They told us that he died from pneumonia. *Pneumonia*, Quigley, do you hear that? The Church lied to us to cover up your sick crimes."

Quigley nodded somberly. John Wesley could see the incredible fear radiating from the man's eyes.

"When I was nineteen I became a nun, a Sister of Mercy, and took the name Sister Lucia in honor of Lucia dos Santos, the child of Fátima. I actually believed priests capable of walking on water."

Now sobbing uncontrollably, Quigley could only nod.

"When I found out the truth," Sister Lucia continued, "it devastated me. I quit the convent. My whole world was shattered, and it became clear to me that the Church had fallen into the hands of the Antichrist."

She turned suddenly and faced Krumenacker, her dark eyes like two smoldering coals from the forges of hell. "Let's get this over with and get out of here," she demanded, glancing down at her watch.

"A few more minutes," John Wesley said. "I don't think Father Quigley realizes how funny this is."

Sister Lucia regarded Quigley with disgust. "I took a

job with the archdiocese—a spy for the Blessed Mother. I made myself indispensable to those robed hypocrites who are destroying the Church, and learned all their secrets. I made up my mind to find out the names of those priests directly involved in Buffo's death. But the Church had buried that information too deeply."

John Wesley fell into a hacking, nonproductive cough, all the while keeping the weapon aimed directly at Hugh Quigley's terrified face.

Sister Lucia smiled at him; there was a wild look in her eyes. "Then the Blessed Mother sent John Wesley to me," she continued. "He remembered my brother, *and* he also recalled every one of the guilty priests by name."

"You know the names . . . " Krumenacker interjected. "Grennan, Gilhooley, Flaherty, Clapp, and, *Father Hugh Quigley.*"

"Let me turn myself in to the police," Quigley pleaded. "Let them put me in jail. I'll tell the whole story. I promise. I swear."

"Go to jail?" John Wesley responded. "Like Father John Geoghan went to jail after three decades as a priest in Boston-area parishes? After a hundred and thirty people came forward, only to let some scummy inmate strangle him to death? I don't think so."

"In any case, it's too late; you know too much," Sister Lucia sneered, again looking at her watch. "It's time, John Wesley," she said insistently.

Krumenacker jerked the pistol in the direction of the driver's door. "Get out," he said to Quigley.

In a voice robbed of all hope, Quigley began to recite the Apostles' Creed. "I believe in God, the father almighty, creator of heaven and earth. . . ."

"Your life is finished, Quigley," Sister Lucia taunted. "You know that, right?"

Quigley continued murmuring the prayer. "And in Jesus Christ his only son . . ."

Krumenacker climbed from the backseat and jabbed the

silencer-lengthened barrel into Quigley's ribs. Pointing
him in the direction of the nearest row of graves, he said,
"Just keep walking until I tell you to stop."

"I have dreamed that this day would come." Sister
Lucia continued to prod and needle the ex-priest, her nagging voice overlying the murmured prayer. "The day when
God would make you pay for all the terrible crimes you
committed against those innocents."

Midway through the seemingly endless row of tomb-
stones, they came to the freshly mounded earth of a recently filled grave.

"Stop here," Krumenacker ordered. "Turn around and
face me."

Standing at the foot of the fresh grave, Quigley obeyed.
"Please, *please* . . . I beg of you. Please don't!"

"Drop your pants," Sister Lucia ordered.

Quigley's eyes narrowed and his frightened gaze
flashed back and forth between Sister Lucia and John Wesley, but he made no move to comply with the order.

"Do what I say, you rotten bastard," she snarled. "You'll
only make it worse for yourself if you don't. I promise
you."

"No," Quigley muttered, his jaw quivering. Then, with
a sudden burst of resolve, he added, "I won't do it."

Krumenacker stared at him, surprised. The man was
getting a spine—too late to help, but a spine nonetheless.

"You think those kids wanted to drop their pants?" Sister Lucia pressed, her voice steadily rising. "Now you see
what it was like for them. I'm telling you, drop those goddamned pants, you miserable excuse for a human being,
and do it now."

Quigley suddenly widened his stance on the frozen
earth and threw his shoulders back in defiance. He stood
fully upright, fingers laced together at his belt line, the
aura of great fear that had enveloped him seemingly gone.
"Tommy Gilhooley died poorly, you said. Well, I won't. If
I must die to make amends for my sins, then I'll die like a

man." His nostrils flared wide then contracted, his chest heaved outward as he took a deep breath. His eyes fell fully on John Wesley. "Do what you have to do."

John Wesley Krumenacker looked intently back into Quigley's challenging eyes. He had never doubted the righteousness of his revenge. His abusers, like the gooks in 'Nam, had to be destroyed. But despite the hatred he had nurtured over the years, he was impressed with the man's defiance. Slowly, he leveled the barrel of the pistol directly at Quigley's groin and began a slow trigger squeeze that brought him right to the brink of firing. . . . But he didn't. After several seconds, he released the trigger.

"What's wrong with you?" Sister Lucia screamed. "*Do it,* for crissakes. What are you waiting for?"

In those seconds, John Wesley Krumenacker realized he couldn't do any more killing. It was insane. . . . He was insane. It had to stop.

"Do it, John Wesley," Sister Lucia screamed again, flailing her arms about in all directions. "There's not a soul around. Do it, goddammit."

"I can't," he said, allowing his hand with the gun to drop limply to his side. "I just can't." He saw a look of tentative relief form on Quigley's taut face.

"Give me that!" Sister Lucia shrieked, snatching the gun from Krumenacker's grip. With both hands, she leveled the forty-five at Hugh Quigley's chest and fired.

The force of the blast threw Quigley's arms outward as he fell backward onto the freshly mounded grave. He lay there, open eyes shifting back and forth involuntarily, mouth open, gasping for breath as a geyser of red pumped from the center of his chest.

When Sister Lucia recovered from the weapon's mighty recoil, she casually reaimed and fired again . . . and again. With smoke still curling from the silencer's tip, she stuffed the gun into her bag.

John Wesley Krumenacker and Angelina Buffolino retraced their steps from the direction they had come. Arriving at the roadway, they bypassed Quigley's Cadillac and continued walking at J.W.'s slow pace two ranges over to row 67J. There they waited, the electric silence between them punctuated every sixty seconds by the screams of Boeing airliners passing immediately overhead, making their final approaches into LaGuardia. At precisely 2:45, a large sedan pulled up. They climbed into the backseat.

"Did all go well?" the driver asked.

"Yes," Sister Lucia responded, with just a hint of sarcasm. "Everything went along just dandy." Glaring then at Krumenacker, she reached into her bag and pulled out the forty-five.

"I used up two rounds on that son of a bitch Clapp the other night," she said in an angry snarl, jamming the gun back in J.W.'s OxyTote. "And three more on this bastard. That makes the clip five rounds short. Take it home and reload it. I'll come by and pick it up tomorrow."

"As long as you're doing that," the driver said, "reload this one too." Reaching into the backseat, he handed Krumenacker the .44 caliber Ruger.

"Can't *you* reload the goddamned thing?" Krumenacker said angrily. He opened the six-shot revolver's cylinder and plucked out two spent shells.

"Hey," the driver said with equal anger. "When you provided the gun, it was fully loaded, but you failed to provide any extra ammunition. I used up two rounds in Boston, and I want that gun fully loaded for Tuesday."

"You couldn't have bought some?" Krumenacker said.

"This is New York City, mister. I just can't go walking into the corner sporting goods store and pick up a box of bullets for a magnum handgun. Not without five different kinds of damn permits."

Realizing the man was right, and in no mood to argue, Krumenacker stuffed the forty-four into his bag.

TWENTY-FIVE

Frustrated, deflated, and pissed off almost to the point of distraction at being a day late and a dollar short to save Hugh Quigley's life, and perplexed by the steadily mounting pressure of the pope's scheduled Tuesday afternoon visit, Savage sat at his desk, peeled the foil from a Life-Saver and popped it into his mouth. It soothed, almost calmed, much the way a first deep drag on a Marlboro used to twenty-plus years ago. He closed his eyes and leaned back for a long moment. Deciding that this would be at least a two-mint call, he peeled the foil from another before putting the roll into the desk's top drawer.

He slowly punched in the numbers to the chief of detective's residence phone, hoping the late-Sunday-afternoon notification call would be short and sweet. It might be short, Savage figured, but he didn't hold out much hope for sweet. This case had put Chief Wilson under a tremendous amount of pressure, probably more than any other case he could recall, and here he was, about to dump on another few hundred pounds of deadweight. After exchanging a few banal niceties with the chief's always engaging wife, Sonya, Savage got right to the point when Wilson himself got on the line.

"The body of the sixth priest, Father Hugh Quigley, has been found in a remote section of St. Raymond's Cemetery up in the Bronx," he said.

"Jesus Christ," Wilson drawled. "And meanwhile, you had half the frigging Marine Corps called out to saturate

St. John's Cemetery in Queens. How the hell did you manage to be fifteen miles and one whole borough off?"

"We got deked."

"When and how was Quigley found?"

"'Bout an hour ago. A caretaker, making his final rounds before closing St. Raymond's gates for the night, came upon Quigley's Cadillac. We're in the process of having the car removed to impound, and Forensics is standing by, waiting to go over it for prints."

"Now, this is the car Quigley used in his limo business?"

"Right. But Quigley wasn't found in or around the car. His body was sprawled on top of a fresh grave several hundred feet away. He'd been shot three times."

"Balls and head?"

"Slight deviation this time," Savage said. "Balls, head, and chest."

"Forty-five?"

"Yep. Three shell casings recovered."

"One of those Lady of Fatima calling cards?"

"Yep."

"So, of course, whoever killed him didn't run into him up in St. Raymond's Cemetery by happenstance," Wilson said tartly, stating the obvious. "Whoever did him, lured him there. The fare was almost certainly the goddamned Soldier."

"That's the way we've got to figure it, Chief," Savage agreed. "When the trip was originally arranged over the phone, the destination of record given to Quigley's dispatch service by a Mr. St. Michel was St. John's Cemetery, which is in the middle of Queens. That's the information the service logged in, and that's the information they provided to Quigley late this morning, hours before he picked the fare up. Once aboard, this St. Michel guy must have simply amended the destination to where he *really* intended to go: St. Raymond's Cemetery up in the Bronx. A perfect deception in case somebody came lookin'."

"Jesus," Wilson blurted, "you're getting me confused with all the damn saints, already—saint this, saint that. How do we know St. Raymond's was his true plan? How do we know he just didn't pick St. Raymond's out of the freakin' blue?"

"Coming to that, Chief," Savage said, nodding to Jack Lindstrom, who had slipped quietly into the office, carrying several freshly typed lists.

"All right, tell me this, then. If the Soldier—aka St. Michel—rode up to a remote section of this cemetery as a passenger in Quigley's limo," the chief continued, agitated. "And the car was found to be still on the scene, how do you figure our boy got his ass home?"

"Hopped the fence and walked. Or had another vehicle already planted nearby. Or . . ." Savage let the thought hang.

"Or somebody else was waiting there to pick him up," Wilson jumped in, right on cue. "I don't even wanna think about that as a possibility; a letter-writing serial killer with a goddamned liveried manservant. *Jesus!*"

"I've got one of my teams up there right now, Chief, along with several teams dispatched from the task force. Officially, of course, this one belongs to Bronx Homicide, but Marcus and DeGennaro are getting first whack at the caretaker and any other staff who might have seen something."

"And so far nobody's seen—or heard—anything. . . . Right?"

" 'Fraid so."

"What about tracks in the snow? Footprints around the body that could match up with footprints leaving Quigley's car?"

"No footprints around the car, Chief. The snow had been cleared from all the cemetery roads days ago. They're very efficient up there."

"Then what about where the body was found. . . . Near

that fresh grave. Don't tell me they plow the fucking snow
from a million grave aisles, for crissakes."

"Probably hundreds of visitors have been through those
grave aisles in the four or five days since it stopped snowing, boss. Everything has been packed down and frozen;
no hope for any usable footprints."

"*Shit!* Keep me right up-to-the-minute on this, Thornton," the chief said, then added sarcastically, "I'm gonna
call the PC at home right now and fuck up *his* Sunday dinner."

"There's a bit more to the story, Chief," Savage said,
popping the second mint. "Quigley's body was found atop
the fresh grave of Father Thomas Gilhooley, who was
buried there on Thursday."

"Oh, *mannn . . .* " Wilson moaned. "That is just fucking
diabolical. Is there anything else?"

There *was* something else; something Savage knew he
wanted to do, something that surely needed to be done.
The idea was not yet completely formulated in his mind, so
he decided not to share it with the chief. Not now, he
thought, not tonight. "No boss," he replied. "Nothing
else." The two-mint call was over.

"What've you got, Jack?" Savage asked halfheartedly,
turning to Lindstrom as he set the telephone receiver back
into its cradle.

"I've put together an alphabetical list of every single
name that appears within the St. Malachy's pictures," Jack
Lindstrom said. He peeled off a typed sheet and handed it
to Savage. "It includes the names of all the boys and any
coaches and staff or priests who were identified. As you
can see, one problem is the use of only a first initial, not
complete first names."

"I see we've got a Father Grennan *and* a Father Quigley
in the mix," Savage snarled, quickly scanning the three
columns of names. He felt his ears getting hot; they were
probably becoming flushed as well. Unless he missed his
guess, his borderline high blood pressure was now redlin-

ing. The "something else" he'd only moments ago declined to mention to Chief Wilson, the idea of paying a quick visit to Monsignor Dunleavy, again lumbered heavily through his mind. Dunleavy deserved a beating; he needed to be kayoed, then tarred and feathered. Of course, the smug bastard's defense would be that earlier administrations had kept lousy records, but Savage didn't buy it. Dunleavy had known all along that Grennan was once a priest in the New York Diocese; he was certain of it. And if Dunleavy knew that, he also had to know that Hugh Quigley could be in great danger. He forcibly stifled the overwhelming urge to hop in his car, go knock on Dunleavy's residence door, and punch the son of a bitch's friggin' lights out.

"Grennan appeared in several pictures," Lindstrom said. "All with the basketball teams from '63 and '64. Quigley appeared only once—debating team, '64. In that one, he's shown accepting an award of some kind."

"Hmm. You couldn't find any of the other victim-priests, though, hah?" Savage asked.

"Nope," Lindstrom replied dryly, offering a palms-out shrug. "Not by name. It's possible they're in one of the photos where *no one* is identified."

Savage studied Lindstrom's list. Minus adult coaches, staff, and priests, the number of individual boys named was sixty-one. Although St. Malachy's was an Irish-sounding orphanage, underwritten by a predominately Irish archdiocese, the boys' names were universal. O'Callaghans, Maughans, Gahans and Smiths were certainly well represented, but there were plenty of Jaworskis, Crapanzanos, and Oberdorffers as well. There was even a Chin, a Chan, and a B. J. Goldfarb.

"Of course," Lindstrom pointed out, "the names we've gleaned from these photos probably only represent a fraction of the total complement of the orphanage. I'm sure not every kid played sports or debated."

"Well," Savage said, laying the list on his desk. "We've

gotta go with what we've got. Get these names over to your friend at the VA right away—"

"It is Sunday, you know, boss," Lindstrom reminded him. "The VA's admin offices are closed."

"Shit!" Savage growled through clenched teeth, slamming his open mitt on the desktop blotter; he'd even forgotten what damn day it was. "Well, then, you be waiting on the VA's doorstep first thing in the morning," he declared. "Get that Lorelei DeKohning to run every one of those names through the VA's health system and see what we come up with."

"We've got two J. Smiths on the list, one J. Jones, and a J. Sullivan," Lindstrom pointed out. "Awful common. Those three names alone could probably spit out five thousand leads."

"Don't bother running them," Savage agreed. "Not this time around. We don't have the time."

Grinning sheepishly like a bashful boy, Lindstrom said, "I happen to have Lorelei DeKohning's home phone number. Why don't I give her a buzz? Who knows? If she's able to get access, maybe she wouldn't mind going in to her office today. I told you, she's very eager to help."

"Go for it. And if she needs transportation, tell her you'll pick up and deliver. When you're finished, call Operations and put yourself off the clock. I'll see you in the morning."

Lindstrom replied with an enthusiastic smile. He snapped a quick salute and turned on his heels.

"Also," Savage called out, stopping the detective in his tracks. "Before I head home, make me up some more copies of that list—minus Smith, Sullivan, and Jones—I'll get with Marcus and DeGennaro's connection over at the Transit Authority. Between the two of us, maybe we can get a few bells to go off around here."

"Ten-four."

TWENTY-SIX

Lorelei DeKohning's usually bustling office, with the grime-blurred seventh-floor view of Tribeca, was strangely quiet except for the rapid-fire click of her IBM keyboard as she typed in *C. Vermeil* and *K. Walterson*, the last two names on Jack Lindstrom's fifty-seven-name list. When finished, she highlighted the long entry, went to SELECT ALL then hit SEARCH. She glanced at a reflective Jack Lindstrom seated several feet away, and flashed him a hopeful smile. There was something extraordinarily appealing about the quiet man.

"How long do you figure this is going to take?" he asked.

"This part shouldn't take too long," she replied, turning her eyes back to the screen. "Minutes, maybe. All I'm asking for now are any matches within our Health Services and Benefits division. This is the key department for us to look at. It would contain the broadest number of names. We can go into the others later, if we have to, but this is where I feel we should begin."

In moments, an alphabetical listing of possible hits ranging from Brennen to Tillotson flashed onto the screen. K. Walterson and C. Vermeil had not made the cut.

"Well," she said, pressing the PRINT button as Jack Lindstrom peered over her shoulder. "Out of your list of fifty-seven surnames and first initials, we've got fifty-one names in our health system which could possibly align. We've got six J. Brennens, Jason P. to Joseph A. Two Michael

Fitzhughs. One A. Hornaday—Alvin. Eight F. X. Jacksons, all Francis Xaviers. We have one R. Kulvane—Ralph; one F. Larouche—Franklin; seven T. Mulligans—Terrence to Twyman; and twenty-three B. Smiths—Benjamin A. to Brian W. We also have one F. Smolenski—a Frederick C.; and one R. Tillotson—Robert. Oops," she quickly corrected, "scratch that last one. It's a Roberta Tillotson, not a Robert; she's shown as having been a Navy Wave. I don't think you need that one."

"That leaves us with an even fifty," Lindstrom said, still peering over her shoulder, studying the names on the screen. "Where to now?"

"Now we go into their individual files," she replied, "where maybe we can narrow this list a little further. That's where we'll get their vital statistics; age, dob, social security numbers, addresses, blah blah blah." Her slender fingers raced across the computer keys. "Let's start with Jason P. Brennen."

In seconds, the screen shifted to a different format.

"Jason P. Brennen is a sixty-one-year-old Vietnam vet confined to the VA Hospital in St. Alban's, Queens," she said. "Of course, he will be included on the printout, but I don't think he's your man."

"Why's that?"

"Quadriplegic," she replied sadly. "Let's try Brennen, James L." She typed the thirteen letters in a blur.

Lindstrom gave out a low whistle. "I don't believe I've ever seen anybody type so fast *and* so accurately," he said, clearly impressed. "My ex-wife used to type very well . . . but not *that* well."

She made brief eye contact and flashed a shy smile. "James L. Brennen is dead," she said, as a new screen page appeared. "He passed away last August fifteenth. Surprised he's still shown in the system. Read me the next name . . . Jack."

"Brennen," Lindstrom called out. "John F."

*   *   *

All too aware of the ticking clock, knowing that in this game of life and death there were no time-outs allowed to ponder strategy and field logistics, Savage slipped through the red lights at Second and First Avenues as soon as the cross traffic had safely passed. Finding the southbound FDR Drive relatively clear, he accelerated the Ford and maintained a steady eighty miles per hour all the way down to the Brooklyn Bridge. Crossing the beautiful span, he allowed his thoughts to wander only briefly to two of his all-time heroes, John and Washington Roebling, the father-son team who conceived and built the incredible span in the late 1800s. He had always been fascinated by their vision, their competence, and their sheer genius. God, how he loved this bridge.

Once in Brooklyn, his thoughts ricocheted between the executed priests, pissed-off police chiefs, and clever calculating monsignors with unclear agendas. Five minutes later, he parked directly in front of the Transit Authority operational offices at 370 Jay Street.

When he entered, he found the place staffed by a weekend skeleton crew that thankfully included Harold Borgen. The big man was very much as Richie Marcus had characterized him the other day. He was smiley, likable and soft-spoken.

"I've got a list of fifty-seven names," Savage opened. "No first names to go along with them, just first and sometimes middle initials. What can you do for me, and how long will it take?"

Borgen set a half-finished liter of Coke Classic on his desktop and pulled his wire-rimmed glasses down over his eyes. "Any SS numbers?" he asked, then jammed the end of a Snickers bar between large teeth and twisted off a good-size chunk.

"Nope," Savage replied, releasing the list into Borgen's free hand.

The huge man chewed casually while scanning the names. Finally swallowing, he looked back at Savage.

"Better give me your fax information, Sergeant," he said. "Hate to tell you this, but our computers are down right now; it could be several hours. If they stay down, as I suspect they will, I might not have all this done till the morning."

"Shit!"

There was no point sticking around the TA watching Harold Borgen desecrate the memory of Dr. Atkins and, Savage decided, there was at least one more stop that he could make tonight. Hell, he was itching for a good fight anyway.

Savage was surprised, and more than slightly relieved, when Monsignor Albert Dunleavy himself answered his own door at his red brick town house on East Forty-ninth, between Second and Third. Maybe the monsignor's housekeeper had the Sunday night off. Who knew? At any rate, it was probably better that no third party would be around to overhear the discussion he intended to have with the priest. It wasn't going to be pretty, and it wasn't going to sit well with Chief Wilson—should he ever find out—but it had to be done.

This section of Manhattan was definitely a high-rent district; Savage recalled that Katharine Hepburn used to live only two doors down. The property, he concluded, was probably one of the Church's many tax-free real estate holdings within the city.

"Why, Sergeant Savage," Dunleavy said, holding the brass-accented, black-enameled door only partially open. "What brings you here?"

As if you didn't already know, Savage thought, his jaw tightly set, his gloved hands balled into fists in the pockets of his topcoat. "Oh," he said, offhandedly. "I was sure you'd already heard, Monsignor."

"Sure I'd already heard what?" Dunleavy countered, his frosty demeanor obvious through the barely cracked door.

The man's snotty attitude seemed a mix of messages.

Annoyance and defensiveness were clearly at the forefront, with curiosity and concern lagging well behind. No question the monsignor had a damn good poker face, but he wasn't a good liar. Savage was expert at reading feigned ignorance; after all, he'd spent a lifetime learning how to cull the truth from genus *Liar erectus*. He'd studied the extremely competent professional ones, the believe-the-lie-themselves congenital ones, and, on the bottom of the heap, the garden-variety, flat-out, everyday bullshit artists. He sensed the lie in the priest's bearing, he heard it in his guarded voice, and, in the glare of the streetlamp above, saw it reflected in his cool blue eyes; Dunleavy knew damn well, *what!*

"May I come in, Monsignor?" Savage said straight out, while trying mightily to conceal the contempt and bitterness he felt toward the man. "Or am I gonna get the Jehovah's Witness treatment?"

"Yes, yes, of course," Dunleavy stammered. He closed the door momentarily, released the chain lock, and swung the door wide. Savage stepped into the warmth of the vestibule. Dunleavy closed the door and led the way into a well-lit wide hallway that fed several side rooms on the left. A staircase with an intricately carved newel and banister led to the upper floors.

Funny, Savage thought, the monsignor did not seem anywhere near as imposing as he had at their first meeting, when decked out in his full regalia. Tonight, the man seemed just a fragile, aging guy, lounging about in casual slacks, a baggy Notre Dame sweatshirt, and corny corduroy slippers. He could hear a TV playing somewhere in another room, a voice-over mentioning the Discovery Channel.

"What is this all about, Sergeant?" Dunleavy asked, his resonant voice gaining timbre, beginning to again exude that confident guile and charm.

"You and I have to come to some sort of understanding, Padre," Savage replied.

"An *understanding*?" Dunleavy grunted in a half-laugh, his superior attitude now fully reassembled, his dynamic composure totally locked in. "I'm afraid I have no earthly idea what you're talking about."

Savage fought the urge to backhand some real-world sense into the deified mortal who was totally unaccustomed to being put on the spot; to make him play, if only for a few minutes, by the rules of Man.

"Does the name Hugh Quigley mean anything to you, Monsignor?" Savage asked evenly, deciding for the moment to continue as Mr. Nice Guy.

"Quigley, did you say?" Dunleavy murmured, making a serious face and gazing off into nowhere.

"Hugh Quigley," Savage repeated acidly. He hated having to witness shitty dramatics, especially when people were dying on his watch. "The Reverend Hugh Quigley, onetime Roman Catholic priest from the New York Archdiocese."

Dunleavy cupped his deeply dimpled chin in his delicate right hand, squinted as if in deep thought, and replied, "No, Sergeant. I can't say that it does."

"You're lying."

"What did you say?" Dunleavy snarled through gritted teeth, icy eyes morphing into incendiary lasers.

"I said you're a liar."

"How dare you come in here . . . into my residence, my home . . . and speak to me in this manner? You'll be hearing from—"

"I could be slapping handcuffs on you, reading you your rights, and dragging you and your corduroy slippers downtown to Central Booking." So much for concealing his contempt, Savage realized after the blast.

"You would arrest . . . *me*?"

"Oh yeah!" Savage responded, locking his eyes on the prelate's beams. "I'd love to put you in irons where you belong, and bring charges of hindering a murder investigation before a grand jury."

"Hindering? Hindering your ass!" Dunleavy growled arrogantly. Turning on his heels, he darted to the telephone on a nearby table, picked up the receiver and punched in 911. "There'll be charges all right," he said, stabbing a manicured index finger in Savage's direction. "But they will be departmental charges against you. Just who in the hell do you think you're dealing with here? Some frightened, flustered, and ignorant citizen who would cave or be intimidated by your badge?"

"You would know about such things, wouldn't you, Padre? Perhaps you think you're dealing with some frightened, flustered, and ignorant parishioner intimidated by your fucking Roman collar?"

Dunleavy glared.

"Let's talk straight, Padre," Savage said flatly. "Let's talk about St. Malachy's Home for Boys. And let's talk about Father Peter Grennan."

It was as if he'd pricked a balloon with a pin. The priest stood silently, phone in hand, still gazing intently back at Savage, who could almost see the gears turning in the man's head. After several seconds, Dunleavy dropped the phone back into its cradle.

"I know nothing about St. Malachy's," he finally said, quietly clearing his throat, his laser beams cooling some. "And I've already told you that we have no record of a Peter Grennan ever being an ordained priest within this archdiocese."

"Don't play stupid with me, Padre," Savage said. "We already know that Peter Grennan worked at St. Malachy's back in the sixties. He worked there with Fathers Flaherty, Gilhooley, Clapp, and Hugh Quigley—now the late Hugh Quigley. We also know that these men were abusing the boys there. That is, until one of those boys took his own life. Then the nasty little lid blew off."

Dunleavy's nostrils flared and his chest heaved. He was involuntarily gulping down the oxygen his heart needed to keep up its stress-driven staccato beat.

"Just what is it that you want from me?" the priest said, reaching out and taking support from the staircase newel post.

"I want you to level. I want to know what—or who—you thought you were protecting while letting people die."

"I was, and I am still, protecting no one," Dunleavy insisted. "And I never had any knowledge that anyone was going to die."

"Yeah, you did," Savage pressed. "You might not have known they were going to die, but you damn well knew they were in mortal danger."

"I'll say no more," Dunleavy said, looking up at Savage with foreboding in his eyes. "I'll say no more until I've spoken with archdiocese legal counsel. I want you to leave. Now."

Standing many inches taller, Savage looked down at the defensive priest and gazed deeply into his eyes, reading him. "I believe that's the first truthful thing you've ever said to me, Monsignor."

Dunleavy thrust out his chin defiantly.

"Now let me tell you something that is an *absolute fact*," Savage continued in an even tone. "I am not going to let go of this. If need be, I will speak to every John Smith and John Jones in the phone book. I will find those who grew up in St. Malachy's Home for Boys, and I will get the truth. And if you, or anybody else, gets hit with the shrapnel, that'll be just too fucking bad." Without another word, Savage let himself out of the town house into the bitter East Side night.

Not a thing had been accomplished by the visit, he thought as he walked to his car, which was parked around the corner on Second Avenue. Not one goddamned thing. It wasn't going to aid the investigation in any way; it wasn't going to help drop a net on the Soldier any sooner.

Why did I do it? Savage asked himself. Why did I come here and possibly put my entire career on the chopping block? He unlocked the Ford, slid behind the wheel, and put the key in the ignition. He knew why. He did it because it was the right goddamned thing to do.

And having done the right goddamned thing, it was time to go see Frankie McBride over at P. J.'s. He needed a drink.

Another life had been taken. Another former priest was now dead. The last of the St. Malachy's five had been viciously killed, his bullet-riddled body found sprawled on the mounded and frozen earth that covered the resting place of Father Thomas Gilhooley, himself senselessly murdered only a week ago.

Dunleavy felt sick to his stomach, weak, as if his life's blood was draining away. What had he done? What had he allowed himself to become part of? In his zeal to protect Mother Church, had he set the stage for Father Killian Flaherty to kill himself? And as a result of his misguided silence, had he played a hand in this latest debacle? He relocked his door and set the security chain.

Badly rattled by the effrontery of the ballsy cop and gripped by the crushing talons of regret and fear, Dunleavy ambled, stoop-shouldered, from the vestibule to the den off the hall, clicked off the television, and fell heavily to his knees. Tormented by the realization that he was unable to alter what had already occurred, he bowed his head and prayed for guidance. "But Lord, maybe I can affect that which still lies ahead. Dear Lord, please help me find some way. . . ."

At 9:45 a.m. Rome time, Alitalia flight 7614 lifted its wheels off the runway at Leonardo da Vinci, scheduled to arrive at JFK at 1:30 p.m. New York time. Colonel George Olmstead, traveling first class as Mr. Armand Ottuso, businessman, gazed out his window as the 777 steadily climbed and banked into a northwesterly course. In only minutes, the Tyrrhenian coastline appeared and Italia gradually faded from view behind the mist and gray of the stalled front that

had badgered metropolitan Rome with a ceaseless down-
pour for the past forty-eight hours.

"Welcome to Magnifica Class, Mr. Ottuso," a broadly
smiling but less-than-attractive flight attendant said. "May
I get you something to drink? A cocktail, some coffee?"

"Nothing right now," he replied.

The attendant turned to the female passenger seated on
the opposite side of the aisle. He heard the woman's soft,
sultry voice as she ordered an extra-spicy Bloody Mary.

Considering the six-hour time differential between the
two cities, it was going to be a very long day indeed. As
Olmstead reclined in the oversized seat to order his
thoughts and ponder strategy for the pontiff's New York
City visit—which was now less than a day away—the
woman across the aisle called to him.

"You really should have one of their Bloody Marys,"
she said boldly. "I know. I make this flight frequently;
they're delicious." The woman was in her midforties, slender, with mile-long legs. She was also darkly beautiful and
smiling warmly. He made her as Italian, southern Italian.

"Perhaps later," he replied.

"I hope the weather in New York will be better than
what we just left," she said in her Mediterranean-accented
English. "I almost missed this flight entirely."

"How so?" he inquired, taken by her aggressive friend-
liness and unmistakable aura of sensuality.

"Terrible flooding and an overturned poultry truck.
There were chickens everywhere," she said, giggling. "But
it was a horrendous, twenty-six-kilometer, bumper-to-
bumper nightmare," she added. "And the forecast is for no
letup. I hope the weather in New York is nice."

"They had a snowstorm last week," he said. "But now it
is supposed to be clear and dry, though very cold."

"That's wonderful," the woman replied. "I've seen
enough rain to last me quite a while. My name is Valerie.
Valerie Palermo."

"Armand. Armand Ottuso." Right again, he thought; the

alluring lady was Sicilian. He'd always had a thing for hot-blooded Sicilian women. He allowed his mind to float momentarily into earthly fantasy.

"Are you going to New York for business or pleasure, Mr. Ottuso?"

"Business, primarily," he replied. He allowed his eyes to wander her full profile, and added, "But I would certainly have no objection to encountering a little pleasure while I'm there. You?"

"Much pleasure . . . I hope."

"Where will you be staying in New York?" he inquired.

"On the East Side. The Pierre Hotel. You?"

"The Palace Hotel."

"Oh, that's not terribly far from the Pierre," she replied, reaching out and accepting her cocktail and a napkin from the flight attendant. Valerie Palermo had long, finely manicured fingers.

"I believe it's only about ten or twelve blocks away. My hotel's right on Madison Avenue and Fiftieth."

"That's right behind that magnificent St. Patrick's Cathedral, isn't it?" she asked, raising her brow in question and sipping at her drink.

"As a matter of fact, yes, it is."

"I've never been inside that cathedral," she said, begging the question.

"I happen to be very well acquainted with it," he replied. "Perhaps we could meet sometime, and I could give you the grand tour."

The dark-haired beauty swallowed him with her eyes. "I would like that." After taking another light sip of her drink, she made a performance of licking her full lips. "I would like that very much."

Olmstead motioned to the flight attendant. "I've changed my mind," he said. "I think I'll try a Bloody Mary."

TWENTY-SEVEN

Monday, December 30, the next-to-last day of the year, and nine days since Father Thomas Gilhooley had been executed inside a confessional booth at Blessed Sacrament Church. It had been seven days since Father Jean Brodeur was found murdered at a debris-filled construction site and, Savage reminded himself, it was also seven days since he'd laid eyes on his pizza-craving, beer-swilling smoky gray roommate, Ray. Also, it was only one day until the pope's much-heralded visit to New York City, and the odds of first collaring the priest-killing machine who called himself the Soldier were getting really long.

The war room at Manhattan South Homicide hadn't seen this much activity in some time, certainly not at six thirty in the morning. Nineteen bleary-eyed detectives from the recently formed task force milled around in small groups. Called in early from warm beds, they downed eye-opening, heart-starting coffees from Styrofoam cups, searched for nonexistent ashtrays, and entertained one another with war stories as Thorn Savage huddled with their boss, Sergeant Terry McCauley, at the far end of the conference table. Jack Lindstrom and Diane DeGennaro sat at the middle of the long table, poring over and cross-referencing names from two separate lists and working the telephone directories from the five boroughs.

The printout of former and current employees Savage had requested from Harold Borgen at the Transit Authority had arrived by fax at Manhattan South at 4:00 a.m.

Hoping that their subject was named somewhere within the lists provided by the VA and the TA was really a stretch, but dammit, it was all they had to go on. The next two days were certain to be pure madness, trying to run down every one of those names. Thank God for the warm bodies of the twenty-five-man task force.

Lieutenant Pete Pezzano barged into the busy room. "Have we arrived at a total name count yet?" he asked Savage. "I've got the chief of detectives on hold."

"On top of the fifty names we had from the Veterans Administration, we now have sixty-seven more from the Transit Authority," Savage replied. "One hundred and seventeen names in total."

"Jesus," Pezzano observed, looking confused. "You'd think there'd be a lot more names on the VA list. Surely there were a lot more Joe Dokes who'd been in the armed forces than Joe Dokes who'd worked for the TA."

"It would seem an anomaly," Savage replied. "But not every veteran takes advantage of VA health benefits. In fact, the actual percentage that do is really quite low."

Pezzano nodded thoughtfully. "I did three years in the air force," he muttered, "but since I got out, I've never once contacted the VA."

"There you go," Savage said.

"Me neither," Richie Marcus agreed in his throaty growl, which always seemed more raucous in the early morning hours. Seated at the table's far end, he looked up from his *Racing Form* and sucked in a final drag of his Winston. "Freakin' VA doctors'll kill ya', for crissakes," he continued, squelching the filtered stub into the liquid dregs of a foam coffee cup. A smoky exhale escaped his nose and mouth in staggered bursts as he added, "Everybody knows that. Nobody goes to the VA unless they're really poor—or really freakin' cheap. You'd have to be a schmuck."

"Have we narrowed it down yet to anyone who appears on both lists?" Pezzano followed up impatiently. "Matching dates of birth, social security numbers, that kind of thing?"

Savage looked toward Jack Lindstrom and Diane De-Gennaro. "Where do we stand?" he asked.

"So far, it looks like the magic number stands at two," Lindstrom said, looking up at Pezzano. "That is, two who are currently receiving medical assistance from the VA *and* who at one time were employed by the New York City Transit Authority." His cell phone rang. "Excuse me, boss," he said, answering it.

"We're gonna visit those two first, right?" Pezzano said firmly, looking to the two sergeants.

"Two three-man teams from the task force have already been dispatched," Sergeant Terry McCauley said. "One team is visiting the last known address of John Charles Jackson up in the Hunts Point section of the Bronx; another team is covering the last known of Brady Patrick Smith out in Elmhurst, Queens." He looked at his watch. "They're probably knocking on those doors as we speak."

"And if they come up with zippo—which they probably will—that still leaves us with a hundred and fifteen names," Pezzano grumbled angrily, his notorious stoic calm agitated. "How are we setting that up?"

"Terry and I are breaking down the lists," Savage replied. "Factoring in a few of our people with the twenty-five from the task force will give us fourteen two-man teams."

"Which will come out to about eight or nine house calls for each team," Terry McCauley said. "We oughtta be able to get that many visits out of each team before Wednesday."

"Actually, there'll even be less," Jack Lindstrom called out, clicking off his cell phone. Carefully aligning a straightedge on the VA list before him, he began lining out names.

"How's that?" Pezzano queried.

"Just heard from my source over at the VA," he said.

"She's still searching through their files and calling in any updates to me as soon as she gets them. She just whittled down the original fifty-name VA list by seven. When we remove those corresponding names from the Transit list, the overall number of possibles is going to drop even more."

"What's suddenly accounting for those reductions?" Pezzano asked.

"Of the seven she just called in to me, three are totally blind, one is dead—killed in a car wreck two weeks ago—and the remaining three all have advanced Alzheimer's."

"Hmm." Pezzano nodded, pensively. "Keep at it. Let's knock these lists down as much as we can." He turned and headed quickly back to his office.

Savage took a long, studied glance around the room and momentarily wondered what it was that made all those present want to be cops. He watched as Richie Marcus lit up another cigarette and began drawing circles on the pages of *The Racing Form.*

Limiting the search to include only those veterans who resided within New York's five boroughs, Lorelei DeKohning had worked back and forth through the computerized files of the VA's Health Benefits records system at least ten times in the past eighteen hours. Four times last night when she came into the office with Detective Lindstrom, when they came up with the original fifty names, and then at least six more times since five thirty this morning. She had actually found some more names that had been missed, but then deleted a few because of updated information. Beyond that, she also searched the active files of all the other VA health-related divisions. In so doing, she had been unable to add any new names, but had reduced the original fifty hits by seven.

Her stomach growled again for the third time in the last two minutes; thank God her office was private. She looked up at the clock; both hands were vertical. She had missed breakfast that morning, having had only one cup of coffee, but wasn't about to miss lunch. After working with five separate clients—one a pathetic Tourette's sufferer with a vast vocabulary of filthy words *and* the world's worst case of body odor—interspersed with the tedious file searches to aid the police, Lorelei DeKohning was ready for a break. She grabbed her pocketbook and strode from the office; a nice hot lunch in the ground-floor cafeteria sounded really good.

Lorelei wondered if Helen Carbone, from Burial and Memorial Benefits, would like to join her today; they often lunched together. She'd swing by her office and ask. Lorelei could barely wait to tell somebody what she had become involved in. She felt a little thrill go through her just thinking about the work she was doing—important work—to help the police solve a brutal crime. She felt an even greater thrill at the thought of the police officer she was working with.

As Manhattan blocks go, Seventy-first between Second and Third Avenues was a nice one. Dead center on the fashionable East Side, there were no tacky garbage cans stacked at the curbs waiting for a noisy pickup, not one scribble of graffiti anywhere in sight, and the only Mexican restaurant was one of those chain places fifteen blocks away on Eighty-sixth Street. Marymount Manhattan College sat right in the middle of the block on the north side, directly opposite the local post office. And, Richie Marcus noted, as apartment buildings go, 234 East Seventy-first was a particularly appealing one. It had that fastidiously maintained, spare-no-expense look, a classy navy blue awning at the entry and a fresh parking space directly in front.

"I don't think we're gonna run into any mariachi bands in this freakin' neighborhood," Marcus said, as Diane De-Gennaro pulled the silver Taurus into the open spot.

Diane didn't respond. Instead she shut off the engine

and slipped the portable radio into her bag. "Let's do it," she said, swinging her door open. Marcus hated when she ignored what he said.

They entered 234 East, tinned the building's uniformed doorman, and had him ring apartment 8C. Mr. Kevin Rombaut was in and would see them. They rode the elevator up.

The eighth-floor hallway was carpeted in a busy paisley print of deep scarlet and hunter green, so thick it was almost difficult to walk on. Soft lighting refracted evenly through sparkling shaded sconces set every five feet or so along the handsomely papered walls. This was definitely not a fluorescent kind of joint, Marcus concluded, as he rapped on the door of 8C.

"Mr. Kevin Rombaut?" Marcus asked the well-groomed man in his early fifties who opened the door dressed in a black silk robe.

"I'm Kevin Rombaut," the man replied. He wore the confused but curious look that noncriminal types always displayed when approached out of the blue by police. "What's this all about, Detectives?" he asked, his brow scrunched in a mixture of concern and wonderment.

"We'd like to ask you a few questions, sir," Diane DeGennaro said, holding up her gold shield. "May we come in?"

Anxious, Mr. Rombaut stepped aside and motioned them into the tasteful, expensively decorated living quarters.

"Questions about what?" he inquired, leading them into a large sitting room that had a gleaming black-lacquered Steinway grand as a centerpiece. He motioned them to two chairs; they declined to sit.

"Does the name St. Malachy's Home for Boys register in any way with you, sir?" Marcus asked.

A sudden defensive pall fell across the man's face. Marcus saw that he'd struck pay dirt. The name K. Rombaut had come off a St. Malachy's debating team photo, but not popped up on either the VA or TA lists. There was, however, only one K. Rombaut in the Manhattan telephone directory. It had been worth a try.

"I was wondering how long it would take until you showed up here asking questions," he said. "It's about those priest killings, isn't it?"

"Yes, sir, it is," Marcus confirmed. "Are you the Kevin Rombaut that was raised in St. Malachy's back in the 1960s?"

Looking for a cigarette, Rombaut tapped and groped at his robe's pockets.

"Marlboros?" Marcus asked.

"Yes," Rombaut replied, looking at Marcus as if he were a psychic.

Marcus nodded toward a pack of Marlboros on a nearby lamp table. Rombaut quickly lit one, inhaled deeply, and exhaled slowly, contemplatively.

"Well?" Marcus pressed.

"Yes. I was raised at St. Malachy's," he finally admitted. "What of it?"

"Did you know Father Thomas Gilhooley when you were growing up there?" Diane inquired.

"I knew him," Rombaut said, sitting down on a curved sectional of deep green brushed suede. He picked up a heavy onyx ashtray from the cocktail table before him and tapped the cigarette into it, attempting to clear an ash that had yet to adequately form.

"What kind of guy was he?" Marcus asked.

"He was a nice guy," Rombaut replied. His words were soft, but his tone was firm. His heavily hooded eyes darted back and forth between the two cops.

"Were you ever molested in any way by Father Gilhooley?" Marcus followed up.

"No. And before you ask," Rombaut went on, "I also knew Fathers Grennan, Flaherty, Clapp, and Quigley." He sucked in another deep drag, covered his lap with both hands, and crossed his right leg over his left.

This guy ain't gonna tell me shit, Marcus suspected.

"And just what kind of guys were they?" Diane asked.

"Which ones?" Rombaut asked, clearly stalling for time to order his thoughts.

"All of them," Marcus said, cranking up his growl just a notch. "Did any of them ever, in any way, molest you? Or do you have any knowledge or belief that any of these priests ever molested any of the other kids at the orphanage?"

Rombaut began to shake his elevated slipper-covered right foot.

The nerves weren't from guilt, Marcus decided. Defensiveness maybe, but not guilt.

"If you know anything, you've got to tell us about these men," Diane said.

"They were all good guys," Rombaut said evenly.

"We have reason to believe otherwise," Marcus said.

"Believe what you like," Rombaut responded. "You're just trying to dig up dirt on these guys. I'm not going to help you." His attitude was strong, but his foot was still shaking.

"You're full o' shit," Marcus said in a sneer. "You could tell us plenty. What are you hiding, Rombaut?"

"I'm not hiding anything," he snapped back defensively.

"Oh yeah, you are," Marcus pressed, certain of his conclusion. Turning to Diane, he suggested, "Maybe we ought to take this guy downtown, where we can discuss this matter on our turf."

"I can't tell you," the man suddenly blurted. He put the cigarette to his lips and took another deep drag.

"Why is that?" Diane asked.

"A confidentiality agreement I signed a number of years ago. That's why." Rombaut uncrossed his legs and leaned forward. The case of nerves was gone; he'd made his decision. His heels were firmly dug in.

"You sued St. Malachy's?" Diane followed up.

"No. I went after the archdiocese. I won an out-of-court settlement."

"How big?" Marcus asked.

"Big," Rombaut muttered. He looked back and forth at Marcus and DeGennaro, raised a brow, but said nothing more.

"Did you go after them alone, or were you part of a group action?" Marcus pressed.

"Alone. But that is all I'm going to say. I can talk to you, but not about those priests, St. Malachy's, or any sexual abuse questions. Besides, they're all dead now. You can't prosecute them anyway."

"They're *all dead*?" Marcus growled, weary of the nonanswers. It was time for some good-guy, bad-guy cage rattling. Cupping his ear dramatically, Marcus glared down at the man and added, "Let me tell you something *Mister* Rombaut. We ain't leaving here until you completely clarify *that* fucking remark."

"What do you mean?" Rombaut said, his tone rising defensively.

"What I mean is this," Marcus went on. "If we come up with another murdered priest tomorrow, I'm coming back here immediately. And I'm gonna hold you and your closed mouth responsible. Do you hear me? And then you might wind up having to sue the fucking NYPD when *I* get done physically abusing you."

Rombaut crossed his legs again and, seeking solace, if not protection, shifted a disconcerted glance to Diane.

"We're not after the priests," Diane said softly, clutching the sleeve of Marcus' coat, as if holding him back. "Try to understand, we're after the person who is killing these priests. We don't need to tell you that, now, do we, Mr. Rombaut? If you have *any* knowledge of *any* additional priests who may be in danger, we need to know that. And we need to know that right now."

"Okay," Rombaut said, caving. He grimaced. "I do not

know of any other priests who may be targeted. Those five were the only priests I remember." He looked up at Marcus with a plea in his eyes—and in his voice—and added, "That's the truth, I swear to God."

"Now, tell us what went on in that orphanage," Marcus said flatly, maintaining laserlike eye contact with the man.

"Look. If I was totally broke," Rombaut said, looking at Diane, but really watching Marcus, "maybe I would tell you what transpired in those years. But, as you can see, I do quite well. By wise investments, I was able to parlay the settlement I got from the Church into a modest fortune. If I were to violate that confidentiality agreement, I would be leaving myself wide open for a legal broadside. To put it simply, I have too much to lose. I can't say any more."

"Let me ask you this, then, Mr. Rombaut," Marcus said, moderating his tone. "Do you have any knowledge of the whereabouts of any of the other boys you grew up with there?"

"None whatsoever," Rombaut replied, with obvious sincerity. "I've not seen, or talked to, or even heard about, any of those other kids in probably forty years." He squashed out the Marlboro, slid the ashtray onto the cocktail table, and stood. "Anything else, Officers?"

"Yes," Diane spoke up. "We have information that sometime back in the sixties, one of the boys at St. Malachy's took his own life. He supposedly jumped from the roof. If you remember that boy's name, we'd like to know it. Surely, recalling *that* information could in no way violate your legal agreements."

Rombaut did not respond. His eyes again darted between Marcus and DeGennaro. Marcus could tell by the thrust of the man's jaw and the flash of his eyes that he held the answer.

"We're not talking about alleged child abuse, pedophilia, or sexual molestation here," Marcus pressed.

"We're talking about something totally unrelated; the suicide of a young kid."

"I think of him often," Rombaut lamented. Swallowing deeply, he uttered, "Buffolino. Emilio Buffolino. Everybody knew him as Buffo."

TWENTY-EIGHT

Lorelei DeKohning was well acquainted with the ambient temperature extremes within the old-fashioned cafeteria of the Varick Street building. During the summer months of July and August, the place was a high-humidity hothouse where one could probably raise world-class orchids, but now, in the dead of winter, it felt like a chill-you-right-through-to-the-bone virtual meat locker. One only found a happy temperate zone there during the transitional months of September and May. Today, she knew to bring along a sweater. The place was noisy too. High, nonacoustic ceilings, stainless steel counters, and hard tile floors made the chatter from fifty-odd tables an indecipherable din, punctuated with the smash and clash of china plates, cups, and saucers being rattled around. But for the workers in 201 Varick and other nearby buildings, the food was hot and cheap, and on bitter cold winter days, convenient.

The steam table offerings were typical cafeteria fare—overcooked chicken; boring, barely passable meat loaf; sodium-loaded packaged gravy ladled over alleged mashed potatoes—and the desserts were only average at best. Lorelei generally stuck with cold sandwiches. Today, it had been tuna salad on whole wheat with a side of raspberry Jell-O.

"So tell me," Helen Carbone said. "This Detective Lindstrom, with whom you seem to be so smitten, is it possible he's married?"

"He's divorced," Lorelei DeKohning replied. "Recently divorced."

"Maybe you can catch him on the rebound?"

"I'm not looking to *catch* him," Lorelei responded, feeling her cheeks blush.

"The way you describe him, he sounds kind of buttoned-up and cerebral. But, if you don't mind my saying so, for you, the guy sounds custom-made."

"Yeah, maybe," Lorelei said, shrugging. "I just wish I could help him more with this case. I'm really finding this all very interesting." She chuckled and added, "Maybe I should have become a cop like my two brothers."

"No real luck helping him?" Helen asked, scooping another forkful of plastic-looking Boston cream pie.

"Mostly a long list of maybes," Lorelei said. "There were one or two who rated slightly better than maybe, but they've already been checked out; nothing. And I've looked everywhere." She fastened one more button on her cardigan, then folded her arms across her small breasts in an attempt to get warm. "I've checked Home-Based Primary Care, Vocational Rehab, Compensation, Pension, Life Insurance, Appeals . . . the entire network."

"Doesn't sound like you checked my division," Helen Carbone said, mumbling through a mouthful of crust and cream. "Why, I'm crushed," she added jokingly.

"Your division is the only one that I didn't check," Lorelei admitted, dipping a spoon into her half-eaten dish of Jell-O. No longer hungry, she played with it for a few seconds then pushed the dish away. "After all," she said with a shrug, "why would I check your division?"

"Why wouldn't you?"

"Burial and Memorial? Why check there? This guy is alive and kicking and out wandering the streets shooting people. He's not six feet under. . . ."

"Yeah, but didn't that 'very nice' detective, Lindstrom, tell you that they believe this Soldier guy might be seriously ill, maybe even dying?"

"Yes," Lorelei replied in a so-what tone. "That's the profile the police are working with. But obviously, he's still very much alive."

Scraping her plate for every morsel of crust, Helen Carbone finished off the pie and washed it down with a last gulp of coffee. Then looking directly at Lorelei, said, "If, in fact, this guy *is* a veteran and, if, in fact, he truly knows he is dying, he may want his veteran's burial benefits."

"Maybe he plans to get buried somewhere other than a veterans' cemetery?"

"Doesn't matter," Carbone assured with a knowing grin. "He would still be entitled to a government-provided headstone, a marker . . . blah blah blah. And he may have already filed in advance. Many vets do."

Lorelei put down her spoon and gazed tightly into Helen's overly large eyes. "Go on," she urged, suddenly charged with renewed interest.

"For many vets, it's the first and only request they ever make to the VA. He would have to submit his DD-214 and file a VA 40-1330 Application for Standard Government Headstone or Marker." Helen Carbone raised her thick eyebrows in how-do-you-like-them-apples emphasis. "That doesn't mean he actually has, but he might have."

Lorelei DeKohning carefully dabbed at the corners of her mouth and dropped the balled-up napkin onto her tray. "Helen, would you mind terribly much if we went right back upstairs to your office and did a quick check through your files? I've got a good feeling about this."

The reports coming in from the field were not encouraging, Savage thought, but not unexpected either. By midafternoon the teams from the detective task force and several teams from Manhattan South Homicide, including Diane DeGennaro and Richie Marcus, had already located and interviewed thirty-five of the almost one hundred remaining candidates. For a wide variety of reasons—death, infirmity, corroborated alibis—all thirty-five had so far been ruled out as suspects.

Jack Lindstrom had remained behind in the Manhattan South squad room. Between update conversations with Lorelei DeKohning, his connection down at the VA, he was also running the tallies and crossing names off the master VA and TA lists as the negative reports from the teams were phoned in.

While handling a nonstop deluge of telephone inquiries from Operations, different branches of the media, and City Hall, Savage had also been casually observing Jack Lindstrom through the glass wall of the sergeants' room. He noticed that in the last half hour, Jack appeared totally rapt during several of the calls he had made. The bit-between-the-teeth expression on Lindstrom's face was one Savage had seen many times in the past on the pre-meltdown Jack. It was good to see that confident demeanor again—the proud set of the shoulders, the intensity in the intelligent eyes. Lindstrom looked just like the Jack of old. And the man was on to something, no question; with each call, he was taking notes as fast as he could write.

Finally hanging up, Lindstrom pushed away from his desk, gathered his papers, and made a beeline for the sergeants' office.

"I think we got us a possibility here, boss," he said, handing Savage a fistful of hastily scribbled notes.

"This guy really stands out?" Savage asked, slipping his half-glasses down to the tip of his nose.

"Like Marcus at a social tea."

"Tell me more," Savage said, flipping through the notes.

"John Wesley Krumenacker," Lindstrom began, sitting down on Billy Lakis' desk. "The name originated on one of the 1965 St. Malachy's basketball team photos. It was one of the names that also popped up on the Transit Authority list, but not the VA's. That is," Lindstrom said with a wry smile, "until a little while ago."

"We sure it's the same guy?"

"Same guy; same social security number. Just to be sure, I followed up by calling the army. Look at this," Lindstrom said, pointing down at page two of his notes. "United States Army, 173rd Airborne Brigade, Vietnam, '66 to '68."

Savage offered a low whistle. "173rd Airborne, pretty tough group. And if this DOB from his Transit records is correct, he was only sixteen years old in 1966."

"Bunch of decorations, including the Bronze Star. And get this: The guy was a damn tunnel rat."

"Jesus, those sonsabitches pissed ice water. What did he do for the Transit Authority?"

"Trackman, '75 to '85. Left the job on his own; doesn't get any pension or anything."

"Time frame's correct for the Transit Authority writing paper," Savage said. "How come the VA just suddenly found him in their data bank?"

"He only recently applied for a burial plot and headstone in the veterans' cemetery out in Calverton, Long Island. The guy's terminal; guess he figures he can occupy it real soon."

"We got an address?"

"Oh yeah," Lindstrom shot back happily. "We got us an address. Down in the good old Ninth."

"Get on the air and raise Marcus and DeGennaro—give them a ten-one. As soon as they call in, give them that address and tell them to meet us there forthwith."

"You want me to contact Emergency Service for a backup?"

"No," Savage said decisively. "They've got enough of their units already backing up the task force. This'll have to be our show."

Savage stepped to his locker, opened it, and plucked Lindstrom's holstered service revolver from the top shelf.

"Here," he said, handing Lindstrom the gun. "You and me are the only two available. After you contact Richie and Diane, go warm up the car. I'll be right down as soon as I speak with the Chief of D. I've gotta let him know what's up."

"Thanks, boss," Lindstrom quietly intoned. He slipped the thirty-eight into his waistband and moved in bold strides back to his desk in the squad room.

Savage reached for the phone.

Sister Lucia's always intense eyes clicked back and forth as she entered the East Seventh Street tenement hallway and approached John Wesley's first-floor apartment. Vigilant, with senses heightened to the level of advanced radar and sonar, she strained for the early detection of someone either entering or leaving the building that might see her there. Despite her big blond wig and heavy makeup, today it was imperative to get in and out of the building totally unnoticed. With her face partly obscured by the extended drape of her dark woolen scarf and her collar pulled up fully in a further attempt to be invisible, she pressed an ear tightly against his door and listened.

The annoying sound effects were there in spades: the choking, the hacking, the disgusting spitting up. She tapped the door gently three times and redirected her senses back to the hallway and nearby stairwell.

Long seconds passed. Open the damn door already, she thought, fuming, sensing J.W. finally at the peephole. She pursed her lips and fought to control rising anger as a series of locks were then slowly unbolted from the inside. Finally the door opened.

"What is it with you and all these locks?" she snarled, pushing her way past J.W. into the tiny hotbox apartment. She pulled off the scarf and jammed it into her coat pocket, then set her large shoulder bag down on the shelf table beside the Underwood. "Besides all of your other problems, don't tell me that you're paranoid too."

"Look who's talkin', for God's sake," Krumenacker replied drolly, leaning against the paint-chipped door until it clicked closed. He carefully reset every dead bolt.

Sister Lucia set her jaw and undid the five large buttons of her knee-length quilted coat; she decided to let the remark go. It was just another indication of J.W.'s rapidly ebbing loyalty to her, and his decreased overall value to the cause. It also underscored her theory that something had to be done—now.

"Have you gotten around to reloading the two guns, as you were asked to do?" she said evenly. She scanned the dreary room, avoiding direct eye contact. The place was as much a dump as it had always been. The big black Hefty bag still sat in the kitchen's far corner, filled with expectoration-soaked paper towels and God knew what else.

"Not yet," J.W. mumbled. He whipped the tether of his oxygen supply tube across the top of his bed as he shuffled to the dresser by the window. Shaking several fish food pellets into his hand and babbling something indistinguishable, he sprinkled them into the fishbowl beside his small television.

"Would you like some tea?" he asked, before breaking into another of his damn never-ending coughing fits.

"No. I don't want any tea," she said loudly over the annoying hack. "I don't want to look at your fish. I don't want any conversation. I don't want anything. I just want you to load up those guns so I can get out of here. Besides getting that forty-four back to where it belongs, I then must get my thirty-eight and your forty-five both stashed in the church today, in case you've forgotten."

"I haven't forgotten," Krumenacker said, gasping the words.

"Remember, we're all three going to need fully loaded guns tomorrow," she said calmly, in a dodge to cloak her intentions. "I will hide your forty-five where we've always hidden it, beneath the votive candles. I'm still working on a place to put my thirty-eight. A place where I can get at it easily when we make our move."

J.W. nodded and shuffled back across the room to the shelf table. He reached inside the OxyTote bag, pulled the forty-five from it, and ejected the ammo clip. He placed the gun back in the bag and the clip on the table. When a gentle knock came on the apartment door, he quickly slipped the clip into his pocket.

"Don't answer that," Sister Lucia snapped in a harsh whisper.

J.W. looked through the door's peephole and began undoing the dead bolts.

"I told you not to open the damn door," Sister Lucia shouted, scrambling across the room to stop him. "I don't want anybody seeing me here. You know that."

"Don't worry," J.W. said. "It's only the spaz from down the hall. He's here to get Charlie." *Cough, cough . . .*

"Who is Charlie?"

"My fish," J.W. replied. "I told this guy he could have him. I know he'll take good care of him. Hell, come tomorrow, I ain't gonna be around to see to him anymore." J.W. swung open the door and allowed a palsied old man to stumble in.

Fuming, Sister Lucia stepped back and turned away.

"Who's the lady?" the man asked immediately in garbled, almost indecipherable speech.

"Just an old friend, Mr. Pitler," J.W. responded. "No one you need to know. C'mon, let me get Charlie for you."

Sister Lucia watched as Krumenacker ambled toward the fishbowl on the dresser. She froze in anger when the palsy-stricken neighbor, fraught with jerky movements and uncontrollable tics, stumbled over to her and got right in her face. "Glad to meet you, ma'am," he stammered, holding out a bony trembling hand. "I'm Alan."

"Unh," Sister Lucia grunted, offering a lifeless grip in return. Why did this fool have to come for this damn fish right at this moment, she thought, her simmering anger about to break into a rolling boil.

"Mr. Krumenacker is so good to me," Alan said, leaning even more into her face, forcing her to lean backward. "When they stole my old three-wheeler, he went right out and bought me a brand new one. It's beautiful. . . . A red-and-white one. Wasn't that nice of him?"

"Very nice."

"Wanna see it?" he asked, pressing even closer still.

"No. I don't think so," she replied sharply, pulling back from the pathetic little man, who was a hopeless space invader with truly terrible breath.

J.W. handed the old man a small box. "That's all of his food and supplies. You carry that back to your apartment, Mr. Pitler, and I'll carry Charlie." Disconnecting the oxygen supply tube at the cannula and draping it over the recliner, he looked over at Sister Lucia. "The top lock'll set by itself when I close the door. Let me in when I get back. I'm only going to be a minute." *Cough, cough.*

"Goodbye, ma'am," the spaz said. "Nice to meet you." Then, as the door was closing behind them, she heard him say to J.W., "What a nice lady, but she smells funny."

It was now or never, she decided, waiting for J.W.'s return. The success of the long-planned mission for the Blessed Mother was at stake. If she were to shoot J.W. with the forty-five, could she place the gun in his hand and make it look like a suicide? She would have to shoot him in the side of the head to make it appear as one. It would absolutely have to look good in order for the police to be convinced and declare that the search for the Soldier was over. The police, the Church, the people . . . everybody would be so jubilant. *The morons.* But the thought nagged: Could she make it look real? It seemed the police always had ways of determining if such things had been staged. . . . What to do? She stiffened when she heard J.W.'s coughing and gagging; he was on his way back to the apartment. She undid the self-setting lock and held the door open a crack.

"Are you still with me, J.W.?" Sister Lucia asked as Krumenacker let himself in. "Are you still with the cause?"

J.W. glanced back at her. "Yeah, I'm with the cause," he said, his response as pale as his suddenly colorless face. "I still support you, but I just can't deal with any more killing."

"You can't deal with any more killing?" Sister Lucia screamed, no longer able to control the anger that had been building since the Quigley affair. "What kind of moronic answer is that?" she demanded, feeling spittle fly. "Killing *is* the cause. This is what we've worked for. If you can't deal with it anymore, how in God's name are we to proceed tomorrow?"

"I'm really not sure." J.W.'s flat reply was spoken just above a whisper. Pulling the Ruger revolver from the OxyTote bag, he moved slowly to the ammo cabinet and, after searching the shelves, took out two fresh unopened boxes of ammunition. He tore open the carton's seals and topped off the Colt's ammo clip with five fresh rounds from one, then slipped two new cartridges into the Ruger's two empty cylinders from the second box.

"I'm not feeling well, Lucy," he said, laying the Ruger back on the table and jamming the clip back into the butt of the Colt. "In fact, I'm feeling very poorly. When I feel this punk it's a bit hard to get enthusiastic about any damned thing." He began another extended coughing spell.

Lucia stepped to the table and picked up the forty-five. She would wait until he turned away to make the reconnect to his oxygen line. Then she would press the barrel against his right temple—she knew he was right-handed—and squeeze the trigger. She hoped too much blood wouldn't fly and get all over her coat.

As Krumenacker reached for the free end of the oxy

tether, he suddenly reared back and clutched at his chest with both hands. Babbling something completely unintelligible, he turned to face her, his taut expression revealing equal parts pain, fear, and regret; the look of one about to be chucked into the fires of hell. His legs went rubbery. He reached out to her for support; she stepped back. Eyes rolling queerly, he stumbled twice, reeled backward, and collapsed faceup on the floor beside his unmade bed. In seconds, his lips began to turn blue.

"Oxygen," he murmured, pointing a trembling finger to the disconnected cannula in his nose. His breathing was coming in very short, rapid, gasps. "Get me nitro . . . in oxy bag."

Sister Lucia quickly put the gun back on the table, located the small vial of pills in the OxyTote, and collected the oxygen feeder tube. As J.W. choked for air, begging with his eyes for her to make the reconnect, she made her decision. She knelt beside him and laying the tube aside, uncapped the vial of pills and spilled them across the floor. She looked down into his dull, pleading eyes and gently stroked his fevered brow, allowing the clock to run.

"It's okay, J.W.," she murmured. "The Blessed Mother has come to take you home to heaven. Just the way I told you she would."

She quickly blessed herself and mumbled a prayer of thanks for the incredible divine intervention. This couldn't possibly have happened at a better time, or without help from the Blessed Mother, she realized. J.W. had been of no further use anyway. Let the cops find him, legitimately dead, without the uncertainty of a staged suicide. They'll now truly think the siege of the Soldier is over. They'll all celebrate like idiots, certain that everything is just hunky-dory.

In minutes, J.W.'s lips had gone purple and he had fallen into total unconsciousness.

Sister Lucia stood, went to the kitchen, and grabbed a dish towel. Returning to the shelf table, she carefully wiped down the grips of the huge forty-five and laid the fully loaded pistol back inside J.W.'s OxyTote. She could barely control her elation; she was ecstatic.

She buttoned up her coat, slipped the Ruger revolver into her bag, and left the apartment. Come tomorrow, ridding the world of the Antichrist pope was going to be a snap.

TWENTY-NINE

Savage and Lindstrom arrived at Krumenacker's Lower East Side address only moments before Detectives Marcus and DeGennaro rolled up in their silver Taurus. After quickly filling them in and formulating a game plan, Savage and Lindstrom climbed the stairs of the stoop and entered the first-floor hallway. Diane and Richie went around back to cover any rear or side exits.

Guns drawn and backs to the wall on either side of apartment 1A's door, they each rapped loudly on it three times; there was no response. Savage rapped again, and called out in a loud voice, "Open up, Mr. Krumenacker, this is the police. We need to talk to you." Still, there came no response from inside the apartment.

"Can I help you?" The abruptly posed question came from a large and slovenly dressed woman. She was standing in the open doorway to apartment 1B, gnarly hands on wide hips, cheaply dyed hair rolled up in a thousand curlers, and wearing way too much lipstick on her fat lips. "I'm the landlady here," she said. "I'm Eleanor Brzazinski."

"And we're the police, Ms. Brzazinski," Savage replied flatly, looking across the narrow hallway. He held his thirty-eight tightly against his belly in his right hand, partially concealing it under his left. "We're looking for a Mr. John Wesley Krumenacker. Does he live here?"

"He lives in that apartment, all right," she said, her pumpkin head bobbing arrogantly on her broad shoulders.

"But if he ain't answerin' the freakin' door, he must be out. Know what I'm sayin'?"

Charming chick, Savage thought. I oughtta introduce her to that prick Sid Fordham.

"Does Mr. Krumenacker live alone?" Lindstrom asked. He reached out the toe of his right shoe and squashed a full-grown roach that was ambling by.

"Yeah," the woman responded sourly. "He lives alone, except for his stupid fish. What do you want to see Krumenacker for?" she inquired, as if actually expecting them to tell her.

"Is there any other way out of this apartment?" Savage asked.

"Only out the front window, or maybe down the freakin' terlit," the woman said, turning to look at Marcus and DeGennaro, who had entered the hallway. "But let me tell ya'," she added, "Krumenacker ain't in no shape to be climbing out of no windows. Know what I'm sayin'?"

"Why's that?" Savage asked.

"Can't hardly breathe," she replied curtly out of the side of her heavily painted mouth. "The friggin' guy's on oxygen, for crissakes."

"You got a passkey?" Savage asked.

"Sure, I got a passkey," she replied, looking down her broad nose. "But only for the house lock." Scuffing into the hallway in open-toe slippers and pointing to the door of 1A, she added, "It's the Yale on top. But old Krumenacker's got a whole bunch more freakin' locks of his own, as you can plainly see. I ain't got no damn keys for them."

"Well, let's just see what happens if we undo the house lock, *okay, lady*?" Savage said pointedly.

"You got a warrant to be goin' inside there?" Ms. Brzazinski asked, her crappy attitude getting nastier by the second. "'Cause if you ain't, I ain't helpin' you get in."

"Mr. Krumenacker's a very sick man, right?" Richie Marcus growled. He shot Savage a millisecond play-along glance and placed his ear to the door of 1A.

"That's what I said!" the landlady shot back, giving Marcus a surly look.

"Well," Marcus said, still holding his ear to the door. "I swear I can hear some moaning and groaning going on inside there. No time for no warrants, lady," he continued, jerking his thumb toward the door. "There may well be a human life at stake here. If your passkey can't get us in, I'm afraid we'll have no alternative but to bust the door down. Diane, go out to the car and bring in the ax." Looking at Savage with flashing brows, he added, "Ain't that right, Sergeant?"

"That's right," Savage said firmly, adding a tone of urgency to his voice. "And we'd hate to have to do that. . . . Doors sure are expensive to replace these days."

Mrs. Brzazinski crossed the hall in a shot, pulling a ring of keys from the pocket of her housecoat. She wound quickly through them until she found the one she wanted; she slipped it into the door's uppermost lock. Upon turning the key, the door released and swung open by itself.

When they entered John Wesley Krumenacker's claustrophobic hotbox of an apartment, they found him stretched out and unconscious on the floor. It was uncertain whether he was dead or alive—enough doubt existed either way. Nobody wanted to call it. To be sure, the man had at least one foot in the grave. Jack Lindstrom and Richie Marcus stripped off their coats and jackets, and both worked up a good sweat taking turns performing CPR on the unshaven and bony man, until an emergency medical team arrived on the scene. They declared him to be still alive, albeit just barely. Comatose, he was transported by city ambulance to Bellevue's Intensive Care Unit, where he was under heavy police guard and considered likely to die.

Although Krumenacker could not be questioned, his stuffy little apartment on Seventh Street spoke volumes. Everywhere the detectives looked, they found the evidence they needed to make a closed case. Savage notified Operations and requested the immediate response of teams from Forensics, Crime Scene, and Photo Unit. The chief of detectives was also notified; he was the first to arrive. With him was a tall, serious-looking man Savage didn't recognize. He did recognize, however, that the man's clothing, shoes, and staid bearing were classic European.

"Tell me something good, Thorn," Chief Wilson said, worming forcefully past Jack Lindstrom and Diane De-Gennaro, who were talking with a few uniforms from the Ninth. "I'm way overdue for some good news."

"This is definitely our boy, Chief," Savage replied. "This place is a treasure trove of incrimination."

He glanced then at the tall man, expecting an introduction before saying anything further in front of him.

"Sergeant Thornton Savage," the chief said, gesturing to the austere man. "I'd like you to meet Colonel George Olmstead, commanding officer of the Vatican's Swiss Guards. The colonel is here on the QT, acting as the advance guard for the papal visit. The police commissioner has directed me to share everything we have with him."

Savage nodded and shook the man's large hand. Olmstead had a viselike grip that suited the stern, no-nonsense demeanor.

"Give me a quickie on what we've got," Wilson said flatly. "I've gotta get right on the horn with the PC. He's standing by with bated breath, waiting to hear *touchdown* so he can get on the horn with the mayor."

Without speaking, Savage led the way to the shelf table in the corner. He pulled open the Velcro flap of the nylon shoulder bag and motioned the chief to peer into it.

"Model 1911 Colt .45 automatic," Savage said.

"*With* silencer," Wilson murmured, turning approvingly to Olmstead, who also glanced down into the bag.

"What is the meaning of the oxygen tank?" Olmstead inquired. His English was excellent, but heavily tinged with Germanic accents.

Lindstrom stepped in to the conversation. "Judging from

all the medications and oxygen equipment, it appears that this man was suffering from some form of COPD. . . ."

The chief cocked an ear toward Lindstrom, his face a question mark.

"Chronic obstructive pulmonary disease," Lindstrom clarified. "I've also found considerable literature scattered around the apartment which would support that."

"I thought the EMTs said this guy Krumenacker had a heart attack," the chief said, turning to face Savage.

"That's what they said," Savage responded. "In fact, it looks like he was trying to get to some nitroglycerin pills; they were spilled all over the floor."

"What else?" Wilson asked abruptly.

"Beat-up manual typewriter," Savage went on. He pointed out the Underwood beside the OxyTote. "Worn out black ribbon. Upper case *T* and lower case *L* have damaged serifs—"

"High-striking lowercase *A*?" Wilson inquired hopefully. Savage nodded. Wilson again turned to Olmstead with an assuring nod.

"Paper the same?" Wilson followed up, indicating several sheets of yellowed stationery beside the machine.

Savage nodded again. "Same Hammermill." He picked up a small stack of Our Lady of Fatima prayer cards that were stored atop the AirSep oxygen machine and flipped through them. "These look familiar?" he asked.

The chief, whose smile was getting bigger by the minute, turned and again nodded confidently toward Olmstead. The foreigner's expression remained inscrutable. If he hadn't known better, Savage mused, he'd have thought the guy must have been from Missouri.

"Boss, come look at this," Richie Marcus called out. Loosely tailed by Olmstead, Savage and Wilson walked across the room and joined the detective inside the small kitchen.

"Looks like our boy was ready for Freddy," Marcus growled, pointing into the open cabinet above the sink.

"Got a little bit of everything in here," he said. "Thirty-eights, three-fifty-sevens, all the way up the bore sizes to forty-fives. Which, by the way," he added emphatically, "happen to be all Winchesters."

Staring into the cabinet, Savage did a rapid scan of the neatly stacked cartons of handgun ammunition. "I see he's even got some forty-fours," Savage said, turning to face Wilson. "Peter Grennan, the Boston victim, got it with a .44 Ruger."

"Winchester ammo?" Wilson asked.

Savage nodded.

"I've seen enough," Wilson said. He reached into his coat pocket and pulled out a cell phone. Stepping from the kitchen and bypassing Olmstead, he began to punch in numbers. Savage followed, but was intercepted by the arrival of Bill Scovers from the Photo Unit.

"How much you want?" Scovers asked casually. He set his hard-sided equipment case down on the open sofa bed and began undoing snaps.

"Give me your deluxe wedding and bar mitzvah packages," Savage responded. "And money's no object."

"Gotcha, boss," the photo tech replied, grinning.

"Listen up," Savage announced, getting everyone's attention. "Before Forensics and Crime Scene get here with their cardboard boxes to start vouchering and hauling everything out, I want Photo to get several shots of every item we intend to take. And I want every one of those items photographed, precisely *as and where* it was found. So please don't go moving anything."

In a most unusual display of blue idiom, Chief Wilson sidled up to Savage and whispered, "The police commissioner's cumming in his freakin' pants." Slipping his cell phone back into his coat pocket, he added, "The press has got it already, so you can expect a mob scene of reporters to show up at any minute."

"*Shit!* You gonna handle them, Chief?" Savage asked.

"You handle them," Wilson replied. "I'm outta here. I'll

get with you later." Turning to Olmstead, he proclaimed, "I think you'll agree, Colonel, looks like your boss is going to be real safe." Flashing a slight smile, Olmstead nodded tentative agreement.

With Colonel Olmstead in tow, the chief of detectives moved for the door, then stopped short in his tracks. He turned to again face Savage, and said loudly, "You and your people have done an absolutely phenomenal job." He looked around the room, making solid eye contact with each detective. "My sincere congratulations to you all."

Savage shrugged and grimaced. Motioning Colonel Olmstead to wait, the chief marched back to Savage, wrapped an arm around his shoulders, and waltzed him into a far corner.

"What's the matter, Thornton?" he asked, flashing a worried frown. "I didn't like that look."

"Nothing, boss," Savage murmured. "It's just that I don't know; I'm not sure. There are a couple of things. . . ."

"Talk to me," Wilson said.

"I'm not sure we should be declaring victory or letting our guard down. Not just yet."

"And why not?" Wilson whispered.

"I really don't know, Chief," Savage said. He looked deeply into Wilson's big dark eyes, grimaced again, and added, "I wish I could tell you. . . . But I think we should pump the brakes."

"I hate when you do this to me," the chief mumbled sotto voce.

"So I don't think I should be the one to talk to the press," Savage said.

"You broke the damn case," Wilson said flatly. "And you always do a good job with the press."

"You know damn well that the mayor and the PC are going to be shouting 'case closed' from the rooftops. I don't want to trip them up, maybe contradict or embarrass them. I think we need to hedge a little on this one, boss, but I don't think they're going to allow that."

"You're right," Wilson agreed. "They want an all clear, no ifs, ands, or buts."

"And I'm not so sure we can give 'em that."

Wilson exhaled hard, turned, and moved purposely for the door. Glancing back momentarily to Savage, he said, "I'll call you later." He collected Colonel Olmstead on his way out and left the apartment.

"Listen up, people," Savage announced. "Before we leave here, I want you to look twice at everything in this place. I want you to scrutinize everything. I want every drawer and closet searched. I want the mattress flipped. I want every pocket of every garment gone through. Twice. Does everybody hear me?" He looked around slowly; all were nodding.

He went on. "If you find so much as a scrap of paper— a lousy shopping list—which you think could be of *any* value to us, I want it itemized, secured, vouchered, and taken in."

Jack Lindstrom pointed to a bulging plastic trash bag in the corner of the kitchen. "What do you think, boss?" he said. "Looks like a lot of nasty stuff in there. You know, medical waste . . . that kind of thing. You'd need a damn hazmat suit to go through it, for crissakes."

"Let's take the whole bag," Savage said. ".We're gonna have to pick it clean eventually."

"Is there something you'd *really* like us to find for you, boss?" Marcus asked. "Something you'd like for Christmas."

Savage mulled that for a second. "A bus, plane, or train ticket stub, to and from Boston, would do me real nice."

Bundled up against the flesh-numbing cold that whipped along darkened Madison Avenue, her small jaw jutted and narrow lips pursed in an expression of frozen determination, Sister Lucia moved steadily, weaving through the slower pedestrian flow with the short, rapid steps of one with a clear mission.

John Wesley had lost his nerve, she reassured herself as she hurried across Fifty-second; he had become a complete liability to the cause. She had had no choice but to let him go the way she did. There was simply no question that his sense of duty had vanished, become completely compromised. Perhaps she had not chosen wisely by enlisting John Wesley in the first place, she mused. That was not true, she quickly realized. It had been J.W. who identified the priests; it had also been J.W. who supplied the guns and taught her how to use them. . . . But the question was now moot. He was gone, and it was time to move on. All in all, things were actually coming together real good.

Sister Lucia turned west at Fifty-first and, when traffic finally cleared, crossed Madison on a diagonal. Halfway through the block, she climbed the stone steps leading to St. Patrick's north transept doors and entered.

The nave was a beehive of worker activity; everywhere she looked, crews of men and women in blue coveralls were busy. Some were mopping and scrubbing aisles, others polished the marble communion rail and anything made of brass, and still others were setting spectacular floral sprays at the liturgical and high altars and around the great bronze baldachin. "Hmm," she murmured scornfully, angry that no expense was being spared for the Antichrist's visit tomorrow. Sister Lucia opened her knee-length coat, dipped two fingers into a font of holy water, and blessed herself. She then made her way directly to the chancel organ enclosure just off the main altar on the St. Joseph's side. She tapped lightly on the age-darkened oak door.

"Yes?" came a mild male response.

"Open up, Philo," she said warmly. "It's me, Angela from the archdiocese."

She heard the lock unlatch. When the small door swung open, there stood Philo Kersey. The lanky, long-fingered, angular man had for many years been one of the two premier organists at St. Patrick's. Of late, he had been bugging the archdiocese, through her, for a small raise and somewhat less playing time. It was rumored that the man was suffering from arthritis and gout.

"How are you feeling today, Philo?" Angela asked, her eyes darting about the small space, taking in every nook, cranny, and pocket. "I must say, you certainly are looking well," she lied.

The taciturn organist shrugged blankly and stepped aside, allowing her entrance into the very cramped space.

"Has all the music been selected for tomorrow's ceremony?" she asked, wide-eyed. She concentrated on keeping her voice soft, her tone friendly and sincere.

"Oh yes," he replied softly, rippling long fingers at a stack of sheet music propped above the multilevel keyboard. "Mrs. McKenna and I have been rehearsing for three weeks. It's not every day that one gets to play for the Holy Father."

"Will Mrs. McKenna be at the choir-loft keyboard for the Mass?"

Kersey nodded. "You know how she is; she has always preferred to be up there," he said. "Surrounded by all those voices. Says it does something for her playing." The man shrugged, nonplussed.

"Then you will be down here at the chancel console."

"Uh-huh."

Closing her eyes dreamily, she sighed and murmured, "There is nothing quite so wonderful, so solemn . . . so sacred-feeling, as when both organs of Saint Patrick's Cathedral are being played simultaneously."

Kersey offered a mild grin. "Seven thousand, eight hundred and fifty-five pipes," he said proudly. "They can make an enormous amount of sound."

"You are blessed," she stated, leaning over to gaze through the mesh screen beside the keyboard. From that vantage point she was but a few steps away from the cathedra, the throne of the Cardinal Archbishop of New York, situated toward the front of the sanctuary. "My, you will have a most wonderful view of the ceremony," she said.

"It's the best seat in the house," he replied, almost showing some level of excitement. "Because this enclosure is hidden by an apsidal column, no one ever sees me. But I'm right here, right on top of everything. I'm going to have a perfect profile view of the Holy Father."

It was true; the mesh screen afforded a full view of the majestic altar. After all, she reasoned, the organist needed to time his playing to the celebrant's every move.

"Are you going to be here to see the Holy Father tomorrow?" Kersey inquired.

"Oh yes," she replied with an anguished sigh. "I'll be here all right, but the best they could do was stick me in a pew fourteen rows back."

"They couldn't get you any closer?" Kersey said, shrugging in disbelief.

"All the front rows have been taken by the money. You know . . . the *Kennedys* . . . "

Kersey snickered knowingly. "So what else is new?" he said, shaking his head. "But fourteen rows isn't so bad. You'll still be able to see everything."

She shrugged and flashed an unhappy grimace.

"Have you been able to bring up my requests to the monsignor, Angela?" he said, doleful eyes set deeply beneath arching brows.

"You mean your request for more money and less playing time?" she said coyly.

"Yes. Everybody knows you hold a lot of sway over at the archdiocese. I just know you could intervene with the monsignor on my behalf. I really must have fewer hours, Angela," he pleaded. "And at least a little bit more money. I haven't had a raise in over ten years."

"Well, I suppose I might be able to do that for you," she muttered, as if weighing his situation. "Tell me," she said. "Would there be any problem if I were to watch tomor-

row's ceremony from inside here, with you, instead of
fourteen rows back? I promise I wouldn't get in your way."

"There's going to be so much security and everything. . . . I don't know if . . ." Kersey began, stammering.

She smirked at the man and glared intense disappointment.

"But . . ." he rationalized, apparently getting the message. "You are a part of the archdiocese inner circle. . . . I
suppose it would be all right."

"Where will I sit?" she asked.

"There's no other seat," he replied. "You might just
have to stand there in the corner and watch through the
mesh."

"Philo," she purred. "Be a dear, will you? Go right now
down into the sacristy and bring up one folding chair.
There are stacks of them down there."

"I'm really very busy right now, Angela—"

"Philo," she barked impatiently. "Do it *right now*!"

The passive man made a pained face but obediently
turned and started from the booth. "Just don't tell anybody," Kersey said. "I could probably get in a lot of trouble."

Sister Lucia smiled broadly. "Philo . . . look at my face.
You have my solemn word."

After he'd closed the door behind him, Sister Lucia
reached into her bag and withdrew the .38 caliber Smith &
Wesson. She planted it in a small recess behind the organ
console.

THIRTY

Clad only in a bath towel tucked at his taut waist and looking intently down his elegant straight nose into the steamed bathroom mirror, Colonel George Olmstead dragged the razor along his raised chin to get the last few remnants of beard stubble. Though he had been up now for almost nineteen hours, he felt strong, energized by the incredible eleventh-hour capture of the priest-killing maniac by detectives of the NYPD. Beyond that, all of the last-minute security plans for the pontiff's arrival tomorrow were now set in stone.

The pope would arrive at JFK shortly after noon, chopper immediately into Manhattan, and motorcade directly to St. Patrick's Cathedral in a limousine arranged for by the New York Archdiocese. For additional security, the vehicle would be driven by the most highly trusted archdiocese chauffeur. Olmstead had been assured by no less than Cardinal Hammond himself that the man knew every street, alley, and avenue in the city in the event of some need to take an emergency detour.

With everything perfectly set and nothing more remaining for him to do until the pontiff's arrival tomorrow, Olmstead decided he could take a deep breath, relax, and reward himself. For the first time in weeks, the pressures that had been steadily mounting on his shoulders had subsided, dropped away like a jettisoned knapsack filled with stone. He still believed strongly in the idea of a far-reaching conspiracy against the pope, but for the moment at least, the

most obvious potential for disaster lying in wait for the pope
had been quelled.

Not that Olmstead could, or ever would, let down on his
sworn mission to protect the Holy Father no matter what;
even at the cost of his own life, if need be. His dedication
to the Vicar of Christ was pure and absolute. And when he
returned to Rome, he would live up to his promise to un-
mask anybody within the papal orbit who could be part of
a conspiracy to bring a new order to the Vatican and to the
Church.

But this night was his, the first free night he'd had in a
long time, and as luck would have it, Valerie Palermo had
been in her room at the Pierre when he called. They were
on for dinner, wine, and . . . He combed his hair, exchanged the towel for briefs, and dabbed some cologne at
his neck. He dressed then in his freshly pressed Armani,
knotted his tie, and left his hotel room. He deserved this
night.

Savage opened the box of frozen waffles and popped two
of them into his toaster oven. He took out the butter dish and
placed it on the counter, then went in search of maple syrup.
He checked every cabinet twice; he had none. *Shit!* Having
waffles for dinner was a crappy idea anyway, he thought, but
it would have been fast *and* he'd be using up old stock. He
dug through his junk drawer and found a menu from Angelo's on Eighth Street. He'd order a pie and have it delivered. As he reached for the kitchen wall phone, it rang.

"Thornton." The caller was Chief of Detectives Wilson.

"Hello, boss," Savage responded. "Glad you got back to
me. I've been trying to get through to you for hours. Did
that hump Crowley let you know that?"

"About ten minutes ago," Wilson advised sourly. He
then got to the point. "Have you been watching TV?"

"No."

"You were a hundred percent right," Wilson said. "The
mayor and PC have pronounced this case closed. They're

giving us all the credit all right, but your words of caution are still ringing in my ears. Let's talk about it."

"Hold on a second, Chief," Savage said. "I've gotta put out a fire." He reached over and shut off the toaster oven and plucked out the two smoldering, blackened waffles. He slid them into the sink and squelched them with running water. "Okay, Chief."

"Are you still thinking about how this guy was able to leave St. Raymond's Cemetery after icing Quigley the other day?"

"Yeah . . ." Savage replied. "A guy as sick as this guy isn't about to be hiking all the way across the expanse of St. Raymond's Cemetery. That place is huge."

"Didn't we think it was possible that he had another car planted?" the chief suggested.

"Still would have had to take the hike . . ."

"What else is bothering you? Give it to me now."

"The guy's got a thousand frigging dead-bolts on the inside of his door, and not one of them is set."

"So what?"

"Anybody neurotic enough to have all those dead-bolts would have damn well had more of them set."

"What are you saying?"

"I don't know what I'm saying. Just seems peculiar that the only lock engaged was the one that would automatically set itself when the door is closed."

"Like maybe someone else had been here?" the chief said.

Savage shrugged. "Besides that, there's also the matter of the second letter."

"What about the second letter?" Wilson asked.

"It was written on the same paper, typed on the same typewriter, but it had a different rhythm . . . a different voice. Know what I mean?"

"Listen, Thornton," Wilson said. "Get yourself a good night's sleep. The pope's security is now in the hands of

the Patrol Division. They'll cover him like a blanket from
the time he gets here until the time he leaves."

"Hmm. But there may be more bogeymen out there."

"Then stay with it. When you get into the office in the
morning, do whatever you think still needs to be done."

The Cafe Pierre was decorated in tones of pale yellow,
green, and gold, and further embellished with Italian gray
marble, etched Italian mirrors, and trompe l'oeil wall and
ceiling murals. George Olmstead thought the ambience elegant European. Almost as elegant as Valerie Palermo in her
daringly low-cut Versace silk sheath. Her tantalizing cleav-
age had turned a number of heads when they entered.

Cocktails before and during dinner were classic marti-
nis. Ms. Palermo preferred Finnish vodka, while Olmstead
went with the Bombay Sapphire gin. He held back; she
drank with abandon. Dinner began with an appetizer of
heirloom tomato and asparagus tartare with smoked buffalo mozzarella and aged twenty-five-year-old balsamic
vinegar. Soup was lobster gazpacho with vine-ripened
tomatoes and guacamole. For dinner, Olmstead selected
braised veal cheeks with pommes puree; it came with
spring vegetables and red wine sauce. Valerie opted for
sautéed Maine lobster served with tomato, tarragon, and
brandy sauce. For dessert they shared each other in Valerie's fifteenth-floor suite. She was truly an experience,
one he was glad he'd had.

As Olmstead stood before a wall mirror tying his tie in
preparation to leave, Valerie Palermo abruptly excused
herself from the bedroom; she disappeared into the outer
room. Moments later, Olmstead was startled by the appearance of a man's image reflected in the mirror. Olmstead turned to face him. The man was well groomed,
nattily dressed, and held a huge revolver in his right hand.
Olmstead recognized him. He had drummed the man out of
the Swiss Guards about ten years prior for spouting radical
and dangerous ideas about the papacy.

"Stronheim," Olmstead uttered.

"Good evening, Colonel," the blond man said, raising the pistol with both hands and aiming it directly at Olmstead's chest. "Did you have a good time this evening with Ms. Palermo?" he asked, then added, "But of course you know that that is not her real name. But she is quite talented though, don't you agree?"

Olmstead's jaw became tight; anger at his own human appetites surged through every cell in his body. Purely and simply, he'd been had, and the clever trap could have only been set in Rome. He glared at the man but said nothing.

"I'm sure you remember me, Colonel. Did I not tell you that our paths would one day cross again?"

"What is your part in all this?"

"Once you announced your determination to uncover a conspiracy within the halls of the Vatican, some of those within the upper echelons decided it would be best to remove you from your post—much the way you had me removed years ago. Turnabout is fair play, or so they say. And, Colonel, it is my pleasure to carry that directive out."

"That is a big gun. It will make a lot of noise," Olmstead advised confidently.

"No matter, Colonel. This hotel was built in the thirties. The walls are virtually soundproof."

"When they find me in the morning, all manner of alarms will go off."

"Valerie is on the phone with the desk right now," the man said, flashing a smile. "She is advising them that she does not want housekeeping to come knocking tomorrow until midafternoon. By that time, it will all be over."

"You miserable bastard!" Olmstead snarled.

"Goodbye, Colonel." The man fired twice, both rounds hitting Olmstead dead center of the chest. He reeled backward from the impact, crashed into the wall mirror, and dropped to his knees. Pitching forward, he fell flat on his face as all went black.

THIRTY-ONE

Monday night into Tuesday morning should have been the first good night's sleep Savage had in more than ten days, but it didn't go that way; he tossed and turned, agonizing about the Soldier case. He was hungry too; he'd never gotten around to ordering that pizza.

Somewhere around two thirty, he'd gotten out of bed and finished off the box of Better Cheddars—and some rock-hard Swiss he'd allowed to age a bit too long in the fridge. He washed down those gourmet delights with the few remaining freezer-burned spoonfuls of Ben & Jerry's Chocolate Fudge Brownie he found hiding behind a package of pork chops and some frozen waffles probably working on their second anniversary. He didn't even look at the ice cream's date code; he didn't want to know.

In a matter of only hours, now, the pope of the Roman Catholic Church was due to make a grand appearance—replete with all the pomp and circumstance that such an occasion would call for—within *his* sector of *his* city. And for the last many hours the police commissioner and the mayor had both been shouting from the rooftops just how safe Detective Sergeant Thornton Savage and his investigators from Manhattan South Homicide had made that sector for the papal visit. He knew it wasn't so. He didn't know how he knew. . . . But, goddammit, he knew. And if he was right, the New Year's Day headlines would prove the mayor and police commissioner both wrong, but all they had to do was turn around and point to him and allow the shit to roll downhill, right into the front door of MSH. He harbored no delusions about who would take all the weight if the pope took a hit.

To escape his thoughts, Savage punched the remote until he caught the tail end of an old Jimmy Cagney film. What was it—*Angels with Dirty Faces*? When the guards at Sing-Sing finally strapped a scowling Cagney into Old Sparky and launched him into wherever—while good priest and childhood chum Pat O'Brien stood by praying for the eternal soul of the good boy gone wrong—Savage clicked off the TV, returned to the bedroom, and resumed his tossing act. The last time he glanced over at the West-clox, it was six fifteen. It seemed like only moments later when the harsh ring of the telephone on the nightstand jolted him from deep REM hyperspace.

"Good morning, Thorn. Father Vinny here. Hope I didn't wake you."

Jesus Christ, Savage thought, grunting out something on the order of, "No, no, Father. Not at all." He yawned so wide, he felt the joint on the right side of his jaw almost give way. The last thing he needed now was a recurrence of his TMJ. He hated when that happened. "What's up, Vinny?" he asked, looking at his clock. It was seven twenty-five. *Shit!*

"Just finished saying six o'clock Mass. I came in and sat down with my coffee and my morning newspaper, and discovered that Detective Sergeant Thornton Savage is New York City's man of the hour."

"Huh? Yeah, well, that's just a bunch of—"

"Then I started flipping through the TV news channels, and the only thing they're talking about is the capture of the Soldier, and how the Holy Father will now be safe during his visit today. I'm very impressed, Thorn. I called to offer my heartfelt congratulations to you. You must be feeling a great sense of accomplishment."

"Thanks," Savage uttered dully. No point in arguing, he thought. Besides, he didn't yet have the energy to explain.

"The article states that the mayor has never been happier or more proud of the NYPD than now," Father Vinny said. "During a press conference, he actually mentioned you by name several times. And Cardinal Hammond has been quoted as saying it was a grand day for the department and the city. You did one heck of a job, friend."

"Unh," Savage grunted. He was still not nearly awake, nor ready to hear any accolades—founded or unfounded as they might be. Something about the damn case just wasn't ringing true. He wished to Christ he could shake the apprehension, but he couldn't. He also wished he could go back to sleep, but he knew he was now up for the day. Dammit.

"Unh!" Vinny grunted. "Is that all you can say? You're the man of the hour . . . front page all the way. In police parlance, this has to be the collar of the century."

"I wish I could persuade myself that this case is closed," Savage said, his wakening tone beginning to reveal those lingering doubts.

"Why?" the priest asked. "You got the guy, you got the pistol, you got the bullets, and you got the typewriter. Newspaper says you even got an identical match on the stationery he used in his letters to that reporter at the *Post*. What the heck more do you want?"

"Is a clear head asking too much?"

"Gee, what's not clear, Thornton?"

"There was a killing up in Boston back on the tenth of December, that involved a—"

"A former priest," Vinny broke in. "A guy by the name of Grennan. You told me about him at Forlini's. It's all in the newspaper article. Says here how you tied that all together with the Soldier. So what's the problem?"

"Several problems, Vinny. First of all, a completely different weapon was used in that one. Secondly, I haven't been able to convince myself that the guy we've got, John W. Krumenacker, was in Boston three weeks ago. I just keep thinking he might have been too sick a man to have made that trip."

There was a long silence on the line. Savage thought he'd lost the connection. "Vinny. Vinny . . . are you still there?"

"I'm here," the priest replied, his tone somehow different, somber.

"What's the matter?" Savage asked. He heard the priest nervously clear his throat.

"I just now realized that I know someone who was in Boston at about that time," Father Vinny said soberly. "And I guess you ought to know about it. Not that I think for a moment that there could be any connection, mind you. It's just for your own information."

"Who is that?"

"His Eminence, Cardinal Dennis Hammond," Vinny replied. "The trip wasn't very well publicized, but the cardinal was up there attending several Church conferences. It's my understanding that he stayed in Boston for two or three days, maybe more."

"Vinny. I hate to put you on the spot," Savage said, suddenly fully awake, "but can you find out for me the exact dates that he was up there? The date he left New York, the date he returned? His means of transportation—did he fly up, drive—that sort of thing?"

Long silence.

"Vinny!"

"Will you be at your office later in the morning?" the priest asked.

"Yep."

"I'll call you there."

Monsignor Albert Dunleavy downed the final sip of his second coffee, set the gilt-edged china cup gently back on its saucer, and dabbed at the corners of his mouth with an embroidered linen napkin. Preoccupied with his own agenda, he listened with only half an ear and nodded respectfully every few moments as Cardinal Dennis Hammond went on and on, postulating on a broad variety of topics that included Church politics, politics in general, and recent archdiocese budget shortfalls. The cardinal always set the tone of their discussions, but Dunleavy thought it very odd that this morning he never once touched on the topic of the murdered priests or their miraculously captured killer; it was as if none of those things had ever happened. Dunleavy fought to control his anger and his temper.

His Eminence had been in a particularly good mood all during their breakfast meeting. And why not? Though he never mentioned them, there were many reasons for the cardinal to feel elated today. The Holy Father was, at that very moment, journeying to the seat of Hammond's archdiocese, and would be there in a matter of hours. What an honor. The Soldier maniac who had been plaguing the city and the Church had been caught. The unbelievable killing spree was over, and the pope's safety during his visit was now virtually assured. And most importantly, the St. Malachy's debacle could again slip back beneath the surface of scrutiny. As far as the cardinal was concerned, it had merely been a close call, but all was well once again within his see. But Dunleavy knew that was not so. All was not well. All would never be well. Not until Hammond did the right thing.

Suddenly, as if someone had turned off a faucet, the cardinal ceased his mundane monologue. Dennis Hammond was a brilliant man, and one of his most notable assets was his remarkable ability to read the mood of others, to see beyond a facade. Dunleavy sensed that Hammond was doing a fluoroscopy of his head, getting a good read on the turmoil and angst simmering inside there.

With quiet concern reflecting from his alert eyes, Hammond softly spoke. "You now know all about St. Malachy's, Albert."

"Yes, Your Eminence. I do."

"And the police?"

"They know some."

Hammond sat back in his chair and folded age-spotted hands in his lap. "Are the police aware that I was the rector of St. Malachy's during the 1960s?"

"I truly do not know," Dunleavy responded, looking tightly into the cardinal's questioning eyes. "However, if you are asking me for my opinion, Your Eminence, I would have to say that the police are not yet aware of that fact."

"Good. And with this matter now closed, there no longer remains any reason for them to look any further. Am I correct in that assumption, Albert?"

"That may be true, Your Eminence," Dunleavy replied. Krakatoa, at least for the moment, still controlled.

"Are you judging me?" Hammond asked.

"I'm trying not to be your judge, Your Eminence. I wish merely to be your conscience."

"Don't flatter yourself, Monsignor," the cardinal responded hotly, revealing for just an instant a flash of his notorious Irish temper.

"I do not speak for me, Your Eminence. I speak for your flock."

"What would you have me do, Albert?" Hammond said, his words sharp. "Lay myself bare before those who would rejoice in seeing the Church take yet another black eye?"

"This is not about black eyes, Your Eminence," Dunleavy offered. "And it isn't even about the five—actually, six—dead priests anymore. Although it must be acknowledged that some of those men might still be alive and breathing if you had been forthcoming."

Hammond opened the bottom drawer of his desk, removed the sterling flask, and poured liberally into his cup. Without offering Dunleavy any, he capped the flask and took a deep gulp of the amber Irish.

"There is a lot at stake here," Hammond said, his tone soft again but persuasive. The cardinal leaned his elbows on his desk, knitted his fingers together, and supported his chin with outstretched thumbs. He gazed intently at Dunleavy. "You are my right hand, Albert. I need you to help me protect Mother Church."

"You used me," Dunleavy said flatly. "Not to protect the Church, but to protect yourself." Inside his gut, he felt the early warning rumblings of an impending eruption of anger.

"I didn't use you, Albert," Hammond said firmly. "I spared you."

"Spared me?" Dunleavy replied. The words started at his diaphragm but had built to an angry snarl while en route to his curled lips. "You pulled me into a conspiracy of silence," he yelled. It was now Dunleavy's turn to display *his* notorious Irish temper.

"You entered willingly," Hammond pointed out, glaring at Dunleavy and sipping again at the whiskey.

"I was seduced by the promise of my being consecrated as bishop. For that, I am to blame. And for that, I will forever be heartfully sorry."

"Nothing has changed, Albert. That promise is still viable."

"You must make a clean breast of the St. Malachy's affair, Your Eminence."

"It all happened over forty years ago, Albert. Leave it lie in its grave. What could possibly be gained by my airing it now?"

"A new beginning, a clear conscience, a soul purified and free of tarnish."

"You speak of the ethereal, Albert. You speak of doctrinal ideals. But as head of this see, I must function differently. I must see the big picture and compensate for worldly realities. You will come to see that as a bishop."

"Will you go forward as I suggest you must? Or do you intend to continue living this lie?"

"I intend to continue as Archbishop of New York. And nothing, or no one, will derail that." Hammond drained his cup and glared at Dunleavy. "You best be getting back to your duties," he said dismissively. "We have a lot to do today. Good morning, Albert."

From the very moment that Savage entered the Manhattan South offices at 0830 hours on the morning of New Year's Eve, the phones were ringing and never stopped. The calls were from media mostly, radio show and print reporters wanting interviews with him and/or his detectives. Not at all ready to go on public record, he nicely fluffed off all of them. Downtown and City Hall, breaking balls and wanting updates every five minutes, kept the phones hot as well; for the most part he fluffed them off too.

He had directed DeGennaro and Marcus to begin sifting through John Wesley Krumenacker's garbage, and had Jack Lindstrom stationed at Krumenacker's bedside over at Bellevue. Lindstrom was there on the very outside chance that Krumenacker might regain enough consciousness to be interviewed, if only briefly, and to take down any deathbed or dying declaration. What they mostly sought from him was information on confederates, if any. That was paramount; the pope was due to land at JFK in about three hours. At nine fifteen, Savage received a call from Father Vinny.

"Cardinal Hammond left New York for Boston on Sunday evening, December the eighth," Vinny said flatly, with no preamble. "He returned to New York on the afternoon of Wednesday the eleventh."

"How did he get there, and where did he stay while in Boston?" Savage asked.

"Private jet, up and back. As to where he stayed, my source was not wholly certain. The belief, however, is that he was put up at the Boston Archbishop's residence. That would be the usual protocol."

"Hmm."

"Surely you don't believe for a minute that the Cardinal could have had anything to do with that killing up there,"

Father Vinny said, his tone unsettled. "That's just totally inconceivable."

"You've got to admit there is some coincidence here, Vinny," Savage replied. "At the very least, I think it would be appropriate for him to account for his whereabouts at the time of that murder."

"Well," Vinny said, sighing. "Lots of luck. I'm just glad I'm not in your shoes. By the way, how are things working out for Jack Lindstrom?"

"Good," Savage replied. "But it seems that he made a remarkably fast recovery; like maybe he went to Lourdes. Only days after starting on those antidepressants, he seemed to be back up to full strength. That just doesn't seem possible. You told me it could take a week or so before discernable improvement. What gives?"

"He's still got his problems," Vinny said. "Depression doesn't go away that fast. But what you're probably seeing are the effects of something known as activated placebo."

"Is that good?"

"It's not bad."

"Take care, Vinny."

Savage hung up, flipped his Rolodex to Boston Detective Teddy Christman's phone number, and dialed.

"Homicide, Detective McNulty." A smooth female voice with a heavy Boston accent answered.

"Detective Christman, please," he said.

"Detective Christman is on his regular day off. He'll be back in for a four-to-twelve on Thursday."

What a set of pipes, he thought, hearing only the few words. Sultry and seductive, the voice could probably talk him into any damn thing. He wondered what Detective McNulty looked like in the flesh.

"Anybody there versed on the Peter Grennan homicide of December tenth?" He hoped she was; he could listen to her talk for days.

"Not at the moment," she replied. "I'm afraid you'll have to speak with Detective Christman; that is his case."

"This is Sergeant Savage, NYPD Homicide. Where can I reach him? This is very important."

"At home, I guess."

"And you're not going to give me that number, right?" he said, knowing what was coming.

"That's right."

"I'm going to give you my cell phone number, Detective," Savage said. "I need you to reach out to Christman ASAP and have him call me *immediately*."

"I'll do the best I can, Sarge. No promises, though. Happy New Year."

"Yeah," Savage groaned. "Happy New Year." He sighed. Detective McNulty was probably a redhead with big green eyes.

Richie Marcus held the swollen garbage bag out at arm's length as he and Diane DeGennaro exited the elevator in the cavernous basement/garage shared by both the Thirteenth Precinct and the Police Academy building on East Twentieth Street.

"Christmas presents from some of your friends, Marcus?" Charlie Huff inquired with a teasing snort. Huff was one of the full-time civilian fuel dispensers who operated the basement gas pumps. He was always trying to get the best of Marcus.

"Nah," Marcus shot back without missing a beat. "It's that bag full of sweaty New York Knicks jock straps you wanted. . . . Where's your car parked?"

Unable to come up with a rejoinder, Huff wilted. He stepped, dejected, back into his small, dark cubicle.

Settling in beside the trash Dumpster just beyond the gas pumps, Marcus set down the Hefty bag and undid the wire tie that had kept it closed. Diane removed a couple of unused plastic bags from her pocket, snapped them both open, and set them on either side of the Hefty bag.

"Hell of a way to start spending New Year's Eve," Marcus grumbled. "Going through some psycho's freakin' garbage."

"You know the boss," Diane replied. "You know how thorough he is. Especially when he's got his doubts. Besides, what's the difference? You wouldn't want to go out tonight anyhow. We *never* go out on New Year's Eve."

Marcus gave her a blasé look while snapping on a pair of long-wrist latex gloves. "That's because New Year's Eve is friggin' amateur night," he began playfully. "No self-respecting, well-trained consumer of the grape—a professional like myself, for example—would ever consider going out on New Year's Eve and rubbing shoulders with a bunch of wanna-bes. Geez, get real."

"So what are you complaining for?" Diane asked.

"Not complaining," he replied, with a dismissive wave of his hand, "just ventilating."

Diane snickered, rolled her eyes, and slipped her grandmother's ring from her third finger. After carefully placing the garnet-and-gold band into her coat pocket, she too pulled on a pair of surgical gloves.

"Ready?" Marcus asked.

"I'm ready," Diane replied.

"Okay," Marcus declared, settling into a comfortable crouch. "If it's total trash, like most every damn thing in here seems like it's gonna be, it goes in the bag on the right."

"But if it could have any value at all," Diane said, "it goes in the bag on the left."

"Let's do it," Marcus said, reaching into the overstuffed trash bag and removing a tightly balled piece of paper towel. He unwound the wad slowly to reveal some ugly dried-out contents. Making a face, he looked over at Diane.

"That's neither a *right bag* nor a *left bag*," she said, chuckling.

"What the hell is it?"

"That's a Lipton *tea bag*."

Flipping the first no-value selection into the open bag on the right, he murmured, "Oh, I can see that this is gonna be great fun." He pulled the wristlet of the snug-fitting glove away from his watch face, studied the time, and added, "We're gonna be here till lunchtime, for God's sake. From the looks of things, we only got about a thousand more wads of this shit to go through."

"Look at this," Diane said, flattening out a crumpled piece of paper. "It's a handwritten sales receipt from Mallory's Bicycle Shop down on Fourth and First."

"What does it say?"

"It says that Krumenacker bought himself a three-wheeler bicycle last Friday; paid two hundred and sixty-eight bucks. What the hell would a guy who can hardly breathe be wanting with a damn bicycle?"

"I remember seeing that bike," Marcus said. "It was chained to the railing in front of Krumenacker's building. It had to be the same one; it was brand new."

"Bag on the left?" Diane asked, holding up the receipt.

"Definitely the bag on the left."

For the next forty minutes, DeGennaro and Marcus picked through each and every item in Krumenacker's kitchen trash bag. Along with the bicycle sales receipt, they also opted to retain several gun-bore cleaning patches they had found and a spent bottle of Hoppe's #9 gun-cleaning solvent.

"The bag empty?" Diane asked.

"I think so," Marcus replied, standing and turning the Hefty bag inside out and ruffling it. A narrow strip of clear plastic dropped to the floor. Diane picked it up.

"What is it?" Marcus asked.

"It's a hospital wristband," she murmured. "Look here. It's got St. Clare's logo in bold lettering." Diane stood and moved directly under the nearest fluorescent fixture and held it up to the light.

"What else does it say?" Marcus asked, dropping the empty sack. He quickly picked up the keeper bag that contained the gun-cleaning evidence and bike receipt, and followed after her.

"It's got Krumenacker's name on it," she answered in a mumble. Squinting her eyes, she then added, "And there's a date of admission."

"Yeah?"

Diane turned a deadly serious glance to Marcus. "December twenty-fourth."

Moving immediately for the elevator and hitting the call button at least a dozen times, Marcus called out to the gas jockey. "Hey, Huff, anything left in them bags is yours."

Having immediately sent Marcus and DeGennaro over to St. Clare's hospital to follow up on the patient wristlet, Savage decided that he would do the follow-up on the bicycle receipt.

Upon arrival at Krumenacker's Seventh Street tenement, he started by knocking on Mrs. Brzazinski's apartment door. When she answered it, he found that the landlady was every bit as good-looking and charming as she had been the afternoon before. She was wearing the same stained housecoat, and still had her overly dyed hair wound up in at least a thousand curlers. She asked him to wait a moment until she put in her teeth.

"What do you want now?" she asked upon her return.

"I want to know what Krumenacker was doing with that three-wheel bicycle that's chained up out front," Savage said.

"That ain't his bike," the charmer replied tersely.

"The serial number on the bike corresponds to the serial number on a receipt that was made out to him on December twenty-seventh."

"It ain't his bike, I'm telling ya'," she snarled out of the side of her mouth. "He bought the damn thing for Alan Pitler." She pointed a fleshy arm down the darkened hallway. "He's the old spaz in 1C. By the way, Krumenacker still alive?"

"He's still hanging in there," Savage responded as he moved down the hallway. Grunting an acknowledgement, Mrs. Brzazinski slipped back into 1B and slammed the door closed.

"I was with him only a little bit before you guys came and the ambulance took him away," Alan Pitler said.

"Where were you with him?" Savage asked. "In his apartment?"

"Yeah." The old man turned away and took several tentative steps into his dingy room. He pointed to a fishbowl atop an old console television. "He gave me Charlie."

"Did Mr. Krumenacker buy you that three-wheel bicycle out front, Mr. Pitler?"

"Oh yes." the man stammered. "Wasn't that nice of him? They stole my other one."

"So I guess Mr. Krumenacker was your friend, is that right, Mr. Pitler?"

"Oh yes," the slight little man replied, nodding his balding head. "My friend. He was my friend."

"Did Mr. Krumenacker have any other friends, Alan?"

"He had a lady friend."

"A lady friend?" Savage inquired gently.

"She was there yesterday when John Wesley gave me Charlie, just before he got sick."

"What was the lady's name?"

"I don't know."

"What did the lady look like?"

"I don't know," he replied, wrapping skinny arms defensively around a bony chest. "Blond," he finally uttered in a frightened little voice. "Lots of blond hair."

"What else can you tell me about the lady, Mr. Pitler?"

The fragile little man fidgeted with his fingers while his head shook involuntarily.

"Concentrate, Alan," Savage said soothingly.

"She . . . she didn't smell good."

Savage cracked a smile. "How do you mean she didn't smell good, Alan? Exactly what did she smell like?"

Pitler shuffled to the sink counter and picked up a near-empty package of bread. Through the clear wrapper, Savage saw that it contained green-molded remnants of what used to be white bread. Pitler opened it, stuck his nose in, and inhaled. With both hands, he held the open wrapper out to Savage.

"Like this," he said. "She smelled just like this."

THIRTY-TWO

The swelling sense of relief sweeping through the city and the Church—and for that matter, most of the NYPD—caused by John Wesley Krumenacker's capture almost twenty hours ago imploded like a house of cards at an 8.8 epicenter when Detectives DeGennaro and Marcus called in their hasty report from St. Clare's Hospital.

A barely conscious John Wesley Krumenacker had been received at St. Clare's Emergency at about ten thirty on Christmas Eve. Hospital records showed that after preliminary examinations by interns and a resident cardiologist, he spent an hour in radiology and was admitted to intensive care shortly after one a.m. Christmas morning. Even though the ambulance had picked him up just outside of St. Patrick's Cathedral, there was simply no way in hell that Krumenacker could have been the trigger in the Father Clapp killing outside Grand Central three hours later.

Back from his interview of Alan Pitler, Savage huddled with Pete Pezzano in the squad commander's office.

"I just got off the phone with the chief of detectives and apprised him of these latest developments," the lieutenant said. He was not a happy camper."

Savage nodded.

"The chief was having his operations office immediately disseminate this information to all the commanders working the papal security force," Pezzano went on. "He figured we'd have enough to do."

Savage remained silent.

"Where the hell do we go to pick up the thread, Thorn?" the normally placid commander asked, clearly frustrated. "The pope is due to land at Kennedy any moment now. Twenty minutes later he'll be at the heliport at Sixtieth Street. Talk about playing *Beat the Clock*."

"The description of the woman with the big blond hair that Marcus and DeGennaro got from McHugh's bartender now takes on tremendous importance," Savage said. "Especially since it gibes so well with the description I just got of a female Alan Pitler saw in Krumenacker's apartment yesterday."

"Do you think Krumenacker would give her up, if we ever get a chance to talk to him?"

At that moment, wheelman Eddie Brodigan leaned into Pezzano's office. "Lieutenant . . . Sarge," he began. "Jack Lindstrom just called in. He's on his way back to the office. Krumenacker croaked ten minutes ago. He never regained consciousness or made any statements."

"Where the hell do we go from here, Thornton?" Pezzano asked dryly. "That son of a bitch was our only hope to show us the way."

"I haven't the foggiest idea, boss," Savage offered, throwing his hands up as he stood to leave Pezzano's office. "But at the very least, I want all our teams inside St. Pat's during the ceremony."

Savage quickly returned to the sergeants' room to get his topcoat. With the small amount of time he had left, he decided to go talk again with the good monsignor. His worst fears seemed to have been borne out. All of the damn hoopla and celebrating over Krumenacker's capture had been premature. The deadly game was on again. Full on. *Shit!*

He had less than two hours to come up with a blond who smelled like moldy Wonder Bread before one of the most important men in the world stepped out before thousands at the altar of St. Patrick's Cathedral; just another fucking average day in Fun City. As he reached for his topcoat, his cell phone rang.

"Sergeant Savage, this is Teddy Christman up in Boston. I'm returning your call. It's all over the news up here that you guys closed that priest-killing case. Congratulations."

"We just reopened it," Savage replied brusquely. "We've got another shooter out there somewhere."

"No shit?" Christman said. "Jesus. I was hoping your collar was going to close my case for me."

"'Fraid not, Teddy."

"What do you need from me?" Christman asked.

"I don't need anything. I just wanted to make sure you were aware that Cardinal Hammond, the head of the New York Archdiocese, happened to be in your town on the night Peter Grennan was offed."

"Didn't know that," Christman said, then added, "Sorry, Sarge, but, ah, so what?"

"I don't know so what, Teddy. But there's coincidence here. And I don't believe in coincidence. Just thought you might sniff around up there and see if you could establish his whereabouts at the time of Grennan's murder."

"I'll do it."

"Good. Anything else doin'?"

"Not really," Christman replied. "Oh, we did get the forensics back on those tire tracks I had told you about."

"And?"

"Michelin tires, size 225/60-17."

"Seventeen inch?" Savage repeated, jotting the info across the back of his hand. "That's a big tire. What do they fit?"

"They're standard equipment on the later-model Lincoln Town Car."

"Nothing else?" Savage pried. "Cadillacs, maybe?"

"Some Caddies came with a seventeen-inch Michelin," Christman responded. "But they used the 235/55-17."

"Hmm."

"And, of course," Christman said, adding the disclaimer, "we have no way of knowing at this point if those tracks have any connection at all with our case."

December 31, 11:55 A.M.

Left foot brake; right foot gas. Savage leaned hard on the Crown Victoria as he stole every traffic light heading uptown on Third Avenue. At Fifty-seventh, he turned east to First, then uptown again to number 1011, the offices of the New York Archdiocese. Seeing no parking spots anywhere close by, he double-parked right in front of the building. He pushed through the front doors and was again greeted by the nice blue-haired lady who looked like his aunt Mae.

"I've got to see Monsignor Dunleavy immediately," he said, in no uncertain terms. Remembering his manners and not wishing to appear rude, he flashed a quick, friendly smile.

"The monsignor is busy in his office just now," the lady said. "He's running very late, and must soon be leaving for the Papal Mass over at St. Patrick's. Can someone else help you?"

Looking into the open office over the woman's shoulder, he asked, "Where is his assistant, Angela?"

"Ms. Buffolino? I'm afraid she's not here. She left for St. Patrick's a half-hour ago."

Savage leaned in close, and asked in a perfectly enunciated whisper, "Did you just say, Ms. . . . *Buffolino?*"

"Yes," the woman replied, shrinking somewhat in her chair. "She's the monsignor's assistant. . . . Angela Buffolino."

Savage took the steps of the winding staircase two at a time. At the monsignor's office door, he rapped twice and let himself in. Dressed in his full ceremonial regalia, the cleric was seated at his desk, talking on the telephone.

"We've got to talk," Savage interrupted. "Right now!"

Dunleavy cupped the phone in his hand. "I have no time. I must be at St. Patrick's in fifteen minutes."

"Make time."

"I'll get back to you," the monsignor said calmly into the phone. He hung up. "What is it, Savage?"

"I came here to talk to you about the cardinal, but right now I want you to tell me about your assistant."

"Angela?"

"Yeah, Angela," Savage replied. "Is her last name really Buffolino?"

"It is. What of it?"

"How long have you known her?"

"When I came here seven years ago, she was already here. All together, Angela's worked for the archdiocese for about fifteen years. She's invaluable to us." Dunleavy focused tightly on Savage. "Please tell me why you want to know."

"When we had our 'discussion' in your residence the other night, we touched on the subject of a little boy who took his own life at St. Malachy's many years ago."

"I recall."

"Do you know what that boy's name was, Padre?"

"No, I don't."

"Buffolino," Savage growled. "His name was Emilio Buffolino."

"Okay," Dunleavy said with an innocent shrug. "It just happens that Angela has the same surname as that boy from years ago. So what?"

"I think the connection may be much closer, Padre." Inhaling deeply, sniffing the room's ambient air, Savage searched for and discovered the same sweet aroma of incense he'd detected on his first visit there. The other scent he associated with the place was as absent as Angela Buffolino—the scent of penicillin, or, as better stated by Alan Pitler . . . that of moldy white bread.

"You said you came here to discuss the cardinal," Dunleavy said abruptly, glancing impatiently at his watch.

"Cardinal Hammond was up in Boston from the eighth to the eleventh of this month," Savage said. "Father Grennan was murdered in Boston on the tenth."

"My God, man, surely you're not suggesting—"

"Krumenacker is dead," Savage broke in. "But we now know that he was not working alone. He definitely did not kill Father Clapp, nor do I believe he was the one who killed Father Grennan.

"Oh my *God,*" Dunleavy uttered, his face drained of color as he again glanced at his watch. "The Holy Father . . ."

"Now you understand why I have no time to fuck around," Savage said. "Where did the cardinal stay when he was up in Boston?"

"He stayed at the archbishop's residence," Dunleavy blurted nervously. "Always does."

"How did he get to Boston and back?" Savage asked.

"He was flown there and back by private jet. A courtesy provided by a very wealthy longtime parishioner."

"Who picks up a full-blown cardinal when he arrives at the airport in Boston? Surely he doesn't take a cab."

"Hans Peter," Dunleavy replied matter-of-factly. "One of our archdiocese chauffeurs."

"One of *your* chauffeurs? Not a Boston Archdiocese chauffeur?"

"The cardinal likes to have his own chauffeur, no matter where he is. Hans Peter drove up to Boston one day before the cardinal left New York, in order to be there for him. He remained there with the cardinal during his entire stay."

"What kind of car did Hans Peter drive up to Boston?"

"The Cardinal's car. A Town Car. A *Lincoln* Town Car."

Savage's computers began to run wild. In an instant, he

was again thrust back eight days to his first visit to the archdiocese building. A kaleidoscope of randomly saved overlapping images flashed across his mental screen. The montage included stills of a fortuitous parking spot he'd found behind a big gray Lincoln that had been parked right out front. Others focused on wide Michelin tire tracks pressed perfectly into virgin snow. There was a man behind the Lincoln's wheel. He was blond, Aryan, reading a newspaper, and wore on his left pinkie a gaudy gold ring with an almond-shaped red stone.

"Where can I get hold of this Hans Peter?" Savage asked.

"I know he's supposed to be driving in the motorcade. Cardinal Hammond was to be at the Metroport to greet the Holy Father when his helicopter arrived, which was probably five minutes ago. As we speak, the cardinal and the pope are probably en route to St. Patrick's."

"Together, in the same limo?"

"Oh yes. Along with several heavily armed Swiss Guards."

Savage turned, bolted from the office, and dashed down the winding staircase. Propelled by pure adrenaline dumping into his system by the quart, he pushed through the glass doors, unlocked and started the Crown Vic, and burned rubber as he raced up the avenue. He reached for the radio.

"Manhattan South to Central, K."

"Go ahead, Manhattan South unit."

"Status of papal motorcade, K?"

"Motorcade has arrived at destination, unit. The principal has left the auto and entered the location at Fiftieth Street."

"Ten-four." Steering one-handed around a slow-moving Saturn driven by a senior with Dumbo ears beneath a shmucky hat, he tossed the radio aside and punched numbers into his cell phone. Chief Wilson picked up on the second ring. He was at St. Patrick's.

"Chief," Savage started. "No questions. Just listen." As he drove westbound like a maniac, running lights and somehow dodging catastrophes at the intersections of Third and then Lexington Avenues, he spelled out his suspicions. He also gave the chief a complete description of Hans Peter, and two complete descriptions of Angela Buffolino.

Savage concluded that if Hans Peter were the ringer, he wouldn't have planned to act during the motorcade while surrounded by armed Swiss Guards. No, it would have been impossible then. The pope would be most vulnerable to attack when he stepped unprotected out before the cathedral's altar, Savage reasoned. *That's* when the ringer would strike.

THIRTY-THREE

East Side traffic was stymied beyond belief by the temporary shutdown of the streets and avenues immediately adjacent to St. Patrick's. Called a "frozen zone," it was a standard NYPD high-security precaution that was sometimes used when the president came to town. As a result, Savage had to abandon car 7146 on Park Avenue near the Waldorf; from there he would make better time on foot. He trotted up the slight incline of Fifty-first to Madison, "tinned" his way through the solid ring of blue uniforms that encircled the cathedral, and entered the building through the north transept doors. The place was packed.

Dozens of Roman collars were seated in the first few rows that faced the main and high altars. Savage was sure they included cardinals, archbishops, and bishops, and other Church high mucky-mucks. Also present ringside were personalities Savage recognized from the worlds of art, politics, and show biz.

Identifying himself to two uniforms stationed beside the baptismal font, he passed then between the chancel organ enclosure on his right and the altar to St. Joseph on his left. In a small office behind the sanctuary that had been pressed into service as a temporary headquarters, he met up with Chief of Detectives Ray Wilson and Lieutenant Pete Pezzano.

"Any luck?" he asked outright.

"No," Pezzano said, shaking his head.

"This guy Hans Peter, the chauffeur, has completely vaporized," the chief murmured. "His limo is parked in front of the cardinal's residence, but he's nowhere around. I've got a team of people keeping the car eyeballed in case he returns."

"What about *her?*" Savage asked abruptly, turning out his palms.

"According to the seating plan," Pezzano said, "Angela Buffolino is supposed to be in the fourteenth row, right-side center."

"And she's not there?" Savage asked.

"Nope," the chief answered. "There is not one female fitting either of your descriptions—in that row or any row near it."

"We located one of the regular cathedral ushers; he claims he knows Angela from the archdiocese and can identify her," Pezzano said. "As we speak, he's weaving the aisles with Marcus, DeGennaro, and Lindstrom. So far, nothing. But as you can see, this place is packed to the freakin' rafters. It seats twenty-two hundred and we've got SRO out there."

Savage nodded. "It may turn out that these two will wind up as pure as the driven snow," he said, shrugging. "But as far as I'm concerned, right now, they're it."

"Understood," the chief said. "Now just to bring you up to date, we've got a whole new complication. Colonel Olmstead, the head of the Vatican Swiss Guards who I introduced you to yesterday, has gone missing."

"I was told he was going to be at JFK this morning to meet the pope's plane," Savage said.

"He wasn't there," the chief replied. "Nor was he at the heliport to meet the pope's chopper."

"And so far today, he has yet to make any contact with his people," Pezzano said. "He's just gone completely MIA."

"Have we checked his hotel?"

"Yes," Wilson replied. "His stuff is still in the room, but

the hotel staff hasn't seen him since around seven thirty last night."

"If this *is* a conspiracy," Pezzano said, "maybe those sons of bitches got to him."

Suddenly, the interior of the church reverberated with thunderous, awesome, and stunning pipe organ music. Voices singing "Hallelujah" rose in the choir loft, and every person in attendance came to their feet. The Papal Mass was about to begin.

Savage, Wilson, and Pezzano left the small office and quickly returned to the nave as a seemingly never-ending two-row procession of clerics, garbed in chasuble, began entering from the west portal. Some at the procession's head carried bronze staffs bearing golden crucifixes and other symbols of the Church. Others gently swung censers hung by chains, dispensing the fragrant smoke of burning incense. The remainder in the long procession stepped in cadence, their heads slightly bowed and hands clasped solemnly at chest level.

Raising his glance to the blue windows below the high-vaulted ceiling, Savage noticed rays of sunlight refracting through them. Like lasers, they traced the length of the nave, splashing against and illuminating—as if they were spotlights from heaven—the bronze baldachin over the high altar. The sight was awesome.

Savage and Chief Wilson took up standing positions at the front edge of the altar's north side. Pezzano, with Marcus and DeGennaro, quickly moved to the altar's south leading edge. All would try to be as discreet and invisible as possible, but they would scrutinize every person in the procession as it reached the main altar and peeled left and right past them.

The procession lasted a full ten minutes. When the last participants had ambled past and formed phalanxes within the north and south transepts, Savage made eye contact with Richie Marcus on the altar's opposite side. An instantaneous exchange of almost imperceptible glances conveyed that neither had seen anything suspicious or observed any lumps or bulges beneath garments that could have been a concealed weapon.

The organ music ceased; then, seconds later, started again with something of an ecclesiastic fanfare, as a second procession of clerics began to emerge from the hidden sacristy behind the high altar.

These were clearly upper-rank guys, Savage decided, counting two separate rows of six priests each. Heading up the row nearest him was Monsignor Albert Dunleavy; it figured that he'd get a good seat. When they had taken their places before small pews set right at the liturgical altar, the Holy Father, Pope of the Roman Catholic Church, appeared at the top of the sanctuary. The fragile-looking man was escorted, one step behind, by Cardinal Dennis Hammond. Dressed from his covered head to his sandaled feet in white satin, the pontiff took his place at the center of the high altar in a chair draped in yellow fabric. Dressed in red, the color of his princely rank, Hammond took his place upon the cathedra, the throne located on the low altar near the front of the sanctuary, only feet from where Savage was stationed. Then the twelve other priests sat. At that point, all organ music ceased, replaced by the solemn vocal music of Gregorian chants emanating from voices high up in the choir loft.

As the audience took their seats quietly, Savage allowed himself a momentary studied gaze of the pope seated a mere fifty feet away. The man had a kindly and gentle face, but he looked tired, if not totally worn-out.

Back to business, Savage had his eyes clicking in steady 180s. Over and over, his intense scan swept across the wide sanctuary and the area of the south transept. Marcus, exactly opposite, had a view of the altar and the north transept. Savage also knew that Pete Pezzano, Diane De-Gennaro, and a retinue of heavily armed Swiss Guards were now ringing the semicircular line of pillars behind the altar, preventing any possible unwanted entrance from the sacristy into the sanctuary. It was showtime, and Savage felt confident that the stage was properly set and well secured.

At the sound of three bells, Monsignor Albert Dunleavy rose from his seat beside the cardinal and moved ceremoniously to center stage. Facing the high altar, he knelt and blessed himself, then stood and turned to face the vast audience. For only an instant, his eyes met Savage's. Standing then immediately behind the liturgical altar, hands clasped in prayer, Dunleavy began to chant in Latin.

Looking across the wide divide that separated them, Savage again exchanged glances with Richie Marcus. Marcus raised his eyebrows and smirked ever so slightly, and folded his hands together at the belt line. He was bored. He was also probably wishing he were at Aquaduct, Savage thought. But then, Richie's whole expression morphed to one of alarm. Raising his chin toward Savage's side of the altar, he pointed a stubby thumb and began taking tentative steps in that same direction.

Savage suddenly heard the sound of a commotion rising over his left shoulder, in the area immediately behind where the cardinal was seated. A millisecond later, Angela Buffolino burst through a stand of floral sprays stacked around the chancel organ house. The woman's eyes were big and alert, those of a starved predator stalking long-awaited prey. After a split second to get her bearings, she began moving in rapid steps diagonally across the lower altar. Dark revolver in hand, Angela headed directly toward the high altar and the defenseless aged pope.

There was no organ music, no Gregorian chants to accompany the panicked scene, only the sound of frightened screams echoing throughout the massive nave.

Savage vaulted over the marble communion rail, leaped the few steps up to the main altar, and set his course directly for intercept. No way he was going for his gun. Bolting past the seated cardinal, he tracked the woman from behind like a relentless linebacker, his sprint across the sanctuary instinctive and effortless. When he hit the bitch, he was going to hit her with every ounce of his power. This was no time to pull punches. He would probably break her back, or at the very least drive her into the middle of next week. But that was her fucking problem.

Though his primary vision was locked totally on Angela, Savage's secondary sight picked up on another figure also moving for the intercept. Dunleavy. Savage calculated that the monsignor's route would bring him between Angela and the pope. It did. Blocking her path and line of fire to the pope, Dunleavy spread his arms, becoming as big a target as possible. Angela raised the gun and fired twice, a mere millisecond before Savage went into a headlong dive and hit her with a devastating broadside. Together they crashed into the unforgiving marble face of the high altar.

Smelling every bit like moldy white bread, Angela lay unconscious, blood trickling from her nose and ears, as a team of Swiss Guards hustled the pope from his chair. Monsignor Dunleavy lay dead.

Marcus arrived in a flash and crushed his cuffs on the woman's wrists. He drew his own weapon and turned fiercely toward the audience, defending the downed Savage.

"You okay, boss?" he hollered.

Savage nodded, scrambled to his feet, and bolted from the sanctuary, gun in hand. The game, he was sure, was not quite over.

Surrounded by dozens of Swiss Guards, the pope was escorted quickly from the sanctuary, down into the relative safety of the sacristy behind the altars, then, in a commotion of bodies that included Savage, up a short flight of narrow stairs into the residence of Cardinal Hammond. Once inside, he was further sequestered within the apartment's private study. Despite the frantic air in the crowded parlor outside the study, the pope's bodyguards then felt secure enough to holster their weapons. Savage did not holster; he merely slipped his .38 Chief into his coat pocket. The hair on the back of his neck was still standing straight up.

Concentrating on every face in the hectic gathering, Savage noticed how the Swiss Guards all seemed faceless and very much alike in demeanor and dress. They were all Aryan featured, all were blond, and apparently all frequented the same tailor and barber. Beyond that, they all wore the same pin of gold and blue in their left lapel.

Savage noticed one of them enter the large busy parlor from the kitchen area; he seemed headed directly toward the study doors. From head to toe, the man looked just like the others, right down to the blue-and-gold pin. But there was one difference: He wore a garish gold ring on his left pinkie, a ring with an almond-shaped red stone.

Savage moved in the man's direction, and their eyes met. The man immediately picked up his pace, still headed for the study doors. As Savage began elbowing his way through the crowd, the man turned, pointed at Savage, and hollered, "Look out, that man's got a gun." He then loudly repeated himself in German, the language of all Swiss Guards.

Pointing back at him, Savage held up his gold police shield and screamed out, "Assassin."

The gathering of Swiss Guards quickly decided to believe the words of the man who had spoken in the same dialect of their native tongue. Which, Savage realized, wasn't too terribly hard to understand. As they surrounded him, Savage frantically tried to explain. He got nowhere. A half dozen of the Swiss Guards immobilized him as others pulled his thirty-eight from his coat pocket. He watched as Gold Ring continued uninterrupted to the far side of the parlor, where he swung open the doors to the study and drew a behemoth Ruger revolver.

"You!" Gold Ring hollered, taking deadly aim.

As Savage was being forcibly hustled from the parlor by three very strong guys with gold-and-blue lapel pins, three shots rang out. Everybody in the room froze and turned toward the open doors of the study. A man, tall, dressed head to foot in white satin, appeared from within. Dressed as the pope, gun in hand, George Olmstead stood over the very dead Hans Peter Stronheim. He looked over and motioned for his guards to release Savage.

THIRTY-FOUR

New Year's Day was as bright and shiny as a new nickel. The temperature was up in the forties, the skies were crystal clear, and the city was still at rest, sleeping off its collective New Year's Eve hangover. Better yet, the pope and his entire entourage were right now winging across the North Atlantic, heading home to Rome, none the worse for wear.

The siege was finally over. Besides the original six dead priests, John Wesley Krumenacker, Hans Peter Stronheim, and Monsignor Albert Dunleavy were all now dead, and Angela Buffolino was somewhere downtown in irons. She better get used to them, Savage thought, sipping at his coffee and looking out the window of Manhattan South Homicide. Despite their differences, he felt bad for Dunleavy; the guy had real guts. Just then, the phone rang.

"Manhattan South, Sergeant Savage."

"Ted Christman from Boston, Sarge. Are congrats finally in order?"

"I don't know if congratulations could ever be in order," Savage said, his voice a monotone, "not when so many have died. But I do believe the siege is finally over."

"Tell me. Did you ask that ex-nun how she was able to locate our victim, Peter Grennan, way the fuck up here in Boston? I'd like to have that information to include in my case jacket."

"She said Grennan called the archdiocese about two months ago, wanting a statement verifying his onetime employment with them. Said he was being screened for a security job."

"So." Christman picked up the ball. "In order for her to send it to him, he had to give up his mailing and job address."

"Right," Savage replied, nodding to Diane DeGennaro and Richie Marcus, who had just entered the sergeants' room. "Then she turned the information over to Hans Peter Stronheim, Cardinal Hammond's chauffeur."

"And he was the shooter," Christman said. "The guy driving the Town Car."

"His .44 Ruger matched your ballistics to a T."

"Thanks, Sarge," Christman said, signing off. "If you're ever in Boston, come look me up. I'll buy you a beer."

"We're finally done with our reports, boss," Diane said, fatigue in her voice. She dropped a stack of DD-5s on Savage's desk. "We are out of here."

"We can't wait to get the hell home," Marcus piped in. "It'll be nice to have a few days off."

Savage smiled broadly in agreement. He too felt the nagging fatigue. Some would say the feeling was just natural letdown at the closure of a heavy case. He knew different; it was just plain old lack of mattress.

"You still think that Krumenacker intentionally loaded those two rounds of theatrical blanks into the Ruger?" Marcus asked.

"The top five rounds in the clip of the forty-five we recovered from his apartment were blanks also," Savage pointed out. "A man with that much knowledge of handguns and ammunition doesn't ever make that kind of error."

"Yeah," Marcus agreed. "You're probably right. That cabinet of his was crammed full of real ammo he could have loaded into both of those guns. All I can say is that Olmstead guy is one lucky fuck. The odds were sixty-six percent against him. The other four rounds in that Ruger were hot loads."

"Now there's a guy who knows how to gamble, Richie," Diane said, teasing.

"Guess what," Savage said. "I came home to a message on my answering machine last night. It was from Ray's veterinarian over on Hudson Street."

Diane's tired face lit up. "Ray's been found?" she asked excitedly. Marcus looked on with anticipation.

"He's been found, all right," Savage said, tongue in cheek.

"Where the hell was the little bugger?" Marcus asked.

"It's not where he was," Savage said. "It's where the hell he is."

"Well where the hell is he?" Marcus said.

"He's in Miami Beach," Savage replied, drolly.

"What?" Diane shrieked.

"What the hell's he doin' in freakin' Miami Beach?" Marcus growled.

"He was discovered inside a moving van," Savage replied. "Lord knows, Ray looks beat up enough as it is, but after a week of no food or water, he must have really been looking bad. The people down there took him right to the local humane society."

"So how did your vet find out?" Marcus asked.

"He implanted an AVID chip in Ray about a year ago. The Miami-Dade Humane Society scans every animal brought in to them. When they scanned Ray, they came up with a nine-digit code that came back to my vet."

"No shit?" Marcus said, beaming.

"How will you get him home?" Diane asked.

"I may just hop a plane," Savage replied. "Besides, the diving's good this time of year down in the Keys."

"What are you doing this afternoon, Thorn?" a bleary-eyed Marcus said, lighting up a Winston. "Diane's putting on a pot of sauce. Maybe you'd like to come over?"

"Jack Lindstrom and that lady he met over at the VA are coming," Diane said. "I can't wait to meet her. She sounds real nice."

"You like Diane's guinea food," Marcus stressed. "Plenty of garlic!" he added, raising eyebrows temptingly.

"Thanks, but I'm already on for dinner," Savage replied. "Otherwise, I'd be more than glad to." He was due at Maureen Gallo's place at two o'clock to dine on re-heated pasty. This time, however, his cell phone was staying home, locked in a drawer.

"Well," Diane said, buttoning up her coat and turning to leave, "but if you change your mind, just show up. There'll be plenty. . . ."

"Happy New Year," Savage said, standing. He reached out for Richie's hand. They exchanged a grip, firm and un-feigned, reserved only for dear friends and old comrades.

"Happy New Year, boss," Diane whispered gently. She put her arms around him and they shared a quiet, tight, and protracted hug.

For the next several seconds, save for the buzz of the ceiling fluorescent, the cramped room fell totally silent, as if none of the three knew quite what to say. The mood was not a somber one, but it was heavy.

God, Savage thought. How I love this job.

The autopsy showed that the dead man
had a simple heart attack.
But the insurance company isn't so sure
it's as neat and clean as that.
When the body is cremated,
all the potential evidence goes up in smoke.
When Detective Sergeant Thorn Savage's
homicide squad gets the case,
little do they know that it will lead
them into the seamy underbelly of Manhattan's

West Side

John Mackie's next novel of the NYPD

Coming in 2005 from Onyx

MICHAEL CROW

"HORRIFIC AND
HIGHLY LITERATE
ALL AT ONCE."
—The Washington Post

RED RAIN

"CROW JOINS
MICHAEL CONNELLY IN
EXPLORING THE...
OUTER LIMITS OF CRIME."
—Boston Sunday Globe

ONYX

0-451-41086-6

ONYX

CHRISTOPHER HYDE

Wisdom of the Bones
A Novel

Master of suspense Christopher Hyde takes us to
Dallas in November of 1963, where Homicide
Detective Ray Duval is about to collide with history.
His girlfriend's mother used to talk about the wisdom
of the bones: "When you're close to dying, you can
see the truth." Now, with six months left to live,
Duval is putting that wisdom to the test. He's trying
to save one last life before he loses his own to a
terminal heart condition. But the President's
assassination has sent shockwaves of panic
throughout the city. The killer has kidnapped another
girl. And—unless Duval can break the pattern—she'll
be dead in forty-eight hours.

0-451-41065-3

An Edgar Award Finalist for Best Novel

Available wherever books are sold, or
to order call: 1-800-788-6262